Stones' Quest

Redemption of the Curse

LaRene R Ellis

www.StonesQuest.com

Gathering Place Publishers, Inc.
Kaysville, Utah

SAN 256-0658

Library of Congress Control Number: 2008904188

ISBN 978-0-9754622-4-9 / ISBN 0-9754622-4-5

10 9 8 7 6 5 4 3 2 1

Contents

Chapter 1

The Mossen Planet

*G*ostler wandered down the corridors of the Liberty Quest, thinking how different this mission felt. Maybe it was the handful of people on board, or what he knew was about to happen? Ghonllier only brought a small staff to man the Med-C. Janet was the only medical tech on board until Adamite decided to join them. He brought Cid for himself in case Ghonllier didn't come back.

Spencer was the only other person on board, since Sunna was taking him with her to Justin's. Ghonllier agreed to drop her off at his legal father's home on their way back. Spencer had been working, as Sunna's assistant since she accepted Justin's new position.

Humphrey had agreed to take over for the security of Ghonllier's family with Sunna leaving but it wasn't going to happen until she physically left the family. Gostler thought about Spencer as he passed him in the corridor. He wondered how he was going to handle the events that were about to happen.

Close to the time of entry into the Mossen planet's atmosphere, Ghonllier gathered his family and Gostler together. As everyone entered the conference room, Ghonllier studied each person like it was the last time he would ever see them all. His thoughts weighed on his mind, as he acknowledged each one. Reading his father's thoughts, he wished his father didn't know about what was ahead of him. Adamite was very troubled, and Ghonllier could feel it.

When Asustie arrived in the room, she gave Ghonllier a hostile look. Instead of sitting next to her husband, she went to him. "Why are you wearing a KOGN uniform?" she glared.

Ghonllier searched her thoughts before he said, "Didn't Jason tell you I'm going behind enemy lines?"

"Jason doesn't tell me anything about you. I would expect you to do it."

Taking his sister in his arms, he whispered, "I'm so sorry, Asustie. You're one of the best things that ever happened to me. I dearly love you. Please know that."

She pulled away and replied, "You talk like you aren't coming back. Why are you talking this way?"

Ghonllier wanted to tell her everything that was in his heart, but couldn't. All he could muster was, "I'm going behind enemy lines, Sister. I'm not invincible yet."

Asustie looked down at his uniform. With emotion, she threw her arms around his neck and pleaded, "Please be careful. I need you to be my brother."

Ghonllier looked tenderly into her face and kissed her on the cheek. "I'll try."

Asustie turned around to see Sunna entering with a KOGN uniform on as well. Ghonllier read her instant dislike for the uniform. He put his hands on her shoulder and whispered softly, "Asustie, please don't say anything to her. She insisted on coming with me."

Keeping her eyes on Sunna, she whispered, "I don't want her to go."

"It's her job. You know how important that is to her."

Asustie faced him. "It doesn't mean I have to like her job." With those words, she left to go sit next to her husband.

Ghonllier took a deep breath and addressed the group. "As you know, we're going behind enemy lines and won't be able to communicate with the ship. Jason is in charge and will be calling all the shots. Gostler might be able to read my mind, but we aren't counting on it. The distance might be too much for the ability the Stones have given him."

Pausing, he continued, "I want you to know how much I love you and appreciate everything you've done for me. I hope this mission goes well. I really can't tell you more about the future. It's being withheld from me. So Sunna and I will be leaving now. Please don't follow. We need time to get in harmony with our new surroundings and each other." Looking at Sunna, he added, "Do you have anything you want to add?"

She looked fondly at Jason and said, "I just want to express my love for you all, since I'm leaving in a couple of days for my new position. I want you to know how much I'm going to miss you." Looking at Asustie, she added, "Especially you, Asustie, I love Jason and you. We will keep in touch."

"Sunna, I don't want you to go," pleaded Asustie, looking between Ghonllier and Sunna. "Do you both have to go?"

Ignoring her question, Ghonllier asked, "Does anyone have any questions?"

Tears welled up in Asustie's eyes, while she waited for more from her brother. She really didn't expect an answer but wanted more reassurance that he would bring them both back alive. Ghonllier headed for the door and didn't quite make it before Adamite asked a question. "Ghonllier, where is the third Stone?"

Stopping to face his father, he answered, "It's in a building housing the museum of ancient history. To answer your other question, once we're out of the ship, Sam is going to hover so he can move in quickly in case we need him."

"Is there any chance the KOGN will discover the ship before you get back?" worried Asustie.

"No, I'm sure of that, Sister. Sunna and I are the only ones in danger," assured Ghonllier, joining Sunna at the door.

"If the KOGN is here, does that mean Gomper is here, too?" asked Asustie.

"Yes, Asustie, Suzair the Great is on the planet," informed Ghonllier.

"Where?" interjected Adamite. "Why didn't you tell me?"

"Jason will explain it to you after we leave," replied Ghonllier, looking at Sunna.

She saw him give her the sign to leave. The two disappeared through the hullercast, making Adamite's heart ache. This might be the last time he saw Ghonllier alive. *Please choose to come home, Son.*

Spencer was waiting for Sunna and Ghonllier outside the door. "Commanders, good luck," he greeted.

The two nodded and kept walking to the OSA. Sunna and Ghonllier were silent, as they retrieved their blasters. Then the two commanders leaned against their compartments waiting for the landing chimes.

Finally, Sunna asked, "Are there a lot of robots in the city?"

Ghonllier signed back, "Yes."

"Why are you signing?" responded Sunna with her hands.

"They're watching us on the server stones. I don't want them to know what we're saying. They are worried enough," signed Ghonllier.

Sunna nodded.

When the landing chimes went off, Ghonllier looked at the door, waiting for it to open. The sun hit them in the face when Sam opened it. Ghonllier exited first with Sunna following.

Being in the office, Adamite looked away from the server stone. He couldn't bear to watch them walk down the ramp. His heart grew heavy and he didn't want Asustie to know how deeply concerned he felt. Listening to the door of the ship seal made him feel like a chapter of his life had just closed. He ached to know if Ghonllier was going to live or die.

Glancing back at the server stone, he saw Ghonllier and Sunna running through the trees heading for the edge of the city. Seeing his son in the KOGN uniform reminded him of something he had forgotten. *The dream!* Adamite ran to Jason and demanded, "Pick him up now! We can't let him go into that city!"

"*No, David!*" responded Gostler, joining them.

Jason looked between the two men. "What's going on?"

"I want you to pick up Ghonllier right now," repeated Adamite.

"No, Jason, don't do it!" warned Gostler. Standing in front of Adamite, he added, "You have to stay out of this, David."

"He isn't your son! You stay out of it!" shoved Adamite, moving around him.

Gostler blocked him again. "I know what is going to happen. You must stay out or you'll end up like Dapper."

Adamite hit his fist on the desk as he sat in the chair, shaking his head.

"Will someone please tell me what is going on?" demanded Jason.

"Right before we went to face Bog, Ghonllier had a dream about picking up the second Stone. In the dream, we were all killed, including Sooner, and Ghonllier couldn't stop it."

"Who killed everyone?" asked Jason.

"A man looking exactly like Ghonllier with his same powers. The man was dressed in a KOGN uniform," answered Gostler.

"Ghonllier is dressed in a KOGN uniform," cried Asustie.

Gostler looked away. "Wait!" responded Jason. "We got the second Stone and nothing happened. Why does this mission have anything to do with his dream?"

Facing Jason, Gostler reminded, "Think! . . . Sunna almost died."

"But Ghonllier saved her life. What does that have to do with the dream?" asked Asustie.

"He made the right decision and saved her life," informed Gostler. "Two Ghonlliers represents two deaths at different times resulting from his actions. The second Ghonllier had on a KOGN uniform."

"Will we all die like in the dream?" asked Asustie.

"No, like he said. This is between Ghonllier, Sunna and the Master Stones," replied Gostler.

"Will Sunna die this time?" questioned Asustie.

"I can't answer because it will depend on his and her choices when they are faced with the opportunity to make them," answered Gostler.

"Why didn't he tell me about it?" shouted Jason. Looking at Ghonllier on the server stones, he added, "Better yet, why didn't he tell me?"

"Didn't he? What did he tell you to do if something went wrong and he couldn't make it back?" questioned Gostler.

"He told me to come and get him at all cost to his life," whispered Jason, looking at Gostler. "He told me to retrieve the Master

Stones and not worry about anything else. They would protect themselves from the KOGN."

"So he told you. Ghonllier knows, he might not come back," affirmed Gostler, sitting while leaning back in the chair, ignoring everyone's stares.

Ghonllier and Sunna arrived at the outskirts of the city to see KOGN uniforms everywhere. They slipped in among the other uniforms unnoticed. Moving through the city, no one paid attention to them.

Sunna studied her surrounding miffed. Finally, she asked, "How long has KOGN been in this city?"

"About a month. It was the first city they invaded. Why?"

"Something's different."

"What?"

"This place is being run very tightly and smoothly. You can tell the shops and businesses weren't looted. When the last leader of the KOGN took over, it looked like a war zone. Windows were broken and buildings damaged. Fires were being set. They must have done things differently," whispered Sunna.

"They landed miles away and walked in shooting everyone they saw. A warning was set and people disappeared."

"Where are the city's people? Is everyone dead?"

"There was a large number of citizen who lost their lives. The others are in hiding away from here."

"Are they okay?"

"They are suffering. Food and shelter is a problem for them," answered Ghonllier, distracted.

"How is Suzair the Great controlling his men so well?" asked Sunna.

"They're too afraid to break a rule. With Bog's stepping stone, he could see everything they did and would punish the KOGN with death. They don't know he can't see them any longer. So out of fear, they obey his orders."

The family members watched the server stone with deep concern. Glancing over at Jason and Adamite, Gostler asked, "Is she right? Does it look different from other invasions?"

"Yes," verified Jason. "Suzair the Great is ruthless and everyone knows it."

"How far away is Gomper from here?" asked Gostler.

"Why? Is he a part of this dream?" asked Adamite, facing him. Gostler looked away.

"Since I'm in charge, I would like to know where he is," stated Jason. Looking at the stone, Jason ordered, "Stone, show us Suzair the Great and tell us what city he's in."

Gomper appeared, sitting on the edge of a desk looking bored.

"Is this what my brother looks like?" asked Asustie, seeing him for the first time.

"Yes," answered Jason distracted.

She saw Gomper stand and walk toward a window. In the corner of the server stone, the name of the city and its coordinates appeared. Jason quickly wrote them down and started to figure the distance.

After Jason did the calculations, he stated, "He's closer than I would like, if I were Ghonllier. I wonder why the Master Stones had him go at this time when Gomper was so close."

"A good question," responded Adamite, wondering if Gomper played a role in Ghonllier's decision to come here now.

This was the first time Asustie had seen her older brother. Fascinated with him, Asustie tuned out the men talking in the room. Without thinking, she started to stare at him with strong intent. She used the intent that it took to magnify her Mingler powers.

All of a sudden, Suzair the Great faced their direction. "I can feel a Mingler close-by," he snarled Suzair the Great. "Bring her to me!"

Adamite jerked his head in Asustie's direction to see her in a trance. "Asustie, no!" yelled Adamite, standing. "Jason quick get her away from the stone!"

Jason grabbed her, causing Asustie to let out a small cry as he forced her out of her trance. Her husband pulled her into his body, holding her tightly. Adamite stood between her and the stone to block Bog from feeling her energy waves. Placing his hand on her shoulder, he apologized, "I'm so sorry, Daughter. Ghonllier warned me to never allow you to look at Bog on a server stone."

"Why?" retorted Jason his eyes flashing with anger.

"Bog is a Mingler as well as a Moveling. He can feel another Mingler's power. He's been looking for her for thirty years. Ghonllier told me."

Staying in Jason's arms, Asustie questioned, "Why would Bog want me, Father?"

"He wants to use you like Gomper to stop Ghonllier from reversing the curse."

Asustie clung tighter to her husband. Jason looked at his father through marriage and snapped, "Adamite, what if this had happened at your home? Why didn't you tell us?"

"It couldn't happen there. I've programmed every server stone not to show Suzair the Great but the one in my office and this one."

In the background, they heard, "Your Grace, I have an urgent message for you."

Everyone looked to see Pursy, Gomper's personal assistant, had joined him. Holding out a message, Gomper glared at him before he took it. The moment, Suzair the Great started to read the message. Pursy disappeared.

The message fell from his hands and Gomper looked at Pappar and Jamham. "My brother is on this planet." Without warning, Bog bellowed, "Where's my pilot?"

"She's on your Galaxy Creeper," reminded Pappar, stepping forward to pick up the message.

"Get her here!" ordered Bog.

Without reading the message, Pappar handed it to Jamham and left to tell Pursy. Gomper watched Jamham read the message. Jamham looked up from the message and Gomper nodded at him. It was their silent signals to let those protecting him know that Bog was gone.

Jamham handed the message back to him while Gomper asked, "Who's Scremper?"

Pappar entered the room in time to hear the question. He answered, "He's a double spy who happens to be your personal contact with I-Force. Is the message from him?"

Gomper nodded handing it to Pappar. He started to read it.

"Do you want Scremper to capture your brother?" asked Jamham.

Gomper shrugged his shoulders while his thoughts became consumed with the knowledge that his brother was here.

"Great!" retorted Jason.

"This can't be happening, he can't be facing Gomper now. Bog will win," feared Adamite.

"Who's Scremper?" asked Asustie.

"Show us Ghonllier," bellowed Adamite.

"He's the double spy who told Ghonllier he was a marked man and that Suzair the Great was his brother," explained Jason, moving away from his wife. "I thought Justin sent him to prison," he added.

"Then why is he out?" asked Gostler.

"I think he sent him to the prison here on the Mossen planet," reminded Adamite. "KOGN must have let him out," he added.

Gostler looked back at the server stone to see Ghonllier and Sunna crossing another pathway. *Now it makes sense. Scremper creates Ghonllier's choice,* thought Gostler.

Ghonllier and Sunna soon arrived at the building they needed to enter. After crossing the pathway, they walked along the building that housed the third Master Stone. Sunna wanted to look back at the guard standing at the front door but didn't. Ghonllier would tell her if they were suspicious of them.

Sunna glanced at Ghonllier to see if he seemed unnerved by the building being so well guarded. He appeared solid and it built her confidence as they turned at the corner of the building. There Sunna asked, "Are the guards at the front door watching us?"

"No," answered Ghonllier.

Sunna looked up at the high windows, as they headed for the back of the building. "Is there anyone inside?"

"No."

"Do we have guards at the back entrance?"

"We have robots," answered Ghonllier.

"How do you want to handle it?"

"We're going to be their replacements. The real ones aren't coming for thirty minutes."

They came into the guards view. Ghonllier was pleased to be dealing with robots with his ability to reprogram them.

Arriving, Sunna spoke, "By the looks on your faces, this must be a fun post."

"You're the first people we've seen. Why are you here? I don't recognize you."

"We are your replacements," answered Sunna.

"No you're not. We don't have—."

In a hypnotic voice, Ghonllier interrupted, "YOU KNOW US. WE'RE YOUR REPLACEMENTS. YOU ARE RELIEVED OF YOUR POST. SO LEAVE NOW."

The robots took on a dazed look. "You're right. It's time to leave."

Without hesitation, they left. Sunna looked at him suspiciously. Ghonllier ignored her and studied the locked door. Since the robots were in his control, Ghonllier didn't hesitate to command the door to open before they had left. Sunna glanced back as they entered to see the robots disappearing around the corner.

Inside, their footsteps echoed loudly throughout the empty halls. The building walls were made of stone, and the floors were made of marble. It was an old building with a musty smell due to a poor ventilation system. Shutting the building up just made the problem worse.

Ghonllier knew exactly where to go and moved quickly down the different hallways. After passing numerous doors, Ghonllier finally stopped. The sign next to the door read "President's office." Ghonllier commanded the door to open as the Master Stones sliced right through the door's locks.

They entered, charging through several rooms. Ghonllier didn't stop until they arrived at a room that was locked. Slicing through the lock, they entered. It was a storage room. The outside walls of stone were lined with large shelves. Ghonllier commanded one set of shelves to move away from the wall. It shook and groaned as it scraped along the marble floor. The move caused some of the items to fall from the shelves.

With the wall of stone exposed, Ghonllier commanded, "STONE, REMOVE YOURSELF."

A stone floated easily out of the wall and hovered in mid-air. Then a container exited out of the wall, where the hovered Stone once occupied, and floated over to Ghonllier's waiting hand. Quickly, he retrieved the key from his pocket that they found on the Hopper moon from the bottom of the pond. He slid the key into its proper place, and the container opened with ease. Ghonllier plucked the Stone out, allowing the container to fall to the floor.

Sunna already had his belt exposed in the back. He reached back to her with the hand grasping the Stone. Then, taking it, she slipped the Stone into his belt pocket next to the second Stone. In the background, she could hear everything moving back into place.

"Ghonllier, the Stones are blinking on and off. What's happening?" asked Sunna, putting his uniform top back.

"They are talking to each other," replied Ghonllier, helping her get his clothes back in the proper place.

"Does this always happen?"

"Only initially," answered Ghonllier.

They wanted his uniform back in place before they left. His uniform out of place meant they weren't in regulations and someone would stop them. They couldn't afford to be stopped. They almost had his uniform in place, when the Stones vibrated.

It frightened Sunna and she jumped back. Ghonllier faced her.

"What's wrong?" she quizzed.

"The KOGN knows we're inside and not at our post. They're looking for us," answered Ghonllier, reaching out to place his hands on her upper arms. He added, "Sunna, we need to split up now."

She saw a pleading look in his eyes. "Why? I don't think it's a smart thing to do. I say no."

"I have to do something alone. Will you trust me?" Reluctantly, Sunna nodded. "Get outside and back to the ship. Do you know the way back?"

"Yes, but I really want you to come with me."

Ghonllier moved his hand to her neck. He ran his thumb along her jaw line. "Sunna, I want you to know that I never hated you like you thought I did. I deeply loved you from the first moment I saw you. I would've made you Sooner's mother if you weren't so resentful toward me. Promise me that you'll stay in contact with him. He might really need you after today."

Stunned, she just nodded. Then he quickly, he leaned in and kissed her on the lips. Stepping back, he added, "Good-bye. I'll always love you." Then he vanished.

Using his Vanisher's speed, Ghonllier arrived at the outside door to the building. The same one they used to enter. Reaching out to open it, he expected to exit the building and face his challenge. Instead, he heard, *YOUR CHALLENGE ISN'T IN THAT DIRECTION.*

At that moment, he felt a hard hit on the back of his head. Confused, he stopped and felt blood running down his neck. Touching the back of his neck, he brought his hand forward and saw nothing.

Staring at his hand, he questioned, "What's going on?"

Then he felt pain in his head and back again. He could feel someone's hands around his neck choking him. However, touching his neck, he felt no one's hands at all. He faced the hallway behind him and whispered, "Sunna! She's going to be captured and tortured before they kill her."

Without thought, he attempted to move but couldn't. *Stones, I need to go back to her. Let me go!*

IT'S TOO LATE. YOU WAITED TOO LONG.

What do you mean I waited too long for what?

WE ASKED YOU TO TELL US WHAT YOU REALLY WANTED AND YOU DIDN'T DO IT. IF YOU HAD ANOTHER CHANCE WHAT WOULD YOU ASK FOR?

Without hesitation, he whispered, "*Sunna as my wife and companion.*"

WHY DIDN'T YOU ASK FOR IT?

Because I didn't want her unless it was her choice. It has to come from her heart.

YOU COULD HAVE MARRIED HER, IF YOU HAD TOLD US THAT WAS WHAT YOU WANTED EARLIER. SUNNA HAS SHUT HER HEART AND WE COULD HAVE OPENED IT UP GIVING YOU A CHANCE.

"She's going to die because of me!"

WE SHOWED YOU THIS IN A DREAM. THE DREAM OF YOU AND YOUR MEN AT THE BEACH FIGHTING WITH THE KOGN.

"No," cried Ghonllier, feeling Sunna losing consciousness. "Am I too late to stop her from dying?"

WE CAN'T GUARANTEE YOU ANYTHING AT THIS POINT. YOU CAN GO BACK TO THE SHIP AND BE THE MASTER OF THE GALAXY OR TAKE YOUR CHANCES WITH SUNNA. YOU MIGHT SAVE HER LIFE BUT IT WILL COST YOU YOURS. IF YOU DIE, YOU'LL NOT BE ABLE TO SEE JENNY UNTIL YOUR APPOINTED TIME OF DEATH.

Ghonllier's head throbbed and his vision blurred because he was feeling what was about to happen to Sunna. It only took him moments to make his decision. "Stones, I choose to die for Sunna. Save her so she can be with Sooner. He'll need her with me gone."

WE AGREE. WE RELEASE YOU. GO TO HER.

Ghonllier disappeared.

"Sunna, I've lost patience with you. Where's Ghonllier?" shouted Scremper, after shoving her against the stone wall.

"He wasn't here, Scremper. Everyone knows he's dead. If you thought, you saw him. Then you imagined it."

"I didn't imagine anything. I saw the two of you walk into this building. I want him now," bellowed Scremper, shoving her harder against the wall.

Sunna wanted to fight back but couldn't. There were two men holding her arms against the wall and twenty-five robots or men pointing their blasters at her. The stone edges seemed to cut into her head and back.

"Where is he?" repeated Scremper.

Sunna was quiet and he shoved her again. Scremper hurt her, causing Sunna to fight to stay conscious. This time the pain was beyond her level of tolerance. She let out a moan, wanting to break down in tears. But her training wouldn't allow it.

The sight of Scremper momentarily vanished. Expecting to hear Scremper's voice, she heard, "Scremper! Touch her one more time and I'll break your neck!"

Scremper whirled around, grinning. "Well, Commander Ghonllier. So it's true! You aren't dead. Your brother never accepted the rumor,"

Scremper moved a short distance from Sunna and then stopped. "It's so nice to see you again." Scremper gestured toward Ghonllier, while he ordered, "Fools, grab him."

The men lunged forward, and Ghonllier disappeared. Reappearing across the room, he startled everyone. The two men holding Sunna pressed her arms harder against the wall and it hurt.

"I never knew you were a Vanisher," responded Scremper, impressed.

"It was a little dangerous to let people know, don't you think?" countered Ghonllier.

Scremper glared at him screaming, "Kill her!"

"No!" responded Ghonllier, appearing in front of Sunna blocking their blasts.

Seeing Ghonllier in the line of fire, Scremper yelled, "Hold your fire!"

"You should've shot me, Scremper," taunted Ghonllier.

"Your brother wants you alive. So no one fire upon him," warned Scremper, pondering. Staring at Ghonllier, he finally added, "I'll give Sunna her freedom if you'll allow me to put restraints on you, so we can take you to your brother."

"We both know that's a lie. We both know the rules for a spy. You'll kill her," countered Ghonllier.

"I'll keep her alive," promised Scremper.

Knowing Scremper had seen the value of keeping Sunna alive, Ghonllier put his arms out and said, "I'll cooperate with you." Scremper grinned and motioned for the men to put on the restraints. While they worked, the new Master warned Scremper. "You touch Sunna in any way or attempt to kill her, and you'll die you right where you stand."

"Agreed," stated Scremper, not realizing Ghonllier had just given the Master Stones instruction on how to handle the situation after he was dead.

The KOGN men quickly placed the restraints on Ghonllier. Scremper walked around him to make sure they were doing it correctly. He didn't want his prize to get away. While he stepped around him, Scremper saw the back of his uniform not quite completely tucked in. He quickly stepped in front of Ghonllier and the two men glared at each other.

"What were you doing in here?" asked Scremper.

Ghonllier just stared and stayed silent. Looking back at Sunna, he saw her looking at Ghonllier with great concern. Thinking Sunna's look meant that she was in love with Ghonllier, Scremper added, "Are you in love with her?"

The Master read Scremper had experience with this emotion regarding Sunna. He answered, "Yes."

"Why did you come in here?" repeated Scremper.

"Why do you think?" challenged Ghonllier.

"Are you trying to tell me that you came in here to be with each other?"

Ghonllier remained silent while Sunna stared at his back. She realized that they didn't get his uniform back in the proper place. The men were finishing up with the restraints. With him not answering, Scremper looked at her and repeated, "Do you love him?"

"Yes," answered Sunna without hesitation, following his lead.

Ghonllier wished Sunna really meant it. With the Master Stones just meeting, he wasn't sure about her thoughts. He wanted to say good-bye to her one more time like he did in the supply room. *If I could give her one more kiss,* thought Ghonllier, watching Scremper with a lament expression.

Stepping toward Sunna, Scremper shouted, "Why were you here?"

"We told you," matched Sunna.

"You expect me to believe that you're behind enemy lines and wanted to come in here just to be together romantically," growled Scremper.

"Why do you think that's so hard, Scremper?" challenged Sunna.

"I know you General. You never date or let anyone get close to you. Have you forgotten how you turned me down? I watched you do it to other men," growled Scremper. Pointing at Ghonllier, he added, "Why him?"

Sunna found herself searching her own feeling. She looked at Ghonllier and her heart seemed to soften seeing him, giving his life for hers. *Oh Ghonllier, why are you doing this? Why didn't you go back to the ship?* Sunna thought.

She came out of her thoughts with Scremper and Ghonllier yelling at each other. "Don't do it, Scremper," shouted Ghonllier.

It was then Sunna realized Scremper had a patch in his hand. The Tron made a dart toward Sunna. The chains on Ghonllier's ankles snapped as he moved to block his path to her.

Fear appeared on Scremper's face and he inquired, "How did you do that? It's impossible to break those chains."

"Remember, I'm cooperating with you. I can break out of these restraints. Stay away from her, if you want me to make it to my brother," reminded Ghonllier.

"So you do love her. I can see it in your eyes," stated Scremper. Stepping in closer to Ghonllier, he added, "I loved her once. Is she worth it?"

Ghonllier didn't answer. Scremper looked at Sunna. "I want to know why she fell in love with you and not anyone else," interrogated Scremper, moving around Ghonllier.

The new Master moved sharply, blocking his path with his body toward Sunna. Seeing Ghonllier was going to give him problems, Scremper shouted, "Then I'll give this patch to you."

Scremper reached up to attach it to Ghonllier's neck. The new Master pulled his head back, hoping the Tron would miss and land on his uniform. Scremper hit his mark and the patch attached to Ghonllier's neck.

Instantly, Ghonllier staggered and then fell to the ground like he was dead.

✳   ✳   ✳

When Ghonllier disappeared at the door, Adamite requested the server stone to follow him. He was shocked to see the server stone take them to where Sunna was captured. Sunna not getting out was a surprise for him.

The brooding father fell into a nearby chair and asked, "What does this mean, Gostler? Has he chosen death?"

"What are you talking about, Father?" asked Asustie, facing her father.

Adamite looked over at Gostler. The former Master looked away from him. Asustie became angry and demanded, "Tell me now! What does this mean?"

"Gostler, I don't know what to tell her," said Adamite.

"I don't know," responded Gostler, looking at her. "Whatever happens is between Ghonllier, Sunna and the Master Stones. I only knew a situation would present itself where they both have to choose something. I can't tell you what it is because I wasn't told. I can't tell you the outcome because it's their choice. I don't know what the Stones are doing."

Asustie looked at her husband. "Jason, what does this mean? Aren't Ghonllier and Sunna coming back?"

"Honey, I don't know. A known spy is instantly killed when captured. Officially, Sunna is a spy. The only reason she's alive is because they're using her to control Ghonllier. Otherwise, she would be dead by now."

"Jason, go get them!" pleaded Asustie.

"I can't," he snapped.

"Why?"

"I'd have to cut the roof to get them out. The debris will kill them if the KOGN didn't do it first."

Asustie started to cry and Adamite stood to comfort her. Jason paged the captains. "Sam, is Ghonllier still broadcasting what's happening?"

"Yes, Commander."

Taking a long pause, Jason finally said, "Wait for my instructions, Sam. I might need you to do some target practice at their coordinates."

"Acknowledged Commander," replied Sam.

Frustrated, Jason leaned forward and placed both hands on the desk, allowing all of the weight of his upper body to be supported with his hands.

Asustie left her father and came close to him. "Please tell me there is something you can do," she choked out.

Looking at his wife with tears in his eyes, he informed, "Honey, he told me to wait until they took them outside, if they were captured. He told me not to interfere with anyone on the inside of that building."

"So he knew about this?" Asustie questioned.

Jason just stared at her. Then taking her in his arms, he answered, "He knew something was going to happen and told me not to come until they were free of a building. They'll take him outside to see Suzair the Great and as you can see, they'll take Sunna so Ghonllier will cooperate." With Asustie in his arms, Jason requested, "Adamite block the server stone from Asustie. I want to see what Gomper is doing."

Adamite blocked Asustie from being felt by Bog while Jason requested, "Stone show us Suzair the Great at the time and place he learns how long his pilot will arrive to bring him here."

The stone showed Gomper being told his pilot would be there in ten minutes. Noticing the time this was recorded and glancing at his timepiece. Jason quickly calculated in his head. "It will take Suzair the Great about forty minutes to get to Ghonllier. They'll take him outside and I'll pick him up before his brother can get to him."

Jason requested the server stone to go back to Ghonllier just in time to see him collapse to the museum's floor. Adamite cried out, "He's dead!"

Asustie broke away from Jason's arms and stepped around her father. They witnessed Sunna shouting at Scremper.

"Scremper, you fool! You killed him!" screamed Sunna.

In his high-pitched voice Scremper screamed, "Get up, Ghonllier!"

"Scremper, you never put a Truth Test on someone without a medical tech," accused Sunna.

Taking advantage of Scremper's hysteria, Sunna kicked her heel into the shins of the man on her left. He let go of her arm to grab his leg. Then swinging her free arm around, she shoved the heel of her hand against the other man's nose, causing his head to hit hard against the wall behind them. He fell to the ground unconscious and bleeding.

The first guard let go of his leg and reached out, grabbing her. Sunna kicked him in the face, causing his head to hit the wall. Being free from her captors, she ran toward Ghonllier, diving for his body. Once, she was on top of him, Sunna searched for the patch, trying to get it off his neck.

In the background, Sunna heard, "Shoot her! Kill her now!"

"Live, Ghonllier. I do love you, too, and didn't mean to push you—" She was gone.

✳ ✳ ✳

The sounds of the blasters echoed on the server stone. Jason paged the captains. "Sam, do you still have a picture?"

"No."

"Do you have their signal?"

"No, they disappeared with the picture," reported Sam.

"Hit your target and pick them up now!"

Adamite sharply looked at Gostler. "Is Ghonllier dead?"

Gostler just looked down at the floor. "Don't ask me, Adamite. You know what having their signals gone means. There aren't any energy waves to track because they are dead."

Chapter 2

Where's My Father?

Sunna's ears pounded from the consecutive blasts, echoing off the building's walls of stone. Afterwards, she expected to hear voices. However, Sunna heard only deafening silence. *I must be dead,* thought Sunna, deciding to move. Sunna slightly moved, expecting to feel the burning sensation from a blast hit. It reassured her that she was dead to feel nothing.

Raising her head, Sunna opened her eyes to find her vision blurred. All she could see were pastel colors. *Scremper succeeded in killing me, even though Ghonllier warned him not to. Ghonllier! Did he go with Scremper to see Suzair the Great?* she wondered, sitting upon her knees. Sunna froze in her fear, realizing that she wasn't in the museum.

Before Sunna saw a slow moving wall made up of some kind of thick substance. The substance had a swirled pattern of pastel colors. Reaching out slowly, Sunna lightly touched it to feel its thick substance, only to feel a sudden pain afterwards. *This is death!*

Sunna wanted to get away from this substance, only to find herself encased in it. The strange room was a very small sized space. She guessed it to be four by ten feet. Looking up, she found a ceiling that would barely allow her to stand up. Deciding to check it out, Sunna attempted to stand, until suddenly feeling something move beside her knees.

Looking down, Sunna saw Ghonllier removing his arm from underneath his chest. *He's here and alive!* Sunna thought. She watched him shift from his crumpled position, and rolled onto his back. She expected him to be looking at her but his eyes were shut. Staring at his chest, she watched his chest start to move up and down, breathing.

Glancing up at his neck, she remembered what happened in the museum. *The patch,* thought Sunna. She knew for sure that she had grabbed it before KOGN fired their blasts. Staring at her hands, she opened them to see the patch gone. Quickly, she shifted a glance at Ghonllier to see he was staring at her. Sunna stopped breathing to see his eerie expression. Ghonllier seemed to look right through her as if she wasn't there. *I am dead and he's alive. But why can I only see him and no one else,* she thought. She looked around again expecting to see or hear Scremper. Silence greeted and she felt a shiver go up her spin.

Slowly, she reached out to touch his face, wanting to say goodbye. Sunna gasped to have Ghonllier grabbed a hold of her wrist. Looking at him, she responded, "Let go of me!"

Instantly, he sat up to face her and expressed, "What are you doing here?"

Sunna pulled her wrist from his grip and countered, "Why are you angry to see me?"

"The Stones told me that you might die but I . . . failed."

"What do you mean you failed?"

"I'm so sorry Sunna. This is my fault you are dead."

"Why did you come back? You are the Master. . . . Sooner? What is going to happen to him without you?"

"I expected you to live so you could watch out for him."

Sunna shook her head. "Why? Why did you do it?"

"I could feel you pain and I couldn't bare the thought of you suffering because of me."

"Why? You really didn't care . . ."

"You were so wrong about me Sunna. I loved you . . . ," interrupted Ghonllier, looking away.

"Loved? You loved me!"

Ghonllier didn't want to respond to her comment. He looked around their small space, trying to avoid her gaze. When he did,

Ghonllier found her studying him. A tear had escaped her left eye. Wishing he had the Stones so he could learn why, he watched it trickle down her cheek. He reached out with his finger to catch it.

"Why the tears?" questioned Ghonllier, moving his gaze back to her.

"I don't have tears," snapped Sunna.

Ghonllier reached up, wiping away another one. Sunna looked away, embarrassed. "Why the tears?" he repeated.

Facing him sharply, she inquired, "I don't know. Knowing that I'm dead. I have some regrets . . . I think."

"What would you regret?"

"That there is a little boy who has lost a father and he will never have a mother or a father again," choked Sunna.

"I know how much you love him and I wished . . . you could've loved his father."

Sunna looked down at her hands. "Why do you think I pulled off the patch from your neck?"

"It was your job."

Sunna shook her head while she kept her gaze on her hands. "I did it out of love for . . ." She looked up into Ghonllier's eyes. He was waiting patiently for her to finish.

When she didn't, he added, "Love for my son."

Not looking away, she said, "I did it out of love for you both."

"You love me!" Sunna nodded. "I could read your thoughts and I knew what was in your heart. There was nothing but disdain for me . . ."

"It's different here," finished Sunna.

"Here, you love me?"

"Yes."

"Are you sure," said Ghonllier, leaning in for a kiss.

Sunna didn't back away but came forward too. They kissed. Then they looked at each other. Sunna smiled, "Oh Ghonllier. I didn't realize until now how much I love you."

He took her into his arms and they kissed passionately. Every hope Ghonllier had ever thought about was coming true for him just then. If he had to wait there for his time to leave, Ghonllier was going to enjoy it with Sunna being in love with him. She was really in his arms, expressing their love for each other.

After a few minutes, they stopped and Sunna cuddled into his arms. Comfortable, Sunna asked, "Ghonllier, if you loved me. Why were you always so angry with me?"

"I could feel your resentment to me. The Stones told me that you couldn't stand to be around me. You were only there because of duty and I was falling in love you. It made me angry with you," said Ghonllier, kissing her on the cheek.

"I was angry with you," whispered Sunna.

"Why were you? I felt like I had done something that had hurt you deeply. The Stones wouldn't tell me what I did . . ."

"I can't tell you why either. You did nothing but you're right. There was a deep resentment toward you . . ."

Sunna felt Ghonllier's body jerk. She moved away from him to see him looking over his shoulder. "What's wrong?"

He looked at her and asked, "Can't you hear them?"

"Hear who?"

"Gostler and Cid."

"I don't hear them."

Ghonllier put his hands on her arms and added, "Please Sunna tell me that you can hear them."

She shook her head. "What are they saying?"

"They are talking about bringing me back and for some reason. I know they can do it." He leaned in closer and added, "Sunna! Come back with me. Please hold on to him tightly and come back with me."

Sunna leaned back further from him. Then she removed her arms from his grip. Slowly she said, "I agree with them. You need to go back and be the Master but . . . For me it's too late."

"What if it isn't Sunna?"

She shook her head. "Ghonllier. For some reason, when I think about returning. I know that I'll return completely. . . . I can't love you there. Not with Sooner . . ."

"What do you mean?" pleaded Ghonllier. She shook her head. "Sunna! Are you telling me that you don't love me?"

"I love you here but there . . . I can't do it. I don't want to interfere with what you have with Sooner."

Ghonllier was stunned. He felt her love for only a moment only to have her rip it away. He felt his heart break. If Sunna was changing her mind, he wished that she had never told him that she loved him. Ghonllier felt betrayed again by her and the Stones. Why had they brought him only to have Sunna break his heart again?

His mind was confused and he heart ached with more pain than it had ever before. Before he could say something, Ghonllier felt a jerk that took him away from Sunna. Looking at her one last time, he whispered, "Please . . . you're breaking my heart . . . I love you enough to make you Sooner's mother."

"Somehow, I know it but I can't come with you . . ."

Ghonllier wanted to plead with her but suddenly, he was jerked through the wall and she disappeared from her sight.

The reality of being alone consumed her. Knowing her last chance to go back was gone; Sunna had remorse and wanted to go with him. In frustration, she let out a long scream. Then she whispered, "Why can't I allow myself to become Sooner's mother? I love them enough. What is wrong with me? Why am I so afraid to give him my heart?"

SUNNA, WE HAVE BEEN WAITING FOR YOU TO ASK THAT QUESTION. DO YOU WANT TO KNOW THE ANSWERS?

"Who is talking to me?"

YOU'VE HEARD OUR VOICE BEFORE. WE HAVE TAUGHT BEFORE.

Sunna recognized the familiar voice. "You are right. You are the Master Stones. Why did it not go the way you promised me?

Stacy had been watching Ghonllier on the server stone, leave the *Liberty Quest* with Sunna. When Ghonllier went back for Sunna, she slumped into her favorite chair in her study. Fear enveloped her. Watching Ghonllier allowing them to place restraints on his body, she thought, *You can't go to Suzair the Great now! Ghonllier! Just leave and take Sunna with you. They won't be able to shoot you and*

live. Think! You have the Stones! That demon will transfer the curse to you. You're letting love blind yourself Ghonllier. Don't do this.

Hitting her fists against the arms of the chair, Stacy blurted, "Honey, please pick him up now!" Bringing her voice to a whisper, she added, "Don't let them take my boy away from us again."

The high-pitched cackling sound of Scremper laughing at Ghonllier's demise brought her back to the server stone. It was then, she heard, "NO!!"

Standing, she turned the server stone off, realizing it was Sooner.

He entered the room, shouting, "Scremper! Father! Grandmother, I heard both their voices . . . He'll kill father!" Seeing the server stone was off, he faced his grandmother. "Turn it back on! I want to see my father!"

She countered, "Sooner, get out! I thought you were over at your friend's house."

"I'm home! I heard Scremper's voice. What were you watching?" demanded Sooner defiantly. Stacy looked away. He pleaded, "Grandmother, please turn it on. I know Scremper wants to kill my father."

Seeing it was too late to hide the truth, she reluctantly said, "Server stone, on to Ghonllier."

The stone came on just as Scremper reached up to place the patch on his father's neck. Stacy let out a cry as Ghonllier collapsed to the floor. They watched Sunna yell at Scremper, while knocking out her captors. Sooner let out a cry to see Sunna fall on his father's back, reaching out for the patch.

Stacy grabbed Sooner and covered his face, when they heard Scremper yell, "Kill her now!"

Tears moistened their cheeks while they listened to the firing of the blasts. The two held each other, hoping somehow everything would be okay. They saw the blaster skip off of Ghonllier's body and go somewhere else. Stacy wanted to ask the server stone to show her where the blasts went so Sooner would see but something stopped her.

The sounds of debris falling caused them to look at the stone. "Finally," expressed Stacy, watching the *Liberty Quest* pick up Sunna and Ghonllier. Stacy ordered the stone to follow Ghonllier. When she saw them in the command center of the *Liberty Quest,* Stacy finally let out a deep sigh.

Everyone but Adamite ran out of the office to see Ghonllier and Sunna. Jason ordered Sam to pick them up the moment Ghonllier went down. He wanted to see where the blasts went when they bounced off Ghonllier's body.

Spencer waited in the command center, watching with the captains what was taking place on the planet. Ghonllier used the Master Stones to broadcast everything back to the captains on their monitor. So they would know where they were so they could pick up the Stones.

When Ghonllier went down, they left to pick them up, using the ships lasers to cut a hole in the roof of the building. The captains flipped on the hullercasts, when they lost Ghonllier's broadcasting the events.

Spencer waited for their lifeless bodies to appear on the beaming pad. When the light dissipated, he stared at Sunna's lifeless body as she lay on top of Ghonllier. Gostler entered the command center first to see Spencer fall on his knees so he could be next to Sunna.

Putting up his hands, Gostler shouted, "Spencer, don't touch them!"

But it was too late. Sparks shot from Spencer's fingertips. He let out a mournful cry and glared at Gostler. "Why can't I touch her?"

"They are being protected by a new I-Force device. When Gostler tells you to do something, Spencer, I suggest you follow his orders," informed Jason, heading for the captains. Arriving, Jason asked, "Are we being tracked?"

"Yes, sir," responded Butler, keeping his gaze on the panel.

Jason looked back at Gostler. "Are you sure the device will work if we're attacked?"

"Yes," assured Gostler, knowing Jason was referring to the Master Stones.

"Even if he's dead?" questioned Jason, seeing Cid and Janet joining them with gurneys.

Gostler nodded as Adamite joined them. Asustie ran to Jason and demanded, "Why are you saying he's dead? He can't . . ."

Jason looked away from the control panel, stopping Asustie from saying more. Softly, he whispered, "Honey, we aren't picking up any energy waves from Sunna and Ghonllier even with them on the ship. The ship knows when it's commander is dead or alive."

"Then why didn't you go earlier to get them?" cried Asustie.

"Asustie, please! This is hard on me, too. It's my sister involved here along with your brother. I do care very much for them both," chocked Jason, leaving abruptly.

Stopping, he faced Asustie and apologized, "Honey, I'm sorry. I shouldn't have lost my temper."

Asustie came to him and he put his arms around her while she divulged, "I'm scared. What is going to happen to us with him gone."

Suddenly the red lights and siren were triggered. Letting go of Asustie, Jason demanded, "Who's firing on us?"

"Commander! We have five incoming quasar cannon fire from the surface of the planet!" shouted Butler.

Jason looked at Gostler. "Are you sure we don't need to fire on them?" he repeated again.

"Yes," assured Gostler firmly.

"Captains. Ignore all challenges and get us into space. Remember to avoid I-Force. We won't want them firing on us, too," ordered Jason, looking back at his sister and Ghonllier.

Everyone looked up to watch the ceiling drop from the ceiling, encasing them in the command center.

Cid nervously asked, "When are you going to allow me to see my patients?"

"When we reach space," assured Gostler.

"Are we going into battle?" asked Cid.

Adamite responded, "Don't worry Cid. This won't be much of a battle. So you don't need to strap in."

"Look!" shouted Cid, pointing at the hullercast beneath his feet.

Everyone witnessed the blasts rapidly approaching them. They were on tract and it was obvious that the blasts were going to hit their ship.

"Are they tracking us with more fire power?" questioned Jason.

"Yes, Commander. We have fifteen more behind these and they are on tract," assured Butler.

Shortly, the first set of blasts arrived at the hull of the ship, only to be reflected off. They headed back for land. Cid was surprised to feel nothing.

Cid questioned, "That's it?"

"This isn't normal. What just happened here?" asked Spencer, looking at Jason.

Adamite, Gostler, and Jason exchanged looks, wondering how to answer. Jason answered, "You seeing I-Force's latest protection shield." Then he faced Gostler and quizzed, "Is this what we expect every time we're attacked?"

"Yes," assured Gostler.

"Commander, we're picking up five Galaxy Creepers coming out of jump speed," announced Butler.

"Can you tell which side they belong to?" questioned Jason.

Butler shook his head. "Not yet, we're running their signal." Then after a moment, he announced, "They're ours, Commander."

Cid pointed behind Jason and asked, "Is this ship one of ours?"

Jason looked over his shoulder and responded, "No."

"The Star Screamer is ordering us to surrender. They want us alive," informed Sam.

"Yeah, I bet they do," responded Jason. Looking at the captains, he ordered, "Don't answer them. Just get us into jump speed."

Everyone watched the KOGN Star Screamer following them. It had no problem keeping up with the *Liberty Quest*. When Sam didn't respond to their request, the KOGN fired at them while in close range. The blasts barely touched the surface before swooping upward, making an arch, and returning to the KOGN ship that fired. The blasts split and spread out, disappearing inside the ship. Moments later, the ship started to break up.

Spencer pointed at the ship. "Wow! Are you telling me that this is part of our new shield?"

"Yes. The stones have the capability to spilt the blast directing them to the ships most vulnerable areas," answered Gostler.

Jason shot a glance at Gostler, before he asked the captains. "How much longer until transition?"

"It's coming up," answered Sam.

"Commander, I have a message from the lead I-Force's Galaxy Creeper. They're aware that we're the *Liberty Quest* and they want us to surrender," informed Butler.

"Are they in range to fire?" asked Jason.

"They are positioning themselves," answered Butler.

"Get away from them. Our new shields will return their blast. I want them to fight with KOGN not us," grumbled Jason.

"Acknowledged, you'll lose them," countered Sam.

Asustie arrived next to Jason and gave him a frustrated look. Jason gave her a half smile as he was searching the hullercast, looking for more ships. Finally, Butler announced, "Transition coming up and we're clear of I-Force."

Suddenly the colors in the hullercast changed to yellow with streaks of blue and green. The colors disappeared to show they were alone in space. Everyone gathered around the beaming pad.

Jason was watching Gostler. The former Master nodded and Jason expressed, "Cid, get your patients. You should be able to touch them."

Spencer had stayed there by Sunna and Ghonllier. Slowly, he rolled her off Ghonllier's back and into his strong arms. With ease, he carried Sunna to the gurney. Jason and Adamite rolled Ghonllier over onto his back.

Butler announced, "Commander, we're now picking up Sunna and Ghonllier's energy waves."

"They're alive!" cried Asustie.

Adamite let out a sigh as he shot Gostler a look. *They're alive. I never want to go through this again,* he thought. Cid and Janet didn't take the time to secure them to the gurney before they hooked them up to the monitors through the analyzer. If they were alive, Cid wanted to know how close they were to death.

Cid read Ghonllier's vital signs the minute they appeared. Looking away, he asked, "Janet, what are you getting on Sunna?"

"It's not good Cid. She's dying. There is poison still entering her body," answered Janet, looking at Cid.

"Still?" questioned Jason, coming to the other side of the gurney.

Jason saw her fist clutched. Grabbing her wrist, he lifted up her hand. Barely sticking out, they saw a piece of the patch. See it, Cid bellowed, "Jason, don't touch it! Janet, get it for me."

Both medics went for the supply closets underneath the gurneys, retrieving protective gloves. Janet pried the wadded up patch out of her hand while Jason held onto her wrist. Moments later, Cid arrived, taking it from Janet with his protective gloves.

He ordered, "Get her hand washed now."

The family watched Cid disappear into the corridor at a run. Adamite faced Gostler and asked, "Are you picking up any thoughts from him?"

"No."

Adamite went to Ghonllier's monitors and looked at his vital signs. *At least, he is alive, but in what condition?* thought Adamite, looking back at Sunna. *What was on that patch and will cause us to lose her? Ghonllier isn't going to be the same if she dies on him, too. I know he still loves her.*

Janet interrupted his thoughts by activating Ghonllier's safety straps. In a daze, he watched her code the gurney to follow her. Shortly she left with both gurneys and Adamite didn't want to be left out. Everyone joined him, including Spencer.

Adamite stopped, waiting for Gostler to join him. Speaking in the ancient language, Adamite asked, "Why can the captains pick up their energy waves, but you're not picking up his thoughts?"

Gostler answered him in the Eraphin language. "It means their bodies are alive for now, but his spirit is somewhere else."

"What do you mean? Where could he be?" asked Adamite, staying in the language.

"Ghonllier could be anywhere with the Stones."

They arrived as Cid appeared from the Med-C. The medic opened Ghonllier's door as Adamite stopped him. They watched Janet take the patients through the hullercast before Adamite asked, "What was on the patch?"

Everyone waited for his answer. "It was a contaminated Truth Test."

Cid disappeared through the hullercasts with the others following. Jason held back to make sure Spencer didn't follow them. When he attempted, Jason ordered, "Spencer, stop. You'll have to stay out with them receiving a Truth Test."

He looked despondently at the hullercast and nodded. Seeing Jason leave, he requested, "Tell me the minute you know which direction she is going into. If they can't save her, please let me say my last good-byes."

"I will," assured Jason, leaving Spencer.

Jason entered to see Janet and Cid applying patches to their necks. After they both studied their vital signs, Cid quizzed, "What do you have, Janet?"

"She's just sitting there, not moving."

"What's her score?"

"Four over ten. What's his?"

"A seven over ten," answered Cid. "I don't like her scores. I want fluid and the bag for her."

Janet immediately left and Cid shut the door after her.

Adamite spoke, "Cid, you're the only one who's allowed to touch my son." Cid nodded. "I want you to be my son's personal medic tech. So you'll be answering directly to him, not me."

"I understand . . ."

"Wait!" reminded Gostler. "He can't accept that responsibility without taking an oath and he needs to know to whom."

"Can we tell him?" asked Adamite.

"I'm not feeling restrained. Tell him," informed Gostler.

Cid faced Gostler and inquired, "Why do I need to take another oath to be the Master of the Galaxy's medic tech?"

"Who told you? Do we have a security problem?" roared Jason.

Cid looked perplexed at Jason's response. "I wouldn't get too upset Jason. In a way Ghonllier told me."

"When did you find out?" quizzed Adamite.

"When you returned from seeing your son, Suzair the Great. Ghonllier gave orders to Janet, regarding Sunna's care. With Ghonllier not being her medic, she had to get my permission first to do any-thing. Sunna was my patient. When she asked, I was so stunned to learn Suzair the Great was your son. I told her to do anything Ghonllier ordered her to do. He superceded me at all times. Remember, I promised you, Adamite, to handle it that way when Sunna almost died from the spider bite."

"So she assumed you knew," whispered Jason.

"And why shouldn't I know? Why didn't you tell me Adamite?" retorted Cid.

"Sorry, I didn't have permission to tell you or anyone on my staff. Ghonllier can only give that permission," apologized Adamite respectfully.

"And he has to have the Master Stones' permission," added Gostler. Facing Cid, he repeated, "So you give your complete allegiance to the Master Stones."

"Yes I do."

"Good from now on, Ghonllier will protect you first because you are close to him," said Gostler. Cid nodded. He added, "I also need to teach you how to work around them. They can be lethal to some people . . ."

A knock came to the door and Cid told Gostler to tell him later. Then he requested everyone leave when he opened the door. Janet entered with everyone else leaving. Reluctantly, Adamite took one last look at his son. Being the last to exit, he heard Spencer asking about Sunna. Adamite sighed wishing the Tron wasn't there. It was stressful, trying to keep the truth away from him.

Jason explained to him what Cid had told him as Adamite half listened. Afterwards everyone just listened to the muffled sounds of Cid giving instructions to the women. Shortly, the door opened and Cid exited.

Spencer started to pepper Cid with questions and Jason held his breath. They didn't have time to inform Cid that Spencer wasn't aware of Ghonllier's title. Watching, Jason was impressed with how Cid handled it. He did not divulge anything of important about them to Spencer. Cid promised if she dropped to a one or two, he could come in. Then he left.

When Cid returned, they were relieved to hear, "Janet paged me. We can enter."

He opened the door with everyone entering but Spencer. Jason glanced back to make sure he wasn't coming and noticed his forlorn expression. For the first time, Jason felt sorry for him. It was obvious that Spencer was smitten with Sunna. *I wonder if she feels the same way*, Jason thought, walking through the hullercast.

He entered hearing Asustie ask about Sunna's future if she lived. Cid wasn't very encouraging. Sunna had been poisoned twice within a short time. It upset him to listen to all the possibilities of Sunna's chances in the future. Jason looked at Ghonllier and decided that he was going to keep her close to him. Maybe, Ghonllier would know of something that might help her have health. So far, he had Cid do things that medic weren't aware of. *The Stones might save her*, he thought.

Jason came out of his thoughts when he heard Cid explain. "If she dies, Sunna will stay unconscious and no one will be able to talk with her."

Those words made him think about his parents. They were going to be devastated. His mother was sure Sunna would die young because she had chosen to be a spy. *Maybe, she was right*, Jason thought, looking at his sister in a bag.

Finally he joined the conversation. Jason asked, "Cid. What contaminated the patch?"

"It was a bacteria that's found in standing water. It is unusual for that to happen. I think someone was trying to kill them and make it look like an accident or they were stupid."

"Let's go with stupid. I know the man and he isn't very bright," stated Adamite.

"Yeah. I agree. He wasn't a medic. I would like to know how he got the patch in the first place," stated Jason.

"How did Scremper see Ghonllier and Sunna go into the building?" asked Asustie.

"I stayed back and asked that question. He was on the roof of the building next to the one they entered," stated Adamite.

"As a Koala?" questioned Jason.

Adamite nodded. Jason sighed. So that explains what happened. Looking at Cid, Jason asked, "Can you tell how old that patch was?"

"Yes. That was the other problem. It was two days old and it looked it had been used before Sunna and Ghonllier got it."

That stupid Tron! Jason thought. He was angry with the Tron for maybe killing his sister. It sounded like something that Scremper would do. Jason had watched him on the server stone go through garbage, looking for item that he might be able to use. Tears wailed up in his eyes as he thought about it.

Jason came out of his thoughts when Adamite asked, "Jason. I want you to take his restraints off."

"I refuse," answered Jason.

"I agree," responded Cid.

"Cid, you need to check Ghonllier's monitor. We are losing him. I can feel it," warned Gostler.

The medic ran to the monitor. Moments later, he said, "You're right."

"The Stones want you to bring him back now."

Cid paused before he left, leaving the door open. Everyone stayed quiet so Janet or Spencer wouldn't hear them. Shortly, the medic returned with a container and closed the door. He looked at everyone and informed them to stand back.

The medic tightened the straps on the gurney while looking at the monitor.

"Gostler are you sure about this. What I'm about to do to him is harsh."

"I can read his thoughts again. He thinks he's dead and he is in heaven. I know he is not. We need to force him to wake up or we will loose him for good."

Asustie moved toward Jason and he put his arm around her. They both needed comfort.

"What's going on?" asked Adamite in the ancient language.

"The Stones have taken his spirit somewhere else. He thinks he's not coming back. If he has no desire to return, then they will lose the connection to his spirit. They can't force him to return but we can," responded Gostler in their common language.

Cid removed the lid as he brought the container close to Ghonllier's face. Ghonllier jerked his head slightly but he did not open his eyes. Cid had placed the lid back on while he studied the monitors. Then he shook his head.

"I need to do it again. If it doesn't work this time, we might be too late," said Cid, removing the lid again.

When he placed the open container close to Ghonllier face, he started to choke and cry out Sunna's name. Asustie left Jason going to her brother's side.

Cid grabbed her. "Move back, he might hurt you."

"He won't hurt me," answered Asustie, trying to get to him. Jason held her back.

After Ghonllier stopped screaming out Sunna's name, he choked and gasped for air. He opened his eyes as Asustie attempted to break his hold.

"Why did you bring me back?" he snarled.

Asustie broke away and joined him. "You're were dying . . ."

"Why didn't you just let go!" snapped Ghonllier.

He glared toward Asustie and Cid. She was stunned to see how glassy and blood shoot his eyes were. The look frightened Asustie and she just froze there. Jason came forward to remove Asustie.

"Honey. He isn't himself. You can get hurt."

With Asustie gone, Ghonllier struggled to get free from the straps on the gurney. Frustrated, he had no freedom. Ghonllier roared, "Get out . . . all of you. . . . I . . . didn't want . . . to come back!"

Medicine used to bring Ghonllier back

35

"Sorry, I had to do it," apologized Cid.

In anger, Ghonllier tried to grab Cid, loosing the straps on the gurney. He attempted to sit up only to find, he had lost his ability to use his hand. The restraints wouldn't allow him to push the straps out of their position.

For the first time, he saw the restraints. In anger, Ghonllier started to pull at them, wanting the restraints off his wrists.

Gostler could read and understand his thoughts clearly. Upset with what he was reading, Gostler wanted to distract Ghonllier by asking, "Ghonllier, why are you so angry?"

"Read . . . my mind . . . old man!" snapped Ghonllier.

"Why is he so angry?" asked Asustie.

Gostler put his hand up and shook his head. Asustie looked back at her brother to see him continuing to pull at his restraints.

"Ghonllier, do you realize that you were given a Truth Test?" asked Cid. Ghonllier stopped while he stared at him. Cid added. "Ghonllier, Sunna is barely alive. She's beyond my skill and equipment. I need you to tell me how to save her."

"I . . . can't . . . help . . . her. Death . . . is her . . . choice."

Gostler closed his eyes now, understanding what happened. It was very clear in Ghonllier's mind and the former Master could see it.

Asustie grabbed her brother's arms and questioned, "Are you going to just let Sunna go without a fight? She saved your life."

He glared at her. "I . . . can't help . . . her . . . if she . . . doesn't want . . . me to."

Asustie wasn't listening to his words as she pleaded, "Why can't you help her? You have the Stones? Are you going to just let her die?"

"I'll . . . never . . . use . . . the Stones . . . again," stated Ghonllier, looking away. "Plus . . . this . . . is . . . what . . . she . . . wants."

Gostler moaned and sadly shook his head. He ached for them both to understand Sunna's choice. Ghonllier's heart was broken and Gostler was concerned that it would take a long time for him to med it. The Stones wouldn't be able to work well with his broken heart. They needed him healthy mentally and spiritually to become the Master in time to save Gomper and the galaxy. The curse had already started to reverse. If Ghonllier stops now, Bog would win. The galaxy would be destroyed.

Refusing to give up, Asustie challenged, "Ghonllier. You love her. I heard you tell Cid and mother. How can you let her just die?"

The questions caused tears to flow from the very corners of Ghonllier's eyes.

In anger, Asustie shouted, "Help her!"

Frustrated with his sister and his ability to communicate, Ghonllier let out a mournful scream.

Gostler put his hand on her arm. "Asustie, please drop it. He asked her to come back with him and she refused. . . . He's right. This time he can't help her. If Sunna lives or dies, it's her choice. The power is in her hands."

Asustie found it hard to hear Gostler's explanation. She was confused. Her brother didn't give her a chance to ask more questions. Ghonllier was letting out his true feeling because of the drug. He had become dangerous to himself, but it wasn't going to stop him as he lifted his head in an attempt to break out of his restraints.

By lifting his head, he instantly was overcome with dizziness. It felt strong, causing his very head to ache. He let out a lowly moan and brought his hand up to comfort his eyes, only to be reminded he couldn't.

In anger, he shouted, "Get . . . these . . . off me!"

"You take them off. Use the Stones to break them. You did it on the Mossen planet," challenged Gostler.

"NO!"

"Why?" matched Gostler.

"I . . . failed . . ."

"You'll only fail if you quit and allow Bog to take over the galaxy."

Ghonllier screamed again. Stepping closer, Gostler warned, "Ghonllier, be careful right now. Trust the Stones and remember what they had told you."

The only thoughts he remembered were the Master Stones telling him he was too late and he should've asked them to help him with Sunna earlier. Pain from his broken heart shot through him again and he let out another painful cry. Then he followed it with deep sobs, which caused his entire body to tremble. This soon brought tears to everyone in the room.

Adamite grabbed Gostler's arm. With tears glistening his cheeks, Adamite pleaded, "Please Gostler, tell me what is happening to him."

In the Eraphin language, he told him everything that he knew. Adamite was saddened to learn Sunna had refused to return to be with him. She would rather die than live. This was how Ghonllier saw it and Adamite wondered if Sunna really felt that way. He knew how much she loved Sooner.

Gostler stopped as Ghonllier let out another pained cry. Then he attempted to break the restraints, using his own strength. The restraints held, causing his wrists to bleed. When blood appeared, everyone expected Ghonllier to stop, but he didn't.

Asustie started to cry, seeing her brother act this way. Wanting it to stop, she pleaded, "Ghonllier, please stop it. You're hurting yourself and I can't watch you do this."

Hearing his sister's pleas, he stopped and looked over at her. Asustie gently wiped away his tears with her fingertip and whispered, "I'm here Little Brother and I won't leave you. I promise to be with you through this. You and I have been apart from each other for so long and I don't want you to ever feel alone."

Asustie's words were soothing to him. There was something between the two of them that they simply couldn't explain. Ghonllier ached to hear those words from Sunna, but Asustie affected him in a way that he didn't understand. He stared at the ceiling while she spoke to him.

Finally, he faced her with bloodshot eyes and said, "I . . . don't . . . have the . . . strength . . . to do . . . this . . . alone."

Asustie leaned over to give him a kiss on the forehead. "I won't leave you, Brother. We'll do this together. You and I. I can feel your power when I touch you," whispered Asustie.

"I . . . know," answered Ghonllier. He added, "Somehow, you . . . are a part . . . of this. Me . . . and the Stones."

Cid looked away from the stats and inquired, "Ghonllier, do you have a headache?"

"Yes."

The medic retrieved a patch from the supply closet underneath his bed on the gurney. While Cid activated the patch, Ghonllier attempted to remove his restraints from his wrists again, by using his strength as a man. His attempt caused more bleeding and it upset Asustie that the blood didn't bother Ghonllier.

She placed her hand on top of his and he stopped. Looking at her, he demanded, "Take . . . them . . . off."

Asustie looked at Jason, while Gostler challenged, "Break them, Ghonllier. You have the power to do so."

Gostler hoped Ghonllier would get back in harmony with the Master Stones and be the Master again. Instead, Ghonllier snapped, "Leave me . . . alone . . . old . . . man. . . . I'll . . . never . . . use . . . the Stones . . . again. You . . . can't force . . . me . . . to be . . . the Master . . . of the Galaxy."

"I guess you'll live with the restraints," replied Gostler in a stern voice. "You're the only one who will take them off."

Ghonllier let out a long and forlorn scream again. With the Truth Test, he had no control of his emotions.

"Stop this!" begged Asustie. Going to her husband, she pleaded, "Take the restraints off."

Jason finally answered Asustie pleading looks. "I can't."

Asustie ran to her father. "How can you stand by and watch this? This is your son."

"Honey, you don't understand. He'll hurt someone if we take them off. He doesn't have control of his anger," assured Adamite.

Jason came forward to comfort Asustie, by taking her into his arms. Ghonllier continued to remove the restraints. Blood increased to soak his uniform. Cid reached out to check his wounds and Ghonllier knocked his hand away.

Using his weight of his body, Cid leaned on his arm to stop him from pulling at the restraints. Then he placed his fingers in four different places on Ghonllier's chest. He held them until Ghonllier relaxed. It caused Ghonllier to drift off into a quiet, peaceful sleep. Cid removed his weight and hands from Ghonllier's body before he looked at the monitors.

"What did you just do?" asked Adamite.

"I temporality blocked nerves, going from his emotions to his brain. We need to stop this until the medicine works its way out of his body," educated Cid.

Asustie faced Cid. "Is there a chance he'll go back to where Sunna is?" quizzed Asustie.

"No, he's tried. The way back has collapsed. I can read that much from his mind," informed Gostler.

"Look, he's through the worst. Why don't you all leave?" added Cid.

"He won't wake up again?" questioned Asustie.

Cid nodded. "He'll wake up again and I'll have to use those pressure points to help him control his emotions. But nothing new will happen."

"So he will be violent again?" asked Asustie, going to her brother.

"Most likely," responded Cid as Asustie ran her fingers along her brother's jaw line.

"Why won't she love him? He's so worth it," whispered Asustie, leaning over and kissing him on the forehead.

Chapter 3

The Fight

*S*ince Ghonllier had come into Gomper's life, it hadn't been the same. With his self-awareness getting stronger every day, Gomper found himself hungering for answers to what had happened to him the last thirty years.

He wanted to know the simplest things like how old he was now. Time was measured differently throughout the galaxy. No one from his staff seemed to know how old he was, since Suzair the Great never celebrated a birthday. Now, Gomper couldn't rely on his memory. It was gone.

In some way, Gomper's mind getting stronger wasn't a blessing. It made him feel lonely and isolated, realizing he wasn't with his family. No one seemed able to tell him about them or what had happened to his life. This was only part of his problem.

Bog, the evil sorcerer who had possessed his body, was still there. He was miserable to live with. When the sorcerer stepped into his body, Gomper shuddered. Bog was cruel to those around him. The three staff members, who were aware of Gomper, called Bog the demon and it got old for Gomper to live with him.

So far, Bog had never spoken directly to Gomper. So he wasn't sure if Bog could read his mind or just listen to their words to know what was going on. He strongly suspected Bog couldn't read his mind and he didn't want to ask him to find out for sure. Every time Bog was about to take over, Gomper would hear a mumbling sound.

The experience was always very unpleasant and Gomper would brace himself for it.

It was Bog who ordered the invasion of the Mossen planet and Gomper wondered why. It didn't make a lot of sense to him and the staff informed him that Suzair the Great never justified his actions to them.

Through Bog's mumbling, Gomper learned the demon wanted the Master Stones and he didn't want to help him find them. Gomper did remember his history that the Mossen planet was the home of Sethus, the first Master of the Stones. *Maybe he thinks they're here*, thought Gomper, waiting for people to bring him what Bog had ordered them to find.

After Ghonllier's appearance on the Jabula moon, Bog moved their headquarters to a Galaxy Creeper. Bog realized it was too easy for Ghonllier to reach his brother if they were on land without him being prepared for it. This time, Bog wanted Ghonllier to find Gomper. If they met, the curse would transfer from Gomper to Ghonllier and the Master Stones. He would finally have them.

Bog was limited in his power to control Gomper, which was why his memory and awareness of himself was emerging. Since Ghonllier had burnt the three books and destroyed his stepping stone, Bog was crippled. The stepping stone allowed the sorcerer to see Gomper and know what was going on behind his back.

When Ghonllier stole the books and burnt them, Bog lost his ability to see things through Gomper's eyes. Now, Bog was frustrated with only being able to hear what was going on in Gomper's life. Bog hoped by transferring the curse to Ghonllier and the Master Stones, he would be able to control him without his tools. Bog desired the meeting of the two brothers and hoped he didn't have to wait long.

Someone interrupted Bog's thoughts with, "Your Grace."

Gomper winced to hear that title. Every time he heard it, Gomper thought about Gostler and his heart ached to know that he didn't save him from whatever happened to him.

Looking over at Pappar, Gomper requested, "Do you have to call me by that name?"

"Yes, for all of our safety. We have to. Please cooperate with us," sighed Pappar.

Gomper nodded and looked away. "What do you want?"

He could hear Pappar's voice, but Gomper found it hard to listen to his words. If Pappar said something that upset Bog, the sorcerer would speak through Gomper and he hated it. During those moments, Gomper felt helpless. Those moments motivated him to find a way to stop Bog from using his body.

Not realizing it, Gomper was getting stronger every time he used his mind. Bog was aware of it and wanted him to stop and just follow orders like in the past.

Since Gomper had become aware of himself and started to think for his own, Jamham, the head of his household, and Pappar, the man in charge of his security, never left his side. Brewster, Gomper's personal medical tech, would trade off with the other two men. The rest of what KOGN considered Suzair the Great's personal staff consisted of fifteen bodyguards and Pursy. He was Suzair the Great's personal assistant and handled his military matters.

For security reasons, Pappar, Jamham, and Brewster were the only ones who knew about Gomper. They kept the others away from Suzair the Great so they wouldn't realize that Gomper was there. If KOGN found out that Suzair the Great had a spilt personality, they would kill him. The law was decreed by Suzair the Great that if a man was killed, so was his personal staff. So these men were very protective of Gomper.

The main reason they didn't want to leave Gomper alone had been because he had no memory of anything that happened to him for the last thirty years. They had to educate him about everything. They hoped to make others believe that he was the feared Suzair the Great.

The biggest challenge they had was getting Gomper to sound like Bog. The two personalities were completely different, including their voices. Suzair the Great had a hard, cold tone in his voice. Gomper was totally the opposite.

Brewster, Pappar, and Jamham had become fond of Gomper and were protective of him out of love. Gomper tried to tell them his real name, but they refused to hear it. Gomper understood their reasoning, but it only increased his feelings of loneliness and isolation.

The staff saw his hurt look and tried to make it up to him. They treated Gomper with respect and warmth because Gomper treated them that way. Gomper developed a love and respect for them very quickly, which made a good team of protecting each other. Their lives depended on it.

Pappar interrupted Gomper's thoughts. "Your Grace, how do you want to handle it?"

Gomper gave him a confused look before he confessed, "Pappar, I didn't hear your question. I drifted off when I heard you talking about the local leaders."

"We just received word that they have all the leaders rounded up that you requested. . . ."

"I didn't request it," reminded Gomper.

"That Suzair the Great requested. Commander Jabolt wants to know if you want to interrogate them or let him do it," repeated Pappar.

Gomper shook his head. "I don't want to do it. I don't want to be here on this planet."

"Then I'll tell Pursy to have Commander Jabolt do it. But I think you should handle it."

"Why?" questioned Gomper, looking at him.

"Suzair the Great always handles situations like this," informed Pappar.

Gomper looked away and Pappar waited for his answer.

"Have this Commander Jabolt handle it. I don't care how it looks. You keep telling me that I don't sound quite like this Suzair the Great and we don't know if the demon will handle it. Besides, I don't understand the demon's purpose for doing this," responded Gomper, going over to the window.

With Pappar leaving, Gomper heard Bog mumbling and braced himself. Moments later, he heard Bog bellow, "I can feel a Mingler nearby. Bring her to me!"

A Mingler, thought Gomper. *There is no one new in this room. What is the demon talking about?* This was the moment Asustie was looking at him through the server stone. If only Gomper had known his family and Gostler were watching him. In a way, it was best he wasn't aware.

Pursy opened the door and gingerly approached his boss. "Your Grace, I have an urgent message for you."

Gomper eyed him for a moment before grabbing the message out of his hand. Then, as he began to read, Pursy disappeared out through the door.

The message was from a Scremper, explaining he had found his brother there on the planet. This affected him so much that the message immediately fell from his hands as soon as he finished reading it.

Then he turned to Pappar and Jamham and uttered aloud, "My brother is on this planet." Though, before anyone could respond, Bog shot back, "Where's my pilot?"

"She's on your Galaxy Creeper," informed Pappar, picking up the message.

"Get her here!" ordered Bog.

Pappar quickly handed the message to Jamham and exited to tell Pursy.

Being alone with Jamham, Gomper watched him read the message. When he was done, Jamham looked up as Gomper gave him a sudden nod. This was a signal to let him know that Bog was gone.

As Jamham handed the message back to him, Gomper asked, "Who's Scremper?"

Pappar entered the room and heard Gomper's question. Shutting the door, he answered, "He's a double spy who happens to be your personal contact with I-Force. Is the message from him?"

Gomper nodded and handed the message to Pappar, who began reading it.

"Do you want Scremper to capture your brother?" questioned Jamham.

Gomper hardly answered him, rather shrugging his shoulders as he thought of his brother being on the planet. Then, pausing for a moment, he asked, "Why did I send Scremper to the Mossen planet?"

"You didn't," informed Pappar, turning away from the message. "When you put a price on your brother's head, Scremper knew him and tried to sneak aboard his ship with a tractor on his body. Your brother found him and put him in prison here on this planet. You released him when we invaded."

The two men watched Gomper respond with a concerned expression. How could Gomper face Ghonllier in front of his officers? It would be too easy for Gomper to expose that Suzair the Great was really two people. They couldn't see Gomper staying quiet when Bog ordered his brother's death.

Wanting to know how Gomper felt, Pappar asked, "You look upset, Your Grace. Why?"

Gomper looked away, shrugging his shoulders. *I can't believe my brother would be that stupid to allow himself to be caught. . . . Unless he wants to see me and I'm afraid to meet him with this demon inside of me.*

"How do you feel about it?" asked Jamham.

Slowly coming out of his thoughts, he answered, "There is a part of me that so desires to see him . . . but alone without my officers and the demon."

"I wish you could do it without the demon, too, sir," interjected Pappar. "Why were you talking about a Mingler?"

Gomper shrugged one shoulder. "Has Suzair the Great ever mentioned a Mingler before?"

"Yes, it's a question he often asks when interrogating someone under the influence of the Truth Test."

"Hum," surmised Gomper, pausing. "Do you know what the demon plans to do with my brother?"

"The rumor had always been that Suzair the Great had killed his whole family before he took on the name of Suzair the Great," answered Jamham.

"Does anyone know his name before Suzair the Great?" asked Gomper.

The two men shook their heads. "He claims it has always been Suzair the Great. But rumor has it that he was another man before the war," said Jamham.

"Yeah, me," said Gomper, keeping his promise to not tell them his true name. He looked at them and quizzed, "Where are the server stones?"

"What's a server stone?" questioned Jamham.

"You have no idea of their existence?" questioned Gomper.

"No. Suzair the Great has never mentioned them," informed Pappar. "What are they?"

Gomper shrugged his shoulders. "Just something from my past is all." *I bet Gostler kept the server stones until my brother could take them. If he has them, then he knows what happened to me. I wonder if the demon felt a Mingler through the stones and if he did, who would be a Mingler? I've never met one before.*

Pursy returned, interrupting his thoughts this time. Going into character, Gomper glared at him. "What do you want?"

"Your pilot will be here in ten minutes, Your Grace," Pursy informed while backing out of the room.

With Pursy gone, Gomper requested, "Pappar, where are my guards?"

"They're out in the entryway of the building, waiting for you," he answered. "Do you want to go to them now and wait for your pilot?"

"Yes," responded Gomper, standing. Heading for the door, he added, "Are you going with me, Jamham, or is it just Pappar?"

"I really don't want to stay here without you," stated Jamham, joining them. "Your Commander Jabolt scares me," he added.

Jamham and Pappar flanked Gomper's sides as they entered the nerve center of the KOGN takeover of the Mossen planet. As they passed, people looked up from their workstations and watched them. Sometimes, when Suzair the Great swept through an office, he would cause anything that wasn't bolted to the floor to go flying through the air. Sometimes, he would accidentally kill someone and Bog did it to intimidate his staff. With Bog being unable to see, he hadn't been doing this since Ghonllier had started the slow reversing of the curse.

They all breathed a sigh of relief to see Suzair the Great and company exit through the doors without incident. Arriving at the front doors, his elite guards quickly stood at attention. Before Gomper could give them a command, they heard a loud rumbling sound. The building's windows shook slightly.

Looking at Pappar, he whispered, "What was that?"

Pappar educated in a soft tone, "Quasar cannon firing. It means an unauthorized spaceship has entered our atmosphere."

Behind them, the door opened. They looked to see it was Pursy. "Your Grace, we want—"

Bog interrupted, "Pursy, I want that ship identified now!"

The frightening glare in Gomper's face let Pursy know that he really meant yesterday. So he quickly disappeared.

With the door shut, Gomper looked outside. He felt a lot of mixed emotions surging inside. What did that unidentified ship mean? Did his brother escape with no intention of seeing him? So why was he here? His heart ached to speak with him alone and he was searching for a way to accomplish it.

The door opened and interrupted Gomper's thoughts. Looking over his shoulder, he saw Pursy standing timidly behind the door. "Your Grace, the ship is the *Liberty Quest.*"

My brother has escaped, thought Gomper with mixed emotions.

Bog ordered, "Arrest that stupid spy, Scremper. I want him in irons and thrown back into prison."

Pursy answered, "Your Grace, Scremper is dead along with the men who tried to arrest your brother."

"How did they die?" asked Gomper.

"From their own blasts."

Good, he's getting stronger. A loud booming sound shook the windows, causing everyone to jump back. Bog had sent a chair flying into a wall, just missing the door. Pursy quickly disappeared while the others looked nervously at Gomper. In his head, Gomper could hear Bog yelling and he wanted to shut him out. It hurt his mind to hear the ranting and ravings of the demon. Gomper decided to focus on something else, waiting for Bog to calm down.

Stepping away from the others, he stood closer to the windows and pretended to watch for his Star Skipper through the ceiling windows. In his heart, he ached to be on the *Liberty Quest* with Ghonllier. Unconsciously, Gomper searched the skies, hoping to see his ship.

Jamham and Pappar joined him. "I'm sorry, sir, you won't be seeing your brother," soothed Jamham.

"It's probably better. You know the demon won't go lightly on either one of us," stated Gomper, suddenly feeling the ground shaking.

A blast from the sky hit the ground. Looking up, Gomper saw more following the first one. With each hit, the ground shook, knocking them to the floor. Fire shot high up into the air. The windows rattled before one broke. Luckily, the window in front of them held.

Standing to his feet, Pappar expressed, "What was that?"

The others joined as the doors of the inner office opened. Pursy shouted, "Your Grace, please don't leave just yet!"

"What do you want?" growled Gomper, searching the skies.

"Our quasar cannon were just taken out and we are tracking five I-Force Galaxy Creepers coming out of the jump fields."

"Coming out! Who fired on our cannons?" questioned Pappar, facing Pursy.

"They apparently were the same blasts we fired at the *Liberty Quest*. Somehow, they deflected the blast, sending them back to the cannons," informed Pursy.

Fire erupted high into the sky and Gomper stared at it with pleasure. *He's just proved to me that he's getting stronger. He would've killed me if we met. I know how the Master Stones work and Bog would try to kill him, causing me to get killed. The demon has lost and doesn't know it. My brother will be coming for me soon and I just hope he'll answer my questions before I have to die for my crimes against the galaxy.*

With Gomper not answering him, Pursy repeated, "Your Grace, what do you want people to do?"

"Evacuate!" snapped Gomper. Then Bog added, "Track the *Liberty Quest*, I want to know where she's fighting."

"Yes, Your Grace," acknowledged Pursy, leaving.

They watched the door close, only to hear another explosion that did shatter the windows in front of them. The shattered window fell upon those waiting for the Star Skipper. Some were hurt, but Gomper seemed to miss most of the flying glass.

The broken window allowed smoke from the fires to fill the room. Gomper thought he saw something in the smoke, but wasn't sure and started to choke for air.

Pappar suddenly got a call. Answering his C-Stone, he listened to the person contacting him. Sharply, he put his C-Stone away and announced, "She's here just outside the door in the smoke. Fran wants us to hurry. According to her reading, the fires are spreading this way."

Coughing, Gomper nodded and bolted through the door into the blinding smoke. Everyone followed to find Fran and the ship just outside. She opened the door, just as they arrived.

Gomper was glad to be inside so he could breathe. The smoke hurt his eyes as they watered. Sitting down, Fran, his pilot, shouted, "Secure yourself. I'm taking off."

After she brought the ship straight up, they could easily see the fires below. Then she banked away from the smoke, leaving it quickly behind. Gomper put his face up to the small window to see fire emergency shuttles flying. They were spraying chemicals on the fire below, trying to put it out. Right before they moved out of sight, Gomper saw a couple of other explosions and wondered what happened. He wondered if Pursy and the others made it out of the building.

Looking at the others, Gomper decided that he wanted to be alone. The three men seldom gave him the opportunity and he figured they would this time. Standing, he headed for the closest door to a storage room. Opening the door, he was relieved to see it was almost empty. Letting out a sigh, he entered and shut the door.

Resting his forehead against the narrow windows, Gomper relaxed his mind and wondered about his brother. It surprised him to feel remorse for not being able to go with him. For some reason, he felt abandoned. *Where's my family and Gostler? Why didn't anyone came to find me? Did they come for him and the demon killed them? Was it just Ghonllier and he who were left alive?*

Jamham watched him leave and didn't like the idea of Gomper being alone. Star Skippers were set up to seat approximately fifteen people, plus they had two rooms for cargo. The loyal servant followed him into the cargo room where Gomper entered.

Hearing the door open, Gomper shot him a glance, acknowledging his presence. Then he stared outside.

Jamham stepped closer and asked, "Is there something wrong? Do you want to talk or can I get you something to eat or drink?"

"Yeah, I'm thirsty and would like something to settle my stomach. The demon's hard on my body."

Jamham paused to study Gomper. Right now, he looked like a sad and broken man. Wanting to remind him that he needed to change his demeanor, matching Suzair the Great, Jamham started, but stopped.

Instead, he informed, "Your Grace, Fran got a report that the *Liberty Quest* has left the planet. She's not a part of the battle."

Gomper nodded while staring outside. The look on Gomper's face concerned him. Pausing again at the door, Jamham glanced at him once more. Then he disappeared to only return shortly. Joining him at the window, Jamham gave Gomper a container of water.

Taking a sip from the container, Gomper asked, "How many people have I killed the last thirty years?"

"Millions."

Quickly removing the container from his face, he questioned, "How did I kill millions?"

"You ordered it to be done for your soldiers. Most of them were robots."

"How many have I killed personally?"

Jamham shook his head. "We haven't kept count. There's been too many."

"How did I start this war?" asked Gomper, facing him.

"You and two other men started the KOGN, claiming you were the new Master of the Galaxy."

"And what does KOGN mean?"

"King of Galaxy Nations."

Gomper snorted, "I don't like it."

"No one questioned it. People joined you thinking you were the real . . ."

Gomper gave him a sharp look and interrupted, "I'm not the real Master of the Galaxy."

"A lot of people believed so when no one challenged you."

"No one? Why did we have a war?"

"Well, there was a large group who didn't believe you, but you forced most of them to join you or be killed."

"Who died?"

"Anyone who knew the former Master of the Galaxy or were gifted," answered Jamham.

Gomper sat on a couple of large containers that were stored in the room. He sighed before Gomper expressed, "Why gifted people? Why did I kill them? Did this include Trons?"

"No Trons. You only killed Vanishers, Movelings, or Control Temps. For some reason, the demon only killed them. The Trons were recruited to spy for you. Scremper was a Tron."

"Where are the three other men who started this with me?"

"You killed them. One by one they had accidents created by you."

Gomper studied Jamham for a moment. "We both know I'm not the Master of the Galaxy. Why did people believe it?"

"When the three of you started to terrorize the galaxy, the Master of the Galaxy didn't appear to stop you. So you announced that the old Master of the Galaxy was dead and you were the new one. Haven't you noticed that you're usually the oldest person in a room?"

Gomper let his back fall against the wall and looked up at him. "My parents were Movelings and knew the Master of the Galaxy. So they must be dead."

"What about your brother? We understood your whole family was killed by you years ago."

"Me!"

"Yes, you killed your family in front of witnesses. They were gifted people and you used it as an example for others to join you."

So how did my younger brother live? thought Gomper, looking outside again.

"Do you think your brother is gifted?" asked Jamham.

Gomper shrugged his shoulders. "Jamham, I have no memory of Ghonllier. I don't know anything about him, except for what I hear from you all. The last thing I remember, my mother was pregnant with twins. So he must be a twin."

"Then you have more than this brother," reminded Jamham.

"Yeah, maybe I do," whispered Gomper.

"I'm sorry you have no memory of anything. We wished you did," sighed Jamham. Studying Gomper for a moment, he saw a painful expression. So he asked, "Are you concerned about something?"

Gomper slowly looked at him. "Our days are numbered, my friend, and I don't think we'll live much longer."

"Do you think your brother will kill you?"

Gomper nodded. "He has to kill me to be the real Master of the Galaxy."

"Will he kill us all?" quizzed Jamham.

"If you'll give him your allegiance from your heart, he can't kill you."

"So why will he kill you? Don't you want to give him your allegiance?"

"Yes, but the demon inside of me will force him to kill me, if we meet," whispered Gomper.

"If you die, the KOGN will automatically kill us, too. They'll send out assassins," reminded Jamham.

"Not by the real Master of the Galaxy. He won't allow anyone else to kill you if you give your allegiance to him."

"Are you sure?"

Gomper nodded. "The real Master of the Galaxy is merciful, Jamham. He isn't like what you have had to live with. Give him your allegiance and you'll live."

"If he's merciful, then why wouldn't he save your life? We both know it wasn't you who has torn this galaxy apart."

Gomper grunted. "Even if my brother can separate the demon from me, how long do you think I'll live, if people learned I was Suzair the Great? There is so much hate toward him. I have no future." He took a long drink of water from his container. Lowering it, Gomper handed it back to Jamham and said, "Thank you. . . . Thank you for all that you do for me."

"It sounds strange hearing those kind words coming from you."

"I guess this whole thing is confusing to all of us," sighed Gomper.

"Can I get you anything else?"

Gomper shook his head. "I need to be alone. I want some time to be me before I have to act like Suzair the Great."

Nodding, Jamham left. Pausing at the door, he watched Gomper go back into the look of being a man totally defeated and weak. Leaving, Jamham felt sorry for him.

Gomper stopped him from leaving. "Keep me informed of the battle. I want to know if it has reached my Galaxy Creeper."

"Consider it done," responded Jamham, shutting the door.

The moment Jamham shut the door, Gomper heard in his head, *I want your brother to kill you.*

The words were clear and Gomper recognized the voice. "I know you want him to kill me, demon. Why tell me?"

It's about time we talk, since I have control of you.

"Why should we talk? I've heard enough of you."

I'm talking because I want you to do something for me.

"Why should I ever do something for you?"

53

I do have control of you.

"No, you don't. You don't have complete control of me. I'm getting stronger and it's just a matter of time until I break the chain that you have on me."

You'll never break it. Death is your only way out.

"I don't believe you," challenged Gomper, hoping to learn something new that would help get rid of Bog.

I can cause you to have pain that will make you wish you were dead. I can keep you feeling the pain, while keeping your body barely alive. If you want me to stop then you'll have to do what I want.

"What do you really want from me, demon?"

I want you to do my bidding without asking questions. I want you to force your brother to face you.

"So he can kill me?"

Yes, if you do what I want, you'll be begging him to kill you. Gomper closed his eyes and wondered what the demon meant by his words. *I can't have anyone kill you, but him. So you will look for him and plead for him to kill you.*

"Why do you want him to kill me?"

If he kills you, then I'll be able to transfer myself to your brother.

"So that's why you're looking for him?"

Yes. That's why I ordered for this invasion of the Mossen planet. He would have to do something about it.

"Not until he's the Master," answered Gomper, knowing why Ghonllier left without facing him.

I want you to come up with a plan to find your brother.

"No!"

Suddenly Gomper felt a sharp, gripping pain in his stomach, causing him to double over.

I suggest you change your mind. Now, you'll really see what I can do to you.

"Kill me, demon. I won't do it," gasped Gomper.

The pain increased within Gomper, causing him to gasp for air. At the same moment, Jamham entered. It frightened him to see Gomper falling to the floor, struggling to breathe.

Running to his side, Jamham questioned, "Sir, what's wrong?"

Gomper couldn't answer him but heard in his mind, *This is your brother's fault. He destroyed my tools that kept you in the dark and unaware of yourself. Then you did my bidding without questions and memory. Blame him, if you're unhappy about your life. You were happy before he entered your life.*

"Your Grace, what's wrong?" repeated Jamham, reaching for his bracelet to page Pappar.

Gomper looked at Jamham, struggling to breathe. Tears glistened his cheeks. Shortly, Pappar entered the room and ran to their side. "What's happening?"

Jamham shook his head. "I don't know."

Gomper gasped, "Kill me . . . demon. I won't help . . . you find him."

Find him!

Gomper felt another shot of pain that rendered him unconscious. Jamham tried to find a pulse on his neck. "Is he alive?" asked Pappar.

"I can't tell. I don't think so," whispered Jamham.

Bog heard them and decided to back off. He couldn't afford Gomper to die on him right now.

"Wait, I think I feel something," responded Pappar.

Jamham looked out the window. "I wonder how far we are from the ship. We need to have Brewster there when we land and we can't let anyone know that he's sick."

"We can't have Brewster there. Rumor will fly and we can't afford that."

"I'll tell Brewster to meet us in his private quarters. We have a whole new problem now," suggested Jamham, looking at his bracelet.

"Sir," shook Pappar, trying to get him to wake up.

When Gomper didn't respond, he looked at Jamham. "From now on, Brewster goes everywhere with him."

"What will it look like? Brewster never went anywhere with him, which is why you and I have handled this."

"We have to change something. This can't keep happening. They can't know that Suzair the Great is weak."

Bog thought about their conversation while the color started to return to Gomper's face. Jamham shook him again and this time Gomper moaned.

"Good, he's coming around," stated Jamham.

Gomper opened his eyes and let out a deep sigh.

"Are you okay, Your Grace?" questioned Jamham.

"I hurt," whispered Gomper.

I'll keep doing this until you give in. Do you want me to do it again?

"Kill me, demon," challenged Gomper.

If I kill you here, I'll go to whoever is around you. Is this what you want? Eventually, I'll make it to your brother with or without you.

In a raspy voice, he said, "I'll find my brother on the condition you leave others alone. You stay with me."

Done.

Jamham and Pappar exchanged looks. Gomper moved and they went back to him. Reaching out, they helped him up. But Gomper couldn't stand up straight. He hunched over, rubbing his stomach. The two men helped him sit on the large container. Gomper rested his head against the wall.

He looked white and tears still spewed out from the corner of his eyes.

"Can I get you anything?" quizzed Jamham. Gomper shook his head. "You don't look well, Your Grace," chatted Jamham.

"I don't feel well," stated Gomper, facing the window.

In the distance, he could see his Galaxy Creepers. There was no battle there and he wondered how long until they had to leave. Where was Pursy? He needed him and Gomper hoped he made it back.

The three men watched their small ship enter the bay area. Pappar and Jamham helped Gomper stand and it hurt more to straighten his back. Inside, he wondered if he could pull off acting like Suzair the Great.

Looking at him, Pappar inquired, "Are you ready?"

Gomper nodded. So he opened the door and stepped outside to wait for Gomper to emerge out. Suzair's elite guard stood at attention while a few unsealed the door. Gomper exited and was pleased to find Pursy waiting for him in the bay.

He stated, "You are here. Did the Star Screamer make it out with all of my staff?" Pursy nodded. "Good, stay with me. I have some new instructions for you."

"Yes, Your Grace."

They left, being flanked by his staff. Everyone moved out of their way. At the lift, Gomper requested, "Pursy, I want to know what is going on with this battle. Give me a verbal report of what you know now."

"I do have the first report. We have lost one Galaxy Creeper and we have reports that I-Force will be here shortly. With you aboard, your captains are leaving."

Gomper looked back to see the bay doors shutting. "Tell my captains to take us out into the middle of space somewhere," ordered Gomper.

Pursy activated his C-Stone and passed on the orders to the captains. Everyone listened to him while they entered the lift that would take them to the upper floors.

When Pursy finished, he looked at Gomper. "Anything else, Your Grace?"

"Yes, I want you to put a report together for me that will tell me every place in this galaxy that we haven't been able to penetrate. I want it as soon as possible."

"Yes, Your Grace. Consider it done. Where will you be?" asked Pursy while they exited the lift.

"In my office."

"I'll do it now," assured Pursy, leaving the group and walking faster.

Gomper continued with the others to his office more slowly. "Your Grace, do you want to be checked out by Brewster in your office?"

"Yes," replied Gomper, watching the people's faces as they passed.

Jamham raised his wrist to page Brewster. They walked in silence to his office. When they entered, Pappar dismissed most of his guards, leaving a few at the door. Before they could shut the door, Brewster arrived.

He waited for them to shut the door before he spoke, "You don't look very well."

Gomper didn't say anything, but reached out with his hand while Brewster pulled out an analyzer from his pocket. Brewster placed it under Gomper's hand while he sat down in his chair. Everyone waited for Brewster to say something.

Finally, he expressed, "You've had a lot of pain in your stomach. The analyzer has never seen it before." Then looking at Gomper, he added, "Do you know what it is?"

"Yeah," answered Gomper.

"What is it?" asked Jamham.

"Nothing," dismissed Gomper.

"Let me go get you a patch for the pain, Your Grace," requested Brewster.

"Thank you," stated Gomper, watching him leave.

Pappar and Jamham waited for him to leave. Then Pappar asked, "What is it?"

"I don't want to talk about it," stated Gomper, standing.

Jamham and Pappar started to talk amongst themselves about how to handle the new problem. Gomper half listened to them. He kept thinking about what the demon said. Now he understood why Gostler never came for him. Gostler had to have known about the penalty of seeing him. It was hard on Gomper to know how dangerous he really was to those around him.

Now he understood the kind of prison he was in. Gomper understood the abilities and ruled the Master of the Galaxy far better than the demon. The demon made a mistake by telling Gomper the truth. Now he understood what Ghonllier had to know. Gomper was determined to help Ghonllier any way he could. Ghonllier had to be aware of the demon that was inside of him and the dangers.

The colors of the jump fields had appeared in the window when Brewster finally returned. Thinking about Ghonllier, he wondered why his brother was on the Mossen planet. More importantly, Gomper wondered if he even cared about him as his brother. Gomper felt a strong kinship toward Ghonllier and doubted his brother felt the same way toward him.

"Your Grace," interrupted Brewster.

"I know," responded Gomper, heading for his desk.

He sat down for Brewster to administer the patch. Instantly, he felt relief and thanked his medic.

Brewster whispered, "I want to know what's causing your pain."

"Maybe I'll tell you someday," answered Gomper, facing his desk.

The three members of his staff watched him start to work on his pile of problems that were waiting for his return. The others talked about how they were going to run Gomper's life and he tuned them out. In the process, he forgot about the report he requested.

Gomper found his ability to work difficult. He was tired from what Bog had put him through. Getting tired of listening to the three men talk about him, he stood. They stopped.

"I want to leave and go to our quarters," announced Gomper.

Jamham glanced at his bracelet. "It's close to dinner time. Are you hungry?" he asked.

"No, I don't feel like eating much," announced Gomper, reaching the door.

A knock was heard and Gomper opened the door. Pursy had the report in his hand. Gingerly, he handed him the memory chip and stated, "I have the report you requested. I also added what happened when we tried to enter and why we wanted to go there."

"That's perfect," glared Gomper, acting like Suzair the Great.

Pursy nodded and left while Gomper slipped the memory chip into his pocket. He followed Pursy out while his guards stood at attention. Pappar and Jamham flanked him as the guards let everyone know Suzair the Great was coming through.

When they entered his private quarters, Gomper handed the chip to Pappar. He knew what Gomper wanted him to do with it. While Gomper got comfortable on the couch, Pappar placed the chip in the amplifier. He started the equipment before he joined him.

Jamham left to order food from his private pantry. Gomper read the report, but was shortly interrupted by Bog. *I want to hear what's in the report, so you need to have him read it out loud.*

So he has to hear our words to understand things here, thought Gomper, glad to finally learn another limitation of the demon. He looked at Pappar and requested, "Would you read the report out loud."

"Why?"

"The demon wants to hear it," replied Gomper.

Pappar obeyed and started to read the report. Jamham returned with food, perplexed Pappar was reading it out loud. In the meantime, Gomper had written a note to Jamham so he would understand. This might be a way for them to control the demon.

When Jamham handed Gomper a plate, he handed Jamham the note. He read it while Gomper looked at his food. He wasn't sure if he was hungry. Jamham sat with his plate and noticed Gomper picking at his food, listening to Pappar.

Finally, he stopped and they looked at Gomper. Pappar asked, "What do you think?"

"Well, I see two possibilities. But with what I know about the real Master of the Galaxy, I think they're on the Xeron moon," guessed Gomper softly.

"Why?" asked Jamham.

"I see things that I understand," answered Gomper, not really thinking he gave any real information to Bog.

Good! Send in a ship and take him, ordered Bog.

"You give me a plan. All you asked for was my opinion," rebelled Gomper, setting his plate down beside him.

Instantly, Bog followed the sound and mentally picked the plate up and flung it. It hit the wall and broke. A piece came back, slicing Jamham's arm. "He's hurt!" shouted Gomper, seeing blood gush from the wound.

Jamham paged for Brewster while Pappar looked at his wound. *I'll kill them and keep you barely alive. You do what I want now!*

"You promised not to hurt them," snapped Gomper.

I don't keep promises. You do what I want or I'll start to kill them.

Brewster was there and Gomper whispered, "Okay, demon, I get the point. I'll come up with a plan to find my brother."

Suddenly, Gomper felt pain in his stomach that was worse than before. Jamham saw his face wretched with agony and shouted, "Brewster, something is wrong with him!"

Pappar and Brewster faced Gomper just as he collapsed to the floor. The medic ran to his side as Pappar finished applying the second skin to Jamham's wound.

"Your Grace!" Brewster shouted, placing the analyzer on his hand.

After a few moments, Brewster said, "Great."

"What's wrong?" asked Pappar.

"The demon can take him close to death so fast," said Brewster.

"Is he dead?" asked Jamham, joining them.

"I think so," whispered Brewster.

Bog heard him and backed off. Without his stepping stone, he wasn't sure how much he was inflicting on Gomper. He didn't want him to ever question him again. Quietly, he waited to learn if he had killed Gomper.

Finally, Bog heard, "I'm getting some numbers."

"Are they moving?" asked Jamham.

There was a long moment of silence, then Brewster answered, "Yes, they're going up rapidly. He's going to live, but I don't know how much more of this he can take without dying."

The three men exchanged looks as Gomper started to gasp for air. They kneeled over him, waiting for him to open his eyes.

Jamham asked, "Why did the demon do this?"

Gomper didn't answer, but closed his eyes. They all waited for him to open his eyes again. When he did, Gomper motioned for them to give him some vanishing paper. When they did, he started to write and then he handed them the paper.

It read: HE WANTS ME TO INVADE THE XERON MOON WITH AN ARMY AND KILL EVERYONE THERE IF THEY DON'T GIVE US MY BROTHER.

Pappar quickly wrote back: What will the demon do if your brother isn't there?

After Gomper read the message, he shrugged.

Brewster looked away from the analyzer and informed, "Your Grace, I think you're stabilizing now. How do you feel?"

"Terrible," whispered Gomper.

"Let me help you rest," said Jamham, giving him a hand.

Gomper was too weak to grasp it. Brewster stood and responded, "I'm getting you a deep sleep patch. Your body needs time to repair the damage it's been through."

"Good," whispered Gomper, closing his eyes. *Brother of mine, I'll do anything I can do to keep us from meeting each other in battle. You have my total and complete cooperation to let you kill me. This galaxy needs to be rid of this curse that has been brought to this galaxy through me.*

Chapter 4

Decisions

*T*he humming sounds of the monitors filtered into Ghonllier's mind awakened him. Evaluating his heart, he found it still aching. The vision of Sunna shaking her head while saying, *I can't come with you,* wouldn't leave his mind. He couldn't believe she would rather stay there then join him. Hurting, he fought to push it away, but it wouldn't leave.

He forced himself to stop thinking about Sunna by wondering, *How long have I been asleep?* He purposely didn't direct the question to the Stones. Sunna wasn't the only one Ghonllier was hurt by. He was angry at the Stones for taking him there only to have his heart broken again.

Wanting to leave and work so he didn't have to think about his pain, he lifted his head. Dizziness consumed him and he let out a moan, allowing his head to fall back. A dull pain in his head increased and he heard someone scrambling toward him.

Expecting to be alone, Ghonllier snapped, "Who's here?"

"You mean you don't know, Your Grace?" countered a familiar voice.

"Cid, don't call me by that name!" warned Ghonllier.

Cid grunted. "It doesn't surprise me to hear those words."

The medic's words angered Ghonllier more, causing his emotions to increase his headache. Bringing his hands up to rub his forehead, Ghonllier saw his wrists wrapped with an artificial skin.

Perplexed, he asked, "What happened to my wrists?"

"You don't remember?"

"No."

Cid stayed silent. Ghonllier looked at him and repeated his question with more force. Quietly, Cid studied him. "You figure it out, Your Grace."

"Cid, I told you not to call me by that name!" shouted Ghonllier.

The medic didn't respond. Instead, he left for Sunna's gurney to examine her stats. Ghonllier watched him adjust her fluids. He was surprised to see Sunna was alive but how close to death she was. Sunna was still unconscious. The new Master debated about getting in harmony with the Master Stones to learn about her condition. Ghonllier quickly dismissed it. The thought of knowing about her resentment toward him wasn't worth it. Sunna had chosen to not be a part of his life and he had given up hope that she would ever change.

But curious to know something, he uttered, "How bad is she?"

"She's barely alive and not responding to anything that I'm doing. I'm in here because I'm expecting her numbers at any minute to drop and be gone. Can you tell me why she isn't moving up or down?"

"No," responded Ghonllier coldly. Cid looked away as Ghonllier added, "Cid, would you page me Jason?"

"No."

"Why?"

"You do it," responded Cid, shooting him a glance over his shoulder.

"I can't!" snapped Ghonllier.

"No you can't or no you won't?"

"Both," answered Ghonllier coldly. Cid ignored him. So he repeated his request.

"You do it," countered Cid, facing him.

"I can't! It hurts too bad to get up."

Cid faced him and responded, "I know you can throw your voice and talk to anyone you want from that gurney. I refuse to do anything that you can do for yourself."

"Cid, you don't understand," pleaded Ghonllier with his voice cracking.

"I think *you* don't understand. Use your powers, Ghonllier. We aren't going to cater to your refusing to be the Master of the Galaxy," replied Cid, heading for the door.

In anger, Ghonllier let out a mournful scream as Cid opened the door. Outside in the corridor, the new Master's scream could be heard. Cid quickly shut the door. At the same time, Jason appeared out of the Med-C. The two men exchanged looks.

"So he's awake," commented Jason. Cid nodded. "Sunna! How is she?"

"The same. I don't know what to do for her or what's happening. She isn't responding and Ghonllier refuses to tell me anything."

"So she's still at a four?"

"Yes."

Jason stared at the closed door and sighed before he went over to a green strip on the corridor's wall. Cid watched him request Gostler to be sent to Ghonllier's quarters. Moments later, the captains paged Gostler over the ship's speakers. Seeing they were going to talk with Ghonllier, Cid decided to stay concerned that he might have to subdue him.

Gostler and Adamite entered the corridor from the dining room. With Jason and Cid standing by Ghonllier's door, they had a good idea to why Gostler got the page.

"So he's awake?" questioned Adamite, arriving.

"Yes, and he refused to use his powers," informed Jason. "Do you want to talk with him?"

Gostler took in a deep breath. "No . . . it has to be his choice. I was afraid of this."

Cid remembered, "He did request to see you, Jason, but I refused to get you for him."

"Let's go see what he wants," suggested Jason, gesturing for Cid to open the door.

The men entered and were followed by Asustie. Running past the men, she went to her brother's side. The two looked at each other. Smiling, she whispered, "How do you feel?"

"I'm in pain, Asustie," snapped Ghonllier.

"You have a headache?" quizzed Cid, coming into his view.

"Yes," glared Ghonllier.

Cid retrieved a patch for a headache underneath the gurney from the supply closet. The others waited out of sight for Cid to make him more comfortable before they let their presences be known to him.

When Cid finished, Jason approached, "I understand you wanted to talk with me?"

"Yes, how close are we to the Jupiter moon?" quizzed Ghonllier.

"Why ask me? You should know that question yourself," reminded Jason.

"Jason! I'm not in the mood for games. Answer my question now."

"We've passed the Jupiter moon solar system. We're halfway home," replied Jason.

"Why didn't you drop Sunna off?" bellowed Ghonllier.

Jason lost patience and matched him. "Ghonllier, I can't believe you said that." He pointed at her. "She's not out of the woods and might still die, saving your life. Sunna took most of the poison that was on the Truth Test. How dare you act this way." He, too, was getting tired of this game.

"What do you mean 'poison'?" questioned Ghonllier.

"Sunna pulled the patch off your neck and the poison went into her," educated Jason.

Ghonllier looked at Cid. "How close to death is she?"

"I wish you would tell us," replied Gostler, joining Jason. "She came in at four ever since we picked you up and she hasn't moved. It's been two days since you two have been unconscious. You're the only one who can reach out to her and ask her to stay."

"I've already done that and she refused," snapped Ghonllier. Looking away, he continued, "I'll never ask her again."

"One way or the other, she's here with you for a while. Your brother is still dangerous to this galaxy. So I suggest you use the Stones and learn about what is going on in your galaxy," warned Gostler.

Putting his hands over his face, Ghonllier roared, "NO!" Removing them, he retorted, "Stop it, all of you. Leave me alone. I refuse to be something . . ." Ghonllier's voice dropped to a low tone.

"I can't get in harmony with the Stones. We don't see things the same anymore."

Asustie reached out to touch him. He glanced at her and he faced Jason and ordered, "Take me into the Med-C. I don't want to see her again. Get her away from me."

"You'll get no rest in Med-C and no privacy. Anyone can walk in on you," reminded Cid.

"I don't care. Get me out of here!"

Bewildered by his behavior, Asustie stated, "Ghonllier. It doesn't have to be this way. I know you love her."

"She doesn't love me and I'm weary of hoping she will someday look at me without disdain."

"Are you sure?"

"Yes." Ghonllier turned his head away, wanting to mourn for his loss in private.

Ghonllier. It can't be this way. . . ."

"Leave him alone, Asustie. He's been through a lot," said a familiar voice from behind them.

Everyone looked behind them to see Sunna. Cid ran to look at her stats while everyone started to talk at once with her. Quickly Cid looked back at her and said, "You are at a ten. It's impossible for you to change that fast."

Gostler started to chuckle. Everyone looked at him wanting to know what he thought was so funny. The former Master gestured toward her and explained, "Sunna has the power of the Master Stones, don't you?"

She nodded. "Why can't I read your mind, Gostler?"

"Ghonllier couldn't either," smiled Gostler.

Sunna took in a deep breath and asked, "So you want to know what happened?"

"Yes," stated Asustie.

"The Master Stones took our sprits somewhere between this existence and the next," answered Sunna.

"Why?" asked Adamite.

"So I could remember something that I had forgotten from my past," answered Sunna. She could read their next question and

Sunna didn't want to answer them. This was between Ghonllier and her. So she stated, "I need to have you all leave or be quiet. We need to finish our conversation before Cid so rudely took Ghonllier away. . . . Everyone move back."

When they made a hole, Sunna commanded Ghonllier's gurney to come to her. It responded enhancing her Moveling abilities. Ghonllier kept his face away from her, not wanting the others to see his tears. Silence hung heavily in the air as everyone backed away to watch.

"Ghonllier, I want you to look at me." He didn't move. So Sunna continued, "Ghonllier. I'm sorry for putting you through so much. I spent time with Master Stones and they showed me that I agreed to be in your life. . . ."

Ghonllier quickly faced her. "Sunna! You are released. I don't want you to be with me out of obligation. Jason. Turn this ship around now and take her to my father's place."

"You are far off on understanding me." Ghonllier looked at the ceiling, blinking back the tears.

"Then why did you come back, Sunna. You told me that you would rather be dead than with me here."

"I came back to tell you why I said that."

Ghonllier closed his eyes, preparing for the worst. He didn't know how much more his heart could take.

Sunna knew Sooner and Stacy were watching and she didn't want him to hear her next words. So Sunna used the Master Stones to speak to him. "GHONLLIER. I HAVE BEEN VERY RESENTFUL TOWARD YOU EVER SINCE I MET SOONER. YET, YOU KNOW THAT I DEEPLY LOVE HIM. THE STONES CAME TO ME AS A CHILD AND ASKED ME TO BE YOUR WIFE DURING YOUR REIGN. THEY REQUESTED I BECOME AND TRAIN SPIES."

Ghonllier faced her with a perplexed expression, "Why?'

"THEY ALSO ASKED ME TO KEEP MYSELF FOR YOU. BEING A SPY, IT WOULD BE HARD. BY ME ACCOMPLISHING IT, I WOULD GAIN A LOT OF INNER STRENGTH AND FORTITUDE. I WOULD BE ABLE TO MATCH YOUR TITLE AND YOU. THEY TOLD ME THAT WE WOULD GO THROUGH A LOT BEFORE WE MET." She paused, "THEY NEVER TOLD ME THAT

JENNY WAS SUPPOSE TO COME INTO YOUR LIFE. THERE IS A REASON SOONER LOOKS LIKE HER."

Ghonllier studied Sunna before he said, "What are trying to tell me?"

"I WAS DEEPLY HURT THAT YOU HAD BEEN MARRIED AND YOU HAD A SON. ON A DEEP UNCONSCIOUS LEVEL, I RESENTED YOU AND I'M SO SORRY." She waited for Ghonllier response, when it didn't come, she added, "JENNY WAS ASKED BY THE MASTER STONES TO COME INTO YOUR LIVE AND GIVE YOU A SON. SHE AGREED TO LEAVE SOON AFTER HIS BIRTH TO HELP YOU DEVELOP. SO THE CHALLENGES YOU HAD TO GO THROUGH WOULD PREPARE YOU FOR THIS MANTEL. JUST LIKE MY SACRIFICES, IT HAS PREPARED ME. I DIDN'T UNDERSTAND. I THOUGHT . . . I ASSUMED YOU BROKE YOUR PROMISE TO THE STONES AND YOU DIDN'T WAIT FOR ME. ALL I KNOW NOW, IT WAS WRONG TO ASSUME. I SHOULD HAVE GIVEN YOU MY HEART WITHOUT QUESTION."

Ghonllier just stared at her. So she added so everyone could hear, "I'm not doing this out of duty. I love you and your son with all me heart. Please forgive me for not understanding you and your challenges."

Adamite's C-Stone started to vibrate, letting him know he had a call. Sunna looked over at him as he retrieved it from his pocket. "It's Sooner. He wants to talk with Ghonllier."

"Ghonllier?" asked Adamite, handing him the C-Stone.

While he brought it up to his ear, he kept his gaze on Sunna. Ghonllier was quiet as he listened. Sunna could hear both sides of the conversation until suddenly it stopped. She looked shapely at Ghonllier with wonderment. Had he taken back the power of the Stones? For a moment, she felt sadness to loose them. She realized that she liked being with them and knowing all. Not sure what Ghonllier was thinking and saying to Sooner, she waited.

Ghonllier brought her out of her thoughts by handing the C-Stone to Sunna. Unsure, she took it. She heard, "Are you willing to be my mother?"

"Yes. I very much want to be your mother," stated Sunna, watching Ghonllier's expression.

She couldn't tell from his face how he felt and she wasn't sure that she had been forgiven. Was Ghonllier going to take her back?

After a long moment, Sooner and Sunna waited for Ghonllier to say something. Finally, he reached over and removed the C-Stone from her ear.

"Sunna. Will you marry me?" She grinned from ear to ear and attempted to raise her head with excitement. Quickly, she let out a moan and so did Ghonllier. "Please be careful, I can feel your pain," he expressed.

"I'm sorry. Ghonllier . . . my answer is yes. I want to marry you today if it will make you happy."

"Father! She agrees with me. Grandfather needs to do it today."

"I don't think that is what she meant Sooner," said Ghonllier.

He had caused it so Sooner could speak with them both by causing the C-Stone to work as a speaker.

"Yes. We need to plan a wedding. I want to help you Sunna," said Asustie, hugging Jason.

"Asustie. Wait! There are strings attached to this. I can't have a wedding reception if we have it soon."

"Why?"

"Ghonllier and I can't let anyone know about our engagement, wedding or friendship."

Asustie looked at Ghonllier. "Is that true?"

"Yes. The Stones want me to keep my personal life away from the galaxy. As far as they know, I have no family, wife or children."

"Why?" asked Asustie, looking at Gostler.

He shrugged his shoulders. Ghonllier answered her. "After my reign is announced, I can tell my city about my family but the Master Stones do not want anyone to know outside the boundaries."

"Why son?"

"We need to keep our relationship a secret now to give us time to build a strong foundation as a family in privacy. It will hurt our relationship in the future if people know that Sunna and I are married or engaged to early."

"I agree," grunted Gostler. "You have a lot of pressure on you when you're the Master of the Galaxy and people know you. I can also see why the galaxy doesn't need to know anything about your personal life."

"So when are you going to get married?" asked Asustie.

"I think you need to do it today, Father."

"There is no one on board but Spencer," stated Jason.

Cid happened to be watching their stats during the conversation. He was curious to see if Sunna numbers were really going to stay up. He saw her stress level increase when Spencer's name was mentioned.

He looked at her and asked, "Sunna. Why does Spencer cause your stress to increase?"

"He asked her to marry him years ago and he still wants to marry her," answered Ghonllier.

She looked at him and shook her head. "I wish I hadn't agreed to let him work with me. He'll want to . . ."

"Ask you out on a date," finished Ghonllier.

Sunna looked away. She knew that she needed to decide what she wanted. She decided working around Spencer knowing she was married was going to be easier than being engaged. The decision was made before she looked at Ghonllier.

He said, "Are you sure?"

"Would you be upset with it?"

"I would like Justin to be here."

"You can broadcast the wedding to a monitor in his office," suggested Gostler.

Ghonllier studied Sunna's face as he examined her and his thoughts and feelings. He so wanted to have Justin in person at their wedding. Having the Stones, he could see into the future and knew it was better for their marriage that Sunna and he had time to come together before the pressures of his title crowded in on them. Reluctantly, he nodded.

Everyone was excited and started to plan how it was going to happen. The two of them just stared at each other. Ghonllier felt weak and so did Sunna. He wondered about the burning fires. They would take a toll on their bodies with them being in space and in this weak physical condition. He talked with the Stones and they seemed to agree with him.

Everything had moved so fast Ghonllier wasn't sure it was happening. He could read that Sunna had made this decision days ago.

She had been with the Stones learning about the role that she was taking on. He debated on saying something about the burning fires but decided he could make it through them and he would help Sunna.

Cid brought Ghonllier out of his thought, when he started to move Sunna's gurney into the Med-C. He reached out to touch her cheek. Sunna was still in the control temperature blanket so he couldn't do more than just touch her cheek. In his mind, he watched her leave the room and was pleased Spencer wasn't there.

Adamite brought him out of his thoughts. "Son. Gostler and I are going to give you a shower. What do you want to get dressed in?"

Ghonllier closed his eyes. "I don't care, Father."

Adamite left while Ghonllier rested his eyes. The roller coaster of emotions had really taken a toll on him. Sleep quickly took him.

Gostler had left with Sunna. He needed to explain to Cid how he had to work with the Master Stones. After Janet took Sunna away to an area in the Med-C for a shower on the gurney, Gostler gestured toward the medic's quarters.

They entered with Cid shutting the door after them. Gostler sat in a chair while Cid leaned up against the wall.

"Cid. The Stones he's wearing are very touchy about how they are treated. They demand respect all the time. So do not touch them or be curious. If you ever have to do something where they are exposed, you need to be alone in the room. If the Stones haven't given permission for someone to see them, the person might become blind, deaf, or both. If at anytime the Stones are threatened, they'll return the attack with the same intent."

"Intent?"

"Yes. If you were intentionally to want him dead and you used a knife for that purpose, the knife would leave your hands and go into you."

Cid moved away from the wall and stated, "That is what I saw happened with the ships earlier."

Gostler nodded. "The Stones returned the blasts with the same intent to those who sent it."

"I see."

"So make sure no one is around you and I doubt you will have to do much with him once we becomes the Master. You need to remember to be respectful at all times."

Cid nodded. Gostler stood and gestured for the door to open. The two men left going into different directions. Gostler went back to Ghonllier. He was in his room with his eyes closed. Adamite paced while talking to Stacy. Gostler thoughts went to his love that he had lost. Ghonllier had told him that she was dead. He wondered if they would be together now, if he hadn't upset the Stones by refusing to give them up. He was deep in thought when he glanced over at Ghonllier to see him opening his eyes.

"Did I wake you?" asked Gostler.

"No. Would you be in contact with Justin during the ceremony so he feels apart of it?"

Gostler nodded as Cid arrived to take Ghonllier into the Med-C for his shower. Adamite followed still talking with Stacy while Gostler retrieved his to inform Justin of the marriage ceremony. He knew Justin would be happy to learn about it. They had talked so often about why Ghonllier wasn't doing anything to find someone to replace Jenny. In their ancestor's language, Gostler gave the details to Justin, hoping to fill him in before Ghonllier entered the shower.

In the Med-C, they had to wait for a few minutes. To Gostler's surprise, Ghonllier requested his C-Stone.

"Let me tell him," said Ghonllier, using the Eraphin language.

Ghonllier continued to speak in the language with Justin and Gostler smiled. Now, Ghonllier had the third Stone. He could understand any language and communicate in it. The third Stone bonded with his intelligence so anything Ghonllier wanted to learn would almost be instantaneous for him. In a way, Gostler missed that Stone the most. He loved what he had learned from that Stone.

Out in the corridor, Asustie promised Cid to bring clean clothes to him for Sunna. Jason was the only one who could enter Sunna's quarters. She refused his offer to let her in Sunna's quarters. Asustie knew that most of Sunna's things were boxed up for her move to Justin's. So she would only have military issued in her quarters. She had helped her pack, spending the last few hours with her. Plus, the containers were in storage within the ship's belly and it would take too long to find something.

Entering her quarters, Asustie was pleased that she had brought some new clothes. Since, Asustie and Sunna had lived together for five years. Asustie knew they wore the same sizes. Jason had given her some new nightgowns that she would be able to keep on board the ship. She remembered one to be a white satin nightgown. Hoping, she had brought it. Asustie raffled through her drawers.

It only took her a few moments to find a couple of satin full-length nightgowns among her unopened packages. She grabbed a white one and left. *I hope Sunna will be pleased,* she thought. Then Asustie stopped. She looked back at the drawer and decided to take all of her new clothes for Sunna. She could tell her what she didn't want to use.

Ghonllier was in the main area of Med-C still talking with Justin, when Cid came to let them know the shower was clear. Ghonllier handed Gostler back his C-Stone and finished his conversation with his legal father, by using the Master Stones. Ghonllier also knew his mother wanted to speak with him. She had some concerns about the their living conditions when they arrived home.

So Ghonllier finished his conversation with Justin to speak with Stacy. She brought up Sunna's parents. He had forgotten about them and he needed to learn from the Stones how much information that he could tell them. It pleased him to learn that he could tell her parents about his title. Ghonllier knew Bonnie didn't like him much. Maybe, she would think differently of him if she knew the complete truth.

When he gave his C-Stone to Ghonllier, Adamite left to retrieve some clean clothes for Ghonllier. Stacy told him that she had sent new pajamas to the ship so Ghonllier could wear them. He was supposed to keep the belt with the Stones covered at all times and she wanted to help him get use to them. Ghonllier had never been a man who liked to wear them.

Opening his son's drawer, he smiled. Ghonllier had promised his mother that he would wear them, but they were still in the packages. Picking out a white satin pair, he left with them to Ghonllier's bathroom. He wanted to get his shaver and anything else his son would need for a shower.

When Asustie appeared in the Med-C main center with Sunna's things, she found Cid alone, resting in a chair. He had a book in his hands while watching all doors in and out of the Med-C. He smiled to see what Asustie had in her hand. Asustie greeted him with a nod while he sat the book in his lap. She handed him everything Sunna would need for her wedding.

Cid accepted them and mentioned, "I'll get them to her."

"Thanks," countered Asustie, disappearing around the wall that separated the medical area from the waiting room.

Cid stood and sat her things on a nearby counter. He paused to listen to the water running for Ghonllier's shower. Then he went back to his chair and picked up the book before sitting.

Chapter 5

Secret Lives

*W*hile reading his book, Cid intently listened to the many sounds around him. Though, one sound in particular stirred him as it sounded like approaching footsteps. Curious, he finally looked up to see Janet charging toward him while wearing a disgusted expression.

Arriving, she snapped, "I went along with Sunna getting a massage. But then I learn that you have ordered the staff from the salon to add makeup and complete style for Sunna's hair. She can't even raise her head. When did makeup and hair become apart of our responsibility? I didn't know it had anything to do with her getting well."

Trying to act nonchalant, Cid responded, "Janet, we both know it's important for a woman to believe she looks beautiful."

"Cid! It . . ."

"Was she pleased?"

Janet folded her arms and glared at him. "Okay. Now, I see what is going on here. You have feelings for her."

Cid started to chuckle from Janet totally misunderstanding. "Look, Janet. Sunna gets anything she wants. If she wants someone to come in do her hair or makeup, she gets it."

"The masseuse told Sunna you gave her orders that she could have a massage as often as she wanted. And she told me privately that you told her to put Sunna above anyone else at all times. What is going on here? We both know that only the commander of the ship gets that kind of privileges."

With a chuckle, Cid answered, "Janet. We know that she's Jason's sister. So don't worry . . ."

"I'm not buying it. Now if it were Jason's wife, I would believe it. She is the sister of the real commander of this ship. Sunna! Jason isn't the one we want or need to cater to and you know it."

Cid grinned, and stated, "Listen. Sunna is my patient and she gets this kind of treatment from now on. Do you undermined me, Janet? I am the head medic."

Janet gave him a smirk before she left. Abruptly, she stopped at the door and expressed, "Right! How dumb do you think I am? Are you attached to her?"

Cid grinned, thinking if only she knew the truth. "Just get her ready the way I ordered. She's my patient and I want her very happy now and in the future."

Janet disappeared, singing, "I think Cid's in love."

Someone behind him started to chuckle and Cid quickly turned in that direction. Relieved to see it was Jason, Cid cajoled, "Come to see for yourself what's happening?"

"Yeah, I'm glad I heard that last scene."

"Why?"

"Now, I know how the crew really feels about me," chuckled Jason, joining Cid.

"Janet now thinks I have a crush on your sister. How long do you think it will take Janet to get that piece of information back to one of us and it's embellished?" Cid whispered.

"I'll give it two hours," guessed Jason softly.

"I think it will take around forty-five minutes," whispered Cid.

Jason looked at his timepiece and challenged, "I'll time it." Looking up, he continued, "Where are we on this? When will they be ready?"

Cid looked in the direction of the showers and stated, "The water has stopped, so they're probably getting Ghonllier dressed. You saw me give Janet Sunna's clothes. So I would expect they'll be right in."

The two men noticed a page coming in for Cid. He left to touch a green strip on the wall. After he took it, he faced Jason. "You heard it. I'll take her back now. Do you mind guarding the area until Ghonllier leaves?"

Jason nodded and took over Cid's post by waiting in the chair.

From the moment Sooner walked in on Stacy watching Ghonllier and Sunna captured, he refused to leave his grandmother's study and she felt the same way. Stacy and Sooner slept and ate in the room, waiting for Ghonllier and Sunna to wake up.

It was hard on Sooner to watch his father under the Truth Test. He had a lot of the same feelings and cried to learn Sunna wouldn't come back with him. Knowing his father's deep emotions for Sunna, he felt closer to him. They both loved Sunna and were hurt by her leaving to work with his legal grandfather, Justin.

Watching Ghonllier's pain hurt Stacy, too. Secretly, she wanted Sunna and Ghonllier to find each other and be happy again. Jenny and he were so happy. She cried for joy when Sunna came back and wanted to be married to him. Stacy knew Ghonllier wouldn't go through with it, unless she truly loved him and he would know it.

Now that they were getting married, Stacy was concerned with Sunna's parents. She knew Bonnie didn't care for Ghonllier because he had a son. For some reason, she was hostel in her behavior toward him. It concerned her for Sooner's sake. Would they accept Sooner as their grandson?

She paced, thinking, as she waited for Gabala to join her in the study. They were going to watch the wedding from here because of the server stone. Sooner was putting his bedding away when Gabala finally arrived.

"Madam, Sunna's parents are here," he informed.

"Gabala, bring them here and I want you to stay with us. I have to give them an oath regarding the server stone and I want you to be a witness."

"Yes, madam," expressed Gabala, leaving.

Sooner joined her, wrapping his arm around her waist. Stacy peered into his happy face and, taking a sigh, expressed, "Sooner, why don't you let me talk to Sunna's parents alone."

"Grandmother, no please don't send me away. If they're going to be my grandparents, I want to be here."

Stacy didn't know how to explain to Sooner that Bonnie might not be as excited as they were about their marriage. Maybe, Sooner needed to be here and see for himself. As she debated it, she finally said, "Then let me do the talking, okay?"

"Sure," stated Sooner, staring at the server stone.

Stacy glanced at the server stone to see Sunna being brought into Ghonllier's room, covered with a blanket. She paused to watch. *Sunna looks beautiful and so happy.* Stacy had never seen a glow on her face before like she saw today.

A knock came to the door and Stacy looked at Sooner. "Shut the doors to the stone. They can't see it just yet," informed Stacy, watching Sooner reluctantly close the doors. Then she announced, "Enter."

Gabala opened the door and explained, "Madam, Sunna's parents are here. Are you ready to receive them?"

"Yes, let them enter," requested Stacy. Gabala nodded. "Gabala." He looked at her. "Please stay with us until I dismiss you."

"I will, madam," nodded Gabala before reopening the door.

He opened the door and stepped back so Bonnie and George could enter. Sooner let go of her waist and she wondered if it was the right decision to let him stay.

Eagerly, Bonnie expressed, "Stacy, Gabala said this is regarding our children. What's wrong?"

Stacy gestured toward the couches. "Please sit. Both your children are fine. Sunna and my son happened to get poisoned is all. Cid is with them and he's taking care of them."

"Poisoned!" repeated Bonnie, sitting on the couch with her husband. "Was it an insect again?"

"No, it was a little different this time," stated Stacy, taking her seat with Sooner by her side. "Sunna and my son were captured by the KOGN. Jason rescued them, but not until they had received a contaminated Truth Test," educated Stacy.

Bonnie gave Stacy a cold stare and questioned, "Why was my daughter with your son?"

"She's his bodyguard," expressed Sooner, getting involved.

Stacy put her hand on his shoulder and reminded, "Sooner, let me talk."

The boy looked up at her and expressed, "Grandmother, she was awesome how she saved my father."

Stacy smiled and looked back at Sunna's parents with questioning eyes. "How did you see what my daughter did?" Bonnie quizzed.

"We—"

"Sooner!" warned Stacy. The boy stopped and Stacy continued, "Gabala, Bonnie, and George, I need for you to take an oath to never divulge what I'm going to tell you."

"Madam, are you sure about me? I have already given you an oath," questioned Gabala.

"Not for this. Gabala, what I'm about to say you don't know," smiled Stacy.

"I will take it," replied George.

"There is more, George. I'm going to ask you if you're willing to give your complete allegiance to the new Master of the Galaxy. He is watching you as we speak," stated Stacy.

"He's here?" questioned Bonnie.

"No, he's watching us from another place in the galaxy," countered Stacy.

The three stated at the same time, "I do."

"Are you willing to keep his identity a secret until he announces his reign?"

"Yes," they all repeated in unison.

Sooner grabbed his grandmother's arms and stated, "Does this mean they agree to be my grandparents?"

Stacy quickly shot a glance at Bonnie. It was obvious she was at a loss for words. But it didn't last long as Bonnie pointed at Sooner and asked, "What is he referring to?"

Before Stacy could get a word out, Sooner continued, "Sunna is in love with my father and I and we love her. They're getting married today and you're invited to the wedding."

Bonnie looked like someone had slapped her across the face. George spoke first. "When did this happen?" Stacy didn't know what to say. So George added, "Is the new Master of the Galaxy with them?" Stacy nodded. "Did he save their lives?"

"Yes, he did," answered Sooner. The boy grinned, "My father is the new Master of the Galaxy."

Stacy watched in wonderment at how Bonnie was taking this information. When she just sat there quiet, Stacy became nervous. She started to say something, but Sooner beat her. He continued, "When Sunna woke up under the Truth Test, she told my father that she loved him. Father and I had already asked her to stay and be my mother."

"And she agreed?" questioned Bonnie, coming to life.

"Yes, Bonnie, my son and your daughter are going to get married. By giving your allegiance to my son, he has asked you all to keep his marriage a secret," stated Stacy.

"Why can't we tell anyone that they're married?" inquired Bonnie with concern.

"Not even his crew will know. They need time to establish a strong foundation for their marriage before his title put pressure on them. They are doing it today because medically it's best for her and Ghonllier is close to becoming the Master of the Stones. Adamite is with them and he'll be marrying them," divulged Stacy.

Bonnie let out a sigh and expressed, "Finally, my daughter wants to get married and I won't be able to see it."

Sooner sat next to her and grinned, "Yes, you will see it, Grandmother. My father's server stones are here in this city. This is his city."

"We knew they here but we didn't' know who had them. Has it been you?" asked George.

Stacy nodded. "We've been keeping them for our son," smiled Stacy.

Sooner grabbed a hold of Bonnie's hand and asked, "Would you like to see them?"

Bonnie nodded as Sooner ran to the doors of the server stone, opening them. On the surface, they saw Ghonllier at Sunna's side. They both were lying on gurneys, smiling back at one another.

Soon Ghonllier reached out to her and she took his hand to kiss it. Then he kissed hers while they glowed, looking tenderly into each other's eyes.

Sunna's mother smiled to see it. Shaking her head, she whispered, "If I hadn't just seen her kiss your father's hand, I wouldn't believe you that our daughter was in love."

"Are they staying on those gurneys while they get married?" asked George.

"Yes, they're too weak to even lift their heads," answered Stacy. Looking at them, she added, "It will be the same for Sunna as it was with the spider bite. They'll be dizzy and weak for awhile."

Stacy looked away from the server stone to see tears streaming down Bonnie's cheeks. "Bonnie, are you okay?" questioned Stacy, getting her a handkerchief.

Sooner met Stacy halfway. Taking it from her, he joined Bonnie to present it to her. "Grandmother."

Blinking back her tears, she accepted his handkerchief. She gently soaked up her tears while looking into Sooner's eyes. Then, suddenly, she opened her arms to him and expressed, "I'm so grateful to have a grandson."

They hugged and Stacy let out a sigh of relief. When they finished, Sooner sat between George and Bonnie.

Looking at Stacy, Bonnie inquired, "When will they be home? Can we have some kind of wedding party for them?"

"Father said we can only have a family party because they have a secret marriage. Do you want to help me plan it?" beamed Sooner.

Bonnie kissed his forehead and expressed, "I would love it."

"Madam, where are they going to live?" asked Gabala.

"Ghonllier's room. When they arrive, please have the staff move her into his room. . . . Ghonllier gave us permission to tell the staff if they'll give them his allegiance," informed Stacy.

"Very good," smiled Gabala.

Bonnie patted Sooner's hand in a nervous gesture. "I hated her career. Yet, through it, Sunna found love and the Master of the Galaxy."

"She's very good at her job, Grandmother. She had to be good to be my father's bodyguard," informed Sooner.

"And yours, Sooner," reminded Stacy.

"How can she guard Sooner when she's not here?" asked Bonnie.

"There are Vanishers who are with me when I leave the house. They have to answer to my mother," smiled Sooner. "She is going to be handling Special Services for my father when he takes over the galaxy."

Bonnie slowly shook her head while peering into Sooner's eyes. "I thought I would never hear that word . . . 'Grandmother,'" she expressed, hugging Sooner again.

Stacy leaned back in a chair, listening to Sooner tell Sunna's parents about the events that had brought everyone to this room. It was interesting to watch Sunna's parents interact with Sooner. She saw something different in Bonnie and George and felt relieved to have this part over with.

✳ ✳ ✳

When Cid brought Sunna back into Ghonllier's quarters, Spencer happened to arrive as Sunna exited the Med-C. Upon seeing her, he attempted to talk with her. Cid knew from their conversation, Spencer presented pressure to Sunna. Not wanting her stressed before the wedding, he intervened by standing between them.

Spencer was furious that Cid wouldn't allow him to talk to Sunna, along with the fact that she didn't stop Cid. She only glanced at him before disappearing. Glaring at the hullercast, he decided to go over Cid's head and talk with Jason. Not realizing that Jason was already inside Ghonllier's room, Spencer waited in vain for him, but he did see Ghonllier.

Soon after Sunna left, Gostler and Adamite brought Ghonllier through the corridor. Seeing Spencer, Ghonllier felt a tinge of guilt knowing Spencer ached to marry her.

The guilt left him when he saw Sunna. She was beautiful and he didn't expect her to look so healthy. The makeup took away her pale look from the poison.

As they moved him next to Sunna, he noticed her eyes were closed. The encounter with Spencer had her upset and Ghonllier could read it. He reached and touched her hand. Sunna opened her eyes. Quickly, she forgot about Spencer.

He smiled and didn't move his lips as she heard, "I LOVE YOU."

She smiled and spoke to him with her thoughts. *I love you and I'm so glad I came back.*

"I GAVE UP ON THIS EVER HAPPENING," expressed Ghonllier.

Me, too.

"YOU LOOK BEAUTIFUL," smiled Ghonllier.

Seeing Ghonllier touching Sunna, Cid released her safety straps and removed her blanket. Sunna carefully moved onto her side so she could face Ghonllier, who reached out to her once more. She responded by taking his hand, kissing it, while he lovingly did the same with hers.

She cracked a beaming smile, gazing tenderly back at him, and ran her fingertips along his face. "You shaved. I wouldn't care if you had left your beard. I don't think we'll be kissing for awhile."

"I know, but our son would've been upset. He doesn't like me with a beard," stated Ghonllier, using his voice.

She giggled. "'Our son.' That sounds wonderful to hear," smiled Sunna.

"Are you really sure about getting married today?"

She nodded. "You can't read it?"

"I was testing you. I wanted to see if there was something deeper that you had hidden regarding me."

"Did you find anything?"

He smiled. "No." Then he paused for a moment and added, "Did you get all of your answers satisfied while you were with the Master Stones?"

"I think so."

"You were concerned about Jenny coming between us, weren't you?"

Sunna glanced around to make sure they were alone before she replied, "I was very concerned. It was my first question to the Master Stones. They assured me of your great capacity to love us both. It was one of the main reasons they picked you to be their Master. Your ability to love others allows the Stones to be more powerful through you. I didn't know love was their source of power.

"They told me, they waited for you over your brothers, Manchester and Astor. The greater your ability to love even your enemies makes it easy for you to utilize all of their power. And revenge wouldn't be a temptation for you."

"Yeah. They warned me about revenge."

"Did you realize that your love is your greatest strength?"

"I never thought about it," divulged Ghonllier, kissing the back of her hand. Ghonllier was grateful for the Stones allowing Sunna to see what was in her heart. He was pleased to learn she wasn't resentful toward him but only a misunderstanding. He thought, *Thank you, Master Stones for giving me my down deep desire.*

YOU'RE WELCOME, GHONLLIER. WE PROMISED YOU THAT WE WOULD MAKE YOUR TIME WITH US WORTH IT. THANK YOU FOR ALLOW-ING US TO GIVE IT TO YOU.

While listening to the Stones, Ghonllier saw love and support in Sunna's eyes for him. It triggered a feeling that he hadn't felt in a long time, the desire to be the best Master of the Galaxy he could possibly be. The thought took him to a deeper level of harmony with the Stones and he knew Sunna was his biggest strength and weakness. Now it made sense to why the Stones warned him that it was important, they kept their relationship a secret from the galaxy. They both knew Ghonllier would sacrifice the galaxy for her life.

Surprised to feel someone touching his face, Sunna brought him out of his thoughts. She expressed, "Did I do something wrong? You looked like you were somewhere else."

He smiled. "I was. I was thanking the Stones for bringing us together. Did I make you feel left out?"

"No," whispered Sunna. "I just want to understand your moods and learn what they mean," she added, lightly running her finger over his lips. Removing her hand, she asked, "When is the cere-mony going to start? What are we waiting for, Ghonllier?"

"Asustie," he whispered. "She's on her way here."

Asustie entered the room and headed for Jason and Cid. They were standing together, quietly talking. Arriving, she spat, "What is this I hear about you, Cid? Is it true?"

"Is what true?" inquired the medic, smiling. He had guessed what she was referring to.

"That you've been in a long relationship between Sunna and you. The two of you have kept it secret from Ghonllier and Jason," commented Asustie, concerned.

Cid and Jason hooted. Nudging Jason, he asked, "How long did it take?"

Jason looked at his timepiece and answered, "You were the closest. It took twenty-five minutes."

"I told you Janet was good," cajoled Cid.

"What is going on?" inquired Asustie.

Jason leaned forward and lightly kissed her on the lips. "I'll explain later, darling."

Seeing Asustie was there, Adamite announced for everyone to gather in a semicircle around Ghonllier and Sunna's heads. Cid, Jason, Asustie, and Gostler made up the semicircle with Adamite standing in the middle. While Adamite collected his thoughts, he stared at his son. It was humbling to see the love that was in Sunna and Ghonllier's faces.

It brought back memories of Ghonllier's first marriage and his own marriage to Stacy. Quickly, he ran through his mind all the things Ghonllier and Sunna went through to get to this moment. Adamite knew by looking at them that the burning fires would appear and it pleased him.

The burning fires were a special binding marriage contract that didn't come to everyone. It was a contract that would continue through death, if honored. This special marriage contract wasn't a choice. It automatically came to those who lived by its rules. The rules were simple but rewarding for those who earned it.

Ghonllier had kept himself for his wives, Jenny and Sunna, and in return they had done the same thing. The contract of the bonding fires would be enforced in the next existence, allowing them to always be together. If the contracts were broken in this existence, Ghonllier would not be married to either woman and they wouldn't be able to see each other.

Sighing, Adamite stepped forward and stated, "With the power invested in me by our society, we're here to bind these two people together. This is an important responsibility that Ghonllier and Sunna are taking and I'm pleased to see it happen." Adamite's voice cracked with emotion.

Ghonllier had married numerous couples while commander of the *Liberty Quest*. He was given the authority since their ship didn't have a home base. Being familiar with the words of the ceremony, Ghonllier half listened to his father. He wanted to be focused on Sunna in her weakened state. The burning fires were going to affect her body. Ghonllier wasn't sure how the fires would affect the Master Stones.

He came back to his father's voice when he heard, "Sunna, is this your own choice to be bonded as one with Ghonllier and to help him carry the mantel of his position of having oneness in all things?"

"Yes," she answered.

"Ghonllier, is this your own choice to be bonded with Sunna to become one with her in all things?"

"Yes."

Adamite stepped back into the semi-circle to make room for the bonding fires. Instantly, they started to appear.

"This fire that's appearing will bind these two people together. It will be a protection and comfort as long as they honor them. By keeping the contract, it will help you become one in purpose, teaching you how to handle your relationship. The only way the bonding fires can leave you is if either one of you breaks this contract by seeking someone else. The warmth and protection of the fire will no longer exist in your life and you'll no longer be married. Darkness and emptiness will replace the warmth you're feeling now."

Ghonllier and Sunna felt the bonding fires the minute they appeared out of the floor. A warm tingling sensation started and quickly spread through their bodies. As the fires matched the height of the gurneys, they could feel the warm sensation coursing through their bodies.

The fires needed to reach into their souls, causing them to wonder where one person started and the other stopped. The Master

Stones magnified the sensation within them, since they were a part of the moment.

Sunna found Adamite's voice fading soon after the fires started. The warm sensation was stronger than Ghonllier remembered. He struggled to stay awake, thinking he was feeling Sunna's health. He, too, was loosing consciousness with her.

The moment Cid saw the fires he panicked. In school, they were taught how the bonding fires ceremony affected the body. *They aren't strong enough for this! Why didn't someone tell me?*

He left the circle, so he could see their faces better. His heart raced when he saw their eyes turn glassy as Sunna closed hers. He searched Ghonllier's eyes, hoping he was in control, but his heart sank. Ghonllier's eyes were shut as well.

Once the bonding fires appeared, no one could interrupt them. The fires were sacred and would hurt anyone trying to interfere. Cid didn't want to ruin the moment for anyone else, but finally he couldn't keep quiet any longer. Looking at Adamite, he saw tears trickling down his cheek.

Ignoring them, Cid asked, "Why are those fires taking so long to go back down? They're still above their heads."

"The Master Stones are being brought into the contract," answered Gostler, realizing Cid was upset. "It will take longer. Is there a problem?" he asked, concerned.

"Why didn't someone tell me that the bonding fires would appear?" whispered Cid through gritted teeth.

"Why would it matter?" questioned Adamite, now paying attention to the conversation.

"If I had known the fires were going to appear, I would've had them on fluids before you started. Normally, the bonding fires drain the body of water. With this taking place in space, the fires are going to task their bodies more than they are capable of enduring," educated Cid.

"Cid, why didn't you ask before we started?" quizzed Jason, engaging in the conversation.

"Sunna's a spy and everyone knows they're—"

"Scum, liars, and untrustworthy in all aspects?" finished Jason.

He faced Jason. "I'm sorry . . . I didn't realize how labeled spies were until you repeated the words people describe them with."

"I know. A lot of men thought Sunna was easy because she was a spy, but they all soon learned," responded Jason.

"Look Cid, what do we need to do?" asked Adamite, concerned.

Cid flashed a glance at the fires and said, "I don't know yet. I hope the Stones have protected them."

"I wouldn't plan on it," interrupted Gostler.

"Great!" expressed Cid.

"The fires are descending," added Asustie.

Everyone looked to see the fires finally dropping. Cid explained that he wanted everyone out when he returned with Janet. Gostler offered to stay since Cid was going to be working around the Stones and the medic accepted it. Asustie was asked to stay to help Janet. She would need her to hand her equipment because they needed to work fast.

Cid left with everyone, watching the bride and groom with concern. Justin wanted to know what Ghonllier was thinking. They listened to Gostler explain what he was reading from Ghonllier's mind.

Shortly, they heard a knock. Jason went to the green stone to talk with those outside the door. "Cid. We can't open the door. We are still having problems," mentioned Jason, looking at the fires a foot above the floor.

He watched the fires slowly disappear into the floor. The moment the fires disappeared, leaving no trace of their appearance. Adamite ordered them to be separated. He put Ghonllier in his dressing area while Sunna was moved over by the wall. Jason was the person who gave Cid the okay to enter.

Cid and Janet entered, carrying their equipment. It obvious that Cid was still angry, as he snapped, "Jason and Adamite! Out!"

The men exited to find Spencer still there. He pounced on Jason, firing questions at him. He didn't answer but exchanged looks with Adamite. Finally, Jason explained that they didn't know. Ghonllier and Sunna just passed out.

Gostler shortly appeared and Adamite demanded, "How's my son?"

Glancing at Spencer, Gostler stated, "Well I learned how to use an apparatus for fluids. Cid will be here shortly. I can't tell you anything, David."

"Is Sunna okay?" quizzed Spencer.

"You'll have to ask Cid," repeated Gostler.

Shortly, Cid joined them. Spencer glared at him, but Cid only ignored him as he said, "Both Sunna and Ghonllier are stabilized. They were quite dehydrated and we are putting fluids into them."

"Sunna? Did this set her back?" questioned Spencer.

Cid looked at him thoughtfully. "The fluids should change their numbers. We better wait until Janet returns and see if her numbers go up. She told me her scores had dropped below a four," informed Cid, glancing over at Gostler.

"What caused this to have both of them drop? I saw the commander a few minutes ago and he looked fine," quizzed Spencer.

Facing Spencer, Cid answered, "This is my fault. I should have put them on fluids after their showers. I didn't take into account being in space and how important water is to you. I'm new at being a medic in space."

Spencer asked the question about Sunna and he going to the Jupiter moon. When Jason informed him that they weren't going and Sunna was going to work from the Xeron moon. Spencer shot Cid a menacing glare before he stormed off. Jason sighed.

"I'm sorry, Cid. I should've told him earlier," apologized Jason.

Cid put his hands in his pocket and responded, "Did you notice the glare he gave me. I think he's heard about Janet's assumptions about Sunna and I. Should I straighten him out?"

"No. It might be a protection for Sunna. Let him think its you," stated Adamite. He shifted on his feet and added, "He is going to make this hard."

"I think we need to run this past Ghonllier. Spencer could start pursuing Sunna harder, thinking he was losing her," expressed Jason.

Gostler, Cid, and Adamite nodded. The door opened and out stepped Janet. She stated, "You can go in now."

They entered to see Sunna covered with a blanket. Asustie was watching the monitors. Jason joined his wife and kissed her on the cheek. Asustie smiled at him. "How's our sister? Did Janet suspect anything?"

Asustie shot a quick glance toward the door to make sure Janet was gone. "She was surprised to see how dehydrated Sunna was and bawled Cid out. She kept saying, the dehydration was high and Cid should've seen it before they had a shower," replied Asustie.

He glanced over at Ghonllier to see them covering him with a blanket. Cid activated the safety strap by the time Asustie and Jason arrived at his side. They could see Ghonllier wasn't awake.

"How long will he be out?" asked Jason.

Cid glanced at him and answered, "I want you to completely leave him alone. Even when he wakes up. Stress will slow his recovery."

"What can we do to help?" asked Adamite.

"I can handle everything until they're off the gurneys," said Cid, looking at Sunna. "Sunna is going to be weaker. If I take her off the fluids, she'll need to be on a schedule where we wake her up to give her water as long as we are space."

Asustie nodded. "I can sleep in Sooner's room and help you, Cid."

"We'll both sleep in Sooner's room," smiled Jason, reaching out for her hand. "I want to be close to help her or Ghonllier," Jason added.

"Jason, eventually I'll need to get coded into Sooner's room. Sometime down the road, we'll have to move Sunna into the other room," stated Cid.

"You don't need to move her into Sooner's room. There is a door that goes between the two rooms," educated Jason.

Cid nodded and expressed, "Why don't you all leave. I'll go get something to eat and come back to stay with them. If anyone needs to come in here in the future, I want to be with you. So I can watch their stress level."

They left while Adamite paused to look back at his son. He was so pleased to be able to marry him this time. He didn't realize how much he desired to marry Sunna and he together.

Twenty hours later, Ghonllier finally woke up. Cid immediately took Ghonllier off the monitors. The new Master moved himself to his bed by using the Stones. He appreciated being able to float himself over to his bed, helping him to avoid the dizziness that came from raising his head. Cid was with him. Ghonllier was disappointed to see Sunna was still unconscious. He connected to her thoughts and decided he wanted her close to him.

Without telling Cid, he moved her to the bed. He knew Sunna would be waking up soon and he wanted to talk with her. Cid wanted to stay in the room with them because Sunna was still receiving fluids. Ghonllier promised to send their stats into the Med-C so everyone would think she was on the gurney hooked up to the monitors.

Cid headed for the door. Stopping at the door, he requested, "She still needs fluids. Don't take her off without telling me."

"I'll let you do it," promised Ghonllier.

Cid left knowing she was in good hands with Ghonllier awake. Ghonllier had a hard time staying awake. He had hoped that he would be awake when she woke up but it didn't happen. Cid entered on a schedule to check on Sunna.

By the third day, Sunna started to wake up on a regular bases. Cid took her off the fluids. She would watch Ghonllier sleep as Asustie or Cid gave her water to drink and food. The Master seemed to sleep through it. For some reason, when he did wake up, Sunna was always asleep.

It had been seven days since Ghonllier and Sunna had their setback. Adamite stepped into Sunna's job. He had it before Justin gave it to her. Often, he was in the office using the C-Stone to communicate with Humphrey. Adamite also kept Spencer business. So he wouldn't hang out around the Med-C. It was obvious Spencer did not like Cid.

Suddenly, the ship's speakers caused him to cut his communication with Humphrey short. Gostler and Jason were being summoned to Ghonllier's quarters. Instantly, Adamite moved out of the office and wondered why he wasn't a part of the page. In away he was, Ghonllier could've talked to them without telling the captains to announce it.

Arriving first at his son's open door, he entered without being invited. The father and son stared at each other before Adamite inquired, "How do you feel?"

"QUITE DIZZY," Ghonllier spoke, using the Master Stones.

Adamite smiled to see him speaking without moving his mouth. Jason, Cid, and Gostler entered the room together and Ghonllier closed the door behind them.

Cid sat on the edge of the bed to monitor his body for stress with his portable analyzer. The medic joined to make sure the meeting wasn't going to be too stressful for Ghonllier and invited himself to it like Adamite had.

It irritated Ghonllier that Cid wanted to monitor his stats, but he wasn't going to say anything to him. The new Master knew it meant a lot to Cid to be his personal medic and Cid wanted to do a good job.

Not wanting to wake up Sunna, Ghonllier projected his voice through the Stones. "I HAD A DREAM THAT WE NEED TO TALK ABOUT." Looking at his father, he continued, "BOG IS FORCING GOMPER TO EXECUTE AN OFFENSIVE AGAINST OUR MOON."

"And he's doing it?" whispered Adamite coldly.

"BOG HAS FOUND A WAY TO FORCE GOMPER TO DO THINGS AGAINST HIS WILL."

"How did he make Gomper do that?" inquired Adamite, upset.

"BOG'S STILL CONNECTED TO THE CURSE THAT IS INSIDE OF HIM. SINCE, I BURNED HIS BOOKS AND DESTROYED HIS STEPPING STONE. HE CAN'T PUT A NEW INCANTATION ON HIM BUT HE CAN USE THE CURSE THAT IS INSIDE OF HIM TO TORTURE GOMPER, FORCING HIM TO DO HIS WILL," answered Ghonllier.

"Why our moon? Why the Xeron moon?" questioned Adamite.

"I TOLD YOU FATHER THAT YOU LIVED IN A DANGEROUS PLACE AND IF I WERE IN GOMPER'S PLACE, I, TOO, WOULD PICK THE XERON MOON. YOU SHOULD'VE LET THEM LAND SOMETIMES . . ." paused Ghonllier. He added, "GOMPER UNDERSTANDS THE SERVER STONES CAN CREATE A SHIELD. SO HE'S QUITE CONFIDENT THAT YOU'RE HERE. BOG CAN TALK THROUGH GOMPER AGAINST HIS WILL. SO HE ORDERED THE INVASION."

"How is he torturing my son?" asked Adamite coldly.

"HE CAUSES THE CURSE TO SURGE INTO HIS STOMACH, WHICH CAUSES A LOT OF PAIN. IT'S TO THE POINT WHERE HE PASSES OUT," answered Ghonllier.

"What kind of offensive are they going to do against us?" whispered Jason.

"GOMPER HAS SENT THREE GALAXY CREEPERS TO OUR MOON TO ATTACK FIRST. HE TOLD THEM TO STAY OUT OF THE ATMOSPHERE AND SEND IN STAR SCREAMERS TO POUND THE SURFACE WITH BLASTS LOOKING FOR OUR SECRET PLACE," divulged Ghonllier.

"Why do they think we're in a protected area?" inquired Adamite.

"GOMPER READ THE SAME REPORT THAT I DID. HE KNOWS THERE IS A PLACE THERE WHERE PEOPLE ARE AFRAID TO ENTER. HE'S FIGURED IT OUT THAT WE MUST HAVE THE SERVER STONES AND ARE UNDER A SHIELD PUTTING US IN ANOTHER DIMENSION. FOR SOME REASON, HE KNOWS IT'S POSSIBLE," said Ghonllier, looking at Gostler.

"I taught him that. He knows the server stones can produce the shield," whispered Gostler.

"The Star Screamers fire power will tear right through our shields. They'll find us," sighed Adamite.

"ONCE THEY FIND THE SHIELD, THE GALAXY CREEPERS WILL ALL POSITION THEMSELVES TO FIRE FROM SPACE ON OUR CITY."

"They would be more effective if they came into the atmosphere," reminded Jason.

"THEY'LL DO ENOUGH DAMAGE FROM SPACE WITH ALL SHIPS CONCENTRATED ON ONE SPOT," reminded Ghonllier.

"Then what will they do?" asked Jason.

"THEY PLAN ON SENDING IN GROUND TROOPS TO LOOK FOR PEOPLE WHO LIVED THROUGH THE ATTACK SO THEY CAN INTERROGATE THEM ABOUT ME."

"No one there knows about you," interjected Jason.

"YOU FORGOT. MY WHOLE CREW IS THERE. UNDER A TRUTH TEST, THEY'LL BE ABLE TO POINT TO THE HOUSE WHERE MY MOTHER AND SON LIVE."

"Why would Gomper come up with such an effective plan to destroy us?"

"HE PLANS ON BEING IN THE LAST WAVE, GIVING ME TIME TO WIN AND LEAVE BEFORE HE ARRIVES. HE KNOWS THAT THE CURSE WILL PASS TO ME IF WE MEET."

Ghonllier didn't tell his father that Bog would probably torture him and his staff with Ghonllier winning.

"So he knows about the curse?" sighed Adamite.

Ghonllier nodded. "GOMPER KNOWS WHAT HE'S DOING AND I APPRECIATE HE IS TRYING TO HELP ME."

"What is your plan to counter it?" whispered Jason.

"JUSTIN IS SENDING HOUSER TO HELP ME, ALONG WITH EIGHT OTHER GALAXY CREEPERS," informed Ghonllier.

"Nine Galaxy Creepers! Why so many?" whispered Jason.

"I have my reasons," stated Ghonllier, resting his eyes.

Everyone started to talk amongst themselves on what would help protect the people from the possible quasar blasts from the ships. Asustie placed her hand on Cid's shoulder. The medic turned his head around to hear her ask, "How is he?"

"Same," answered Cid.

Ghonllier opened his eyes and Cid requested, "Ghonllier, I want to check your eyes."

"Go ahead," mentioned Ghonllier, watching Asustie join Jason.

Cid raised his eyelids more to examine what lines were developing in his eyes. "Cid, I can answer your question for you," responded Ghonllier, reading his mind.

Letting go of his eyelids, he challenged, "Answer it."

"You're concerned about the increased fatigue suddenly appearing on the analyzer?" Cid nodded. "I added the third Stone. Every time I add a Master Stone you'll see my blood change. It will cause some fatigue, but nothing like the first time."

"How's the dizziness?" quizzed Cid quietly.

"I'm tolerating it better. I understand why Sunna would try to push it when she was poisoned before."

"You were close to being too stressful moments ago. I'm concerned about this up-and-coming battle. Even for you, stress is going to set you back and we need you to become strong quickly."

Ghonllier softly snapped, "I know."

Cid saw his stress levels increase. "Ghonllier, do you want me to stay during the battle?" asked Cid.

"No, it would stress me more. We'll be in battle shut down mode. You need to be in your quarters in a chair or on your bed. Butler is going to be doing some fancy flying. If you aren't using the safety straps, you'll be thrown around and possibly killed," answered Ghonllier, seeing Cid's concern. He added, "I'll be mindful of the stress and find ways to not let it get to me. Thank you for reminding me."

Cid looked down at the analyzer before he spoke again. "Ghonllier, I'm concerned that you aren't being totally honest with yourself. I can see you have a lot of concerns."

"CID, I'M A LEADER, A PROTECTOR, A FATHER, AND NOW A HUSBAND. WHAT DO YOU SUGGEST I GIVE UP?" snapped Ghonllier, using the Stones so others wouldn't hear.

In a whisper, Cid countered, "You aren't the leader yet. So let it go. You're not being a father right now with Sooner gone. After this moment, I wouldn't take being the protector that serious. Enjoy the moment of being a husband before you have to add the job of being a leader, protector, and father. You need a strong foundation with Sunna first."

He shifted a glance at the analyzer, wondering how Ghonllier took his speech. Ghonllier broke the silence with, "THANK YOU, CID, I NEEDED TO HEAR THAT." The medic raised his head and smiled. Ghonllier added, "I'M IMPRESSED WITH WHAT YOU SAID, BEING A SINGLE PERSON."

"My mother taught me well."

"You're a good man," whispered Ghonllier as Cid gazed at Sunna.

Looking back at Ghonllier, he commented, "I'm concerned about her. She isn't doing very well. What's your opinion?"

"YOU'RE RIGHT. HER BODY IS STRUGGLING TO PUSH OUT THE POISON. I'M AWARE IF WE DON'T REMOVE IT BY A CERTAIN TIME, IT WILL DO SOME SERIOUS DAMAGE," answered Ghonllier.

"Have you talked with her about it?" Cid asked.

"No, she is always asleep when I've been awake."

Cid stared at Sunna, not liking her skin color. Ghonllier heard the Master Stones speak to him. *CID IS RIGHT. YOU NEED TO REST. WE'LL CARRY THE LOAD OF THIS BATTLE FOR YOU AND LET YOU KNOW WHAT WE NEED FROM YOU INSTEAD OF THE OTHER WAY AROUND.*

Ghonllier smiled to feel the load lift off his shoulders. With the pressure leaving, Ghonllier realized how much stress he was feeling.

Cid stood to realize Adamite, Jason, and Gostler were gathering to speak with Ghonllier.

"Son, do we need to notify the leaders of our city?" inquired Adamite.

"I WOULD. I CAN'T GUARANTEE THEIR SAFETY," answered Ghonllier.

"Men," announced Cid, stepping in front of him. "I don't want you to bother him any further. You all know what needs to be done. I want you to leave. He needs his rest."

They nodded. Ghonllier interjected, "Jason, would you get me my field glasses? Sam and Butler will want to talk with me during this battle. They don't know how to contact me mentally yet." Jason nodded and joined Gostler at the door. Ghonllier opened and requested, "Gostler, stay here for a moment. I need to talk with you."

Gostler watched everyone leave and the door shut. He joined Ghonllier and being able to read his mind, he ordered, "Roll over."

Ghonllier reached up and took out the second pillow before rolling onto his side.

Now, he faced Sunna sleeping. While Gostler took the third Master Stone out of his belt, Ghonllier ran his fingers lovingly through the ends of her hair, trying not to wake her up.

While Gostler held the Master Stone to authenticate it, Sunna opened her eyes. Ghonllier spoke in sign language, warning her that they weren't alone. When he finished signing, she closed her eyes again. Ghonllier could read that she was deciding if she should go back to sleep or stay awake. He hoped she would stay awake and regretted asking Gostler to stay.

"I see it," whispered Gostler. Smiling, he faced Ghonllier to see Sunna lying on his arm cuddled into him. "Hi, Sunna. Did I wake you?" he greeted.

"No," she smiled.

"Would you like to see what you risked your life for?"

"Please," responded Sunna.

Gostler commanded an orbiter to follow his hand. He held the Master Stone between Sunna and the light. Sunna grinned and asked, "Do all the Stones have raindrops on the inside?"

"No, just the third one," answered Ghonllier. "The first and second have a snowflake and the wind."

"The fourth?" inquired Sunna.

"The sun," answered Gostler. He ordered the orbiter to return to its original place. "Roll onto your side so I can put this back. Then I'll answer your questions."

Sunna rolled over on her back while Ghonllier went to his side. His lips touched her head and he gently kissed it while Gostler placed the Stone in the belt. Then they rolled back to see Gostler watching them.

"What's your first question?" Gostler asked.

"Tell me everything about what you understand the third Stone can do," requested Ghonllier. "Especially, if it pertains to this upcoming battle," he added.

"Battle?" questioned Sunna.

Ghonllier put his hand up and signed he would tell her later.

"Well you have already seen its protection. Your body has the same protection that your ship has now. You'll be able to see farther into the future than you did before. This Stone bonds mostly with your intelligence. As you noticed, you instantly understood our Eraphin language that we've been using around you. It will be an easier Stone to adjust to compared to the first two Stones."

"How far into the future will I be able to see?"

"I'm not sure how to explain it."

"Can he see anything he wants in the future?" asked Sunna.

"It depends on the Stones and why you want to see it. They have a mind of their own and will refuse to show you some things from the future, as you already know that about me. Just remember, if they refuse to show you something, they have a very good reason. I suggest you trust them."

"Weather, what can I do with it?" asked Ghonllier. "Will I need the Movelings to start something?"

"If the elements are already there, you should be able to enhance and/or control them. You can't create anything that isn't there. But you can move the weather you want into the area. When you're the Master, you'll be able to summon the elements to create whatever you want."

"Will I be able to bring in asteroids from space into the atmosphere on my own?"

"No, remember the temperatures are the hardest elements to control."

"Can I produce rain?" Gostler shook his head. "And what about lightning?"

"You should be able to make lightning if the clouds and wind are just right. Wind is the easiest weather-related element to control. You have clouds usually that can make lightning."

"How fast can I move clouds over our city if I have to bring them in from a distance?"

"You really need to ask the Stones that question. I never was in the situation where I had to test it with the third Stone," reminisced Gostler.

"Can the Stones enhance the fire power of the *Liberty Quest*?"

"Yes."

"Thanks, Gostler. You've given me some ideas."

"Good luck," waved Gostler, leaving. Stopping before Ghonllier opened the door, he asked, "Would you two like something to eat?"

"Please, I'm so hungry. This will be our first time that we have eaten together, since we've been married," smiled Sunna.

"Open the door for me, Ghonllier," requested Gostler.

"Hullercast, open," spoke Sunna.

Gostler smiled and left.

Chapter 6

Xeron Moon

*I*n his private quarters of his Galaxy Creeper, Gomper waited for the battle to begin at the Xeron moon. While nervous, he waited patiently, wondering if he could really help his brother save the people's lives and escape. In his mind, Gomper could hear Bog mumbling about how much he despised Ghonllier.

The sorcerer was furious about Ghonllier escaping from the Mossen planet and not fighting. He planned the whole invasion, hoping to have a confrontation with the *Liberty Quest* and Ghonllier. Among Bog's mumbled words, Gomper started to get an idea of what Ghonllier had done to him in the past. He understood that Ghonllier had met Bog and Gomper was perplexed. The thought intrigued him and he wanted to know more.

He strongly suspected Ghonllier was aware of the curse from Bog's mumbling. Gomper wondered if Ghonllier would ever find a way for him to learn what really happened to him before he died. Sometimes, the thought crept into his mind that Ghonllier would find a way to rid him of the demon so he could go home. Every time he got that thought, Gomper pushed it away. He didn't want to think about ever being able to go home.

A request for Suzair the Great to come to the bridge brought Gomper out of his thoughts. Pappar looked at him, waiting for an answer. Gomper shook his head. "Tell Commander Jabolt that I'm watching it from here," replied Gomper, knowing Bog would punish him and he didn't want others to see it.

Commander Jabolt and those with him were pleased. The last time Suzair the Great was on the bridge, Bog didn't like the message Commander Jabolt delivered. Bog sent a sharp object through the air and embedded it into the commander's arm. Jabolt ordered the captains to send all information to Gomper's quarters.

It wasn't long until the bridge was sending pictures showing the Galaxy Creepers coming out of jump speed. Gomper told Brewster, Pappar, and Jamham to leave, not wanting them to get hurt. They all shook their heads and while telling him that they didn't wish to leave, Gomper shook his head at them and pointed to the door. Jamham went to retrieve vanishing paper. He wrote: Sir, we won't leave you. If the demon hurts you we want to be here. If you die, we all are dead. So don't worry about us.

Gomper read the note and rubbed it between the palms of his hands, causing it to disappear. The voices of the captains on the Galaxy Creepers were talking to each other and they could hear the conversation. Gomper sighed, wishing he were with his brother now. Someone turned the volume of the monitor up. Gomper looked up and wished they hadn't done that, but didn't say anything.

Quietly, he waited. When they heard the captains of the KOGN Galaxy Creepers had picked up the *Liberty Quest* signal, he looked back at the monitor. Quietly, he listened to the *Liberty Quest* taking out their Star Screamers.

Nervous about their time of arrival, he broke silence and asked, "Pappar, how far away are we from the Xeron moon?"

Pappar checked with the time sync stone before he answered, "We'll be there in three hours, Your Grace." Gomper tapped his fingers on the arm of the chair. "Do you want me to find out any other information?" asked Pappar.

"Yes, find out if she's there alone," requested Gomper.

He was concerned that he didn't give Ghonllier enough time to take out the KOGN Star Screamer before they arrived. Bog moved up his time table and he was concerned.

Pappar returned, "She's alone, Your Grace."

"Tell them to keep the *Liberty Quest* busy until we arrive with the next wave of ships."

Gomper listened to Pappar passing his order on to Pursy. Brewster offered him some water in gesture. If he had enough in his body when Bog attacked, it helped with the pain. Reluctantly, Gomper took it, not speaking so the demon wouldn't know they all were there. If he wanted to hurt them, Bog would follow their voices and move anything to hit them with a flying object.

With each KOGN ship Ghonllier destroyed, Gomper felt the pain in his stomach increase. When the bridge reported the news regarding nine I-Force Galaxy Creepers appearing, Gomper suddenly lost consciousness, falling forward onto the floor.

Jamham saw him fall forward first and nudged Brewster. The men quietly leaped to his side. Brewster quickly put the analyzer on his hand to see what he could do this time to keep him from dying.

He had patches already made up and used the one that the analyzer suggested. Everyone waited patiently to see if it worked. Brewster knew Gomper was going to come out when he saw tears flowing out from the corners of his closed eyes. Gomper curled up into a ball, trying to get relief. Then he went unconscious.

"Is he dead?" questioned Jamham.

"Very close," replied Brewster.

Hearing them, Bog backed off, not wanting to kill him. Those around him didn't understand that they could stop the pain simply by pretending it hurt worse than it did.

✻   ✻   ✻

Adamite had an ache in his heart while he told the leaders of his city about the impending battle. The leaders were relieved to know that I-Force would be there. A battle was a concern for the moon, since it was neutral territory. The moon had no weapons to defend its people. All Ghonllier's city could do was go underground and protect their windows from flying debris.

Stacy wouldn't leave Adamite's thoughts. What would he do without her if things went bad? Would he be able to pick up his life and go on like Ghonllier did? Frustrated, he pushed through his concerns about the battle, wondering if he had done enough to protect his beloved city. Since he talked with his city, Adamite hadn't left the server stone. He touched the time sync stone. It revealed *Thirty minutes. Xeron Moon.*

The *Liberty Quest* was the safest place to be now with Ghonllier having the third Master Stone. He ached to have his wife beside him. *I wish I knew what our son is going to do to protect us against my other son. I wish Ghonllier was the Master now,* thought Adamite, looking away from the desk.

The Master of the Stones couldn't always control people getting hurt or killed. They could only fight to protect the masses in the galaxy. Feeling frustrated and helpless, Adamite felt like he had to do something physically. Reaching over the desk, he paged for Jason.

"I was on the bridge when you paged. What do you need, Adamite?" entered Jason as he finished the page.

"I want news. Has my son talked to you at all?"

"No."

"Is Gostler still with him?"

"No," answered Jason. "I don't know anything more and I've talked to Gostler since he came out. He doesn't know anything either. Apparently, Ghonllier has his mind blocked to him, since he got . . . hurt." Being careful, he didn't say *marriage*.

"Do the captains know what is going on?" asked Adamite.

"No, they told me Ghonllier tells them less and less these days. He only involves them if it's necessary for them to participate with him."

"Are you going to tell those on board what is going to happen?" asked Adamite just as Butler made an announcement for a meeting.

The two men stared at each other, waiting for Butler to finish. Then Jason turned, "I've got to go, Adamite."

Adamite decided to follow, mainly to feel like he was doing something. He felt antsy and unsure about the future. Walking into the dining room, Adamite realized how small their crew was on board. Ghonllier was right. There were enough people to tell the KOGN where his son and mother lived, if they survived the blasts from the KOGN Galaxy Creepers.

While Jason spoke, Adamite rolled his C-Stone over and over in his hands, trying to channel his nervous energy. It felt strange that he was going into a battle for survival with two sons leading each side and his wife as the prize. His thoughts kept going between Gomper and Stacy. He wondered if Ghonllier would be forced to fight against his brother.

The meeting wasn't helping him feel any better, so he left quietly while heading for his server stone. He desired to talk with Stacy, hoping to find peace for his heart. Sitting in the chair behind the desk, Adamite commanded the server stone to show him his wife. The sight of her did bring peace to his heart. He knew it was wrong for him to follow Jason to the meeting. The only thing that would make him feel better would be to hear her voice, so he activated his C-Stone.

Stacy happened to be outside, walking in the garden while holding onto Sooner's hand. She was making sure the metal shields had covered the windows properly. This house had so many windows that she wanted them well protected.

Gabala came out on the patio, informing her that Adamite wanted her. Being finished outside anyway, she squeezed Sooner's hand before they headed indoors. The minute the two entered the house, Gabala locked the door and palmed the wall, placing the last metal shield into position. With no light coming in from outside, every aurora orbiter in the room came on. The orbiters automatically lit up any area when someone entered.

Paging the lift, Stacy spoke, "Sooner, I don't want you to leave my side until we see your parents. Do you mind?"

"No, I want to stay with you, Grandmother. Have you been in a lot of battles on the ground?"

The door to the lift opened on the fourth floor. Stacy answered, "A few. You haven't been in any on the ground during a battle, have you?"

"No."

"Would you rather be here or on the *Liberty Quest*?" quizzed Stacy.

"The *Liberty Quest*."

"I would rather be where your father is, too," stated Stacy, entering her study to grab her C-stone from the desk.

Gostler happened to walk in on Adamite and Stacy talking. Glancing at the server stone, he listened. Just like Adamite, he, too, was nervous. But he wasn't feeling better listening to their conversation. So he left, heading for the bridge. If anyone would know something, the captains would.

Arriving, he sat in Ghonllier's flight chairs, deciding to watch the battle from the hullercasts. Nervous, he stared at the stones operating the ship that were in the console beside his chair.

Earlier, Gostler had brought brought in food. Ghonllier propped his head up to eat. The dizziness bothered him, but he was forcing himself to get used to it, in hopes it would go away. He decided to stay in this position while he waited for the battle to begin. Trying to keep his stress levels low, Ghonllier closed his eyes, watching his enemy.

To his disappointment, Sunna had fallen asleep during Gostler's stay. The former Master stayed with them, helping Sunna eat something. Every time she tried to raise her head, the dizziness was too much for her. She fell back asleep after a few bites.

Soon after Gostler had left, Ghonllier felt the bonding fires because Sunna had moved her hand next to his so she could feel them. They were soothing and she loved them as much as Ghonllier did. It was what he missed the most when Jenny died.

He watched Sunna sleep and found it comforting. Suddenly, the Master Stones reminded that they would be coming out of jump speed at the Xeron moon. Mentally, he requested his field glasses to float over to him from the nightstand. It was time to talk with the captains.

As he placed them over his eyes, Ghonllier felt Sunna move her hand up his arm. His mind went back to her and he realized she was dreaming. He desired to hold her hand, but knew he would wake her up.

Turning his attention back on the Xeron moon, he waited for them to come out of jump speed. Knowing they would appear right behind a newly arriving KOGN Galaxy Creeper, he activated his comset and whispered in a tired voice, "Sam. When we come out of jump speed, leave the *Liberty Quest* in code blue. I want to make sure that everyone can see us. Bring us right past the KOGN Galaxy Creepers."

"What should I expect to happen with them?" asked Sam.

"Expect them to send out Star Screamers to fight with us. We're going to be doing a lot of target practice with this battle. We aren't hiding this time," informed Ghonllier.

"What about I-Force? Are we still hiding from them as well?" asked Sam.

"Commander Houser is in charge of the Galaxy Creepers from I-Force. He could recognize us, but the ships won't be able to pick up the signal. I'm blocking it."

"The *Liberty Pursuit* captains knows us, with you and Houser being close friends. Are you sure Commander Houser won't order them to fire on us? You'll take out his ship," reminded Sam.

"No, my father, Justin, warned him to never fire on my ship. If they can't pick up our signal, it won't force Houser to fire on us."

"Acknowledged," replied Sam, speaking to Ghonllier over the bridge's comset or loudspeaker. Butler didn't have his earpiece in and Sam wanted him to hear the conversation.

Jason had joined Gostler on the bridge during the conversation. The two men exchanged glances as Butler turned on all hullercasts in the room. The room filled with the scene from outside as they heard the announcement telling everyone to go to their stations for security. Jason sat in the other flight chair by Gostler.

The hullercasts showed them in jump speed. Shortly, the colors disappeared, exposing the moon, the KOGN ships, and black space. Sam noticed the KOGN Galaxy Creepers pick them up immediately, causing the *Liberty Quest* to automatically go into shut-down mode. The ceiling opened up, allowing the wall to descend next to the corridor.

Jason and Gostler watched them speed past a KOGN Galaxy Creeper. Gostler studied the Galaxy Creeper, expecting it to fire upon them. Instead, he saw two Star Screamers leave the ship in pursuit of them. Gostler smiled as he thought, *Okay, smart move, Ghonllier. Keep them busy so they don't blast the surface of the moon.*

Moments later, the *Liberty Quest's* stones knew the KOGN Star Screamers had them in their sights. It caused red warning lights and sirens to blare throughout the ship. The warning triggered safety straps for those on their beds and in chairs that weren't on the bridge. With the ship being able to spin during a battle, it was the safest place for the crew. Today, she was really going to be diving, spinning, and rotating. The captains were ordered to be aggressive in their fighting.

The commotion woke Sunna up. She raised her eyelids to look up at Ghonllier. From her angle, she could see he had his eyes closed underneath his field glasses. Sunna wondered if he was awake or asleep and why he had field glasses on. Wanting to know what was happening, she gingerly rested her hand on his chest.

Opening his eyes, he moved his glasses to the top of his head and smiled, "You're awake?"

"Yes."

"Do you want to see what's happening?"

"Please."

"Hullercast, on," commanded Ghonllier.

The whole room turned into one big hullercast, not hiding the artwork and furniture. It unnerved Sunna for a moment. "Wow," she responded, "this isn't in my old quarters."

"You aren't the commander of a ship. I installed the hullercast in case I couldn't make it out in time for a battle."

"Do the red lights mean the whole ship is in shut-down mode?"

"Yes. No one can come into our room right now," informed Ghonllier as he slipped the field glasses back over his eyes. Afterwards, Sunna caught a glimpse of the KOGN Star Screamers pursuing them. White wispy clouds caused her to lose sight of the ship momentarily. Her attention went back to Ghonllier when she heard him say, "Slow down, Butler. I want them to fire on us."

Sunna glanced back to see two Star Screamers emerge from the clouds at a much closer range. Instinctively, Sunna tensed up and

Ghonllier physically felt it. Using the Stones, he soothed, "RELAX, YOU'RE WITH ME. NOTHING CAN HURT YOU."

His voice was hypnotic, causing her to relax as he took her hand in his. Relaxed, she watched the *Liberty Quest* change positions. Sunna rolled over on her other side to watch the Star Screamers better, making it hard for Ghonllier to hold her hand. Four blasts left both the KOGN Star Screamers and Sunna tightened up her body, bracing for the impact.

Ghonllier reached out to her and placed his hand on her shoulder. "SUNNA, RELAX. THIS ISN'T HEALTHY FOR YOU. DO YOU WANT ME TO CAUSE YOUR MIND TO GO BACK TO SLEEP? YOU'RE NOT SUP-POSED TO BE STRESSED RIGHT NOW."

Before Sunna could answer, the four quasar blasts reached the surface of the *Liberty Quest,* only to skip off while returning to their origin. The blasts separated, moving toward different parts of the ships, causing the KOGN ships to explode.

"Sam, track their other Star Screamers in the atmosphere and take them out. Engage them as fast as you can in battle. I want them out of the sky."

Sunna rolled back over to look at her husband. He moved his glasses once more to the top of his head and smiled, "I can see you want to talk."

"Is this what it is going to be like for us in this battle?"

Ghonllier nodded. "Do you want to stay awake?"

"Yes, I want to see you in all your glory," smiled Sunna.

"It's going to be awhile before we find another ship to battle. Do you want to talk? You have questions that are causing you stress."

"Are you always going to know what I'm feeling before I do?"

"Yes, does it bother you?" reached out Ghonllier. She watched him take her hand in his.

"I would like to talk and didn't realize it until you said it," she stated, raising her gaze to meet his. "Now probably isn't a good time."

"It's a prefect time. No one can interrupt our conversation."

"Don't you need to concentrate on the battle?"

Ghonllier shook his head. "I can do two things at once with the Master Stones, Sunna. I won't always be shutting you out."

"It seems strange to know you're reading my mind. What do you know?"

Ghonllier didn't know if he wanted to answer that question. The third Stone had increased his ability to understand those around him. He didn't know if he wanted people around him to know how much he understood. Deciding not to tell Sunna everything, he shrugged his shoulders. "I don't know how to explain it."

"I feel troubled when I wake up. I wanted to talk about it, but you've been asleep. Can you tell me why?" she challenged.

"There are two things. Which one do you want to talk about? Your desires or fears?"

"Fears?" He looked away. "Ghonllier, what do you see I'm afraid of?"

Watching a cloud pass by, he stated, "You're still afraid of me and being married has you more nervous than you want to admit."

"Why?"

"Down deep you want to know what I expect from you as my wife. You're afraid that you'll let me down. You're also afraid of getting hurt. I'm the first person who has come into your life and I'm staying."

"Hmm," paused Sunna. Looking up at him, she added, "You're right on all accounts. But, why am I afraid of letting you down?"

"You're afraid that I'm going to compare you against Jenny. Another thing that has you upset is not knowing what I want or expect of you."

Sunna rolled on her back to watch the clouds and sky go zipping by. Without looking at him, she stated, "So this is what it is going to be like living with you."

"Tell me more about what you mean by that statement?"

Her eyes flickered toward him briefly. Then she stated, "You know so much about me. I'm not used to people knowing more about me than I do myself."

"Please forgive me, Sunna. I shouldn't have been that revealing," apologized Ghonllier.

She looked over at him and stared. "I would've been disappointed if you had held back and I think you knew it."

"You're right," smiled Ghonllier.

Facing him, she asked, "What do you really expect of me?"

"I want to get closure with how I treated you on the other two Stones. Do you mind talking about that first?"

"Go ahead."

"With the third Stone, I won't treat you like I did with the first and second, Sunna. The first two Stones are the roughest."

"Why were you so rough on me?"

Ghonllier looked past her. "At first it was because you were a spy."

"You bought into the story about spies?"

"Yes, I did. Dapper told me I was wrong. Until you came along, spies had always proven to me to be dishonest and immoral."

"Why did you fight with Spencer from the moment you met him? Was it because he was a spy?"

Ghonllier gave her an embarrassed smile before he explained, "Jealousy. Spencer had hoped of a future with you. Down deep, I wanted the same thing, but felt doomed to a life of loneliness with Jenny gone and the Stones in my life."

"Why did Gostler take your belt away from you on the Zuffra moon?"

"Jealousy again. I knew Humphrey liked you and you enjoyed his humor. I knew the two of you would be friends in the future. At the time, I didn't believe I would have another friendship with a woman. Until I received the first Master Stone, I didn't realize how lonely I was without Jenny. With the Stones, I felt trapped in my state and I wanted freedom to follow my heart."

"You felt you were going to be like Gostler?"

"Yes and it made me angry. I blamed the Master Stone for my situation, not realizing I had control. But I wasn't using my power to choose."

"Are you saying you were in love with me before we went to the Zuffra moon to see Bog?"

"Oh, yes. I was in love with you on a deep level and wouldn't have realized it for months. But the Stones made me see it quicker than I would normally," replied Ghonllier. "The way I behaved is how a typical man in love acts when his love isn't returned. The Stones just magnified it, that's all."

"You had a lot of anger when it came to Jenny? Why?"

Ghonllier looked at her sharply. "You asked her that question, didn't you? You talked with Jenny while you were with Master Stones."

"Yes, she told me to ask you that question. She wanted to know."

"I hadn't mourned properly for Jenny and let her go. It stopped me from moving out of the moment when she died. My mind was frozen in that moment and I carried it until I finished bonding with the second Stones."

"That's it?"

"I was angry with myself for letting her go on that mission," he stated, looking at Sunna. "I had a choice and I hadn't forgiven her and myself for her dying."

"What did you know about my feelings during that time of the second Stone?"

"I was completely aware of your resentment and the Stones couldn't tell me why you felt that way. You deeply hurt me because you wouldn't give me a chance."

"I saw it in your face at times and thought it was there because of Jenny," whispered Sunna.

"No, it was there because of you."

"I was really taken back to watch Cid wake you up while you were under the influence of the Truth Test. I saw and felt how painful the whole experience of my being in your life had been for you. I'm so sorry, Ghonllier."

"What do you mean you saw what happened under the Truth Test?"

"The Master Stones showed me what was happening to you from the room we were in. I never realized how deeply I hurt you. It wasn't my intent."

"I know. What did the Stones tell you during that time with them?"

"Like you, I forgot about why I made the oath with them. I didn't remember consciously that I agreed to walk beside you on this journey. I made such a strong commitment to not break my oath to them. My walls were high and strong. My walls became more important than my commitment." Then, pausing, she asked, "When did you remember your promise to them?"

"It was like you. I didn't remember until the Master Stones played it back to me after I realized what had been given to me."

Ghonllier touched her cheek and Sunna smiled. "Why did you talk with me with some kindness after we returned to the ship with Bog's books?"

"There I was being myself. I knew from being with you on the Zuffra moon that you were different from my other women officers."

"How was I different?"

"You weren't intimidated by my position. Your skills were good and you were a dedicated officer like I was. You also knew as much as I did. In spite of me disliking spies, I was trained with your skills."

"Yes, from a legend. Dapper was the best."

"After being with Bog, I knew I needed you to replace Dapper and it didn't make me happy because you made me feel vulnerable."

Sunna chuckled, "So you felt vulnerable around me?"

"Yes, we both felt the same way."

"Are you going to be able to still feel my physical pain in the future?"

"Yes, until the day you die. Even after I give up my reign, I'll feel or be aware of your physical pain."

"Why?"

"Because of the way I treated you when we met."

Sunna gazed deeper into his eyes and asked, "When did you fall in love with me?"

"The moment I saw you."

Sunna smiled and moved her hand from his chest to run her fingers along his collarbone. Underneath his clothes, Sunna felt a patch. "What kind of patch is this?"

"It's a body power patch. You have one, too."

All of a sudden, the ship started to sway and Sunna tried to raise her head to see. Ghonllier quickly placed his hand on top of her head. "Please don't do that. I can feel it," he spoke softly. "Let me show you everything on the ceiling."

"What hit us?"

"A Star Screamer's blast just bounced off of us from the side," educated Ghonllier. She rolled onto her back and could see it. Then she heard Ghonllier say, "Time your firing next time, Sam, to return your blast with their blasts bouncing off the ship."

Sunna looked at him to see his glasses covering his eyes. When he finished, Ghonllier placed them on top of his head. She smiled and cajoled, "This is impressive, but I think it is dirty fighting."

Ghonllier slipped his arm underneath her neck and forced her to roll onto her side, pulling her into him. He commanded his second pillow to leave so his head would be on her level. "Why do you think this is a dirty fight?" he quizzed.

Sunna smiled to get a rise out of him. He pulled her in tightly and started to tickle her ribs. Giggling, Sunna requested, "Please stop." Ghonllier stopped and the two locked gazes. "What area of the galaxy are we stopping KOGN from attacking?"

"Our home," answered Ghonllier softly.

"Why are they attacking our home?"

"This is a war now between Bog and I."

"Is he here?"

"No. Gomper has orchestrated it so I can get rid of the KOGN before he arrives. Gomper knows we can't meet as long as Bog has control of him."

"Are you strong enough to do it with three Stones?"

"What I need now is courage and a belief in me. I have it now with you by my side." Then Ghonllier paused while studying her. "Are you concerned?" he asked.

"No, I'll never be concerned as long as you're close by."

The rumbling sound of the ship firing her quasar cannon interrupted their conversation. The ship swayed at the same time. Ghonllier flipped his glasses down on his nose and ordered, "Captains, there are eight more Star Screamers entering our atmosphere and I need them eliminated now. We're running out of time."

"Jason wants to know if we are going after the KOGN's Galaxy Creepers," stated Sam.

"Only if we finish with the Star Screamers and Houser isn't here," explained Ghonllier, removing his glasses.

"Who's this Houser? I've heard both you and Sooner use his name before." Sunna inquired.

Looking at her, he said, "A close friend and rival of mine."

"Rival?"

"Where women are concerned, he's a rival."

"This sounds interesting. What did you boys do to be rivals?" teased Sunna.

"If one of us happened to be with a new woman or we got a new one on our staff, we wanted to find if the other liked her romantically. We had our ways of testing each other's resolve about her."

"What would he do if he saw me?"

"He would flirt with you in front of me to see if it gave me a rise."

"That's not professional."

"We both know what's a rise with each other. It's very professional. We're the only ones who understand what is going on."

"How would he treat me if I was introduced as your wife?"

"He would be very respectful toward you and not flirt."

"Where did you two meet?"

"We roomed together at the academy and graduated at the same time."

The ship rumbled again, startling Sunna. She grabbed hold of Ghonllier's arm while watching the *Liberty Quest* fire on Star Screamers ahead of them. Four blasts left their ship and upon impact, the KOGN ship exploded.

"Do you ever get used to the rumbling sounds of your ship firing?" asked Sunna.

Ghonllier whispered, "SUNNA, RELAX YOU'RE GETTING UPTIGHT AND IT ISN'T NECESSARY."

She looked at him. "It's because you're used to this and I'm not. I've been on land most of my career."

"Focus on something else and not the sounds of fighting. Some new recruits to space get nauseated and lose their stomach. It will happen to you if you don't relax."

"Help me relax so I won't have to watch this," she challenged.

The ship fired again while the two gazed into each other's eyes. Before the KOGN ship exploded, Ghonllier leaned over to kiss her on the forehead. "Does that help?"

"A little."

Ghonllier kissed her on the cheek. "Does that help?"

"A little," said Sunna, wanting a kiss.

He leaned into her for a kiss on the lips. Sunna kissed him back like she did when they believed to be dead. He kissed her a few more times and stopped before moving back to lie on his pillow.

Surprised, Sunna quizzed, "Why did you pull away? Is the dizziness getting to you?"

"I can tolerate the dizziness if I'm kissing you," he answered, facing her. Then he added, "I can read your mixed emotions."

"Like what?"

"You want me to kiss you, yet I detect deep fear from you. I love you, Sunna. I would like to get over you being afraid of me. Can we talk?"

"What are you reading from me exactly?"

"This whole experience of you being close to me is very emotional for you, which is why you're feeling fear. It isn't this battle. It's me."

"Ghonllier, that sounds silly," stated Sunna, embarrassed.

Ghonllier shook his head. "No, the Master Stones are telling me this is a common emotion for women. Being with me is emotional for you."

"It isn't that way for you?"

"No, not really. I'm a little nervous about being alone with you like this. It's been a very long time since I've opened up my heart. I can see with the Master Stones that I respond differently to you than you do with me," explained the Master. Then Ghonllier shook his head. "This is incredible," he added.

"What are the Stones doing?"

"They are answering my questions about the difference between men and women that I've always wondered about ever since I discovered girls."

"What are they telling you?" asked Sunna.

"We function differently." Ghonllier smiled. "You walk into a room in your uniform and I think about you entering my personal space. It stimulates me physically to want to be with you. You don't even have to look or say anything to me. Men function totally physically."

"And for us?"

"With you, a woman gets excited emotionally and enjoys the moment through her feelings. You love romance."

"Why do I fear you?" repeated Sunna.

"Women fear being physically close to men at first," whispered Ghonllier.

"Why?"

"First, let me explain the laws that govern a man and a woman coming together. The Stones are telling me a man and woman come together on different levels. For a man it's physical and for a woman it's emotional. And the emotions are a higher level than physical. If the man chooses to join her, then they can . . ."

"They can what?"

He looked at her and stated, "They can have a spiritual experience—"

Ghonllier stopped and Sunna quizzed, "What's wrong?"

He looked at her and stated, "The Master Stones are telling me that we move in different circles. I wish I would have known this when I was married the first time. You need to feel validated at your pace, not mine. If I push you too fast, it will either anger or frighten you. Or both." Ghonllier ran his fingers along her chin and listened to the Stones. Slowly, he commented, "I never knew there was so much in a kiss."

"Is physical bonding important to a woman like it is to a man?"

Ghonllier waited for the answer to come from the Master Stones and when it did, he raised his eyebrows. "You just asked a very good question. I don't think I would've asked that question."

"What did the Stones say?"

"It's very important to a woman if it's handled right. Bonding between a married couple is extremely important to their relationship. The act binds the two people together mentally, emotionally, and physically, reminding them of their contract."

"How does a married couple get a spiritual experience?"

"If a man chooses to bring his emotions into the moment and give them to the woman, he matches the woman's level. Then, together, the couple can raise themselves to—" said Ghonllier, stopping.

"Why did you stop?" asked Sunna.

Looking at her, he answered, "I really didn't know that physical bonding is meant to be a spiritual experience."

"Spiritual, really?"

"Yes, a spiritual experience that can only be achieved by a married man and woman who are together emotionally during bonding. From there, the two reach a spiritual experience that's sacred," responded Ghonllier with his voice drifting off.

"Why does being married make such a difference?"

"A marriage is a contract of living commitment between two people, where they agree to sacrifice and give to each other. The physical bonding cements the contract of commitment and loyalty. They are giving everything to each other. This is the whole reason for a marriage contract. Anytime someone bonds outside of marriage, there is no contract to be committed to each other. Their relationship is based on selfishness and indifference. It's totally physical and leaves them feeling empty. The man has brought the woman down to his level.

"At the moment, they're pretending to commit, but down deep the act is based on total selfishness. Bonding represents commitment and it's a lie. There is no commitment. Any lie destroys your self-image, their self-love, and self-worth. So you miss the important part of bonding."

"Why?" asked Sunna.

"Because bonding between a man and a woman are supposed to bind them together spiritually, physically, and emotionally. A couple who has a spiritual experience doesn't care to be with anyone else. They'll crawl on their hands and knees upon a hot desert to reach each other, if that's what it takes. It's impossible to have a spiritual experience when the reason of being together is based on selfishness. Now I understand why the bonding fires don't come when you bond out of wedlock," whispered Ghonllier thoughtfully.

"Selfishness is really what stops the bonding fires from coming?"

"Yes. It's easy for a man to pull a woman down to his physical selfish level. When it happens, it's impossible for them to have a spiritual experience," replied Ghonllier. "And the laws that govern it can't be changed. It is what it is. A marriage based on selfishness can stop a couple from having a spiritual experience. Now I understand why you can break the bonding fires contract by seeking someone else even in your heart. You're seeking someone else out of selfishness."

"And people are being told that it's acceptable to bond outside of wedlock or cheat on each other. How sad," commented Sunna. Ghonllier smiled. "What happens to a couple like us? We kept the laws. What do we expect if we have a spiritual experience?" Sunna asked.

"It binds them spiritually, mentally, and physically and it is the whole purpose of bonding. So it's very powerful and important to a marriage. It's what holds them together during the rough times, especially when the spiritual experience is repeated often."

"That's powerful," said Sunna, hoping to get Ghonllier's attention.

He was looking past her. The battle was raging on the hullercast behind Sunna and he found himself looking at it while thinking about what the Master Stones were teaching them.

She reached up to touch his face and he looked at her. They waited for Sam to stop firing the ship's cannons before she inquired, "Ghonllier, have you ever had a spiritual experience?"

"No, Sunna," smiled Ghonllier. "I'm not going there with you. It's for me to know and you to never be concerned about. I refuse to compare our relationship to what Jenny and I had. I deeply love you and that's all I want you to know and feel," assured Ghonllier as he ran his fingers through her hair. Then he added, "Don't worry about what I expect. I just want to love and take care of you."

Sunna smiled. Ghonllier leaned in for a kiss as he heard from the Master Stones. BONDING OUTSIDE OF MARRIAGE FOR YOU WOULD'VE DETERIORATED YOUR SELF-IMAGE TO THE POINT WHERE IT WOULD'VE WEAKENED YOUR INNER STRENGTH. THEN WE WOULD NOT HAVE ACCEPTED YOU AS OUR MASTER, NOR WOULD YOU BE WITH SUNNA NOW.

They stopped kissing when the ship was hit by something that almost threw Ghonllier forward on Sunna. The safety straps held him.

"What was that?" asked Sunna, frightened.

"A Galaxy Creeper's blasts just skipped off our ship."

"Are we fighting with them now?"

"No. Houser has engaged them in combat and we happened to pick up a stray shot."

"Ghonllier, how is this going to end? Will our son be okay?"

Rolling on his back, he said, "Look back at the ceiling. We're coming up on our home now."

Sunna joined by rolling onto her back. All she saw was a blue sky, which quickly changed. A dark wall of clouds appeared. Lightning fulgurated in the clouds to light up simultaneous in completely different places, creating a pattern. The pattern of rhythm gave the storm a different, almost frightening, appearance.

"Are you controlling everything there?" pointed Sunna.

"Yes. I used the winds to bring the clouds over our city. I'm causing the lightning show. Right now, that is all I can do," divulged Ghonllier. Moving his glasses back onto his nose, he ordered, "Sam, there is a Star Screamer. If it stays on its path, it will hit our home. Follow him into the storm. It won't hurt us."

Looking back at him, Sunna stated, "Do you realize that you just told your brother where our home is?"

"Yes and this is why," responded Ghonllier, expanding her picture.

Sunna could see a KOGN Star Screamer skimming the surface of the moon, blasting away. A Star Screamer could fly through a rough storm in the atmosphere made by nature and not be affected.

Ghonllier knew when the captain's instruments picked up his storm that they were hesitating flying into it. Ghonllier wanted them to enter the storm. The new Master listened to the communication of the Star Screamer to the Galaxy Creeper where it came from. To Ghonllier's disappointment, the Star Screamer veered away from the storm.

Sunna heard, "Sam, move in on that Star Screamer. It's headed for space."

The *Liberty Quest* took a dive through the clouds and Sunna could see why they needed safety straps. They didn't move as they spun through the atmosphere, taking out the ship. Suddenly, the hullercasts stopped spinning and they could see another ship skimming along the surface, firing.

Ghonllier could see Sunna was upset. "SUNNA, RELAX. TELL YOUR BODY THAT IT'S OKAY," he whispered while running his finger along her cheek.

She smiled, her body instantly responding to his words, and felt better. Sunna asked, "How do you handle this without the Stones?"

"You have to stay relaxed and focus on something else."

"Okay, how is the battle going with Houser?" Ghonllier didn't answer, but removed his field glasses. They floated out of his hand and back to the nightstand. "You're not going to talk to the captain anymore?"

"No."

"What about the battle?"

"What battle?" he smiled.

"Aren't you concerned about Houser?"

"No, he's done this many times before. He knows what he's doing by now," answered Ghonllier, getting caught up in her gaze.

Mentally, she asked Ghonllier to kiss her. He leaned in to kiss her and during the kiss, she heard his voice next to her ear. "I LOVE YOU, SUNNA. I'M TOTALLY COMMITTED TO YOU AND OUR CONTRACT. I WAITED A LONG TIME FOR YOU AND IT WAS WORTH IT."

Sunna answered him back by kissing him passionately. Pleased to know she wanted to try for a spiritual experience, Ghonllier kissed her back passionately while reaching out to the captains. "I WANT YOU TO BEAM MY MOTHER AND SON UP TO ME. WOULD YOU PLEASE TELL MY FATHER TO JOIN THEM IN HERE IN MY QUARTERS AFTER THEY BOARD MY SHIP?"

Sam smiled to see a new talent of the Master of the Stones. As the ship took another dive after the last of the KOGN Star Screamers, the hullercasts in their quarters and the bridge showed the big battle raging on outside. Everyone watched it, but Ghonllier and Sunna.

On Suzair the Great's Galaxy Creeper, things weren't going as well for him as they were for Ghonllier. Brewster was working hard to revive him. Finally, he let out a sigh after seeing Gomper was out of danger and eventually would be coming around. The other two men sat back on their heels and watched Brewster keeping vigilance over his analyzer.

Finally, the medic looked at them and informed, "He can't take much more of this and live. Somehow, this has to stop. He's going to die and I can't keep him alive."

Bog heard them and decided to stop hurting Gomper with such vengeance. He didn't want to kill him, not yet. It angered him to know Ghonllier had smashed his stepping-stone. Bog heard Brewster set his analyzer on the floor as they talked about moving Gomper to the couch.

It was a strong enough sound to make Bog aware of where it was as he mentally picked it up and flung it out of anger. The analyzer hit Jamham in the arm. He let out a moan, almost dropping Gomper. When they had Gomper safely on the couch, Brewster went to Jamham to find he had a nasty cut.

At the same time, a page came in from Commander Jabolt. Pappar took it.

"I need to talk with His Grace," requested Jabolt.

"He's busy," answered Pappar. Looking at the others, he added, "What do you want and I'll give him the message?"

"With all our ships destroyed in the battle on the Xeron moon, does he want to continue to it?"

There was silence as the three men looked between each other, wondering what to do. In the moment of indecision, Pappar made up an answered. "He says yes."

After Pappar hung up, Jamham commented, "I hope you made the right decision for us."

"Yeah, me, too," responded Pappar, looking at the unconscious leader.

Chapter 7

Good-bye

*S*tacy felt nervous about being beamed up to her son's ship, since this was her first time. Sooner excitedly explained the process to her. His enthusiasm helped by giving her the confidence to try.

It pleased Sooner to share his love for space with his grandmother. His emotions really heightened when they arrived on board and when he showed her around the command center. It felt strange, yet wonderful, to Stacy to be at the place where she had watched Ghonllier work and live from the server stone.

The Stones vibrated lightly to let Ghonllier know his son and mother were on board. It pleased him to see Sooner taking his time. They weren't quite ready to receive the family.

Sunna didn't want to meet Sooner the first time as his mother in her nightgown. Asustie was summoned to their quarters to help Sunna get dressed. Ghonllier waited in bed, feeling Sunna's dizziness. To help him deal with his wife's pain, he focused on Sooner and his mother working their way to him.

His excitement to see his son mounted as he watched him get closer to his room. Opening his eyes, Ghonllier saw Sunna was about to crawl over him. He reached out to move the blankets back, but Sunna stopped him.

"No, Ghonllier, I don't want to meet your family today being inside your bed."

He recoiled his hand and requested, "Asustie, get her a blanket for me."

Asustie left to go get the blanket from Ghonllier's closet. When she returned, Asustie spread the blanket over Sunna as she lied on top of the blankets next to Ghonllier.

He startled Asustie by grabbing a hold of her hand and requested, "Please stay with us, Sister."

Before Asustie could answer, the door opened and in bounded Sooner. "Father!"

After greeting his father with a hug, Sooner looked at Sunna and grinned. "Hi, Mother."

Sunna grinned. "Hi, there, Sooner. How's my boy?"

"Great!" he responded, leaving his father and going to her arms. "I'm so happy that you decided to be my mother," he expressed, lying down next to her.

Sunna smiled. "Me, too," she stated, wrapping her arms around him.

Sooner snuggled into Sunna with delight. Ghonllier looked at him as he grinned. Facing his mother, he said, "Mother, I watched you take out those men. Did they hurt you before Father came for you?"

"Yes, they hurt me," replied Sunna as her eyes shifted toward Ghonllier. She added, "But your father took care of them, didn't he?"

"What made you change your mind about being a mother?"

Peering into his eyes, she answered, "When I was faced with dying, I regretted telling you no . . . and I discovered I would miss your father because I loved him."

"I love you," said Sooner, wrapping his arms around her neck.

Sunna tightened her hold on him and whispered, "I really love the two of you. I'm so sorry for pushing you both away."

"I forgive you, Mother," responded Sooner, still snuggling her.

Sunna was taken back on how wonderful it felt to have a family and to be a mother to that little boy.

Ghonllier intently watched the two of them, reading the joy they both had at that moment. It meant a lot to him to feel their love for each other. The three of them together did feel right and he was glad Sunna chose to come back. He felt getting married like they did was right, even though Justin couldn't make it in person.

Interrupting his thoughts, Sooner asked, "How long will you both be sick this time?"

Sunna looked at Ghonllier as he responded, "We'll take each day at a time. I'll get better first. Your mother received more poison than I did." Ghonllier reached out to give his son a light squeeze on his arm. "She'll really need your help to get well again."

"Good, I like taking care of her." Then Sooner saw Asustie and he added, "Hi, Aunt Asustie."

"Hi, Nephew," she smiled.

"With Sunna living at our house, what do I tell my friends?" asked Sooner.

"Tell them Sunna is in charge of the family's security and needs to be close by us," answered Ghonllier quietly.

"Will they accept it?" questioned Sooner.

"I think they will. Most of your friends are from the *Liberty Quest* and their parents already know that's Sunna's job," smiled Ghonllier.

They heard a knock and Ghonllier opened the door. Stacy entered the room and Asustie left Ghonllier's side to greet their mother. The two hugged while Adamite entered. "Do you want Gostler in here?"

"Yes, and Jason," confirmed Ghonllier.

Adamite went to the nightstand to page them. Stacy let go of Asustie to greet her newly married son. Stacy smiled to see Sooner cuddled in Sunna's arms between them. Sitting on the edge of the bed, she reached over Ghonllier to hold Sunna's arm.

"Welcome to our family. I'm so glad to see the two of you together. I've secretly wanted it from the moment I saw you two together on the *Liberty Quest*," divulged Stacy.

"Thank you, Stacy. I've known you ever since I was a little girl and never dreamed that I would become a member of your family."

Suddenly, Ghonllier commanded his field glasses to float over to him right before a page. Activating his comset, he stated, "Sam, I know what you're going to ask. I'll send Sooner to get the message."

"Acknowledged," replied Sam.

"From now on, direct all messages to me that are in a foreign language," informed Ghonllier. Turning off his comset, he asked, "Do you mind, Sooner?"

Sooner pouted, "Do I have to? I like it where I am."

Ghonllier removed his glasses, giving him a stern look. Sunna leaned into his ear and requested, "Please Sooner, go do what your father wants and then you can come back here."

"Okay," responded Sooner, getting off the bed.

Ghonllier rolled his eyes to see Sooner respond instantly to Sunna's request but not his. It irritated him a little, but nothing like it would with the earlier Stones. Before Sooner reached the door, it opened for Cid, Jason, and Gostler. Ghonllier acknowledged Jason and Gostler as Cid pulled out his analyzer. Stacy stood so Cid could take her place.

Cid put Ghonllier's hand on the analyzer while he closed the door. Quickly, Cid raised his eyebrows and looked at Ghonllier. The new Master saw his expression and knew his thoughts.

Cid whispered, "I can see you found a way to stay calm during the battle."

"YOU BETTER KEEP IT TO YOURSELF, CID. I DON'T NEED YOU HERE. I ALLOW YOU TO BE HERE BECAUSE I LIKE YOU. SO BE CAREFUL," warned Ghonllier.

The medic smiled and looked back at the analyzer to watch Ghonllier's stress levels during the meeting.

Jason spoke, "Ghonllier, the I-Force Galaxy Creepers are moving into position and are awaiting instructions."

"We have two hours to move this city. That's the time frame the captains have. So Father, you better know how you want it moved," informed Ghonllier.

"I do. Is this why you called this meeting?" commented Adamite.

"Yes. Mother, where do you want to live?" asked Ghonllier.

Stacy shook her head. "I don't care. You pick, Son," she assured.

"Gostler, I want you to tell Justin that I want the captains to take us to the Suzair planet, to the very place where Dapper crashed and picked up the first Master Stone," requested Ghonllier.

"Why there?" questioned Jason.

"The KOGN won't expect it. They combed that area already with equipment looking for the Stone. Plus it's in I-Force territories and it's close to a small town. Gomper won't guess we went there if Bog pushes him to keep looking for me."

Adamite nodded. Ghonllier reached for his mother's hand and asked, "Mother, is the Suzair planet okay with you?"

Stacy smiled and answered, "As long as we're together, I'm fine."

The door opened and Sooner entered. Handing the message to his father, he crawled back to Sunna's arms. Ghonllier didn't look at it, but mentally floated it into Gostler's hands. He requested, "Would you answer this for me?" The former Master nodded, reading Ghonllier's mind. The new Master added, "Father, you better get going. They will want your direction on how to move my city."

Adamite and Gostler left while Ghonllier looked at Jason. The commander asked, "I heard the captains say you wanted us in code red with I-Force here. Are we traveling ahead of the Galaxy Creepers or are we going to land in one of them?"

Ghonllier looked at Sunna. "Do you want to stay here or move to the house?"

She glanced at Sooner and he waited for her answer. Knowing how Sunna felt, Ghonllier answered, "We'll land on the *Liberty Pursuit*. Jason, you handle it with Houser. Tell him you need supplies."

Jason left, leaving Stacy and Asustie there. Sooner asked, "What are you talking about? Are you moving our house?"

"Yes, we're going to go live next to Jasper."

Sooner sat up with excitement. "Are you sure?" Ghonllier nodded. "Oh, Mother, you need to meet Jasper. He's my first and best friend." Sooner looked back at his father and added, "Will I be able to go to school with Jasper?"

Ghonllier grinned, "Probably."

Sooner went back to Sunna. "Mother, I can hardly wait for you to meet him and he'll be so surprised to learn . . ."

"You can't introduce her to him as your mother. Only as your bodyguard," reminded his father.

"Can I call and tell him that we're coming?"

"Let's wait until we're closer to the Suzair planet," replied Ghonllier.

Sooner gave his father a perplexing look and asked, "Father, are you supposed to still be dead?"

"Yes."

"Shouldn't Butler be beaming you down to the house now?"

Ghonllier thought and smiled, "Very good, Son. Your grandfather has already moved the house to the *Liberty Pursuit*. So we'll have to do it another way."

Cid looked away from the analyzer and offered, "I can call in emergency shuttles to take you to the cargo bay before we leave."

Ghonllier nodded. "Let's do it," he affirmed, looking at his mother. "Do you mind helping Cid, Mother? We need to move Sunna's things from her quarters to the house. I want the staff to unpack her things and put them in my room."

"I'd be glad to," responded Stacy, reaching over to Sooner. She requested, "Would you come with me and show me how to get to Sunna's quarters?"

"Sure," stated Sooner, sitting up. He looked at Sunna and asked, "Do you mind?"

"No, please take care of my things, Sooner," smiled Sunna.

Sooner bounced off the bed and ran for the door with Cid and Stacy following. Ghonllier let out a sigh at being alone. It frustrated him to feel so weak. Closing his eyes, he lowered his stress levels and decided to take a nap. It didn't last long. Ghonllier received a message of danger from the Stones. Instantly, he opened his eyes and looked at Sunna.

Relieved to see she wasn't asleep yet, he rolled over onto his side and quizzed, "Sunna, do you know of a spy in I-Force by the name of Bennett?"

Sunna opened her eyes with a questioning look. "Bennett, no, I don't. Why?"

"I see you don't know him because he's new to I-Force," responded Ghonllier, opening their door.

"Ghonllier, what's going on?" questioned Sunna.

"I'm too tired to go through it twice, honey. Wait for Gostler, please," answered Ghonllier, closing his eyes.

Shortly, Gostler entered and inquired, "What's the problem, Ghonllier? Why are you saying it's an emergency?"

Closing the door, he answered, "There are KOGN spies on the *Liberty Pursuit* and most of the other Galaxy Creepers here."

"How many KOGN spies do we have here?" quizzed Gostler.

"I can see ten spies scattered throughout the ships. The *Liberty Pursuit* has three and the most dangerous one is on Houser's ship."

"Why is this spy so dangerous?" asked Gostler.

"He's a paid assassin with a contract for a David."

"My David?"

"Yes, your David and my father."

"When did it happen?"

"I should've insisted Father stay on the *Liberty Quest*. Bog put it out on him after he woke up from the Truth Test I gave Gomper. When Bog ordered the contract, Gomper had no idea it was his father."

"What about me? Is there a contract out on me still?"

"Yes and no. Bog would love to find you, but thinks you're still on the Zircon moon. With the virus, they can't go there to find out for sure. So he's backed off on you."

"Have any of the spies broadcasted out that I-Force is moving this city?"

"No, they're waiting for the information on where I-Force is taking us," answered Ghonllier.

"Okay, so what do you want me to do?" asked Gostler.

"I want you to contact the *Liberty Pursuit* and ask for Commander Houser. When you speak with him, tell Houser that you're requesting a Mandatory Transfer for the spy Bennett."

"What is a 'Mandatory Transfer'?"

"Mandatory Transfer is a code word that means 'Trust me and loan me one of your men. I'll explain later why.' It was something that was just between Houser and I, so he shouldn't give you a bad time about it," answered Ghonllier.

"He'll do it for a stranger?"

"Use Dapper's voice. In fact, I'm going to need your Mimette abilities. I need you to be Dapper for a short time," replied Ghonllier.

"Ghonllier, what are you thinking about doing here?" quizzed Sunna, listening.

"I want to hold court on him here in my presence and I need Gostler to be Dapper."

"Okay, what do I need to do?"

"Tell Jason that he is conducting court for me. I'll tell him what to say."

"Where are you going to be?"

"Here. I want to be in the room," answered Ghonllier.

"What about Houser knowing who you are?" asked Gostler.

"I'm going to let him learn that I'm alive, but he can't know I'm the future Master."

"Ghonllier, he already knows Jason is the commander of the *Liberty Quest*. How are you going to get around to why your ship was taken away from you when he sees you?" asked Sunna.

"I'm going to make Jason look like he has my powers, so he won't suspect me," answered Ghonllier.

"Why does Gostler have to be Dapper?" asked Sunna. She added, "Aren't you putting Gostler in a situation where Houser will pump him for information about you?"

"Yes," answered Ghonllier, looking at his mentor. "I'll tell you what to say or what he's thinking, Gostler. You'll know how far you can go on telling him the truth, since you're still tied to the Master Stones."

Gostler nodded. "Be careful, Ghonllier," he reminded.

"Why?" questioned Sunna.

Looking at Sunna, Gostler educated, "During the time of bonding, you can't tell people around you that you have the Master Stones. Having people know distracts you from the bonding process."

"Then why does Ghonllier have so many people know about him being the Master of the Galaxy?" questioned Sunna.

"In Ghonllier's case, it's unheard of to have as many people know the truth. As you remember us telling you five years before Ghonllier knew, you were told to not interfere with the bonding process by asking him questions."

Sunna nodded. "You're right. I think that was another reason I pushed you away."

Ghonllier smiled. "You're a very loyal person and I loved that about you."

"Why do I need to be Dapper?" questioned the former Master.

"Houser knows Dapper as well as he does me. I don't want him to know that he's dead right now. Legally, Dapper is alive and it's a secret within our circle."

"That's right," remembered Gostler. He nodded, "Is there anything else you want me to do?"

"Tell Jason to contact Humphrey and get all the Vanishers on board my ship. My whole family is aboard. So they need to be here now," reminded Ghonllier.

"I'll go do it now," said Gostler, leaving.

"Wait," warned Ghonllier. "I want them a part of this court and I want everyone wearing field glasses so they can ask me any questions."

"Yes, Your Grace," said Gostler, heading toward the door.

"Gostler, tell Jason to have Asustie keep our parents and Sooner on the bridge. I'm going to have the captains put the ship in shut-down mode for everyone's protection."

"When do you want this court?" asked Gostler at the door.

"The moment the captains land us in the bay of the *Liberty Pursuit*," said Ghonllier, opening the door.

Gostler disappeared and Sunna expected him to close the door, but he didn't. She was about to ask him a question when Asustie entered the room.

"What do you want, Brother?"

"Help Sunna out of here. She needs sleep and it won't happen here," informed Ghonllier as Asustie came forward.

Sunna started to float off the bed. Then Ghonllier allowed her to stand slowly. Sunna reached up to grab a hold of her head while letting out a moan. A strong sensation of dizziness consumed her. Asustie quickly put an arm around her to give Sunna support.

"I've got you, Sister," soothed Asustie.

Together, they left the room through the adjoining door. Ghonllier knew Sunna needed water and made sure Asustie gave her enough before she lied down. He was relieved to have her settled down. He closed the door between their rooms, forcing Asustie to leave through Sooner's door.

Shortly, Jason entered with his weapons belt on. "Ghonllier, I have Humphrey with me. Can he enter?"

"Yes."

The commander disappeared and returned with Humphrey by his side.

Ghonllier responded to his thoughts. "General, I'm putting the ship in shut-down mode and I want your men guarding it everywhere, from the ramp to my room."

"Out of sight?"

"Yes, except for you and four guards at the base of the ramp. Tell them to keep their weapons holstered," informed Ghonllier.

"Is there anything else you need?" asked Humphrey.

"Yes, I want your men getting all of my things out of here, except for a reclining chair for me to sit in." Humphrey looked around. Ghonllier added, "Keep the nightstand here, too."

"Consider it done," said Humphrey, disappearing.

Jason waited for his instructions. Ghonllier requested, "Jason, help me get up and dressed in a uniform."

Heading for his closet, Jason asked, "Which one do you want?"

"Get me Special Services so I blend in with you," answered Ghonllier.

Jason returned with the uniform and placed it on the foot of the bed. Then he went to Ghonllier and reached out his hand. "Do you still need help to stand?" he asked.

"Yes," answered Ghonllier, accepting his help.

Soon after Ghonllier was off his bed, Humphrey entered with his men. Immediately, they started to move out his artwork and furniture. The general was giving orders to his men while Jason helped Ghonllier change clothes. While he dressed, Ghonllier answered Jason's questions about his role in court. By the time Ghonllier was dressed in a uniform, Jason understood his role.

The Vanishers placed a reclining chair in the corner by the door. As Jason helped him to it, Ghonllier checked on Sunna to see she was in a deep sleep. Sitting, Ghonllier leaned back and closed his eyes, waiting for the dizziness to settle down.

In the background, he could hear his elite force talking about where to place the chairs for court. Mentally, Ghonllier watched everyone and gave instructions to those helping him through the Master Stones.

When Ghonllier opened his eyes, he saw his quarters transformed. Everything but his chair and nightstand was gone. In the place of his furniture were chairs from the dining room. A few Vanishers were finishing up and Ghonllier knew they would be staying in the room with him hiding within the walls.

Checking on his key people, Ghonllier found Jason in the corridor, answering Humphrey's questions that he still had. They weren't too far from where Spencer happened to emerge out of Med-C.

Ghonllier told Jason to send Spencer into his room. The Tron entered and found Ghonllier quickly. "Commander, you wanted me?"

"Yes," said Ghonllier, looking up at him. "Spencer, do you know a spy by the name of Bennett?"

Jason arrived at that moment, wanting to hear Spencer's response.

"I know of one. What does he look like?"

"Jason, open the door of the monitor. His face is there," informed Ghonllier.

The commander opened the door to expose Bennett's face. Instantly, he nodded. "I know him and I've worked with him before. It wasn't a pleasant experience."

"Why?" asked Jason.

"Once, when we were paired up together, he disappeared on me and I happened to walk into a trap."

"You got yourself out of it," finished Ghonllier.

Spencer nodded. "I don't trust him."

"What else do you know about him?" asked Ghonllier.

Spencer was quiet, but Ghonllier could read what he didn't want to say about Bennett. They weren't positive. Bennett had a hot temper and was very skilled with different weapons that he had created himself. Jason got impatient with Spencer's silence and repeated Ghonllier's question.

"I don't trust him," responded Spencer bluntly.

"Did you know he was a paid assassin?" shot back Ghonllier.

Looking sharply at Ghonllier, he retorted, "No, I didn't. But it doesn't surprise me. Is he here somewhere?"

"Yes, he's on the Galaxy Creeper we are landing on," said Jason, following Spencer back to Ghonllier.

Spencer looked around the room for the first time. "You're going to hold court on him, aren't you?"

"Do you want to stay, Spencer, and help me?" asked Ghonllier weakly.

"Yes," replied Spencer firmly. "What do you want me to do?"

"I want you to go with General Humphrey and bring him on board. His commander is going to be bringing him to our ship. Once he's in here, I want you to stand guard on me. I'm too weak to protect myself."

"You shouldn't be here, Ghonllier," reminded Jason.

Ignoring Jason's comment, Spencer replied, "I'll be glad to help you, Commander." Looking at Jason, Spencer added, "Do I have time to get my weapons belt?"

"Yes, get it and come back here," replied Jason, seeing Ghonllier's eyes were closed.

Ghonllier had his eyes closed because he was reading Spencer's memories of the spy. There was a lot that Spencer wasn't telling him and it wasn't necessary to pry. He was pleased that Spencer was there with so much valuable information.

With Sunna comfortable, Asustie shut her door and left to go find her mother. She found Sooner and her in the game room. Asustie was surprised to find her mother interested in looking around the ship. She seemed to want to touch everything.

After watching them for a few moments, Asustie requested, "Mother, the ship is going into shut-down mode. We need to leave."

"Why is it doing that?" questioned Sooner.

"More KOGN Galaxy Creepers are on their way here. Would you like to show your grandmother to the bridge so she can be with her husband?" requested Asustie.

"Sure, now you can see what it's like to be in a battle on a ship, Grandmother," responded Sooner, reaching for his grandmother's hand.

Stacy gave her daughter an unsure look. Asustie smiled. Sooner led her away with Asustie following. They entered the command center to witness all the hullercasts on. Asustie paused, staring at the floor. They were flying over the city and it was interesting to see their house from the sky without the shield. Jason and her parents' homes were gone, along with most of the buildings and the land around their homes.

Hearing Stacy's voice, Asustie looked up. "Sooner, I would like to sit close to my husband."

Sooner followed her to the chair next to Ghonllier's flight chair. Adamite was sitting in Ghonllier's chair, talking to the captains of the different ships. Stacy sat down with Sooner commanding the safety straps to appear. It startled her.

Looking at Sooner, she asked, "Why did you activate the safety straps?"

"You need to be safe, Grandmother. A Galaxy Creeper blast can really toss you around," informed Sooner, sounding like his father.

"Okay," replied Stacy, knowing the blasts wouldn't affect the ship now that they had three Master Stones on board.

It was then that Sam announced over the ship's comset, "All crew members, we are going into shut-down mode in two minutes. Everyone to your stations."

Asustie went to sit with Sooner in the flight chairs along the outside wall. Asustie was fascinated in watching the city continue to disappear into the Galaxy Creepers. It was moving faster than she thought it would. Suddenly, the city disappeared as the *Liberty Quest* entered the *Liberty Pursuit*.

Moments later, the warning signal was sounded and everyone looked up to see the wall exiting the ceiling. Looking away from the descending floor, she heard Sooner ask, "Why are we seeing the city again on the hullercasts?"

"It's your father, Sooner. He's helping your grandfather by showing him what is outside the Galaxy Creepers," smiled Asustie.

"My father doesn't have that kind of power," informed Sooner.

"Yes, he does," assured Asustie.

Sam shut everything down but Ghonllier's door. All the Vanishers lined themselves along the corridor, except for Humphrey. He was with Ghonllier, Cid, Jason, Gostler, and Spencer in his quarters. All the hullercasts were on in Ghonllier's room, so they could watch Houser and Bennett enter the bay. Nervously, Gostler pulled at the collar of his uniform.

Jason noticed and cajoled, "You look happy."

Grunting, he commented, "I don't know how you guys do it day in and day out. I still don't like wearing uniforms. They're too tight on my neck."

"We're just tough," responded Humphrey, keeping his gaze on the hullercasts.

"Right," countered Gostler.

Jason questioned, "Humphrey, do your men have their restraints?"

"Yes, they are behind you," answered Humphrey.

Jason looked behind him to see no one. Taking in a deep breath, Jason knew if Humphrey said they were there, it meant they were.

Looking back, Jason asked, "Cid, are you ready?"

"Yes," answered Cid, making sure he had the patch in his pocket.

Spencer pointed, "That's Bennett. The right man is coming here."

Everyone joined Spencer to see Houser beside him. Jason looked over at Gostler and informed, "The man on the left is Houser."

They heard Ghonllier speak behind them. "Gostler, go alone to bring Houser back here first. Then I want Spencer and Humphrey to bring me Bennett."

Humphrey looked at Spencer while Gostler nodded and left.

He thought about being Dapper on his way to the OSA. Before he arrived, Gostler activated his field glasses comset. He wanted to listen to Ghonllier talking to anyone. He promised to broadcast to everyone if he was going to speak with one person.

Standing in the OSA, Gostler watched Houser and Bennett arrive at the ramp. The four Vanishers stopped them.

"I'm Commander Houser and this ship requested a—"

"We know who you are, Commander Houser," answered one of the Vanishers as Dapper appeared in the doorway.

Bennett beamed to see Dapper. He was on the KOGN list to capture and he was pleased to be receiving the reward for the general. Then Bennett realized that they were standing in front of the *Liberty Quest*. If they were talking to General Dapper, then this had to be the *Liberty Quest*. With a reward for Dapper and the *Liberty Quest*, he was already imagining himself spending it.

Surprised Dapper didn't motion him to board, Houser uttered, "General Dapper, may I talk with you?"

"Commander Houser, just send Bennett up."

Houser stopped Bennett. "Dapper, I need to talk with you about this Mandatory Transfer first."

"Later," countered Dapper.

"No! I want to talk first."

"Not this time, Commander."

"A Mandatory Transfer is my choice. I don't have to do it. This time we need to talk or I'm leaving with Bennett now," threatened Houser.

After listening to Ghonllier, Dapper nodded. "Men, let only Commander Houser through until we get this straightened out."

Two men moved aside, allowing only Houser to enter the ramp. Bennett beamed to watch him go up.

Houser arrived at the door and Dapper stepped away to allow him to enter. Dapper took off his field glasses and closed them up. "Houser, this is dangerous for you to fight with me on this. Why are you doing it?"

"We've been friends for a long time. I need answers about my closest friend. He was like a brother to me."

Dapper let out a sigh. "I only have a minute to talk before I have to get Bennett back to see the commander of this ship."

"How did the *Liberty Quest* enter my ship without us picking her up?"

"I can't answer that question."

"Dapper, I have orders to fire on this ship. You know I'm a man who follows orders," reminded Houser.

"We both know you wouldn't do it," said Dapper.

"Is that why she landed on my ship?" asked Houser.

"Maybe."

"Are you the ship who needs supplies?" asked Houser.

"Yes, we used that excuse, but we don't need anything except this Mandatory Transfer."

"First, tell me about Ghonllier? How did he die?"

Dapper shook his head. "I can't. He doesn't exist." Gostler could see his field glasses were paging him. Putting them on, he answered, "Yes, Commander." Then he paused. "Are you sure?" He paused once more, nodding. "Sorry, sir, I'll ask him." Looking back at Houser, he stated, "Since you know this ship so well, you need to give me an oath right now that you'll never talk about seeing this ship or me—"

"I will," interrupted Houser.

"Houser, you didn't let me finish. I need to tell you that if you break the oath, it means instant death," warned Dapper.

Houser stared at him and then leaned closer. "You found the Master Stone. That is the only thing that can cause instant death."

Dapper shook his head. "I can't validate that comment with a yes or no."

Instantly the door started to close to the OSA. Houser looked at the main loading sealing. "What is going on?" he demanded.

"Take the oath and mean it with your heart or you'll never be able to leave this ship again," rushed Dapper.

Houser had already locked looks with Dapper before gradually nodding. Moments later, his field glasses let him know that he had a page. "Yes, Commander," said Dapper. Then he looked at Houser. "Your oath has been accepted," he informed.

The door opened as Dapper ordered, "Follow me, Commander."

"Where are we going?"

"The commander of this ship wants to meet you," informed Dapper.

Houser started to ask another question, but stopped when they soon entered inside. That was when he noticed the ship in shut-down mode. "What is going on here? Is this ship prepared to fight with me?"

"This ship just came out of a big battle. We took out twelve Star Screamers," reminded Dapper.

"I noticed her. Why couldn't we pick up your signal?"

"What did you get?"

"You appeared on their equipment as a foreign and unidentified ship. We would've taken you for a KOGN ship if we didn't see you taking them out," answered Houser. Dapper looked at him and Houser added, "And you did it with so much ease. What is your secret?"

Gostler looked straight ahead, refusing to answer. Houser joined him to see Ghonllier's hullercast. He got emotional to see it. It was still the same mountain scene he had since Jenny's death. "So Commander Jason has taken over Ghonllier's old quarters," Houser whispered.

"Yeah," responded Dapper, disappearing through it.

Houser paused, thinking about Ghonllier before he followed. Upon entering, he was taken back to see everything looked different. He wanted to take a quick glance around the room, for there were quite a few people around. However, he soon noticed Jason standing by the nightstand, glaring at him.

Jason gestured toward a single chair in front of him. "Sit, Commander Houser."

Houser knew that chair was meant for the person on trial. Who did they want, him or Bennett? With Ghonllier telling Jason his thoughts, he waited for his response.

"I would rather stand, Commander."

"Look, Commander Houser, you insisted on seeing me. I didn't want the meeting," sneered Jason.

"Maybe I made a mistake," countered Houser.

"You made a lot of mistakes and we need to talk about them," replied Jason.

"What do you mean by that statement?"

"Bennett is a paid assassin for the KOGN. Why do you have him on your ship?"

Houser shook his head. "I didn't know that."

"You didn't know because you run a sloppy ship. Maybe I should just take it away from you right now," bellowed Jason.

"You can't do that," matched Houser.

"YES, HE CAN," said a weak voice behind him.

Houser recognized the voice and spun around to see who said it. All he saw was Spencer standing in front of a reclining chair with a man lying in it. Spencer blocked Ghonllier's face.

"Commander Houser, I think you better pay attention to me if you ever want to see your ship again," ordered Jason.

Facing Jason, Houser asked, "Who gave you the authority to be the Commander of this ship?"

"Sohmer," responded Jason. "I have the orders to prove it. I can commandeer any ship I want and no one can stop me. Do we understand each other?"

He has the Master Stone, thought Houser. *So Squirt found the Master Stone and its owner.* Jason brought him out of his thoughts by saying, "You have ten KOGN spies here on this mission and you're in charge. Three of them are on your ship."

"Bennett is one of them?" questioned Houser.

"Yes, and as we speak the other spies are being rounded up, including the other two on board this ship. I want them handled according to the laws that govern our galaxy."

"Then why did you bring Bennett and me here?" asked Houser.

Jason looked past him and said, "I've granted a wish and you have a few minutes to talk with him. Spencer and General Humphrey, go get Bennett and take your time."

Humphrey nodded and left with Spencer following. It was then that Houser saw Ghonllier. Stunned, Houser stared while Ghonllier remained still. Peering back at him, Houser could hardly believe his eyes as they grew wider with wonder.

"Squirt?" he uttered faintly, running off to his side.

"Hi, Beanpole," whispered Ghonllier.

"You look so pale and weak. You've lost a lot of weight," gasped Houser.

"I lost more weight than this. I'm finally putting it back on," informed Ghonllier.

"Why are you listed as dead?"

Ghonllier looked at Jason as he joined them. "Commander Houser, if you ever mention to anyone that you've seen him, you're a dead man and I'll have your ship."

Houser looked away from Jason and asked, "Does your father know about this?"

"How do you think I got this ship?" smiled Jason.

The commander watched Jason leave through the hullercasts. Then he looked at Ghonllier. Biting his lip, Houser asked, "What's wrong with you?"

"Poison," answered Ghonllier.

Ghonllier knew Houser was blaming Jason for him being poisoned. Jason reentered and ordered, "Take your seat, Houser. Bennett will be here shortly."

Reluctantly, Houser left and sat next to Dapper. The two exchanged looks before Houser asked, "Where is his son?"

Going to the front of the room, Jason answered, "His son is in my safekeeping. It gives me control on I-Force from firing on my ship."

So that's why Justin told me not to fire on the Liberty Quest. *He knew he was going to be here,* thought Houser, looking back at Ghonllier. It angered him to see Ghonllier in this situation and he was helpless to do anything about it. Dapper caught his attention and gave him a pleading look. Now, Houser understood why Dapper didn't want him to board the ship. It would've spared him from seeing his beloved friend in this condition.

Jason brought Houser out of his thoughts as he heard, "General Humphrey, please sit."

Immediately, the door closed and Bennett looked sharply behind him. Spencer stood there between Ghonllier and Bennett. As Bennett faced the front of the room, weapons came flying out from their hiding places on his body. Three strange-looking devices floated over to Jason's open hand.

Jason held them up and said, "Only a paid assassin uses these kinds of weapons and we both know what side you're on."

"Yes, I'm an I-Force spy," assured Bennett.

"No, you're not. You're a KOGN spy who wanted to turn this ship in, along with General Dapper, to Suzair the Great for a hefty reward."

Bennett started to panic. Cid stood with his patch. Seeing it, Bennett went into a defensive stance, preparing to fight with everyone in the room. Spencer, being taller and stronger, wrapped his arm around Bennett's arms and chest from behind. Tightly, he held him with one arm while he placed his other hand on his shoulder, a technique that made it impossible for the spy to move his arms. The pain from the hold made him give out a moan while his arms went limp.

Vanishers appeared out of the walls and in seconds had the spy in restraints. Houser, in amazement, grabbed Dapper's arm and slowly looked away from them.

"Where did those men come from?" he whispered. Dapper looked away. "Dapper, are they Vanishers?"

Knowing it was okay from Ghonllier to answer him, he nodded. With the Vanishers finished, Jason ordered, "Go ahead, Cid. Administer the Truth Test."

Spencer still held Bennett while Cid applied the patch. The spy tried to bite Cid, but couldn't reach his hands. A Vanisher stepped in and held his head for Cid. The medic stepped back so Spencer could release the spy. In anger, Bennett thrashed his body around, trying to do some damage. Houser and Dapper moved out of his way. Seeing they were going to have problems, Spencer placed his arms around him again and this time, he picked the man from off the floor and carried him to his seat. At the chair, Spencer dropped Bennett. The spy almost fell to the floor but stopped himself.

Sitting up, the captured spy glared at Jason as the commander looked at one of Bennett's weapons in his hand. Looking at him, he asked, "Bennett, is it true that you're a KOGN spy?" The spy stayed silent. So Jason demanded, "Answer me now! Is that true?"

The man refused to answer, trying to use his will over the medicine. "How long have you been working for KOGN?" continued

Jason, watching the Tron's eyes. He knew it was only a matter of time when his eyes would become glassy. When they did, the Tron would start talking.

"You might as well start talking, Bennett, because I already know that you have been in KOGN's services for three years. Tell me who the other KOGN spies are on Commander Houser's ship?"

The Tron still didn't answer and Houser shot Bennett a menacing expression. Jason continued. "I believe there are three of you altogether."

"That . . . fool Scremper," Bennett finally said. "He . . . must have . . . told you."

Jason looked at Houser before he asked, "Who's your mark now?"

"It . . . keeps . . . changing."

"You now have a man named David, correct?"

He nodded without control of his neck muscles. His head flopped around more than he wanted.

"If you found this David, would you kill him?"

"Yes."

"Do you still have Commander Ghonllier as a mark?"

"No, he's . . . dead."

"But your leader doesn't believe he's dead, does he?"

Bennett's head flopped around once more as he answered, "Commander Ghonllier . . . is . . . supposed to . . . be turned . . . . over to . . . Suzair the . . . ."

Jason interrupted, "General Dapper is also someone who KOGN has placed a price on his head. Do you plan on killing him?"

"No, Su . . . zair wants . . . . him alive."

"If Suzair the Great was dead and a new Master of the Galaxy appeared, would you give your allegiance to him?"

"No."

"Why?"

"If . . . he . . . would . . . pay me . . . . to kill," responded Bennett, now rocking his whole upper body back and forth from the drug.

"Why do you want to continue to kill?"

"I hate . . . and don't . . . . care . . . who I . . . kill."

Jason looked at Houser. "You know the rules. You'll find the same attitudes with all the other spies," responded Jason, taking a list from his pocket. He handed it to him and reminded, "Commander Houser, I want you to make sure court is carried out on all of these people and tell the commander what questions to ask, but do not mention Commander Ghonllier's name. Do you understand me?"

"Why did you mention it?" asked Houser, standing to take the list.

"For your benefit," answered Jason, removing his hand.

"You have ten minutes, then I want you off my ship," ordered Jason.

He left while Humphrey and his men were taking Bennett out of the room. Spencer, Dapper, and Cid left, leaving the two friends alone.

Houser arrived at his side, shaking his head. "You're really stepping into it this time, Squirt."

"I know," whispered Ghonllier.

Jason reentered the room and Houser faced him. "Since we're guests on your ship, we better have extra protection in this bay. I don't want anyone in here who hasn't taken an oath regarding my ship."

Houser nodded and Jason disappeared.

Going back to Ghonllier, Houser held up the list and expressed, "Squirt, you wrote this. I know your handwriting. What is going on here?"

"Please don't say anything about it. Dapper gave it to Jason. I wanted to find a way to let you know that I was alive in case Jason changed his mind on letting me talk with you," said Ghonllier weakly.

Putting the list in his pocket, he inquired, "What happened, Squirt? How did you get yourself into this mess?"

In a raspy voice, he answered, "I met Jason off my ship. I was rendered unconscious and Jason boarded my ship through Dapper."

"Why would Dapper allow them on board?"

"I was unconscious and just like he said to you, I live if you do what he wants," reminded Ghonllier.

"Where is Sooner? Is he on board?"

"We're together, but I don't always get to stay with him."

Houser placed a hand on his arm. "I'm sorry, my brother."

Ghonllier took a deep breath. "Please promise that you'll do everything to make Jason happy and don't mention me to anyone, not even to my father. He won't be able to talk about it with you."

Houser nodded. "He knows?"

"Yes. Justin knows and can't do anything about it," said Ghonllier.

"Is this Commander Jason taking care of you? You look so weak."

"I can't talk about it. Just don't upset him, is all I ask. Don't ask Dapper or I any questions. Let's say, I'll pay for it."

Seeing Houser wanted more information from him, Cid entered the room at Ghonllier's request. Cid brought a gurney and Jason followed. Houser glared at him and reminded, "It hasn't been ten minutes."

"I changed my mind. I want you off my ship now. Suzair the Great will be here shortly and you have courts to oversee," reminded Jason. Houser looked at Ghonllier and Jason added, "I didn't poison him, like you think I did."

"I didn't say you did!" snapped Houser, facing Jason.

"You thought it," responded Jason. Looking over at Ghonllier, he added, "Wrap this reunion up. I want you back where you belong."

Ghonllier watched with Houser as Jason left. It was Cid who spoke first. "Commander, do you want me to move you onto the gurney?"

"Yes," answered Ghonllier, telling Cid what to say.

Using the Stones, Ghonllier moved himself over to the gurney bed by floating over to it. Houser raised his eyebrows to see him float over while Cid covered him up with a cloth blanket. Houser placed his hand on Ghonllier's arm while Cid activated the safety straps.

"I'm glad you're alive, Squirt," he smiled.

"Thanks, Beanpole. It's like old time seeing you again," answered Ghonllier.

Cid started to move him out into the corridor with Houser walking beside him. There against the wall was Sunna asleep with Jason standing guard. Cid stopped and Houser did as well.

"Commander, do you mind staying here while I remove Commander Sunna out of here first?" requested Cid.

"No, go ahead," replied Ghonllier.

"Commander Sunna!" Houser responded. "I have orders to see her."

"No you won't," answered Jason, stepping forward.

Cid left with her while Houser watched. He stated, "Commander Jason, I have a package for her from Justin. I was told to give it to a man named Adamite." Houser grinned and added, "I would like to give it to her in person."

"Why?" questioned Ghonllier.

"I heard she was beautiful, and she is," said Houser, looking at Ghonllier. "I also heard she did anything to get her commission. I want to see if it's true."

Jason grunted, "You give all packages to me for Commander Sunna."

Houser nodded and Jason left as Ghonllier looked away. Houser noticed it. Leaning over, he whispered, "I know that look. You're in love with her."

Looking at Houser, Ghonllier informed, "It isn't exactly what you think, my friend."

Houser shook his head. "There was a glow to you when I mentioned her name. I know. And it's easy to see with your coloring so pale."

"Houser, never say that again. Commander Sunna is Commander Jason's sister."

"What's wrong with her? She looks like you, very pale."

"We were together . . ."

Houser interrupted, "Squirt, how could you do that? How could you do that to Jenny? She's a spy. You hate them and you have good reason to do so."

Ghonllier looked back at him, reading that he totally misunderstood Jason's remarks. There was nothing he could do to correct them. Houser had thought Ghonllier broke his marriage contract with the bonding fires and lost Jenny.

"Do you love her?" he asked.

Ghonllier looked away and answered, "Yes."

"So I see," said Houser, disgusted. "Jason is just using you both." Ghonllier faced him and Houser shook his head. "You really stepped into something this time."

"I know," said Ghonllier. "You better get out of here. Jason wants those other two spies taken care of now."

Houser nodded. "Bye, my friend."

Ghonllier watched him leave and it hurt to see him think so poorly of Sunna and himself. He didn't even know her, only judging her because of her profession. He saw his old self in Houser and it bothered him.

Shortly, Jason arrived. "Ghonllier, how did it go?"

Ghonllier studied him for a moment. He wanted to tell him about what Houser didn't say, but stopped himself. This was the burden of knowing too much.

"Fine. Thanks Jason. We put enough fear in him so he won't be asking questions about me," assured Ghonllier.

"Your mother has two emergency shuttles here. Sunna's things are being put on one as we speak. Who do you want to take the emergency shuttles?"

Ghonllier paused and then ordered, "First, contact Houser and tell him that you want everyone out of the bay and then bring them back after they take the oath." I don't want them to see my family or me getting on the shuttles. Put my son, mother, Asustie, and Gostler on the shuttle with me. Father, you, and the Vanishers can arrive by walking through the ship."

Activating his comset on his glasses, Jason ordered the Vanishers to stop Houser and pass on the information. When he finished, Jason said, "It's done."

"Tell the Vanishers to stay invisible with you when you return home," answered Ghonllier.

Jason nodded. "Consider it done."

"Tell the captain to secure the ship and that Houser will send guards to keep people out of the bay. I want them to stay on board."

"I understand."

With everything completed, Ghonllier closed his eyes, wanting sleep. The whole experience took a toll on him.

Chapter 8

Jasper

Gomper arrived at the Xeron moon right after I-Force's last Galaxy Creeper moved into jump speed. Ghonllier made sure the KOGN weren't aware of their departure. Brewster was concerned about this last ordeal with Bog, as Gomper wasn't doing well. The patches for nausea were only taking off the edge. At least, the cramps and pain had stopped. Gomper had become non-talkative and Brewster wondered just how much more his patient could handle. No one really understood why the demon was punishing Gomper, but he seemed to be doing what he wanted and when he wanted to.

Something deep inside of him kept Gomper moving forward and he wasn't sure what it was. Somehow, he felt a strong connection toward Ghonllier and wanted to help him. Believing he had purpose seemed to ease his suffering.

With them arriving at the Xeron moon, Suzair the Great was expected to appear on bridge to give his officers instructions. Gomper was on his way there, looking mean. He hurt and it showed on his face.

Pappar and his bodyguards flanked him, clearing a path for him to walk through unbothered. Jamham and Brewster were going with him. More bodyguards were escorting them to his Star Skipper.

Everyone they passed ran. Usually it bothered Gomper, but today he really didn't care. People expected Suzair the Great to be very upset with the KOGN losing all of their ships at the Xeron moon. They didn't want to be a part of his blind anger.

Pappar took in a deep breath as they entered the bridge, hoping Bog would leave Gomper alone while they were with his officers. They were always in fear that the officers would find out about Gomper. His voice wasn't quite the same as Suzair the Great's and Pappar worried about it. They avoided going out as much as possible because of it. Today was one of those moments. Gomper had to make an appearance or people would wonder.

Gomper's appearance with his entourage caused his officers to grow quiet. They acted uncomfortable to see him, almost like he had interrupted something. Pappar wondered why. What were they talking about? Glancing at Gomper, he wondered if he had noticed it.

Suzair the Great stepped away from his men and stood in front of Commander Jabolt. Glaring at him, they saw fear in Jabolt's eyes.

"Your Grace," greeted Commander Jabolt, giving a slight nod.

Gomper stayed quiet, thinking about a dream he had the night before. Everyone was standing in the exact place they were in his dream. In it, Gomper was aware of the conversation. They were planning on getting rid of him during this invasion and he could see it in their eyes it was true.

Ghonllier had given him the dream, using the Stones. If Gomper didn't pay attention to the dream, he would only have hours to live. Ghonllier had replaced Bog's stepping stone by telling him what was going on around him thought dreams. He picked dreams over speaking directly because Gomper wasn't ready for it.

Glaring down Jabolt's nose, Gomper ordered, "Pappar, I want weapons out and a man on each captain and one on Commander Jabolt. Escort the others out. I want to have a personal conversation with Commander Jabolt."

Pappar snapped his fingers and pointed to the three men who would guard the captains and Jabolt. They took their positions while the rest of the bodyguards removed the other officers, shutting the door. Gomper and the commander stared each other down while the other officers reluctantly left.

With the door closed, Gomper looked over at the captain's monitors to see them come out of jump speed. Gomper's heart stopped beating for a moment to see the Xeron moon. He expected to see the *Liberty Quest* waiting for them and felt relieved to find her gone.

He ordered, "Send out a Star Screamer to the coordinates where the unnatural storm was reported."

"Yes, Your Grace," responded the captain, following orders.

"Captains, turn on our hullercast," ordered Gomper, wanting to make sure the *Liberty Quest* wasn't there. Gomper knew Ghonllier could disguise her signal.

Relieved to only see the KOGN Star Screamers leaving the ship, he ordered, "Captains, broadcast to the large monitors what the different Star Screamers' stones are seeing on the surface."

On the large captain's monitors, they could see the terrain of the ground. The monitors soon split, showing the different visions of the Star Screamers. Gomper lightly bit his lower lip, watching the proceedings.

Nervously, Gomper asked, "How close to the location of the storm are they?"

One of the guarded captains announced, "They're coming up on it now. Our instruments are showing the storm is gone, Your Grace."

"Gone?" questioned Commander Jabolt with Gomper glaring at him.

"The city is gone," whispered Pappar, causing Gomper to look at the monitors.

One Star Screamer was actually flying over the ground that showed scars of a once rooted city. Gomper let out a silent sigh of relief. He stared at the scars left in the ground, knowing this had to be his brother's city. *So it means he knows about the curse*, thought Gomper. Seeing the scars let him know how badly he wanted answers to his many questions.

One captain interrupted his thoughts. "Your Grace, the captains are asking permission to land and check out the area. What do I tell them?"

"Denied!" snapped Gomper. He added, "Tell them to return now." Then he ordered, "Tell my pilot, Fran, that I'm leaving like we planned and I'm on my way."

Gomper looked back at Jabolt to see him smiling, just like in the dream. So he said, "Commander Jabolt, now we'll have our private talk."

"Yes, Your Grace," nodded Jabolt. "What would you like me to do for you?"

"I'm taking all of my bodyguards and personal staff with me, except for these three," gestured Gomper.

Jabolt looked at the three guards as they held their blasters on him and the captains. "Why are you so hostile? We're friends here."

"Friends?" glared Gomper. "I don't have friends. When I leave the bridge, the captains better keep the door locked. If you dare give the order to the captains, my men will shoot all three of you." Stepping closer, he added, "You better be here when I return. And don't even think about giving the captains the order to fire upon my Star Skipper. Do we understand each other?"

A stunned expression appeared on Jabolt's face. Gomper had expressed exactly what they were planning on doing. Trying to cover his tracks, he stammered, "Your Grace, do you think I would do something like that?"

Gomper grunted and left. Jabolt called after him. "Your Grace, is there something wrong? Have I done something to offend you?"

Gomper faced him. "Let's say, Commander Jabolt, we don't know each other that well to trust." Looking at one of the captains, he asked, "Where is my ship?"

"You'll find her on Deck Six, Station Three."

Pappar opened the door and they saw the officers all look in their direction. Gomper exited and stopped to stare at them. When the door was closed, Gomper informed, "Anyone even attempts to go in there, the captains and Commander Jabolt will die. If they die, I will end everyone's life here. Do we understand each other?"

The stunned men nodded. Some stared at the closed door while the others watched Gomper and his entourage leave.

Once they were alone in the corridors, Pappar whispered, "Was that you, sir, a moment ago?"

"Yes, Pappar."

"Why did you do that?"

"Was it out of character?"

"No, just the opposite. Why did you do it?"

"I don't know. Something bothers me about Jabolt and the officers who constantly hang around him. I don't trust them."

Pappar agreed with him. They always seemed to slink around him, but he didn't realize that Gomper saw it, too. When they arrived at the ship, the rest of his bodyguards were waiting for him outside of it.

Gomper stopped in front of them and asked, "Did you check it out?"

"Yes, Your Grace. We found an explosion device right where you said we would."

"What kind was it?" asked Gomper.

"The kind that attack-blasts, just like you said."

Gomper nodded and entered the ship with everyone following. The pilot sealed the door and went to her seat. Gomper sat next to the window and rested his elbow on the armrest. Lightly, he tapped his finger against the window without realizing what he was doing. His thoughts were on his past.

Bog was impressed with Gomper's behavior on the bridge and knowing about the explosion device. Without his stepping stone, he wasn't aware of it. Seeing Gomper through a new light, Bog decided that he needed him. He was more valuable alive than dead.

This was what Ghonllier wanted to create for Gomper, hoping the demon would stop torturing him. Bog decided to leave him alone for a while and watch him. Not wanting to admit it, Bog was relying on Gomper more each day and he didn't like it.

Quietly, Pappar joined Gomper, but he didn't acknowledge him. Brewster and Jamham sat across from them. All three men wondered why all of a sudden Gomper seemed to know things like the old Suzair the Great. Yet, he was sounding very much like Gomper.

Pappar leaned over and asked Gomper if Jamham could get him something to drink. Gomper ignored him and kept looking outside. As they traveled along the surface, Fran, his pilot, sent back a message. Pappar was more forceful this time. "Your Grace, Fran wants to know if you want her to land."

Gomper nodded. Moments later, they landed. Pappar stood and moved out of the way while watching Gomper pass him. Then Gomper stopped to stare at an open door to one of the cargo rooms.

Pappar joined him and asked, "Sir? Do you want something?"

"I want to take that single transport and do my own search," replied Gomper.

Pappar snapped his fingers and pointed at one of guards to get it out of the cargo room. Gomper left the ship with Pappar following. Seeing the transport passing through the door, Pappar said, "I'll be the one to take you, Your Grace."

Gomper faced him. "You don't understand," whispered Gomper. Then he added, "I'll take myself, Pappar."

Pappar matched him. "Your Grace, these men don't know about you. Suzair the Great can't use a single transport."

"I lied," bellowed Gomper, wanting everyone to hear. "I can use a single transport and anything else I want. I do not want people to figure me out. So bring me the transport."

The guard with the transport gave it to Gomper and he got on it. Pappar quickly ordered the second one to be brought out. Before it arrived, Gomper had left on the first transport. Everyone was shocked to see Suzair the Great alone and using a transport. The concerned head officer briefly eyed them to watch their reaction. This was something Suzair the Great had never done before.

Gomper was lost in another place for a few minutes. The speed took him back to his youth. At a very high speed, Gomper traveled the circumference of the city. The speed thrilled his soul and for the first time, he felt like he had freedom to express and be himself. It felt wonderful.

Once he had the thrill out of his system, he slowed down to look closer at the ground. Meticulously, he studied the surface. It surprised him to see that they moved this city, taking everything. For them to take pathways and everything underground, they had to have a lot of Galaxy Creepers.

It frustrated him that they had taken everything. Any clues left behind would be few and far between and he wanted to prove to himself that this was the Master of the Galaxy's city. Moving down one particular pathway, he smelled a fragrance that he hadn't smelled for years. It was a flower from his childhood.

A second transport arrived at his side. Gomper saw it was Brewster. He quizzed, "Are you okay, Your Grace?"

Gomper nodded and looked back in the direction of the fragrance. He divulged, "I smell a flower that was my mother's favorite."

Leaving in that direction, Gomper went slowly where a pathway was a few hours ago. He wanted to find the flower and didn't stop until he reached a particularly large hole left by a very large building. Scanning the size of the hole, Gomper slowly rode around the outer edge of it with Brewster following.

On one side of the hole, Gomper moved away, stopping at a place where a few plants and flowers had inadvertently been left behind. In the hurry to get out, the ships crossed beams, leaving a patch of ground. Gomper got off his transport and Brewster copied him.

Gomper stopped in front of the few plants, staring at them.

"Your Grace, this place can't mean anything. That hole left by a building can't be a home."

Not taking his gaze off the flowers, Gomper answered, "It could've been my parents' home. It was an excessively large house."

Brewster looked back to see Gomper had stooped down, picking a flower. Slowly, Gomper brought it to his nose, taking in a deep whiff. The smell brought back so many memories of his childhood. His mother loved gardening and shared it with her sons. They each had a place among their mother's gardening that belonged to them.

Each boy created a design with flowers and plants. The colors would change, but never the design.

Holding the only tie to his past, Gomper left to look at the other spots missed by the Galaxy Creepers. At the next place, Gomper's hands started to tremble. *This is part of Manchester's design.* His body tingled with the sight of something having belonged to his brother, Manchester. Seeing more in another place, he moved quickly to see what could've belonged to his brother, Astor. Stepping closer, he saw part of his own design.

Stacy kept their designs in the garden as a memorial for her sons. *This is my family's home. Are they alive or is Ghonllier just living here?* thought Gomper, falling to his knees. Shoving his fingers in the dirt that he loved, he let the soil fall from his hand.

Tears fell from his cheeks. Brewster was concerned and joined him by saying, "Your Grace, what's wrong?"

Without thinking, Gomper choked out in a raspy voice, "This is my family's place. They're alive."

NO!! Gomper heard in his head. Instantly, Gomper felt pain from Bog, causing him to faint. Falling forward, he landed on top of his design while clutching his flower. Brewster reached for his analyzer from his pocket and knelt beside him.

After getting a reading, he said while running to his transport for some medicine, "Great, I think he's killed him this time."

In anger, Bog hit Gomper harder with the curse than usual. He felt his stepping stone had lied to him and if he had it, Bog would've thrown it against the wall like Ghonllier already had done.

✳   ✳   ✳

By the time Ghonllier had reached the house, he was asleep. The experience of court had drained him. Cid wasn't happy with the stress court had caused. So he took things into his own hands. Without Ghonllier's permission, he placed a deep sleeping patch on him.

Cid kept a deep sleeping patch on both he and Sunna, changing them every four hours. Every four hours, Sunna was awakened for water. He couldn't have her dehydrating, putting her back on the fluids. Her arm was becoming bruised from the stopping and starting of the apparatus entering her veins.

With Ghonllier asleep, the Master Stones monitored everything for him that they understood to be a concern to the Master. They watched out for Gomper, giving him dreams of what his officers were plotting. So he could take the necessary steps to avoid their traps.

It had been days that Cid kept the couple sleeping. Suddenly, Ghonllier woke up on his own accord to the sounds of the monitors running. At first, he thought the monitor was for Sunna. But as he looked over at it, he realized they both were on the monitors. Reaching up on his neck, he took off the patch that Cid's staff had placed on and disconnected his hand from his monitor.

Standing, Ghonllier found the dizziness gone. Feeling strong, he gazed at Sunna sleeping, studying her body. Then he left for the bathroom to enjoy a shower while thinking about her condition.

When he exited, Cid pounced on him. "Did you realize how frightened I became when I saw your monitor go blank?"

"I'm sorry, Cid. I don't stop to think about you," apologized Ghonllier, going to his drawers. "Your idea worked. I feel great, thank you," commented Ghonllier, taking out some exercise clothes.

"Do you feel strong enough to use those clothes?" questioned Cid.

"Yes, I want to start to build my muscle tone, especially since we're in space," stated Ghonllier, heading back to the bathroom with his clothes.

"What about Sunna? What do you see in her future?" Cid asked, looking at her.

Ghonllier stopped to join Cid, looking at her. Letting out a sigh, he divulged, "Her health isn't good. I see two areas in her body where it's having a hard time healing. She received too much poison from having the two so close together."

"Her liver?"

"Yes, it's going to scar if we don't do something soon," replied Ghonllier.

"What's the other area?"

"I don't like her spleen."

"I agree. It's weak and sluggish and not producing enough red blood cells. It should've changed by now," stated Cid.

Ghonllier paused. "I don't see her changing a lot when I look into the future."

"What do you want me to do?" asked Cid, glancing over at Ghonllier.

"I want to give her a couple of days and let's see if her body can rally on its own. If I don't see improvement, I want you to make me up a patch with Sweet Dumble and Sutter Mood."

"Cleansing medicine?" Ghonllier nodded, continuing to the bathroom.

Cid watched him shut the door. When Ghonllier returned, Cid was still there. He looked at him and asked, "Why are you still here, Cid?"

"You're going to work out. No one is supposed to use the machines without me monitoring their workout," reminded Cid.

"Not me. I can monitor myself better than you can," countered Ghonllier.

"Please, do you mind if I monitor your workout?"

Ghonllier could see Cid was making a documentary on how the Master Stones affected a man's body during the bonding process of man and Stone. The new Master commanded his shoes to come to him from the closet as he thought about it. Plucking them out of the air, he answered, "Cid, I'll let you do it as long as you don't irritate me too much. If I ask you to leave, I want you to."

Cid smiled, "Thank you, Ghonllier."

The medic had kept every examination with his analyzer, including Ghonllier's first visit. No one had the opportunity before to monitor a man bonding to the Master Stones and Cid was excited Ghonllier allowed him to continue. In the past, the Stones bonded with a man in total secrecy. With the Stones being lost for thirty years, Bog could easily stop them this time. There had to be a nucleus of people protecting and helping Ghonllier become the Master of the Stones. Cid was well aware of this golden opportunity.

At the lift, Cid expected Ghonllier to page for it. Instead, he stared at a different hallway. Shortly, Cid saw Gostler come around the corner. Gostler seemed pleased to see Ghonllier.

Arriving, he grinned, "Well, you're feeling better."

"Yes, I'm over it," replied Ghonllier, requesting the lift.

"Sunna?" quizzed Gostler.

"She's still pretty bad," informed Cid, entering the lift.

Ghonllier entered, "I see you're still wearing a uniform."

Gostler hurriedly followed and retorted, "Yes. When I agreed to be Dapper, you didn't tell me how long my role was going to be." Ghonllier chuckled as Gostler added, "You knew what I was getting into, didn't you?"

"Yes, I knew. Sorry, Gostler," apologized Ghonllier, watching the rail come up.

"Why does Dapper need to be at these meetings?" asked Gostler.

The lift disappeared. When it arrived on the main floor, Ghonllier answered, "Dapper had extensive knowledge of the area we are moving to. He walked out of there with Jasper. So Houser thinks you need to be at the meetings."

"How does Houser know that?" asked Gostler.

"He was with me when I picked up the boy, Jasper. He helped me interrogate Dapper and Jasper on what happened on the Suzair planet."

Gostler grunted, "Why is he requesting Jason to be there?"

"He wants to study him. He thinks Jason has the Master Stones and he's the new Master. He's hoping to get Jason to release me to him."

"Why release you to him?" questioned Gostler, following him out of the lift.

Ghonllier looked at Gostler thoughtfully. "Jason confuses him. He's not sure about him. One moment, Jason appears compatible and then he acts ruthless. He suspects Jason has the Master Stones. If he does, Houser wants to find away to give him his allegiance."

Exiting the lift, Gostler headed toward the dining room. Ghonllier stopped him. "Do you have time to go with me so we can talk?"

"Yes," answered Gostler, following them down the hallway that led to Cid's medical center.

Entering the glass-walled exercise room, Ghonllier asked, "How are you handling being Dapper for a long period of time?"

"Adamite and Jason watch me closely. They get me out of there when I need a break. Jason's job is to never allow Houser to follow me," answered Gostler.

"That's good. Houser really wants to get you alone," replied Ghonllier, getting on a walking machine. He looked at Gostler while Cid hooked him up to the monitor. Gostler was about to ask why he was letting Cid do this, when Ghonllier said, "At the next meeting, I want you to request a Star Skipper from him."

"Who's the pilot?"

"Tell him you are."

"Dapper can fly a Star Skipper?"

"Yes, we took lessons together. I can see he joined me so he would have an excuse to be with me. It was fun learning how to fly at the age of sixteen."

Cid finished and Ghonllier started his exercise. "I can't fly, you know," warned Gostler.

"I'll be flying the ship. Just check it out in your name and go with me," stated Ghonllier.

"Okay, is there anything else?"

"Yes. I can see you're holding the meetings in Father's office. How was he introduced to Houser?"

"He was introduced as an city official of your city. He knows nothing about Adamite being your father. Did we do it the way you wanted?" asked the former Master. Ghonllier nodded. "We only allowed Houser to come to the meetings because of the server stone. Did we make a mistake by letting him be aware of them?"

"No. We can trust him," answered Ghonllier. "I'm sorry that Houser's being burdened with so many secrets. The KOGN would find a fountain of information if they could get their hands on him."

"We didn't feel the restraint from the Master Stones when we talked about it, so we went ahead."

Ghonllier nodded and changed the subject. "I need to have you tell Father that I want our home and his office placed close to Jasper's home."

"Now he's . . ."

"The boy who found the first Master Stone," reminded Ghonllier. Gostler nodded. "Why?"

"So Sooner can be close to him. They still talk with each other."

"How?"

"Jasper has a C-Stone programmed to Dapper's old one. Sooner has it," answered Ghonllier.

"I was on my way to see Adamite now. I'll tell him," responded Gostler.

"If he wants to talk with me, you know where to find me." Gostler started to leave. "Gostler." The former Master stopped. "I want to leave with the Star Skipper twenty-four hours before the Galaxy Creepers arrive."

"Why do you want to go ahead of Houser? It isn't necessary for you to do that."

"Yes it is. I want to talk with Jasper's family before we land. And I want Sooner to go with us."

"I'm going as Dapper?" questioned Gostler in a down tone.

"Yes. The whole family only knows Dapper, and they haven't met Sooner or me."

"Why not wait until you land to see the family?"

"The whole family is suffering because the KOGN took their home. I don't want them to wait any longer to get help. I owe it to them."

Gostler nodded. "I'll make the arrangements," stated the former Master, leaving. At the glass door, he stopped and added, "Ghonllier, did you realize that some of your old crew is on board the *Liberty Pursuit*?"

"Yes, the Stones warned me. Why did you bring them up?"

"A woman came up to me asking about you. When I told her you were dead, she started to tear up. I thought you never dated. It was obvious that she had some strong feelings for you."

"Anna," whispered Ghonllier, getting a little winded.

"Who's she?"

"She was my medic tech who took care of me with the first Stone." Ghonllier slowed down his pace. He added, "It surprises me that she would tear up. She thought I was going to die from what was in my blood from the first Stone."

"That explains why she looked so shocked to learn you died in a battle with the KOGN."

"I'm sorry it was Anna you saw," replied Ghonllier. "I can see she still blames herself for not helping me get better. Now, she blames herself for my death."

"Is your father still in the dining room?"

"No, he's now in the library," stated Ghonllier, looking at Cid recording his stats.

Feeling like Ghonllier was through, Gostler left. He shut the door and paused to take a quick glance at him. Ghonllier was talking to Cid. *He has more patience than I did. It would upset me to have someone do what Cid is doing,* thought Gostler, heading for the library.

With Ghonllier awake, Cid took Sunna off the monitors and stopped placing a patch on her neck. She wanted freedom from the monitors, so Ghonllier kept her stats appearing in his office.

Schools were closed during the moving, so Sooner stayed with his parents and helped Sunna drink and eat. Now with Ghonllier and Sooner there, the ailing woman had things given to her before she realized she needed them. It bothered her on one hand, yet, she embraced the chance to understand Sooner and Ghonllier.

The time came for Ghonllier to leave for the Suzair planet. Cid happened to find Ghonllier paging for the lift with Sunna's breakfast. Seeing Cid, Ghonllier spoke, "Go ahead, Cid. Make up the patch of Sweet Dumble and Sutter Mood root. She needs it."

"We were taught to use it in a drink. Why a patch?"

"I'm increasing the formula on the first patch. It will make her violently sick, causing her to throw up."

"Are you sure about increasing the medicine?"

"She can't wait any longer. The Master Stones are going to aid the medicine and move the poison to her stomach quickly. So she can expel it."

"Are you going to explain to her what to expect or are you going to let her find out?"

"I refuse to force it on her. I'll give her a choice."

Cid nodded, returning to his clinic while Ghonllier entered the lift. Opening the door to their room, he found their bed empty. Checking with the Stones, he saw Sunna was in the bathroom. He sat the tray on the nightstand and entered the closet to retrieve his old uniform.

When he came out, Sunna had just exited and watched him past her carrying it. She inquired, "Ghonllier, what are you doing with an I-Force uniform?"

"I brought you some breakfast. I'll be back and we can talk," responded Ghonllier, entering the bathroom.

Listening to the shower, Sunna stopped at the nightstand. She drank her water before lying down. Sunna dozed off and was awakened with Ghonllier tossing his cloak and weapons belt on their bed. Startled to see them, she inquired, "Why are you leaving us?"

"I'm taking a Star Skipper to see the family who gave me the first Master Stone. I need to talk with them."

"I was really hungry this morning. Why didn't you bring me much?"

Before Ghonllier could answer, Cid entered with his assistants. They were carrying equipment that Sunna recognized. "Why are you giving me fluids?"

"Only if it's necessary," replied Cid.

"What's going on here?" she asked, looking sternly at Ghonllier.

Sitting on the edge of the bed, Ghonllier stated, "Sunna, I didn't bring up anything but water for your breakfast, because you're going to get very nauseated shortly."

"Nauseated? Why?"

"I had Cid make up a powerful cleanser for your body. The Stones are telling me that we need to get the poison out of your liver now or it's going to lead you to a very painful death in the future."

Sunna gazed at the patch in Cid's hand. "Are you going to force me to take it?"

"No, I'm giving you a choice."

"Are you sure it will work?"

"The Master Stones are going to help your body through this patch. So it will be rough in the beginning, but then you'll be like me, strong and healthy."

"Why the fluids?"

"We're in space. I don't want you to dehydrate. I want them close by if you need them," answered Cid.

She searched Ghonllier's face and asked, "You're leaving the Galaxy Creeper, if you have your weapons belt and cloak out. When will you be back?"

"Maybe four hours or so. I'm taking Sooner. When I return, we won't leave your side."

"How long will I be really sick?"

"I hope not too long. I'll be able to feel your illness, Sunna," answered Ghonllier.

She touched his face with her hand. "So we'll be going through it together."

"Whether I'm here or not, I'll feel your discomfort. I've waited as long as I dare."

"Stay away until I'm through the worst. I don't want you around, Ghonllier, seeing me be that sick."

He leaned in to kiss her. "You might change your mind." The two gazed into each other's eyes before he let go of her hand. Slowly, he stood before they looked away from each other. While Ghonllier picked up his weapons belt, Cid sat in his place to start the procedure.

"Ghonllier," requested Sunna. He looked up from his belt. "How strong are you going to feel my discomfort?"

"I'll feel your nausea, but I won't hurl like you," he informed.

Sunna watched Cid apply the patch to her stomach area. Ghonllier paused at the door and Sunna gazed up at him before he left. He nodded and went out the door.

He exited the lift to find Sooner and Gostler waiting for him in uniforms at the front door. Sooner's uniform was a little small on him. It had been a while since the boy had worn it. Ghonllier put his field glasses on and asked, "Sooner, do you mind being with Gostler looking like Dapper?"

"We have been talking about it. I'll be okay."

"Gostler, you and Sooner go first and I'll follow. Whatever we do, people can't see the three of us together," said Ghonllier. Gostler nodded and he added, "There are a lot of people on board who know Sooner and Dapper." Looking at his son, he reminded, "Sooner, people are supposed to think that I'm dead. Remember that if they talk with you, you can't tell them I'm alive. Also tell Gostler the names of the people because he won't know them."

Sooner nodded. Gostler placed his hand on Sooner's shoulder, like Dapper always did. Then Gostler responded, "See you there."

Ghonllier opened the door as Gostler changed into Dapper. A sudden strong presence of his beloved bodyguard and friend was felt. The third Stone had increased his sensitivity because Ghonllier felt Dapper's presence. Watching Gostler disappear around a building let him know that Dapper had stayed with him.

Soaking in the moment, Gostler mentally contacted him, interrupting his thoughts. "Where is the Star Skipper checked out to Dapper?"

"It's on Deck Eight, Station Six," answered Ghonllier, using the Stones.

Ghonllier felt a chill race through his body as Dapper walked right through his energy space. *So this is what he was talking about when he tried to teach me to be invisible. Today, I wished I had learned.* It felt strange to see Dapper walking away and to feel his presence at the same time.

The new Master waited for Gostler and Sooner to enter the bay's lift before he departed from the house. Dapper's presence felt like the old days. Getting off the lift in the upper corridor, Ghonllier used his Vanisher speed to maneuver his way through the corridors. Many familiar people, he passed. He knew them because Ghonllier had been on the *Liberty Pursuit* many times.

Finally, he arrived at the corridor that would take him to the Star Skipper. Reappearing, he startled one of the guards. Ghonllier nodded and entered the adjoining corridor. Looking at what they were guarding, Ghonllier could see it was his ship. He smiled to see Houser trying hard to please Jason.

Ghonllier could see Houser thought he was still on board the *Liberty Quest*. *I wish I could tell him the truth,* thought Ghonllier, arriving at the bay of his Star Skipper.

Entering the bay, he knew Gostler and Sooner were behind him. Quickly, he hid behind a nearby transport, knowing part of his old crew were in the bay at this very moment. Jackson, one of his generals, was the man from his old crew. He was a friend who knew Jenny and himself. Ghonllier watched him from his hiding place and smiled.

Ghonllier was pleased Houser got him. He was a good officer and Ghonllier could see that Houser requested Jackson when he heard about his crew being broken up.

Seeing in his mind that Gostler was close to entering the bay, Ghonllier warned him by explaining to Gostler the relationship and promised to talk him through it. Dapper knew the man as well as Ghonllier did.

The bay was so large that Jackson didn't see Ghonllier when he appeared from using his Vanisher's speed. The crew around the Star Skipper didn't know Ghonllier and didn't pay attention to him. He walked around the ship, checking it out, while he watched in his mind Sooner and Dapper greet Jackson.

Immediately, Jackson asked about Ghonllier. It hurt to see the grief on his face, regarding Ghonllier's alleged death. Jackson constantly encouraged Ghonllier to find another wife and he would be happy to know about his new marriage. He wanted to leave and go see Jackson, but Ghonllier kept his promise to the Master Stones.

When Dapper and Sooner arrived at the Star Skipper, Ghonllier wasn't there. A man came forward to have Dapper sign a tablet checking the ship out to him. Then the man unlocked the ship and moved out of the way. Dapper opened the door and felt someone move quickly past him.

Entering the ship, he closed the door to find Ghonllier reaching the pilot's seat. Gostler took the seat next to him, with Sooner standing between the two men.

Glancing over at Gostler, Ghonllier replied, "I need Dapper to call in for a systems check and a release of security."

"Why do we need to do that? You can check out the ship yourself by using the Stones?" questioned Gostler.

"They don't know that. Remember protocol, General Dapper. Just read my mind and follow my words."

Reluctantly, Gostler put his field glasses on and started to sound like Dapper, following Ghonllier's thoughts. Once they were out of the Galaxy Creeper's bay, Ghonllier looked at Sooner and asked him to contact Jasper. "Tell them I want to see his parents and him at Dapper's crash site."

"Can you tell them that you're alive?" asked Sooner, retrieving his C-Stone.

"Yes, Son. They aren't a part of the military and don't know I'm supposed to be dead," replied Ghonllier.

Ghonllier half listened to Sooner talk with Jasper as he went into jump speed. It was a short jump as he quickly came out to see the

Suzair planet. Again, he felt Dapper behind him as the Suzair planet appeared. Reminiscing, he thought, *A lot has happened to me since I last landed on this planet.*

Sooner rested his head on his father's shoulder after talking with Jasper. He informed them that they were going to call him back after Jasper spoke with his parents. Sooner added, "It feels strange to be back here, doesn't it, Father?"

"Yes," whispered Ghonllier, knowing Sooner was feeling Dapper, too, but didn't understand it.

When they were about to travel through transition, Sooner got his call. "Tell him we'll be there in twenty minutes," informed Ghonllier before Sooner activated the call.

Sooner took the call while Ghonllier smiled to see the colors of transition. Being in the atmosphere, Ghonllier departed into a different direction, heading toward a brilliant pink sunset. The blue sky quickly changed to blackness allowing the stars to appear. Ghonllier kept his eyes on the numbers moving swiftly, trying to match up with the stationary numbers.

On the right side of the ship, one of the two moons of the planet appeared. Ghonllier headed in a slightly different direction and the second moon appeared in front of the spaceship.

A few minutes later, Ghonllier headed for the surface of the planet. Treetops appeared as they skimmed the surface, arriving at Dapper's crash site. With this being a clear night with two moons, they could see everything on the ground. When Dapper's crashed Star Skipper appeared, sadness shrouded Ghonllier's heart.

He circled it once before landing next to the rubble. Out his window, Ghonllier noticed a light glimmer through the trees. He felt excited to see the boy again who changed his life. Jasper was a good experience for Sooner and Ghonllier and he would always mean a lot to him.

Looking at Gostler, he requested, "I need Dapper to meet them."

"Do you know the parents' names?" asked Gostler, standing.

"No," replied Ghonllier. "Jasper is the only one who Sooner and I know. I don't know if Dapper learned their names."

Gostler left while Sooner ran to the window, waiting for Jasper. They came out of the trees and the boys could see each other. Jasper ran for the ship while Sooner met him at the door. Jasper and Sooner leaped into each other's arms. Ghonllier smiled to know how excited they were to be together.

When the parents entered the ship, Ghonllier reached out his hand to greet his new neighbors. He assumed, "You must be Jasper's parents."

"Yes, and you must be Commander Ghonllier," answered Jasper's father, accepting his hand.

"I am," responded Ghonllier, gesturing for them to sit.

"We have heard so much about you, Commander, and your ship, the *Liberty Quest,*" smiled Jasper's mother, sitting. In the background, Dapper shut the door before joining them.

"Jasper told us that you have something to ask us," mentioned Jasper's father.

"We're moving our city here to your valley and wanted you to know about it." Reading their minds, he quickly added, "Our city is in a different dimension, so you won't see us."

"Then why are you telling us?" asked Jasper's mother.

"We know what you have been going through since being captured by the KOGN. Also, since we are in a different dimension, it's going to be hard on the boys to know how close they are without being able to see each other—" informed Ghonllier.

"You don't live on the *Liberty Quest* anymore?" interrupted Jasper.

Sooner grabbed Jasper's arm and said, "We live on land now, so I can go to school. And Father still has the *Liberty Quest.*"

"He's still the commander of her?" questioned Jasper. Sooner nodded.

"Why are you moving the city?" asked Sooner's father.

"The KOGN decided to move to our moon. It was neutral and we didn't want them to find us. So we left before they arrived," answered Dapper.

"How did you know about it before the KOGN arrived?" inquired Jasper's mother.

Ghonllier surprised Gostler with his answer. "We live in another dimension in a city that belongs to the future Master of the Galaxy."

"Why are you moving it here?" asked Jasper's mother coldly.

"The future Master brought the city here out of respect to Jasper."

"Have the Master Stones been found?" asked Jasper's father.

"I can't deny or confirm your question. Jasper accidentally met the new Master before he received the first Stone. The new Master knows how you have been suffering, since he didn't have the Master Stones to stop the KOGN from kidnapping you. He wants to make it up to you."

"He knows?" questioned Jasper's mother.

"Yes. He sent us because we know Jasper. He's aware of your nightmares, madam. He wants to invite you to live in his city and enjoy peace," stated Ghonllier. The couple looked at each other while Ghonllier continued, "He also knows the town people are afraid of you. They think you caused KOGN to take your home and they're afraid that they will come back and take the whole town."

"How did you find his city?" asked Jasper.

Ghonllier smiled, "The new Master found me after Suzair the Great put a contract out on my ship, along with General Dapper and me."

"How soon will you be here?" quizzed Jasper's mother.

"We'll be there in twenty-four hours," answered Ghonllier.

"How many people are with you?" asked Jasper's father.

"About fifty thousand people," Ghonllier answered.

Jasper grabbed his mother's arm. "Please, Mother. Can we join them? I want to go to school with Sooner."

She looked at Jasper and smiled, "We'll talk about it."

"Please do. Your other children need to be a part of your decision." Then Ghonllier took a moment before adding, "Please know they will have more friends in his city than they could have here."

"We have all lost our friends," grunted the father.

A tear escaped the mother's eye. She quickly wiped it away as Ghonllier assured, "The Master wants you to know that you did nothing to have the KOGN kidnap you. It was a mistake on their part."

"Thank you for bringing us back and putting my family back together, Commander," said Jasper's father.

"You're welcome," smiled Ghonllier.

In a raspy voice, the mother asked, "What kind of people are in this city?"

"People who have been marked for death by Suzair the Great. They're mostly gifted people, so you won't find my old crew, Jasper," informed Ghonllier, reading his mind.

"So there aren't families?" responded Jasper's father.

"On the contrary, the city is made up of mostly families," answered Ghonllier.

"What about my work? Do you need my skills?" asked his father.

"What do you do?" asked Dapper.

"I work with energy, cold fusion. I repair and design energy fixtures."

"We can use you. I'll get you a job," responded Ghonllier. The couple looked at each other. "Please don't feel like you need to give me an answer right now. You need to talk it over with the rest of your family. But if you decide not to join us, we can't have you telling anyone about us."

"If you decide to join us, it will take us about twenty-four hours after we arrive to bring your house into our dimension," informed Dapper.

The mother looked at her husband and he gave her a solemn expression. Ghonllier started to answer his questions. "If you join us, your town will never see you again. Your home and you will disappear and they will assume the KOGN came back."

Letting out a sigh, he revealed, "That might be good. The town is so afraid of us and I'm tired of it."

"Jasper can contact us when you're ready to let us know your final decision. In the meantime, we'll be moving in right next to you, unseen," said Ghonllier.

"Please thank the new Master of the Stones on behalf of my family for being concerned about our welfare. We'll seriously consider your offer," stated Jasper's father.

Jasper's mother stood up and everyone joined her. Smiling, she came forward to give Ghonllier a hug. "Thank you for saving my family's lives. Jasper told us so much about what you did. I'm grateful to you."

Releasing her from the hug, Ghonllier assured, "We think so much of Jasper. We are here because of your sufferings."

She wiped away a few more tears and nodded. Looking at her son, she hugged him. "I'm so glad you went with General Dapper. Normally, I would've been furious. You made the right decision at a tough time in your life."

Jasper smiled, hugging her, while Jasper's father put his hand out to Ghonllier and said, "Thank you so much. We'll let you know."

They passed Dapper and repeated the same thanks to him. The mother leaned in and kissed Dapper on the cheek. It surprised Gostler and he almost lost Dapper's look. She didn't notice Gostler's struggle because she went back to kiss Ghonllier. "Thank you, Commander, for getting permission for us to join you."

"Madam, it's the least I could do. Our boys are good friends and I would like it to continue," smiled Ghonllier.

Dapper opened the door and the couple exited. Ghonllier stopped them. "If we're going to be neighbors, will you please tell me your names?"

The parents laughed. "Our names are Barney and Louise, and welcome to the neighborhood," smiled Barney.

"Thank you for welcoming us. We're glad to be here," replied Ghonllier, reaching out to accept a handshake.

They left and those inside the ship watched the small family melt into the night. Gostler secured the door while Ghonllier went back to the pilot's seat to enter the coordinates for the ship. Gostler joined him.

When Ghonllier finished, he looked past Gostler and through the window. Ghonllier stared at Dapper's crash site.

Reading his mind, Gostler stated, "Ghonllier, break the tie to that picture. It isn't healthy for you to keep going over that moment. It was Dapper's choice to leave you the way he did. It wasn't your fault."

Ghonllier looked away and started the ship. *I forgive myself for putting Dapper in that kind of decision,* thought Ghonllier, lifting the ship off the ground.

Chapter 9

The Letter

*W*hen Ghonllier and Sooner arrived home, they stayed by Sunna's side. Entering her room, Sooner politely requested Cid's staff to leave so they could take care of her. Ghonllier applied the patches that Cid made as Sooner entertained her. At first, it made Sunna feel uncomfortable for Ghonllier to see her so sick. Seeing the love and support in both Ghonllier and Sooner's eyes made the whole experience worth it.

Sunna was sick for about eight hours. It went better than Cid had thought. It didn't stop him from giving her fluids. With them being in space, Sunna's body had problems. Once Sunna stopped expelling the poison, she slept for a long time. Ghonllier and Sooner stayed close by and watched her. It was good bonding time for the father and son as they played games near Sunna's bed.

The next morning, Sunna awoke feeling stronger. Sooner and Ghonllier were pleased to see Sunna with some energy and good color to her skin. As the day wore on, Sunna's energy increased as the new family spent the day together. This time allowed the family to gel together as they talked and played games.

When Sunna awoke the following day, it felt different to her. Ghonllier moved back the drapes to show the clouds back up in the sky. She smiled to see it. It was like an old friend, knowing they were on land. School was still out, with the city getting back to being in its proper place.

Looking back at Ghonllier, Sunna asked, "How long did I sleep? The lights indicate it's late morning."

Ghonllier smiled. "You didn't sleep that long. The time is different here. Everyone is going to be confused for a couple of days."

"Well it's good to see our sky."

"It's good to see you with some color back in your skin."

The two gazed tenderly into each other's eyes as Ghonllier commanded the drawers to open. He requested a white lightweight shirt to floated out of the drawer and came to him. He snatched it out of the air, causing his robe to slightly open. From this view, it showed Ghonllier had only his pants on with the belt of the Master Stones just above his pants. He looked at his shirt and then at her.

"Still walking around exposing those Stones, I see," teased Sunna.

He grinned at her. "Are you afraid?"

"Should I be?" she countered.

Ghonllier allowed his robe to fall off his shoulders and floated it back to the bathroom, while he pulled the shirt over his head. When he finished, Ghonllier gazed into Sunna's eyes before he headed for the bathroom. They kept their gaze on each other as he paused by her nightstand. He picked up her container and disappeared into the bathroom. Sunna could hear water running as he returned a moment later. Taking the container, she questioned, "I need this?"

"Your body needs it and I'm leaving," smiled Ghonllier.

After Sunna took a gulp, they heard a knock at the door. "Who's there?" asked Sunna, moving the container away from her lips.

"Your son," answered Ghonllier, mentally opening the door.

Sooner entered and greeted his parents. Smiling, Sunna handed Ghonllier the container and opened her arms to Sooner. Ghonllier sat her empty container down while Sooner crawled into her arms. After becoming comfortable, he gave his father a pleased grin.

Smiling, Ghonllier inquired, "Did you come for just this?"

"No. Jasper's father, Barney, wants to talk to you," Sooner said, bringing his hand out of his pocket to expose his C-stone. "Is Jasper going to join us?"

Not responding to his question, Ghonllier took the C-Stone and requested, "Make sure your mother gets more water, would you?" Then he stepped away from the bed and greeted, "Good morning, Barney. How's the family?"

"We're good and ready to talk further with you about your proposition. May we meet with Dapper and you again in the grove of trees?"

"When do you want to meet?"

"Are you comfortable with fifteen minutes?"

"Yes, I'll see you there," answered Ghonllier, returning to the bed to give Sooner back his C-stone. He found the boy gone, along with the container from the nightstand. They heard the water running as Ghonllier gazed into Sunna's eyes.

When Sooner returned, he handed the container to his mother as Sunna asked, "How long will you be this time?"

"Not long."

Sooner looked at him and inquired, "Is Jasper's family coming with us?"

Ghonllier handed him his C-stone and didn't answer his question. "Sooner, would you go down to the dining room and get Gostler. Tell him Barney wants to meet with us now."

"Is Jasper going to be joining us?" repeated Sooner, putting the C-Stone in his pocket.

"Yes," smiled his father. "Congratulations, Son. Jasper and you will be going to the same school."

"Yes!" shouted Sooner, running for the door.

Sooner exited with Ghonllier mentally closing the door. Looking back at Sunna, he stated, "You're wondering how much you'll be able to do today?"

"Yes."

"Go ahead and start exercising, if you go to the roof. I'll come back and walk with you . . ." Reading her mind, he added, "If you like, we can have breakfast there, too."

Smiling, she replied, "I'd love that." Ghonllier reached down to the bed and picked up his uniform top. "Thank you for staying by my side," said Sunna. "Is all the poison gone?"

Ghonllier nodded while slipping his I-Force uniform top over his shoulders. Then he sat next to Sunna on the edge of the bed. Leaning over her, he kissed her good-bye. Standing, he responded, "I'll be back soon."

"I'm going to miss you."

"I'll hurry back," replied Ghonllier, leaving the room. As he reached the door, his weapons belt floated out of the closet. Without missing a step, he exited the room with it.

Jason's right. He does like that belt. He doesn't need it, thought Sunna as she stretched. *If it were me, I would leave it home.*

Ghonllier didn't stop again until he reached the front door. Gostler leaned against the door, waiting in the same I-Force uniform. Seeing Ghonllier, he stated, "How much longer do I need to be Dapper and be in a uniform? I keep thinking I'm through."

"I promise, this is your last time," informed Ghonllier, opening the front door.

A huge bouquet of flowers blocked their exit. Being aware of who was behind the flowers, Ghonllier cajoled, "Spencer, flowers, how nice."

The flowers moved to the side to expose Spencer's face. "Commander Ghonllier," replied Spencer. "I didn't hear the door open. These flowers are for my superior. Sarah mentioned when I stopped by yesterday that Sunna was having a hard time. I hope she feels better today. Do you know what her condition is this morning?"

"You ought to ask Cid that question. He's her medic," informed Ghonllier, passing him.

Spencer entered the house while Ghonllier paused to watch him disappear with the flowers. Once he was gone, Ghonllier and Gostler continued on their way.

"Why didn't you answer his question about her? You know better than Cid how she was doing," asked Gostler.

"I won't talk about Sunna to anyone outside of our circle. If anyone wants information about her, they won't get it from me."

"Is that your plan?"

"Yes. I'm handling it the same way I did in the past. I wasn't a source of information about Sunna and I'm not going to start it."

Gostler nodded. "Does it bother you that he is giving your wife flowers?"

"Do the moons revolve around this planet?" Ghonllier answered sarcastically.

"You're good. I really thought you didn't care."

"Thank you," responded Ghonllier, looking at the shield as they walked.

"What are you going to do when Sunna feels better and she goes back to work? Spencer isn't going to believe all of sudden she doesn't like horseback riding with him."

"We'll take one day at a time," countered Ghonllier, looking at Gostler. "We haven't talked about it. Sunna isn't emotionally ready to face it right now. She's still in shock of having Sooner and I always there crowding her space."

Ghonllier headed between two buildings. He paused just past the building and stared at the shield. Gostler watched him before he asked, "Is this where they are waiting for us?" Ghonllier nodded. "Where are they meeting us?"

"Right in the middle of a grove of trees," said Ghonllier, moving toward the edge of the shield. He was feeling the energy wavelengths of the shield before he matched it. Being in harmony, he passed through the shield with Gostler following him.

When they exited, Barney and Louise had just arrived and were startled to see Ghonllier and Dapper appearing from an unseen place. Coming forward, Louise greeted, "Thank you for coming."

"We'll come anytime you want, if we're here," replied Dapper.

"How soon can we join you?" inquired Barney, joining his wife.

"Are you sure about it?" questioned Ghonllier.

Louise nodded. "It was unanimous. We're tired of being excluded. It's hard and our children are taking the brunt of it."

"I quit work this morning," informed Barney.

"We'll start today to pull your home into our protective shield," responded Dapper.

"Do we need to do anything?" asked Barney.

"No, just relax and watch the sky. When you see a huge cloud with light shining through it, you'll see our homes soon after. Contact us as soon as you would like. We'll introduce you to some of your new neighbors," smiled Dapper.

"When Jasper calls, we'll pick you up and bring your family to our home," assured Ghonllier. "You'll need to meet my mother, since the two of you will probably be talking a lot together."

Louise smiled, "Please tell His Grace, thank you."

"I will," smiled Ghonllier.

Barney reached out for his wife's hand and they left. Gostler and Ghonllier watched them walk through the trees. Louise looked over her shoulder to see if they were really still there. Ghonllier didn't move, knowing she needed reassurance.

The minute she was satisfied, Ghonllier left with Dapper beside him. Gostler asked Ghonllier a question and he didn't answer. Looking at him, Gostler saw Ghonllier in a trance. It meant he was in a discussion with the Stones. The former Master knew not to bother him during this time.

He kept glancing at him and was concerned with Ghonllier's expression. The new Master glanced at him. Without thinking, Gostler asked, "Ghonllier, is there a problem?"

Ghonllier answered, "Yes. We need to have an emergency meeting now. Call Father and tell him to have Jason there. We're on our way to his office now."

Gostler reached into his pocket as Ghonllier walked across a pathway. Adamite and Gostler finished their conversation as they arrived at the office building. When they entered his office, Adamite and Jason were already waiting for them. Immediately, Adamite shut the doors, using his Moveling abilities, while everyone waited for Ghonllier to speak.

Quietly, he paced behind one of the couches. Adamite leaned over to Gostler, wanting to know what the meeting was about. Gostler shook his head, as he watched Ghonllier.

Getting impatient, Adamite asked, "Son! Does this have to do with Gomper?"

Ghonllier faced his father. "In a way, yes. Do you remember when we talked about Gomper's baby?"

Adamite went white. "Has the baby been born? Does Bog have him?"

"No, he's close to being born and Bog has spies watching the mother."

"Why?" asked Jason.

"He plans on taking the baby so he can transfer the curse to him, stopping me."

"How?" asked Adamite.

"He'll bring the curse back after I'm not the Master of the Galaxy."

"Can he do that without his stepping stone?" asked Jason.

Ghonllier sighed before he answered, "The curse will transfer and will come out at the same age as when Bog put it on his daughter."

"You won't be the Master," reminded Gostler.

Ghonllier nodded. "It will quickly go out of control, killing everyone in the galaxy but the Master whoever he is."

"Will he be able to stop it?" asked Jason.

"No."

"You never told me that Bog knew about the baby!" demanded Adamite.

"I know. The stepping stone informed Bog that she would get pregnant if he had Gomper force himself onto her that night. After they left, Bog sent spies to watch her to see if she went through the pregnancy. Spies have been sending reports into Gomper's office and he has no idea that they're talking about his own son," replied Ghonllier. Watching his father's expressions, he added, "Bog has ordered the spies to pick the baby up the moment he's born and bring him to Gomper so the curse will transfer. Killing Gomper."

"No!" snapped Adamite. "I want that boy."

Ghonllier looked at Jason and ordered, "Get my ship ready to leave within the hour."

"Who do you want?" asked Jason.

"Family and Cid . . . bring no other medical staff with us. I don't want anyone to see what we are about to do."

"What are you going to do?" asked Adamite.

Ghonllier ignored his question and headed for the door. As he left, Ghonllier reminded his father that he better tell his mother about the event. The new Master could read from his father's thoughts that he was coming with him and Stacy knew nothing about her grandson.

He wanted to go talk with Sunna. She was waiting for him on the roof. He used his Vanishers speed to arrive at the steps of his home. He appeared in time to see Spencer exiting the house.

Ghonllier nodded at him as he passed. *GHONLLIER. INVITE SPENCER TO GO WITH YOU.*

Not taking the time to question the Stones, Ghonllier stopped to look for Spencer. He was about to step off of the last step, when he stopped him. Ghonllier was surprised that Spencer readily accepted his offer. The new Master could see that Spencer wanted to go every time with Ghonllier so he could earn points faster. Spencer wanted to become a general so he could ask Sunna to marry him again. He felt their rank had something to do with her indifference toward him.

Watching him leave, Ghonllier wondered why the Master Stones wanted him to join them. He really didn't want Spencer there with the baby and he wasn't planning on taking Sunna. Thinking about it, he entered the house and went directly to the roof to tell her about his change of plans.

Being on the roof, Sunna didn't hear Ghonllier exit the lift. She was on the opposite end of the roof, enjoying her leisure walk along the stream. The house had a garden on the roof and a stream to water the plants before it cascaded down to the reflection pool in the garden.

Softly, she heard, "YOU'RE SO BEAUTIFUL. I LOVE YOU."

Sunna jerked her head to the side to see no one there. Stopping, she looked around to see she was alone. When she went to resume her walk, Sunna found Ghonllier blocking her way. Instantly, she put her arms around his neck and kissed him. After a couple of kisses, Sunna smiled at him and expressed, "I'm glad you sent me up here. I didn't know that your parents had such a beautiful garden on top of their home. It's a romantic place to have breakfast. Are you hungry?"

Ghonllier looked over at the table waiting for them. "Honey. Something has come up and I need to leave right now."

"Leave where?"

"Space. I need to intervene with Bog trying to stop me from reversing the curse."

"When do we leave?"

"Now. I wasn't going to ask you to do go . . ."

"Who are you taking?"

"Cid and family. None of my elite force is coming."

"Then I want to go. We can be together . . ."

"It could be hard on your health . . ." interjected Ghonllier.

"I want to be with you."

Ghonllier nodded. "My heart wants you there, too."

Gabala appeared out of the lift to find out what they wanted to eat for breakfast. Ghonllier apologized for not eating. He explained that he was leaving with Gostler and his father. Gabala nodded and brought his bracket up to page staff to remove the table.

Ghonllier put his arm around Sunna and answered her questions to why they were leaving. By the time, they reached their room. Staff members were waiting to help them pack. Ghonllier kissed Sunna and left to go talk with Cid. He didn't know that he was leaving and Ghonllier wanted to speak to him personally.

When Ghonllier retuned, the staff was leaving with their things. She came over to Ghonllier and put her arms around his neck. She expressed, "Thank you for the flowers."

Ghonllier looked at them and answered, "Sunna. I did not give you the flowers. They came from Spencer . . ."

"Spencer!"

"Yes . . . I can see he's on his way over here to give you a letter."

"Why?"

"He's coming with us on this flight. I was told by the Stones to bring him and I don't know why."

Sunna stepped back. "Why would they do that?"

Ghonllier wished he had an answer for her. It was confusing to him, too. Before he could answer her, Cid entered the room with a gurney. Sunna looked between the two men in horror.

"Why is that here?"

The Master stepped toward her and said, "Spencer is on his way here to tell you something. Do you want to greet him looking and feeling well?"

Sunna sighed knowing Spencer would be everywhere she was and she wasn't ready to face him. The thought seemed to drain away her newly found energy.

Cid expressed, "Sunna. This gurney came form the emergency shuttle. It's waiting for the two of us. Maybe we can get you out of here before Spencer arrives."

Sunna nodded as she headed for the gurney. Ghonllier picked her up in his arms and sat her on it. She asked, "Where are we going?"

"The Omattures moon."

"What's on the Omattures moon?"

The new Master did not want to discuss it in front of Cid. So he promised to tell her later so she could leave for their ship now. Sunna laid down while Cid covered her up with a blanket and requested the safety straps. Ghonllier and her held hands until Cid was ready to take her to the emergency shuttle.

When Sunna left the room, Ghonllier looked over at the flowers from Spencer and wondered how this was going to turn out. Spencer was definitely going to cause a problem for them. He had been asking the Stones about how to handle it and they told him not to worry about it. They promised him that it would all work out.

A knock came to the door and Ghonllier opened it. Gabala asked him if he was ready to leave for his ship. He nodded knowing the staff had already placed their bags in the transport. Ghonllier told him to bring in around to the front of the house and he would be there.

He wanted to take a moment and talk with Sooner. Using the Stones, he explained to his son that Sunna and he were going into space. He promised that he would return shortly and Sooner assured him that he would rather stay home.

Letting out a sigh, Ghonllier left his room to meet Gabala out front. As he walked to the lift, he saw Gabala had already taken his father and Gostler out to the ship. He could see that Jason was bringing Asustie. It pleased him to have his sister with him. For some reason, Ghonllier didn't understand. He always wanted Asustie to fly with him. Maybe, it was because they hadn't grown up together and it gave them time to be together.

Ghonllier attempted to exit the house when he heard his son calling after him. Sooner ran up reminding him of Jasper and his family coming into their dimension. The new Master apologized to him and asked Sooner to express it to them. Then he requested Sooner head up the party and help Gabala plan it. He told him to invite his grandmother but she would be busy getting a room ready for a baby. Ghonllier didn't tell Sooner that the baby was a relative. It was something he wanted to explain, when he had enough time to answer all of his questions. Sooner could possible have a lot.

Father and son had finished when he heard a commotion outside. Sooner would not be able to hear it. Ghonllier's hearing was far better than his son's, now he had the Master Stones. Ghonllier watched Sooner leave as he listened to the scuffle outside.

He saw with the Stones that Cid had Sunna in the emergency shuttle when Spencer arrived at the house. Spencer wanted to give her something and Cid refused to let him in the shuttle. The other medics came to Cid's aid, when Spencer tired to force his way past Cid. He could read that Sunna was upset and so was everyone in involved. In away, he was glad that Sooner had stopped him from going outside. He would've been caught up in the scuffle and he really didn't want to be forced to come to her defense. Spencer might suspect something.

Leaving the house, Ghonllier watched Gabala pace by the transport as he watched Spencer. He was standing not to far from the transport, looking up in the sky. Gabala was relieved to see the commander. When he greeted Ghonllier. Spencer turned to face them.

"Commander?" Ghonllier looked at Spencer at the door of the transport. "Do you mind if I go with you to the ship?"

"No, please join me," offered Ghonllier, entering the transport.

Gabala waited for Spencer before he shut the door. Cid, Ghonllier and Sunna's bags rested against his leg. Spencer stared at them before he leaned forward, rubbing his hands together. Ghonllier asked the Master Stones one more time, if he could tell the Tron about their marriage. The answer came back, "NO," and Ghonllier decided not to read his thoughts.

After Gabala drove away from the house, Ghonllier heard Spencer sit up and he looked at him. Spencer spoke, "Thank you, Commander, for the ride."

Ghonllier nodded as he happened to pick up Spencer's thoughts. "Spencer. Why did you agree to go with me on this mission?"

"Why did you ask?"

"I knew you were trying to pick up extra points."

"I'm close to becoming a general. I'll go anywhere with you so I can earn my points faster."

Ghonllier smiled and said, "I remember when I was in a hurry. . . ."

"I've heard about you, Commander. I researched how you received your commission so fast. You took on some very dangerous missions."

As Ghonllier asked why he wanted to hurry, the new Master could see it was more about Sunna. Quickly he shut down his ability to read his mind. He was about to look away when Spencer reached into his vest pocket and pulled out an envelope. The Tron held it out to him. "Commander. Would you please give this to Sunna?" Ghonllier accepted it as Spencer added, "Why is Sunna here then? I was told by Jason she wasn't coming."

"I told Jason that she wasn't coming. But when I ordered Cid to come . . ."

"Sunna needed Cid," finished Spencer.

"Probably so," said Ghonllier, leaning back.

Spencer went back to staring at the bags. Ghonllier looked out the window, finding it hard to talk to Spencer about Sunna. He was relieved to see the *Liberty Quest* in the distance. When Gabala stopped, Spencer grabbed his bag and left the transport first. Ghonllier and Gabala exchanged looks as he exited with everyone's bags. Reading his mind, Ghonllier assured, "It's okay, Gabala. You did the right thing."

"Thank you," nodded Gabala.

Ghonllier headed for his ship while Gabala returned to the driver's seat.

After boarding his ship, Ghonllier took his time leaving the OSA. The only people entering the room were the medics from the shuttle, leaving with Sunna's gurney. The men slightly nodded in acknowledgment as they passed him. He watched them leave the OSA before he shut the door to his compartment.

He had mentally told the captains that he was there. So when the medics cleared the ramp, the captains started to seal up the ship so they could leave. Ghonllier left to greet Cid exiting from Sunna's door. He paused, giving Ghonllier a concerned expression. Then he continued toward the Med-C. The new Master was well aware of what had him so upset. Now, he was going to learn how the scene with Spencer was affecting Sunna.

He opened the door and quickly shut it behind him. Sunna ran to his arms. Tightly, she wrapped her arms around his neck, burying her face into his neck. He mentally sent their bags to the dressing areas so he could hold her. Softly, he asked, "I'm sorry Sunna that you didn't get away in time."

"Oh, Ghonllier. Spencer was so angry to see me with Cid"

"I know. He's heard about the rumor about Cid and you."

"Why was he so upset? It's happened before and I never seen him act this way before."

"Maybe, this will tell you way," educated Ghonllier, removing Spencer's envelope from his pocket.

Sunna stared at the paper envelope. Then she looked up at him. "What is he giving me?"

"A letter."

"How did you get it?"

"With Cid telling him that he had to get his permission to see or talk with you, he decided that I could superceded Cid."

Sunna lamented at it and shook her head. "Ghonllier. What does it say?"

"You need to read it yourself." Ghonllier sent it to the nightstand and took her into his arms. "You're too upset to read it now. Let's easy your stress."

She thought about how he had done that in the past and Sunna smiled. Ghonllier leaned in for a kiss. Sunna kissed him back. Then he picked her up in his arms and carried her to the bed. They stopped kissing and gazed into each other's eyes. *With Spencer on board, I don't want to leave this room. Will you be able to stay here with me?* Sunna thought. Ghonllier nodded, reading her mind.

Gently, he let go of her and she floated down to the bed. Ghonllier joined her as they went back to kissing. Suddenly, he stopped and looked at the doors.

She followed his gaze. "What is wrong?"

"Jason needs me to give the captains the exact coordinates to the Omatture Moon." Then he looked at her. "Would you excuse for a moment to give all of my instructions. Then I'll stay here with you for the whole trip."

"Good," grinned Sunna.

Ghonllier got up and left closing his door behind him. In at the corridor, he saw Spencer coming from the commander center. Letting out a sigh, Ghonllier headed in the same direction. Spencer called out to him.

"Commander."

He stopped to wait for Spencer to come to him since he could read his mind. When he arrived, Ghonllier greeted, "Spencer."

"I've written an note of apology to Sunna and I wondered if you would give it to her."

Ghonllier did not like the idea that he was quickly becoming a channel to her. So he responded, "I'll give it to Cid. He's her medic right now."

"Will he give it to her?"

Ghonllier nodded. "I promise she will get it."

Spencer shoved the vanishing paper into his hand and stated, "Please get this to her."

"I'll do it after I speak with Commander Jason."

Ghonllier stepped around him and continued onto the command center, while Spencer watched him disappear. Then he entered the dining room to get something to eat.

Arriving in the command center, Ghonllier noticed Gostler and his father at the message center, talking. They stopped when Ghonllier entered and stared at him while he walked over to the NV table.

They joined him and Gostler asked, "Are we going to see each other on a regular basis on this trip?"

"Probably not," countered Ghonllier, retrieving vanishing paper from the NV table.

Gostler and Adamite exchanged looks while he wrote down the coordinates. They watched him leave to hand them to the captain. "Sam, here you go. Tell Jason that I want a meeting right before we come out of jump speed. Will you announce it," informed Ghonllier, readying to leave.

"Commander!" Butler said, stopping him. Ghonllier looked at him. "Who do you want at the meeting?" he inquired.

"I want everyone but Spencer. You both need to be there."

The captains nodded. This time Ghonllier left.

"Take care, Son," said Adamite, watching him walk past him. Mentally, he added, *Take care of Sunna, too.*

Ghonllier smiled at them picking up on his father's words. Sunna and he hadn't had a honeymoon. They were hoping this flight would give them one. With Spencer, he made it a little harder. He reached into his pocket to remove the vanishing paper from the Tron.

Ghonllier entered the Med-C so he could keep his promise to Spencer. He went to Cid's quarters and knocked on the door. Cid opened the door to see Ghonllier holding up the vanishing paper.

"Give this to Sunna," ordered Ghonllier.

"Is this from you?" quizzed Cid, with questioning eyes.

"Spencer," answered Ghonllier, leaving.

The corridor was empty when Ghonllier returned. When he opened his door, he found Sunna leaning against the headboard, writing.

"What are you doing?" he asked, seeing her mood had completely changed.

"I finally read Spencer's letters," commented Sunna, staring at letter.

"Are you upset?"

Sunna looked at him and asked, "He says that he wants to talk to me when he gets back being on his mission with you about us. He wants to know if he can become closer to me. . . . Where is he going with this?"

"He's been upset to see you almost die twice. He wants to know if you have changed your thoughts about your career. Do you want a personal life? He wanted you to know that he would be a general soon and maybe, you would you consider him? He doesn't want you taking anymore-dangerous missions. He still loves you and he wants to get married . . ."

Ghonllier drifted off, seeing Spencer had asked her before. Sunna had turned him down. Spencer had been in love with Sunna for years and for some reason. He couldn't get her out of his system. The new Master liked Spencer and he felt for him. He knew what it was like to be love with a woman who you might not see again.

He debated about telling her about the second letter, when they heard Cid enter her room, requesting entrance to theirs.

"Come in, Cid, it's okay," greeted Sunna.

Cid entered their room with the new letter. He glanced at Ghonllier before handing it to Sunna. Ghonllier knew he wanted to know what was in the letter, since he had the fight with Spencer.

"What's this?" questioned Sunna, taking it.

"It's another letter from Spencer," answered Ghonllier.

She looked at the folded letter. "Why is he giving me another one?"

"Read it Sunna. I think it will help you understand Spencer," answered Ghonllier.

Slowly, she opened it and started to read. Ghonllier already knew about the contents of the letter and listened to Sunna's feelings as she read.

When she finished, she looked up. Cid asked, "What does it say?"

"I'll read it to you. Then I want both of your opinions on how I should answer him."

"Okay," said Cid.

Sunna read:

My dearest Sunna,

I'm so sorry for what happened at the shuttle. Please forgive me. I didn't mean to make a scene. I didn't realize you were going on this mission and I was coming to the house to tell you that I was leaving with Commander Ghonllier. I had it in a letter that I wanted to give you myself.

Since your first accident, I've felt shut out of your life. I've been so worried about what you've been through. It upsets me that I can't get to you to learn how you're feeling after these near death experiences. We used to talk and I miss my friend.

Seeing you go through your first near death made me want to be more than a co-worker again. I thought my feelings had changed for you, but I've been lying to myself. I need to know if you have any romantic feelings for me. Is there any change in your desires to have a life outside of work?

Sunna, I'll do anything for you, even leave my career, if it was the only way we could be together. If you are ready for a change in your career, I'll be a general soon. I can afford to take care of you if you want me.

If you're still interested in your career, I'll still be honored to be a part of your staff, but I want more and I'm determined to find it somewhere. I hope for what's best for you and I hope to be apart your life somehow. Please let me know how you feel as soon as you can.

I love you and a friend always,

Spencer

Sunna put the letter down and stared at her husband. Ghonllier wouldn't look at her, knowing she wanted to know his feelings. Now wasn't the time. Ghonllier knew Sunna had to search her own feelings and not rely on him. If she didn't handle this right, Spencer would always haunt her and it would probably hurt their working relationship.

Cid broke their silence. "What are you going to do?"

"I started to write something because I suspected Spencer wanted more than just friendship. Would you men like to hear it and give me your opinion?" asked Sunna.

"Sunna, tell me first what you want to accomplish with your letter," said Ghonllier, looking at her.

"I want him to move on with his personal life and stop wanting me to be apart of it. Spencer's friendship is important and I don't want to lose him."

"You can't have both," replied Cid.

"I want to be friends with him like I am with you Cid. We were kids . . . somehow, we stayed friends. I don't mind working with him, if he stops wanting more from me."

Ghonllier stayed quiet, reading Cid had a crush on Sunna as children. They went to school together. She liked him, too, but she stayed true to her promise to the Master Stones. When she started to have feelings for him, she cut them off, hurting Cid. Being young, Cid got over Sunna and moved on.

Cid brought him back, when he heard, "Well let's hear what you have so far."

Sunna read:

My dear friend Spencer,

You have no idea just how much it meant to me to hear you say that you love me. I'm sorry that my accidents have made it difficult for us to renew our friendship, since you transferred here. I've always been fond of you and that hasn't changed. Despite my difficulty with Commander Ghonllier, I can say this has been my favorite assignment. I enjoy being in charge of Justin's spies and I'm looking forward to getting back to work. Thank you for helping General Humphrey to keep the job going in my absence.

I'm sorry I couldn't tell you in person that there have been some changes in my life. For the first time in my career, I'm staying close to my family. The near death experiences have changed me there. Being close to those you love is important.

I still deeply love my career. The near death experiences have taught me that I need balance in my life. I'm satisfied right now with pursuing and developing my relationship with my family. I'm not interested in pursuing anything deeper in my personal life than what I already have.

I would like you to stay and work as my assistant. I hope you find the peace and happiness in that role. It's obvious; you're a man who needs to be married. I would like you to find that person. Please forgive me for not being her. I wish I could, but I'm not.

I'll always love you as a brother. You've been a good friend over the years and I cherish our relationship dearly. I would like to be able to count on you as a valuable co-worker, but I do understand if you want to leave.

Thank you for your concerns and friendship. I value both of them deeply.

Your friend always,
Sunna

She looked at Ghonllier first, wanting his approval. Seeing she wrote what was truly in her heart, he smiled and responded, "Very good, honey. I like it."

"Do you think it will help him move on and keep his friendship?"

"Yes, if he wants it to," commented Cid. "It's a good letter."

"I have some mistakes, Cid. Let me rewrite it before we give it to him."

"Let me know," said Cid, leaving.

Ghonllier decided to go into the bathroom, waiting for Sunna to finish. He took his time. When he came out, Sunna was re-reading her words.

"We never ate breakfast. Would you like me to go get you something?" asked Ghonllier.

"Yes."

"What would you like?"

"Get me the breakfast special," answered Sunna, handing him the letter.

Taking the letter, Ghonllier slipped it into his top uniform pocket and left. Entering the Med-C, Cid was there. The two men exchanged looks as Cid took the letter. Without a word, Ghonllier left and headed for the dining room.

He was pleased to run into Jason and Asustie exiting. "Asustie, would you help me with Sunna's breakfast?" asked Ghonllier.

"Sure."

"How is she doing?" whispered Jason, following Ghonllier and Asustie to the counter. "We saw the gurney. I thought . . ."

Ghonllier interrupted, "IT WAS FOR SPENCER'S BENEFIT."

Jason leaned into him and whispered, "Do you know why he is here?"

"No."

While Jason waited for Ghonllier and Asustie to get Sunna and his breakfast, he noticed Cid entering the room, heading for Spencer. He sat alone at a table, drinking from a container.

Without a word, the medic dropped the letter on the table and left. Spencer didn't watch Cid leave. Instead, he stared at the letter on the table. Slowly, he picked it up.

Ghonllier lightly nudged Jason to let him know that they were leaving. Jason wanted to watch Spencer read the letter, so he walked slowly. Spencer finished reading it before they exited. He lightly tapped the letter on the back of his other hand, staring at it.

Out in the corridor, Jason stepped close to Ghonllier and whispered, "What is going on between Cid and Spencer?"

"Why do you think anything is going on?"

"Cid and Spencer don't seem to be too friendly toward each other."

Stopping in front of their quarters, Ghonllier glanced down the empty corridor before he whispered, "They had a fight on the way to the ship."

"Why?"

"Over your sister," answered Ghonllier as he watched Asustie enter Sooner's door with Sunna's food. Then he opened his door.

The two men entered and Ghonllier shut the door.

Chapter 10

A Baby

No one saw Ghonllier during the trip, expect when he came out to get food from the pantry or galley in the dining room. Sunna wasn't seen at all. When they were about to come out of jump speed at the Omattures moon, the captains announced the meeting like Ghonllier requested. Sam especially was looking forward to the meeting, wondering exactly what was going to be expected of him this time.

It bothered Spencer that he wasn't asked to be at the meeting, but he was relieved to hear that Cid wasn't invited either. He wondered why Ghonllier had requested Cid, if he wasn't being called to the meeting.

Asustie was pleased Spencer wasn't at the meeting. She needed something from the galley and couldn't get it without someone in the military. To use the galley, you had to be scanned into the ship so the stones could read your energy waves. The other problem with not being scanned into the ship was that the captains didn't know where to direct pages for you. Therefore, if they wanted you, the message went over the ship's con-speakers. Asustie strongly disliked being paged to the meeting over the loudspeakers.

Everyone called to the meeting waited quietly for Ghonllier to join them. Though, soon, someone entered the room from the corridor and everyone looked over, expecting it to be Ghonllier. They were surprised to see Sunna.

Jason stood to move out a chair next to him. "Sister, I didn't expect you to be here. How do you feel?"

"Stronger. I thought I would surprise you all and come to the meeting," divulged Sunna, searching for Ghonllier. She didn't tell him.

"Is this permanent? Are you going to be out and about from now on?" asked Gostler.

"I don't know," stated Sunna, sitting. "I thought I would try today and see how I do."

"Did you see Ghonllier out there anywhere on your travels?" asked Adamite.

"No, I expected him to be here."

Adamite looked at his timepiece and was getting nervous. The concept that he was about to see a grandchild seemed unreal to him. He thought about Gomper and wished they were picking him up, too. He missed his son so much and didn't realize it until now. They had so much joy with Gomper's birth and so much pain losing him. Adamite hoped that the experience with this grandson would ease some of their pain of losing so many children.

Suddenly, the door between the office and conference room opened, interrupting Adamite's thoughts. Ghonllier entered, carrying a thin, flat container in his hand. At the same moment of entry, he apologized. "Please forgive me for making you wait. I needed to take care of something with Justin before we started this meeting." Closing the door, he stopped and blurted, "Sunna, you're here! Are you up to this?" He really had no idea that she was going to be there.

Sunna refused to look at him. With Sam there, she was concerned that her feelings for him might show on her face. She smiled, for it did please her to hear Ghonllier genuinely surprised. She did take a quick glance to see his equally surprised expression.

The couple decided not to act like friends, even in front of family, so they wouldn't ever make a mistake in front of the crew. Today would determine how well she could pull it off with a few members of the crew.

Ghonllier didn't look away, but held his gaze on her for a few moments longer. Moving to his seat, he said, "I'm glad you're here, Commander Sunna. And since you are, I'll add this to our meeting and get started with it now."

He let go of the thin metal container in his hand, sending it to Jason. The commander plucked it out of the air and smiled. "Where did you get this?" he asked.

Sam answered, "I found it. Commander Houser gave it to me, along with Sunna's new commander uniforms, while we were on the *Liberty Pursuit*. Since we were the only ones on board, I put the container in a drawer and forgot about it. I happened onto it and gave it to Commander Ghonllier." Sam looked at Sunna. "I'm sorry, Commander. I should've given it to you with your uniforms."

Sunna smiled, gazing at the container in Jason's hand. Ghonllier sat while he expressed, "Jason, I feel you should handle this, since you're the official Commander of the *Liberty Quest*."

"Thank you, Ghonllier," replied Jason, standing. Looking at his sister, he ordered, "Stand, Sunna, and take the swearing-in as a full-fledged commander on the *Liberty Quest*."

Sunna stood, facing Jason. He raised his hand and she mirrored him. "Commander Sunna, as commander of the *Liberty Quest*, I'm asking you to give an oath to the security and safety of those on board this ship, that you will do your best to execute your job at all times, and that you'll always be loyal to I-Force and will fight to preserve our freedoms."

"I do," replied Sunna.

"Welcome aboard, Commander. From now on, the ship will read your commission as commander," Jason grinned. The two saluted and Jason handed her the plaque. Sunna took it and smiled at her brother. He broke military protocol and gave her a hug. "Congratulations, Sister. This is a great achievement."

"Thanks, Jason," responded Sunna, overcome with emotion.

"Sister, I'm pleased to have the opportunity to swear you in. I'm grateful we're together."

She flickered him a glance as she lovingly ran her fingers over the plaque. To be the first woman to become commander in Special Services had been her goal from the beginning of her career. Now, she had it. Though, being a mother and wife meant more to her and she smiled at the change of heart.

Adamite interrupted her thoughts. "Sunna, congratulations. It's nice to have you alive so you can receive this officially."

Looking at him, she answered, "Thank you, Adamite."

"Sam, make it official in the ship's records," ordered Jason.

"Glad to. Congratulations, Sunna," responded Sam.

She grinned at him. Everyone but Ghonllier wanted to look at it and congratulate Sunna. He sat quietly and watched, disinterested. But Sunna did hear, "CONGRATULATIONS, HONEY, YOU DID EARN IT AND YOU DIDN'T GET IT BECAUSE OF WHO YOU KNEW."

Sunna chuckled, because she told Ghonllier that was how he got his commission. Justin, his father, was their superior until Ghonllier announced his reign to the galaxy. The whole experience started to bring tears to her eyes.

Seeing that she had enough, Ghonllier started the meeting. "People, we're close to our destination and we need to talk about what is about to happen here." Everyone stopped talking and looked over at Ghonllier. Commanding the doors to the monitor to open, Ghonllier continued. "Sam, I want you to indigo beam this woman to the bay."

The monitor showed a woman, her belly big, as though she was about to have a baby at any moment.

"Sir, she looks pregnant. Why are you beaming her to our ship? Why not land and pick her up?" quizzed Sam, looking at Ghonllier.

"Sam, I want you to fly into the place under a code green."

"Why are we going in looking like a KOGN Star Screamer?" expressed Sam.

"Yes, why are you doing this?" asked Jason, curious to hear his reasoning.

"I-Force has our signal. They're not going to believe we're a KOGN ship and they'll shoot anyway, with us listed as a rogue ship. Why are we going in?" questioned Sam.

"Sam, you forgot who he is," answered Jason.

Sam blushed. "Sorry, Commander Ghonllier."

Ghonllier leaned back in his chair and explained, "We're going in under a code green and I'll show you the right woman to beam up. You're going to have to do it on a sweep, no hovering."

"That's dangerous—" said Sam, stopping himself. "But you already know that." His voice drifted off.

"Sam, the Master Stones will work the ship's stones to make sure there isn't a mistake. Just do your job and I'll back you up," assured Ghonllier. He nodded. Ghonllier looked at Jason and added, "Ask me the question so everyone can understand my answer."

Jason glanced over at him. "Why are we acting like a KOGN Star Screamer in an area held by I-Force?"

"I want the KOGN spies watching her to think Suzair the Great took her. So, they won't contact Suzair the Great about the kidnapping," answered Ghonllier, looking around the room. "Once she's on board, I want everyone in KOGN uniforms, including the captains."

"How long do we wear KOGN uniforms?" asked Sam.

"As long as she's on the ship. She needs to believe she's on a KOGN ship."

"Even yourself?" asked Jason.

"Yes."

"What about Cid?" asked Jason.

"Especially Cid. He'll be the one who sees her the most. We should have enough on board that everyone should find one that fits," informed Ghonllier.

"Wait, does it mean all of us?" asked Gostler.

"Especially you, Gostler. I need your abilities as a Mimette to portray someone she knows from KOGN."

"Like who?" asked Gostler suspiciously.

"Your choice is Suzair the Great—"

"NO!"

"Or this man, called Jamham. He is the head of Suzair's household," informed Ghonllier, pointing to the monitor. The monitor showed Jamham's face. Gostler studied the man while Ghonllier continued. "Sam, to answer your question, she'll be walking along a pathway. There will be other people around her, so you do the sweep and I'll guide the beam so we don't accidentally pick up someone else." Sam nodded. "Does anyone have anymore questions?" asked Ghonllier.

"Who's going to be in the delivery room?" asked Jason.

"Cid, Asustie, and I," answered Ghonllier.

"Can I come?" asked Sunna, finally looking at him.

"Sunna, do you have any experience delivering a baby?" Ghonllier asked.

"No, but Asustie doesn't either," reminded Sunna.

Thoughtfully looking at her, he finally said, "Sunna, I can use you in the delivery room, as a guard. It would make us look more authentic. Suzair the Great would have someone there to make sure everything goes the way he wants it." Ghonllier glanced around the room and then added, "If there are no more questions, then this meeting is over."

Everyone stood up but Sunna and Gostler. He was still studying Jamham on the monitor. Sunna stayed seated to avoid Ghonllier. She wanted him to leave first. Sunna felt everyone was watching them, including Sam. It was the newness of her feelings for him and she was grateful not to be engaged to him.

Ghonllier slowly walked past her, watching Gostler master the mannerisms and voice of Jamham. Stopping behind Sunna, he placed his hand on her shoulder. They instantly felt the bonding fires. He expressed, "Congratulations, Commander. I'm glad you're on the team." Then he left.

Cid looked up from his book as he heard footsteps around the wall separating his part of the Med-C from the waiting room. He noticed it was Ghonllier, who took a quick survey of the room while saying, "Cid, I need you to do a job for me."

Putting his book on the counter next to him, he asked, "What do you need?"

"I want you to deliver a baby for me."

Giving him a concerned look, he stood while stating, "We don't have anyone on board who's pregnant. Where are you getting this woman?"

"In less than thirty minutes, we're entering an atmosphere to pick up a woman who's in labor at the moment. I want you to deliver the baby."

"Are you saying she hasn't seen a medical tech yet?"

"No, she has one."

"Then why do you want to land just to have me deliver this baby?"

"Cid, we're going to indigo beam her up so you can deliver the baby."

"We are delivering in space?!"

"Yes."

"Are you crazy, Ghonllier? Do you realize that will cause her to go into fast delivery before her body is ready?!" shouted Cid. "It will kill her and the baby before she can give birth."

"I know. I believe I can control her mind to not panic and stop the chemicals in her body that will kill her."

"Are you positive?" retorted Cid, opening up closets to take a survey of the right equipment. In frustration, he faced Ghonllier. "Footsack, Ghonllier! I can't believe you're doing this and didn't tell me until now."

"Cid, relax. There is no reason for you to get upset. I need you to be calm and stay that way," said Ghonllier in an altered voice, using the Stones.

Cid let out a deep sigh and responded calmly, "Who is this woman and why are you doing this?"

"The woman's name is Suzette and she's carrying my nephew."

He nodded. "Okay, I understand why you're taking the risks."

"I'll set up your room for delivery. I need you to make up a patch for heavy bleeding, shock, and severe pain. I'll show you on the monitor in the medicine room how strong to make the patches," informed Ghonllier.

"I need assistants to successfully handle a dangerous delivery like this. How are you going to handle that?"

"I'm your assistant, Cid. Asustie will be here for the baby," assured Ghonllier.

Cid grunted. "I hope you can pull this off."

Facing the closet, he tossed Ghonllier sterile gowns to wear before leaving to make up the patches. Stopping, Cid asked, "Are you going to show me how bad her bleeding will be?"

"Yes. You'll see her stats on the monitor, as if the delivery is over with," informed Ghonllier.

Cid left, relieved that he did have Ghonllier. *His help's worth five assistants*, thought Cid, disappearing into the medicine room. Taking the gown with him, Ghonllier left to change his clothes. While he was gone, the examination table changed into a birthing chair, with Ghonllier using the Stones. Equipment floated out of the closets and into place.

Using his Vanisher's speed, Ghonllier was dressed and back into the room before everything was set up for delivery. Ghonllier watched everything, surveying the room to make sure the right things were there. Satisfied, he commanded a gurney to come to him. Cid returned with the patches and was surprised to see a privacy screen come out of the wall without anyone pulling it out. He took a quick survey to make sure he had everything he wanted. If he thought about something that wasn't there, the item would float out of its place of storage.

Finally, Cid handed Ghonllier the patches. Just then, Sam announced over the ship's con-speaker that everyone on board was supposed to be dressed in KOGN uniforms until further notice. Cid looked sharply at Ghonllier. "Does that mean me, too?"

"Yes."

"Why KOGN? What are you doing?"

"I want her to think Suzair the Great has her son. Go get ready in your sterile gown. We have ten minutes left," informed Ghonllier.

Cid left while Ghonllier turned on the monitors to view the present status of the baby and mother. He was staring at them when Cid returned. "Cid, I want everyone to wear complete surgery gear."

"No! Not the headgear! They are designed for standing, not moving around."

"We have to, unless—"

"Unless what?"

Ghonllier was quiet and eventually said, "We don't need to wear headgear. The stones just showed me how to erase her memory so she won't remember us or the baby."

Cid looked at the monitors and was pleased to see the stats. The woman was in the beginning stages of labor. "Is this her first baby?" he asked.

"Yes."

The medic faced Ghonllier and stated, "I still think this is cruel, Ghonllier."

"I don't have any choice, Cid. This baby right now is the key to stopping this war."

Suddenly, they heard someone enter the room and Cid turned to see it was Sunna dressed in a KOGN uniform. "Are you going to be here, too?" he snapped.

"Yes."

"She's Suzair the Great's representative. Sunna will be taking the baby to my father."

Cid handed a sterile gown to Sunna. "Give this to Asustie when you see her."

She took it, looking at Ghonllier's back. Right now, she wanted him to hold her and wished they had a moment together. She was thinking about how it would feel, when she heard, "I WANT TO DO THE SAME THING. I LOVE YOU."

She smiled to know he had acknowledged her. *Are you comfortable with this delivery?* Sunna asked mentally. Ghonllier nodded. *Good, because your father heard your conversation with Cid and wasn't happy.*

Ghonllier faced her and answered, "I know."

"Where do you want me to be during the delivery?" she asked.

"Move Cid's chair in front of the privacy screen."

She mentally expressed, *I want to be with you. Part of me wants to watch you two deliver and the other part is afraid.*

"I KNOW, HONEY. IF YOU WANT TO WATCH, BE CAREFUL. IF SHE SEES YOU, IT WILL FRIGHTEN HER MORE," warned Ghonllier, stepping behind the privacy screen.

Sunna could see his feet and wanted to see what he was watching. The sounds of the baby's heartbeat pulled at her emotions. She had never heard them before.

Peeking around the corner, she saw the baby on the monitor. She could actually see the baby as it moved in its mother's womb. It was so real. She smiled to see the movements of its hands. For a moment, Sunna felt the baby was looking at her. Someone had entered the room and Sunna looked behind her to see it was Asustie.

"Is she here?" whispered Asustie, hearing the heartbeats of the baby behind the privacy screen.

Sunna shook her head while handing her a gown. "Cid wants you to get dressed in this," informed Sunna.

Distractedly, Asustie took it and peeked around the corner of the screen. Seeing it was only Ghonllier, watching the monitors, Asustie left, taking the gown with her.

Before Asustie returned, Cid and Ghonllier left with the gurney for the bay to meet the mother.

Entering the bay, Cid asked, "Ghonllier, can I watch you pick her up?"

Commanding the doors to the monitors in the bay to open, Ghonllier started to broadcast the woman on the ground. Ghonllier sent the same picture to the command center for the captains to watch on their huge monitor.

Seeing it, Sam took in a deep breath and hoped Ghonllier could pull off what he said he could. Not ever seeing a Master of the Stones at work, he wasn't sure.

Adamite stayed in the office to watch the woman carrying his grandson on the server stone. Seeing her caused him to think about the night he accidentally looked at his older son kissing her. Then Bog took over and he hurt her so deeply that Adamite carried the pain ever since then. Back then, he thought it was Gomper, but Ghonllier told him it was Bog and not his son.

He smiled at the woman, so grateful she didn't abort the baby. Ghonllier said he was an important key for the healing of his family. The new Master told him that this baby would bless many people's lives, including his birth mother. The whole idea of holding him was getting emotional for Adamite. Maybe, he was getting Gomper back through him.

Gostler and Jason entered the office, talking about how close they were to the moon. It brought Adamite out of his thoughts as Gostler joined him. Seeing a city on the server stone, Gostler asked, "Is this her city?"

"Yes," answered Adamite.

Adamite asked to see what Ghonllier was showing the captains. The stone showed the city a blur, due to the speed the ship was traveling. Suddenly, the speed slowed down, allowing things to come into focus. Adamite recognized Suzette and ordered the server stone to follow her.

When they slowed down, it caused people on the ground to recognize a KOGN Star Screamer. Everyone started to run, leaving the pregnant woman alone. She froze, thinking the baby's father was there to take her away.

Without stopping, Sam hit his mark on a run, capturing the frightened woman, and disappeared.

As the colors dissipated in the bay, they heard the frightened woman's screams. Instantly, Ghonllier used the Master Stones and talked to her in his hypnotic voice. Moments later, she collapsed into his arms and closed her eyes. The new Master picked her up and carried her to the gurney. Cid quickly requested the safety straps and they left.

As they ran into the corridor, Cid asked, "Is she alive?"

"Yes, hurry," urged Ghonllier.

"What did you do?"

"I just hypnotized her mind to relax so her emotions won't kill the baby. They both are relaxed and asleep right now."

"Is she still in labor?"

"Oh, yeah," answered Ghonllier, entering Med-C.

Arriving in the Med-C, Ghonllier mentally moved the back of the privacy screen enough to get the gurney next to the birthing chair. Sunna stayed out of the way, staring at the unconscious woman, wondering if she was dead.

Before she could ask, the woman floated above the gurney, turning on her side. Ghonllier pulled up her shirt, exposing her spine. Cid administered the patch for pain.

Stepping away, Cid ordered, "Asustie and Sunna, get her ready for delivery."

Asustie joined Sunna as Cid left for a gown. Ghonllier moved out of the way and Sunna purposely bumped into him. She smiled to herself to feel the burning fires. He felt it, too.

While they worked, Ghonllier paced behind the privacy screen. Cid joined him and asked, "What's happening to her labor?"

"The beam caused her contractions to go from fifteen minutes apart to five. They are hard and if she was awake, the pain patch might not be helping. It's going to take her longer than normal to not feel the contractions."

"I told you this would be hard on her. How long are you going to keep her asleep?"

"Until the patches stop the pain," answered Ghonllier. Suddenly, he shook his head. "Cid, you need to go back and give her a patch for shock. Her body is confused from the environmental change. She's going to have this baby too fast and we need to slow it down or stop both their hearts from beating," informed Ghonllier.

Leaving, Cid grunted, "Great, how do I slow it down now?"

"I'LL DO IT. YOU APPLY THE PATCH," said Ghonllier, going into a trance.

Cid paused to watch him.

Ghonllier hooked into the mother and baby's minds. He talked Suzette's mind into a state of calmness, allowing the mind to take control over the body. Cid sighed to hear both their heartbeats change.

"Do we still need shock?" asked Cid.

The new Master nodded, staying in the trance. Cid was glad he had it ready and waiting. He paused at the edge of the wall and asked, "Can I come back?"

"Yes, Cid. We're just finishing," said Sunna.

He went back and picked up the patch for shock and administered it. Then he went to the monitors to watch, wondering what the patches were doing. It made it hard to know with Ghonllier there. He was staring at it when Asustie touched his arm. He gave her a startled look.

"Cid, look," stated Asustie, gesturing toward her.

Suzette was floating over to the chair. So Cid removed the gurney while Sunna came out. She wanted Ghonllier's attention, but he was still in the trance. Asustie moved the screen back and Sunna moved her chair into place, brushing against Ghonllier again. He didn't respond to her while in the trance.

Then she sat, watching her husband in awe with what he was doing. Suddenly, he came out of the trance and winked at her before going behind the privacy screen. Sunna smiled as she watched him disappear.

When he joined Cid, the medic commented, "I can see you slowed her contractions."

"That's not all I did. I increased her body to properly prepare her for delivery. With us surprising her, the mind and body stopped working together. I think it's the way it should be," informed Ghonllier, taking a deep breath.

Cid faced him. "You're right. I can't believe you did all that."

"The mind can do anything if it understands what you want it to do."

Pointing to the monitors, Cid questioned, "Look at those numbers moving. Is this what you asked her mind to do? Her cervix is moving faster than I've seen, softening and expanding."

Ghonllier nodded. "Watch and you'll see the baby drop down into its correct position and probably break her water."

The Master hadn't finished his words, when they saw his predictions appear. Cid looked at him. "Then I need her awake. Are you going to wake her up?"

"Yes," answered Ghonllier, stepping closer to her.

"Ghonllier, she just moved to an eight," said Cid. "We're going to have a baby real soon."

"I know."

Moments later, she moaned. Then, opening her eyes, she gasped. Ghonllier read something in her mind that he didn't expect. Looking behind him, he saw Sunna standing there. The KOGN uniform was what he was reading.

"Commander, get behind the privacy screen. You're frightening her." Sunna left and Ghonllier continued in an altered voice, "DON'T BE AFRAID. I'M HERE TO PROTECT AND HELP YOU. I WON'T ALLOW ANYONE TO TOUCH YOU, AS LONG AS YOU'RE WITH ME."

"Can you help me against his father?" she asked, frantically searching the area.

"I KNOW THIS IS SUZAIR THE GREAT'S CHILD. HE ISN'T ON BOARD THIS SHIP. YOU'RE SAFE WITH ME," informed Ghonllier.

Suzette relaxed and Cid saw her go to a ten, allowing the baby to enter the birth canal. "Suzette, are you feeling anything?" asked Cid.

"No," she answered.

"Well, I need you to push in a few minutes," answered Cid, placing his hand on her stomach so he could feel her contractions. He couldn't see the monitors. The moment he felt her muscles tightening, Cid encouraged, "Push. I need you to push hard."

Suzette did what he asked. Ghonllier had the Master Stones aid her. "Stop!" shouted Cid. The baby had crowned.

Waiting for the next contraction, Ghonllier said, "SUZETTE, ON THIS NEXT PUSH, THE BABY'S HEAD WILL BE OUT. PLEASE KEEP YOUR EYES ON ME IF YOU DON'T WANT TO SEE THE BABY."

She momentarily closed her eyes and whispered, "Thank you."

Keeping his hand on her stomach, Cid ordered, "Push."

Suzette did and the head came out, just like Ghonllier said it would. Cid cleaned out the baby's mouth while Ghonllier said, "STAY RIGHT WITH ME, SUZETTE. THIS WILL BE OVER WITH IN A MINUTE AND YOU'LL FORGET ANYTHING HAPPENED."

Mesmerized by his voice, Suzette held her eyes on Ghonllier. Hearing his voice caused her to relax and take her to a place of safety. She watched to see if his mouth moved, but it didn't. Yet, she heard his voice next to her ear, like a whisper, and it felt soothing.

She was so caught up in the moment Ghonllier was giving her that Suzette didn't notice Cid take the baby and cut the cord. Handing him off to Asustie, Cid said, "This is the last push. Give me one more."

This time, she looked at Cid and pushed. Cid stopped her shortly afterward. He had the placenta and didn't need more. Ghonllier reached for two patches and activated them while Suzette watched him place them on her stomach. She didn't know it was for bleeding and hormone balancing.

Sunna spoke, causing her to come out of her trance. "Why are you here?"

"I want to talk with Suzette," said Gostler in Jamham's voice.

Suzette stopped breathing, recognizing the voice. Ghonllier noticed it and grabbed a hold of her hand. She looked at him. "I WON'T LEAVE YOU. BUT I DO THINK YOU SHOULD FIND OUT WHAT HE WANTS."

A strong feeling of security swept over her. So Ghonllier ordered, "Enter and be quick."

Gostler entered and nodded in respect. "Madam, the father wants his child. He sent me to pick him up," stated Gostler as Jamham.

"And me?! What about me? Does he want me, too?" she asked.

"He didn't expect you to survive the delivery, so no, madam," expressed Jamham.

"I don't want to go to him. Don't take me back to him."

"I agree. Where would you like to go, madam? I'll have the captains sworn to secrecy and we'll take you anywhere in the galaxy, without Suzair the Great knowing about it."

She stared at Jamham and eventually asked, "Why are you doing this?"

"Madam, I was there and know what he did. I couldn't stop him without him killing us both. I've been looking for a way of ending my guilt for not having the power to stop it. Please let me drop you off somewhere and let him think you died," soothed Jamham.

Ghonllier looked at her. "Suzette, take the offer. Where do you want to go?" he suggested.

She looked away. "I'll think about it," she replied.

Jamham bowed and left with Ghonllier reading from her where she wanted to go. Instantly, he told Jason so he could chart it for the captains before telling Gostler that he didn't have to play Jamham again.

Cid watched Gostler leave and looked back at her. "Why didn't you tell him? It was your chance," he said.

"I don't trust them," she said.

"YOU DID THE RIGHT THING. WE'RE GOING TO PUT YOU TO SLEEP AND YOU'LL WAKE UP NOT REMEMBERING ANYTHING THAT HAPPENED HERE," hypnotized Ghonllier.

She looked at him, dazed, before closing her eyes. Cid watched the monitors before he asked, "I can't believe how fast she is healing. Is that the Stones?"

"Yes, they're programming her mind."

"What do you want me to do next?"

"I want you to put her in one of the medics' rooms. Keep her asleep and give her fluids, since we're in space," said Ghonllier, moving her to the gurney.

"Do I need to wear a KOGN uniform?"

"No, since we're close to Zircon moon, we'll keep her asleep until she reaches her aunt's place."

"Will the KOGN ever find her?" asked Cid.

"No, she picked a place that the KOGN are afraid of entering, since I caused a virus to enter the air that paralyzes all newcomers."

"What about her?"

"I'm going to give her a patch that will make her immunized to the virus. It isn't as strong as it used to be, but the KOGN don't know that fact."

Cid left with Suzette while Ghonllier went to the next room to stare at the baby. Asustie was cleaning him before placing him into a temperature control blanket. Sunna wasn't far from her, watching. He could see Sunna excited about holding the baby.

The medic returned to examine the baby. He stopped next to Ghonllier and asked, "Is the boy okay?"

"Yes, he's healthy," assured Ghonllier, looking at him. "I'll leave both the mother and baby's vital signs on the monitors. So don't worry about handling it."

Watching Sunna take the baby into her arms, Cid stated, "Good, because I doubt I'll see the baby much."

Sunna paused and beamed at Ghonllier before she left with the child. Ghonllier stated, "Yeah, I think you're right."

"Where are we going to put the baby while we're on board the ship?" asked Asustie, joining them.

"He can't stay in Sooner's old room, like Sunna is thinking. If Spencer weren't here, Sooner's room would be good," whispered Ghonllier. He faced them and added, "There is a baby's gurney in storage. Get it up here and put him in it so everyone can get to him," answered Ghonllier, looking at the mess he had to clean up.

"Give me all the patches the baby and mother will need and I'll go make them up now," said Cid, leaving for the medicine room.

Asustie touched her brother's arms and smiled, "I'm going to see the baby. Have fun cleaning up."

"Change your gown and thanks for helping me," grinned Ghonllier, watching Asustie leave.

He went behind the privacy screen to decide how he wanted to clean up. Ghonllier could hear someone entering the room as he commanded the cleaning products and equipment to leave the closets. The person came around the edge of the privacy screen and watched everything float over to Ghonllier.

"Hi, Jason. What can I do for you?" asked Ghonllier, starting to clean.

He had a tablet in his hand and Ghonllier knew what he wanted. "Ghonllier, I need to write up a log of what we did here. I was thinking about putting into the log that we transferred a made-up name of a person. Do you agree or do you want something else?"

Ghonllier flicked him a glance while cleaning. "I don't even want that in the ship's log that we picked up someone. Just say that we're spending time together as a family," answered Ghonllier.

"I can't do that. That's against military rules," reminded Jason.

"This is my ship and I can use it for a family outing. Remember who I am."

Jason smiled. "Sorry, I forgot. Please forgive me, Your Grace," apologized Jason.

"You call me that one more time and I'll leave you with Suzette on the Zircon moon, without my sister."

Jason chuckled, realizing what Ghonllier was doing. "Why aren't you using the ship's cleaning and sanitizing system?"

"The sounds of the system irritates me to hear it now," answered Ghonllier.

"Really? I can't hear the cleaning system."

"I didn't hear it until I received the Stones," said Ghonllier, turning the orbiters up brighter so he could see better.

Jason watched for a moment longer and then left to write up the report. Seeing Sunna's chair, he decided to sit right there to write the report, in case he had another question for Ghonllier. After he sat, Jason watched Ghonllier's silhouette behind the privacy screen, working. *Here he's the most powerful man in the galaxy. All living matter will obey him and he's cleaning,* thought Jason, going back to the tablet.

Hearing someone enter, Jason looked up to see Sunna. He smiled at her and she joined him. "Do you know where he is? I have a message for him from his father," whispered Sunna.

Jason pointed at the silhouette and Sunna smiled. Quickly, she slipped behind the privacy screen, putting her arms around his waist. It pleased Ghonllier to see his wife as he faced her. She moved her arms to his neck and they kissed.

This was the first time Jason had ever seen Sunna kiss a man. He stared, thinking about them. Shortly, he heard Sunna say, "You were incredible to watch delivering that baby. I want you to deliver ours."

Ghonllier kissed her, instead of responding to her comments. Behind him, Jason heard someone gasp. Facing the noise, Jason saw Spencer. In the background, they could hear Sunna divulge, "I love you and I want you to give me a baby as soon as possible."

A hurt look consumed Spencer's face and then he bolted for the corridor. Jason knew they were in trouble now. Jumping up, he tossed his tablet in the chair and pursued Spencer.

Exiting the Med-C, Jason saw Spencer disappearing down the corridors toward the sleeping quarters. Running, Jason yelled, "Spencer!" The hurt man kept on going. "Spencer, stop now! You were in an unauthorized area. We need to talk!"

This time Spencer whirled around and shouted, "How long has this been going on?!" Jason froze, unsure how to answer him. With Jason's silence, Spencer choked out, "How long has she been in love with Cid?"

Jason was stunned by the word "Cid," and just stared at Spencer with his mouth open. The Tron was impatient and wanted answers now. "Come on, Jason. Everyone knows that he's in love with her. When did she fall in love with him?" he repeated, his voice becoming even angrier.

Slowly, Jason said, "You want to know how long Cid and Sunna have been in love?"

"Yes, you heard me!" snapped the Tron.

"Since we picked her up on the Mossen planet, she has been in love," answered Jason gradually. "What did you exactly hear?"

"I heard her tell him that she loved him and that she wanted him to give her a baby," repeated Spencer. "Is she pregnant?"

"NO!" affirmed Jason, putting up his hands. "Why did you come into the Med-C? I gave strict orders to have everyone stay out of there."

"I saw Sunna enter and I knew the baby was gone. I wanted to talk with her. It's been so long . . . then I saw her kissing him," choked Spencer, his eyes watering up.

"Spencer, what are you the most upset with? I really need to understand this right now. My sister's personal life is supposed to be private."

He looked away, blinking back his tears. "I asked her as we left for this mission if there was any chance that she would ever consider having a personal relationship with someone. She led me to believe that nothing had changed in her life, except for family." Giving Jason a glare, he continued, "Cid isn't family. Why didn't she just tell me that the answer was *yes* and she was in love with another man? It would have been easier on me. . . . I could've . . . It would've helped me move on and showed me that she respected our friendship," said Spencer, choking on his words.

"So you feel she doesn't respect your friendship, and that hurts you more than Sunna not being in love with you?" repeated Jason. Spencer nodded while staring at the floor.

"It hurts to know how little she thought of our friendship," whispered Spencer.

"I know for a fact she has a lot of respect for your friendship, Spencer. Right now, she can't have you telling anyone about her being in love. You and I are the only ones who know about what you saw in the Med-C," divulged Jason.

"Why can't I talk about it?" snapped Spencer, looking at Jason. "If Sunna doesn't respect our friendship, why do I need to be loyal to her?"

"Spencer, Sunna does respect your friendship. Right now, she's under oath to keep her private life a secret."

"Who would she give an oath to?"

"Me," responded Jason, trying to give an excuse for Sunna.

"You?" retorted Spencer.

Jason put his hands up. "Look, I did it so Commander Ghonllier wouldn't find out about it. He breaks up relationships within his crew if he finds out about it. I didn't want him to send her away."

"Why would he do that?"

"Sunna is his bodyguard. You're in Special Services. It's dangerous to have your bodyguard in love with someone close to their client. Cid can't leave so she would have to leave."

Spencer looked away. "We both know the rules of spies. I want Sunna to stay with the family. It has been years since we've been together. I love her and when I saw her falling in love, I made her promise that she wouldn't tell a soul, so Ghonllier wouldn't find out," finished Jason, hoping Spencer would accept his answer.

"I don't see why he would care, but . . ."

"But what?"

"I know he doesn't like crew members fraternizing with each other," whispered Spencer.

"Know that she would've told you if she hadn't promised me."

Spencer looked away and started to leave. Jason shouted, "Second Cadet, I didn't dismiss you."

Spencer spun around. "What do you want?"

"You and I are the only two people who know about Cid. My wife doesn't even know about this. I want you to take an oath right now that you won't tell a soul, including Sunna. If you change your mind, you have to talk with me first."

"And if I don't?"

"You're off this ship now. I'll drop you off at the next solar system and you'll lose points. I do have the power to make your life miserable anywhere I drop you," reminded Jason, coming forward. He added, "Spencer, I don't want to do that. Please, if you're a friend who truly cares about your friendship with my sister, give Sunna this one moment of happiness. I've never seen her this happy."

Spencer put his hands in his pockets and stared at the floor. Jason continued. "Spencer, do you see Asustie and I showing any affection on board, except when Asustie thought her brother was dead?"

"No," answered Spencer.

"It's because of Ghonllier and we're married. Asustie isn't a part of the crew and she's here out of his good graces. He runs a tight ship and we do some dangerous missions on this ship. Let Sunna stay. She'll turn on you if you ruin her happiness," reminded Jason. Spencer nodded. "Please give her this moment until Commander Ghonllier doesn't need her as his bodyguard. I know she will tell you."

Spencer bit his lower lip, keeping his gaze down. "Are Cid and Sunna going to get married? It sounds like they're talking about a baby."

"It was the first time I've ever seen her kiss someone. I don't know how to answer you," said Jason. Spencer was quiet and didn't move. Jason added, "It has been a long time since I have seen or worked with Sunna. Please let her stay with her family."

"Is she truly happy?" choked Spencer.

"You heard her. I've never seen her this happy before. Please don't ruin her working relationship with Ghonllier and her future happiness. If she's finally found love, let her find out what it's like," pleaded Jason as Spencer looked away. "Let her have it. Pretend she told you the truth. How would you handle it?"

Eventually, Spencer nodded and said, "I'll take the oath to not talk with anyone but you."

"Thank you," responded Jason, relieved. Then he added, "You're dismissed."

Spencer left while Jason watched. The minute he was out of sight, Jason ran for the Med-C to find Ghonllier. Entering the Med-C, Jason was disappointed to only see Sunna standing in the middle of the room.

She smiled at him and Jason came close and whispered, "Where is he?" Sunna pointed back to the area where patients could get dressed in gowns. Jason added, "Get out of here and go to your quarters. We have a problem and we need to talk."

Sunna expressed a look of concern as she headed for the corridor. With her gone, Jason took in a deep breath while going back to the chair. He picked up his tablet and stared at it, thinking.

Shortly, Ghonllier walked into the room and Jason faced him. "Jason, you're upset."

The commander mentally said, *We need to talk in your quarters now.*

"Why?"

Look at what happened in here while you were behind the privacy screen, cleaning, thought Jason.

Ghonllier stared at the floor while going into a trance. He knew when Ghonllier saw the part about Spencer. His head came up sharply as he looked at Jason with concerned eyes. Then he bolted for the corridor with Jason following.

Ghonllier's hullercast opened the moment he entered the corridor. When they entered his quarters, Sunna was pacing. Relieved to see them, she ran to Ghonllier. "What's wrong? Why the emergency?"

Sunna, being taken into his arms, expected him to say something, but he didn't. Instead, Jason asked, "Will he talk?"

"Will who talk?" asked Sunna, moving back.

"Spencer," said Jason.

"Someone tell me what is going on!" retorted Sunna, expecting her answer from Ghonllier.

Jason could tell Ghonllier was deep in thought. So he answered, "Spencer followed you into the medical center and saw the two of you kissing. He heard you tell Ghonllier that you loved him and wanted a baby."

"When?

"While you were behind the privacy screen."

She faced Ghonllier and grabbed a hold of his arm. "How is Spencer handling it? And are the Master Stones upset?"

"Sunna, Spencer thinks it was Cid, not Ghonllier, you were kissing," answered Jason.

"Cid?! Why him?"

"Mainly because Ghonllier never spoke and we could only see your silhouettes. Ghonllier had on a Medical Tech's gown. The rumor is out that Cid is in love with you. Why would he think anything else?"

"Is that good or bad, honey?" questioned Sunna, looking back at her husband.

Ghonllier finally looked at her and put his arms around Sunna. Knowing how upset she was, he soothed, "Sunna, let go of your guilt. You didn't do anything wrong. The Master Stones are pleased. . . . In fact they set this up. This is why the Stones told me to bring him. Spencer now knows that there isn't a future with you, without having to tell him about my title or us. I feel this is good."

Sunna asked, "Are you telling me the Master Stones set it up so Spencer would walk in just as I was in your arms?"

Ghonllier nodded. "I asked them to help stop Spencer from chasing you and get him to move on. He is looking for something and doesn't understand what it is. So he keeps forcing something that isn't good for him or you."

"Will he be okay?" asked Sunna, concerned for her friend.

Ghonllier nodded slowly. "He'll be fine, if he makes the right choices that will take him to where he needs to go."

"Will he?" asked Sunna.

Ghonllier shook his head. "I don't know. What I do know is he's tired of making the wrong choices. He now realizes how many he has made. Spencer's ready to go into the right direction now."

Looking at Jason, Ghonllier grinned, "Thank you, brother of mine. You handled it very well with him."

"You're welcome," beamed Jason.

"I'll be so glad to have this over with. I'm so tired of this secret marriage. It is a lot harder than I imagined it to be," grumbled Sunna.

"Luckily, it isn't going to be forever," stated Ghonllier. *It'll be worse for you, Sunna, when everyone around learns you're my wife . . . Except for my elite force. They already accept Sunna as being next to me.*

Ghonllier watched Sunna worrying about Spencer. It was going to be hard for Sunna to be around Spencer and not be able to tell him. They were good friends and she didn't want to lose his friendship. For some reason, Ghonllier felt the same way.

Chapter 11

The Dream

*G*ostler was right. The third Stone was different to bond with than the other Stones. The best part was Ghonllier didn't feel as tired as he felt with the other two Stones. He liked the Stone bonding to his intelligence. No matter what he looked at, the Stones would give him in-depth information regarding it. He understood the complete makeup of all elements, instantly, that went into anything living or non-living.

Another ability that increased for Ghonllier was the ability to interpret dreams. The sounds, smells, and meanings were stronger than the first two Stones. Ghonllier was taken back by the change in his dreams compared to the first Stone.

One night, he found himself in a dream that woke him up. It troubled him so much that he decided to get up. He sat in the chair by the windows that looked over his city. The sight of his city usually soothed him, but not this time. The Stones had shown him that there was a problem with reversing the curse. If he didn't stop Bog, he would lose the war, with the evil sorcerer winning. Deciding a solution to the problem was more important than sleep.

Ghonllier tried to relax, wanting to go into a state of meditation so he could find an answer. But it wasn't happening as quickly as he wanted it to. Looking away from the window, he watched Sunna sleep. After a long gaze, Ghonllier decided he wasn't going to lose her to this war. *One wife is enough*, thought Ghonllier, standing. He dressed and left their room.

Arriving at the door of the garden, he stared at the reflection pool as it mirrored the shimmering lights of fireflies. Walking down the steps, a flower with the scent of fresh baking bread caught his attention. He paused at the bottom step, looking away from the reflection pool. The flower was one of his favorites, but it didn't draw his attention for long. He was focused tonight as he traveled down the pathways that wound through trees, flowers, and bushes.

Stopping, he stared at some fireflies lighting up a flower. He asked out loud, "Stones, are you really telling me it's time to move onto the next step with Gomper?"

Yes.

Why so early? I've had this Stone shorter than the other two.

We have sped up your learning with the third Stone. Your brother isn't going to live if you don't move ahead now.

"Where is the fourth Stone?" whispered Ghonllier.

You'll find the fourth Stone in the fourth solar system from the Xeron moon.

Ghonllier thought about the fourth solar system from the Xeron moon in all directions. The Stones verified to him when he had picked the right solar system. Instantly, he started to shake his head. *No, it can't be there!*

Yes, countered the Stones.

It was a planet that was controlled by the KOGN and his least favorite place in the galaxy. He was stationed there when he was a first cadet. It was the same place where Jasper gave him the first Stone. Now, he had to go back.

"Stones, where on the Jasmine planet is the Stone hidden?" snapped Ghonllier.

A valley appeared in his mind with a tall tree standing alone. These clearings and valleys were where the bases were built. This was a tropical planet and Snacker Vines thrived there.

Is this how it looks today?

No.

I want to see it today.

The valley changed and reappeared, showing a large KOGN military base at one end of it, by the lone tree. His senses became consumed with studying the base. Ghonllier let out a sigh, learning this base was their largest.

Where is the Stone hidden here?

UNDERNEATH THE BASE, IN A CAVERN.

Knowing that Jasmine in some places had numerous caverns underground, he asked the Stones to tell how many were there. He understood why the KOGN had placed their base there. The whole valley was honeycombed with caverns. It disappointed him to see the KOGN had been storing most of their fuel for ships and transports there. The flammable fuel was needed on the ships to operate the hullercasts and camouflage gels. The ship's stones handled everything else.

When Ghonllier was stationed there, he stayed only shortly because I-Force finally developed fuel that no longer needed to be stored in the cool temperatures of the caverns. So I-Force left, allowing the KOGN to take over. Only Trons were left behind so they could keep an eye on them.

If Gostler was right, Ghonllier was upset about having to pick the fourth Stone at the Jasmine planet. It was a very powerful Stone and had a hard time adjusting to the other three Stones and a man. Ghonllier shook his head as he thought, *This was the wrong place to hide the fourth Stone.* In his mind, he could see the person who hid it was thinking it would be one of the safest. The Snacker Vines kept people from building cities.

Gostler warned him to disappear shortly after receiving that Stone. If it feels just the slightest disloyalty, it becomes violent. The fourth Stone could be very dangerous to those around Ghonllier while bonding. This was the Stone that controlled the weather, matter in space, and everything under his feet.

To get control of this Stone, Ghonllier was aware that there would be a cost. This Stone would require things that meant a lot to him. Ghonllier wasn't sure he was ready to face that decision.

This Stone had the most influence in picking the Master who ruled over them. They needed a man who was strong on the inside. He had to have a great capacity to love and discipline. Jenny paid a price to help develop this in Ghonllier. With Jenny dying, it left Ghonllier to be a single parent with a baby. They needed Ghonllier to be in the military and know this galaxy and her people. Ghonllier chose to keep his son with him on the *Liberty Quest* and Justin made it possible. Everything else, Ghonllier had to achieve by himself. He became the youngest commander to ever be commissioned.

Those trials had built character and they would carry him through the challenge of controlling this fourth Stone. As Ghonllier reminisced about his life, he saw it had been his choices that brought him to this point. His dedication to Sooner, Jenny, and his bonding fires contract made him a tower of strength. He could see the Master Stones could only enhance what he already had, not giving him anything he didn't earn. If he had made the choice to not prepare properly, they would've passed him by and gone to another man. He wouldn't have Sunna. She went with the Stones because of her strength to keep her oaths and commitments. He was pleased to see he had innocently chosen to match her.

The third Stone showed Ghonllier how every law and choice had brought him to this point. He was awe-struck to understand everything had its purpose, even the unpleasant moments. He paused to evaluate what he had just learned, when the visions of his dream returned.

Determined to find an answer, Ghonllier continued his walk, thinking about the dream. He wished the Stones would just give him the answers, but they didn't work that way. He always had to study the situation and they would only verify if he had made the best choice. If he was told the choice was okay yet not the best, he would keep searching. Ghonllier quickly caught on that they were making him look at all angles before coming to a final decision. They were teaching him a lot.

To give his mind a break from the dream, Ghonllier went back to the fourth Stone. He saw the cavern it was hidden in. It was the only cavern the KOGN hadn't used to store their fuel. The cavern was made out of limestone and he couldn't understand why they weren't using it.

He searched the cavern to find something that upset him. Ghonllier shook his head and sighed. "There's too much flammable fuel in this area for the fourth Stone. If the base weren't there, maybe it would be easy," Ghonllier whispered, deciding to come out of the vision.

Dawn was close at hand and he wanted to talk with someone. He looked up at Gostler's room that overlooked the garden. The former Master was usually an early riser and Ghonllier hoped it was the same this morning.

Gostler was on his way to the bathroom, when he glanced out the window. It surprised him to see Ghonllier in the garden, walking. *He hadn't done this since he has been married. So why now?* thought Gostler, grabbing a robe and leaving his room.

By the time Gostler entered the garden, Ghonllier was sitting on the edge of the reflection pool. Without moving, Ghonllier greeted, "Hi, Gostler."

"Are you okay?"

"Maybe."

"What has you out here this early?"

"Dreams."

"Dreams! You're not supposed to have dreams this early, unless they're important."

"You're right," replied Ghonllier, gesturing to a spot next to him.

"Tell me about your dreams," requested Gostler, sitting.

Ghonllier took in a deep breath and stated, "In my dream, I saw two men walking down a road, arguing with each other. I could tell from their words that they had been together for a long time. One man had power over the other and he was being brutal to him. He was causing the man to suffer and was gloating over his ability to hurt this man.

"The trapped man was trying to convince the other man to leave him alone. When the man with power laughed at his offer, the trapped man slipped a knife between the other man's ribs. They struggled, but the man with the knife in his ribs fell to the ground, lifeless," stated Ghonllier, becoming silent and staring at the water.

"Is that the end of the dream?"

Shooting his eyes in Gostler's direction, he responded, "The man who stuck the knife in the ribs stood there, looking at the dead man. I came up closer to look at the dead man's face. It was Bog's. I turned to look closer at the man standing over him and saw it was Gomper."

"So your brother is thinking about ending his life?" assumed the former Master.

"Yes. Bog is hurting him for fun and I don't know how much more he can take."

"Why is he taking it? It wouldn't take much to get himself killed."

"The men with him, his personal staff. If he dies, they will be killed, too."

"Why?"

"Suzair the Great set it up that way so his personal staff would be motivated to be loyal to him," whispered Ghonllier.

Gostler grunted, "It's the only way he could get anyone to be loyal to him . . ."

He paused and soon added, "How is Gomper handling his situation?"

"He's a strong man and I'm in awe of my older brother. You know what it's like to have the Stones. I know everything he's going through and he's doing it with strength. I think he would've been a better Master of the Galaxy than I. He has strength that's being tested and I can't stay back and do nothing much longer."

"You can't stop it, Ghonllier, or Bog will win," reminded Gostler.

"I know."

"Are you talking to him while he's asleep?"

"Gomper has other problems besides Bog. This new commander is plotting to kill him and take over the KOGN. With me destroying Bog's stepping stone, he has no idea of what is going on. So I'm giving Gomper dreams, telling him about the traps."

"And he's believing you?"

"So far, he is. When I see his future in the short run, I give him a dream showing him the same thing. As he sees it play out, Gomper isn't dumb. He's playing it very smart and is following my suggestions on how to foil their traps. But one little mistake and he's gone, and so is the curse. It will be out of control and Bog won't be able to control it."

"Does Bog understand that?"

"Yes and no. He's aware of the consequences of Gomper dying on him, but he has so much hate in him. It's blinding his judgment."

"Wow," sighed Gostler. "What is he remembering about his life?"

"He remembers everything up until Bog stepped into it. He believes his family is alive and that they abandoned him because of what he's become."

"Is that what triggered his depression?"

Ghonllier nodded. "I knew he would feel that way and it broke my heart not to help him," he whispered.

"Is he expecting you to save him?"

The new Master shook his head. "Gomper wants me to kill him. He's ashamed of what happened to him. He hangs on for us to meet, long enough for me to tell him why this happened to him."

"I can't imagine Gomper not coming home. I've always felt like the Stones would release me when he's home," whispered Gostler.

"That's my problem, Gostler. Gomper doesn't expect to come home again. Even if Bog leaves him, he doesn't see himself or his life having any value now," choked Ghonllier with emotion.

"You've got to get him to see it differently," pleaded Gostler.

"I can't force him, Gostler, and you know it."

"This has been so hard on me over the years. I loved Gomper like he was my own boy," whispered Gostler.

Ghonllier put his hand on his shoulder and the former Master looked at him with tired eyes. "I know you love him, even though I can't read his mind." The new Master removed his hand and added, "Look, I need to ask you some questions. I didn't mean to burden you with problems that aren't your responsibility."

"What do you want to know?"

"How long does it take to bond with the fourth Stone and become the Master?"

"At least a couple of months at the minimum. You've got a lot of power to control with that Stone." Gostler studied Ghonllier. "Do you think Gomper will hold on that long even if you had it today?" he added.

Ghonllier shook his head. "There must be something else I can do for him. I feel like there is something and I've missed it. . . . I haven't asked the right question. That is why I can't sleep right now."

Gostler changed the subject. "Where is the fourth Stone?"

"On the Jasmine planet, right underneath KOGN's largest military base."

Gostler grunted, "Are you serious?" Ghonllier nodded. He added, "When are you going?"

"As soon as I figure out how to get Bog to leave Gomper alone long enough for me to become the Master."

"Are you taking your wife with you when you get the fourth Stone?"

"No."

"Has she agreed to it?"

"No, you're the only person who knows about it."

"Is there anything that I can do for you?"

"Would you contact Jason for me after breakfast and tell him to have a small crew on standby? I'll need to leave at a moment's notice."

"He'll want to know who you want to take with you. What do I tell him?"

Ghonllier was quiet as he talked to the Stones. "Tell Jason that anyone can come who wants to in the family. But outside of them, I'm being told to have Spencer and Bert there," answered Ghonllier.

"Why the Trons?"

Shaking his head, he replied, "I don't know."

"I'm going in for some breakfast. Do you want to join me?" asked Gostler.

Ghonllier shook his head. "I'm not ready to eat. I'll be in later, thank you."

"Do you want me to tell Sunna about the Trons? You know how upset she gets if Jason tells her."

Ghonllier didn't answer him and Gostler couldn't read his mind. He assumed he was talking to the Stones and Gostler left to enter the house. Moments later, Ghonllier decided to answer Gostler's question but realized he was gone.

Realizing he was alone, Ghonllier was pleased. He felt exhausted and wanted a break. The new Master wanted to take a nap before he went back to tackling his problem. Ghonllier headed for a bench that was close to the patio. As he arrived, Ghonllier commanded a pillow from the chairs on the patio to come to him. Sleep came quickly.

Gostler paged for the lift, planning to head to his room and freshen up before breakfast. Though, when the lift arrived, Sunna exited. "Gostler, do you know where my husband is?"

"You lost him already?" winked Gostler.

"Yes, I did."

"He's out in the garden," informed Gostler, entering the lift.

Sunna quickly thanked him and headed for the patio, excited to see her husband. However, stepping outside, she found no Ghonllier. It angered her that he wasn't there. She glanced back at the lift to ask Gostler more questions, but he was gone. In frustration, Sunna ventured out onto the patio and down the steps.

Arriving at the reflection pool, she scanned the area. When she didn't find him, Sunna headed for the house. It was then she noticed him half hidden by bushes, asleep on the bench. Relieved, she went to his side to see if he would awake at her presence.

When he didn't, Sunna reached out to touch him, but stopped. Rethinking, she withdrew her hand. Not being sure if he would be happy about her waking him up, Sunna decided to eat breakfast alone.

When she entered the family dining room, one of the chefs came out to greet her. "Good morning, madam. Would you like breakfast now?"

Deciding that she didn't want to eat alone, Sunna answered, "Maybe later. I would like to start off with just some fruit. What do you have?"

"We have a good selection. Would you like a bowl with different ones? That way, you can return what you don't want."

Sunna smiled. "I'd like that."

He nodded and left. Sunna looked around the room and wondered how long Ghonllier would be sleeping. However, after the chef returned with her fruit, she soon decided that she wanted to be there when Ghonllier woke up. Therefore, Sunna headed for the outdoors.

It upset her that he was outside. *I wonder if I've done something to upset him or is it something else?* thought Sunna, arriving.

Across from the bench Ghonllier was asleep on, Sunna found a grassy place by a tree. She leaned her back up against the tree and started to eat some fruit. Sunna didn't take her eyes off of him, wondering what had driven him to this.

Someone passed by the windows, capturing her attention. It was Sooner, who suddenly waved back at her. Quickly, her son joined her. Falling on his knees, he asked, "Why are you out here, Mother?"

"I'm having a little snack before breakfast. Would you like some fruit?"

"Yes," answered Sooner, taking a piece. It was then Sooner noticed his father. Between bites, he said, "Father must have a problem."

"Why do you think it's a problem? Is this normal for him to leave his bed and sleep outside?"

Sooner nodded and Sunna wrinkled up her forehead. The boy noticed it and asked, "Does it bother you that he is out here and not in his bed to sleep?"

Surprised he would ask that question, Sunna nodded. "Does it bother you?" she asked.

"It did. Father does this all the time, when he has to figure out some kind of military strategy. Every time he was working on something, I found him asleep in his office after working way into the night. Do you know what he is working on now?"

Sunna shook her head. "I was going to wake him up, but decided not to. Is he easy to wake up? Would you do it?"

"No, I wouldn't wake him unless you have to. He gets really short and angry now he has those Stones," reminisced Sooner, taking another bite.

"So I should expect this on a regular basis? When he doesn't stay in bed, I'll find him down here, sleeping?"

Sooner swallowed his bite. "I would plan on it," he stated, looking at his father. "It used to upset me, too, that he would sleep in the office. Now it doesn't."

Sunna smiled. "Why did it upset you?"

"I learned it embarrassed me to have my father fall asleep in his office, when he should've been in bed."

"How did you discover that?"

"One of the times, when I discovered him asleep in his chair, Dapper was on his way out and stopped to see what I wanted. I asked him why my father did it. Dapper started asking me questions that let me realize his behavior embarrassed me." Sooner took another bite. "Dapper asked how I would handle the situation if I were in my father's shoes. I told him if I were tired, then I would go to bed. Then Dapper asked me if my way was the only way to handle the situation and if it was better than my father's."

"That's an interesting question to ask you."

Sooner nodded. "It was hard to answer. Dapper helped me to see that I was judging my father on how I would handle the same situation. Because his behavior was different from mine, then my father's must be wrong. He told me I wasn't being fair. I should stand in my father's shoes and understand him before judging and condemning his behavior. When I stood in my father's shoes, his actions made sense."

"That was a powerful lesson," replied Sunna, impressed. "Did you really like living on the *Liberty Quest*? Do you resent your father at all for keeping you there for so long?"

"No, I think it was wonderful," smiled Sooner. "The whole crew was my family. I went to work with my father every day and we are close because of it. Now, I realize what a special privilege it really was."

"Did your father teach you to be grateful for everything in your life?" asked Sunna, wondering where his wisdom came from at such a tender age.

Sooner paused. "Dapper taught me and Father sold me on the idea."

"Dapper? What did he tell you?"

"He told me if I was grateful, it would keep my mind and body healthy. I would always be happy. More important, it would build and keep my self-love strong."

"Very wise words," smiled Sunna.

"Grandmother tells me that Dapper was one of my father's teachers, when he was a boy like me. I should cherish everything he taught me."

"When did you decide that you wanted a mother?"

"After the crew was gone, I missed all of the attention from the women. Most of the women were single and they liked my father. They would fuss over me. Dapper told me that they were trying to get my father's attention through me. I didn't realize what I had until they were gone."

"How did you know the women liked your father?"

"I would overhear them talking about him."

"Did they know you could hear them?"

"Yes. This one time, Dapper was with me and we talked about it after they left. He told me not to tell my father, like they wanted me to. He would transfer them out if he knew they had feelings for him."

"Why?" asked Sunna, knowing why Ghonllier would do it.

"He wanted a professional crew. Once a woman was transferred out and it upset me, so Dapper explained to me why he did it."

"I guess I wasn't in danger of being transferred out, since your father wasn't aware of my feelings."

"My father requested for you to be transferred out the moment you stepped on the *Liberty Quest*."

"Why?"

"Because of me. I wanted you to be my mother and this time Grandfather refused his orders," grinned Sooner. "I'm glad Grandfather Justin didn't do it."

Sunna grunted, "So he really tried to get rid of me."

"Yes. That was why we were fighting. It was over you staying. Father was angry that Grandfather listened to me and not him."

"What was he like with the women who were a part of his crew? How did he treat them?"

"He was very business-like. He treated them the same as he did the men. He expected them to do their job and always be ready. They knew it and wanted to please him."

"Did any of the women tell you that they were in love with him?"

"Yes, they did," said Sooner, looking at her.

"Did it happen a lot?" asked Sunna, watching his expressions.

"Sometimes."

"Did your father ever seem to look at other women or seem interested in a particular one?"

"No, he didn't. Why do you think I had to find me a mother?" Sunna smiled and nodded. Sooner continued, "Gostler tells me that Father treated you the way he did because that was how a man in love behaves when first getting the white Stones." Sooner watched her for a moment and then asked, "What about you, Mother? Why didn't you want a family?"

Sunna shrugged her shoulders. "I never found a little boy who I wanted to be a mother to," she smiled. Wanting to know more about Ghonllier through Sooner's perceptions, she quizzed, "What was your father like before the Master Stones?"

"About the same," answered Sooner. "My father's always been a man who understands the laws of the universe. I understand more than the kids in my school because of my father. It's easy for me to find the energy wavelengths of things and command them to obey. I watch some of the kids struggle and I know it's because I was taught by Dapper and my father. I really don't know anything else. In the military, all your equipment works on being able to feel the energy waves. I didn't appreciate my past until I watched other kids not understand their life through the laws that governed them."

"The laws that govern your life, you understand that?"

"Yes. Father always said you understand the laws so you have the kind of life you want. They're always at work and you can use them against you if you don't understand how they work. So I decided to learn them so I could create the kind of life I wanted." Sooner looked at Sunna and added, "They work. I got you."

Sunna giggled and played with the fruit in her hand. "Do you talk about your life on board the ship with your friends here?"

Sooner shook his head. "Jasper and I talk about it when we're alone, since he lived there with me for awhile. But we don't talk about it with the other kids. They don't understand and don't like it."

"Who taught you to sit back and study and learn to understand other people?"

"Dapper did."

"How did Dapper to that?"

"Well, it started with me getting upset with my father sleeping in the office. Dapper told me we're all different and differences are very good. We should appreciate it in others. Dapper taught me that it was the secret of having good relationships."

"Did Dapper teach you how to be happy?"

"Yes. He taught me that there are steps. The most important one is to love myself and the life that has been given to me. From there, I can create anything I want if I'm patient enough."

"What're the first rules of the universe that govern humans?" tested Sunna.

"We all want to feel accepted and acknowledged. If I accept myself and love my situation, I'm calm and this makes people feel comfortable."

Impressed, Sunna leaned back against the tree again. "You're right."

"Dapper taught me that everyone does things differently than I do. Methods of doing things are what most people argue about between themselves. Father and I understand this law. I know my father accepts me totally and he trusts me. I don't want to do anything that would cause him not to mistrust me, and I know he feels the same with me. He doesn't want to break my trust."

"Is that why your father always makes sure he has his face shaved?"

"Yes. He promised me to never let his beard grow."

"Did he ever break that promise?"

"After he promised me, no he's never broken his promise." Sooner looked at Sunna and asked, "Do you like a beard, Mother?"

She shrugged her shoulders. "I've never kissed a man with a beard, so I don't know." Sooner took another fruit and started to eat. Sunna asked, "Do the other boys understand their fathers like you do?"

"No. They misunderstand their fathers."

"Why do you think the other boys don't understand their fathers?"

"I think they haven't spent enough time working beside them and they don't communicate with them."

"Did Dapper teach you to communicate with your father?"

Sooner nodded. "I wish he was there when I thought Father wanted to kill you."

"I heard about that. You misunderstood your grandparents' conversations, didn't you?"

Sooner nodded. "It reminded me that my perception isn't always right and I need to look at things through someone else's eyes."

"I'm impressed. You understand so much at such a young age, Sooner," mentioned Sunna, thinking about her mother and her. "How did Dapper teach you to stand in your father's shoes?"

"When I would get upset with him, Dapper would talk to me about it. He let me express my point of view. Then he would have me play the scene back in my mind. He told me to go stand behind my father as I pictured the situation. Once I was behind my father, Dapper told me to step into his shoes. It surprised me to see that I could understand my father's thoughts and desires. I learned how my father felt. I learned to understand him. Then, I understood myself."

Sunna let out a big sigh. "Dapper was one incredible man. I wish I could've met him."

"I do, too. I would like to meet Becker," said Sooner.

"Who's Becker?"

"I've heard Grandfather Justin, Dapper, and Father talk about him. I don't know him personally." Sooner looked at his timepiece. "Mother, I need to leave. It's time for school. You have a good day. Get stronger." Sooner jumped up and disappeared into the house.

Sooner's talk left her stunned. Seeing into the house, she watched Sooner run to Gabala as he waited at the door. They left and her thoughts went to her mother. *Maybe it was wrong for me to put up such a wall between my mother and myself. Maybe I need to stand in my mother's shoes and understand why she criticizes me so much. I would like to stop fighting with her.* Since her spider bite, Sunna had spent more time here than at home. She wondered if her mother agreed with her choice of a husband. They had hardly talked since Ghonllier and her returned from being married.

Taking a moment and doing what Sooner suggested, she could see that her mother didn't like her career, because it took Sunna away from her. The loss of Sunna being gone hurt and frustrated her. It was easy to see why she lashed out at her career, not knowing how else to express her fears and love. Her mother hardly realized that she was pushing Sunna further away by criticizing her choices in life. It was her mother's way of communicating her love for Sunna. *We both need to spend time together and get reacquainted,* thought Sunna, sighing.

It was then she saw someone new pass by the windows. Recognizing Gostler, she jumped up to join him in the house. Seeing her coming in, he stopped to wait for her. She greeted, "Gostler, do you mind if I have breakfast with you? I need to talk."

"I thought you would be eating with your husband," replied Gostler, entering the family dining room with Sunna.

"He's asleep on the bench outside," replied Sunna as the chef came out to get Sunna and Gostler's order.

The chef left with Sunna's partially eaten bowl of fruit and their orders. Gostler pulled out a chair for Sunna and she sat. While Gostler joined her, he asked, "Did you get a chance to talk with him?"

"No. He was asleep by the time I found him."

Knowing they hadn't talked, Gostler decided to change the subject. "How do you like being a mother?"

"I love it. At least to that little boy. He is an incredible child. His understanding of life and learning is far beyond mine at his age. It gives me some insight into what Ghonllier was like as a young boy, I think," said Sunna.

"You're right. He's very much like his father at that age. They both had the same tutor though," commented Gostler.

"Yes, I'm jealous. I wish I could've met Dapper. I've heard so much about him, even before I came here. He was held up as one of the greatest in our business. I'm more impressed with him as a man now, since I heard Sooner talk about him. You made the right decision to take him out of the spy field to be Ghonllier's trainer and bodyguard," said Sunna.

"Thank you, but it was the Master Stones who requested him."

"Gostler, what do you know about this Becker?"

Giving her a sharp look, he asked, "How would you know him?"

"Sooner mentioned him. Who is he?" Gostler shrugged his shoulders. "Where did he go?" Gostler looked away and didn't answer her question. "Do you know him?"

Looking at her, he answered, "Yes, I know him."

"What happened to him?"

"What did Sooner say about him?"

"Not much. He said his father would mention him from time to time. I can't get anyone to tell me anything about him, including my husband," said Sunna. "Can you tell me about him?"

"I can, but I won't. It is something that is a part of Ghonllier's training to become the Master of the Stones. You'll have to wait and ask him."

Sunna's eyes were fixed on Gostler. "Then tell me what you talked about before he fell asleep."

Seeing she was determined to know, Gostler spoke, "Not much. He had a bad dream about Gomper. The Stones are giving him permission to go get the fourth Stone. He told me to tell Jason to bring Spencer and Bert."

Not paying attention to the information about the Trons, Sunna asked, "Why this quick? He hasn't had the third Stone for very long."

"You'll have to ask your husband."

"Where is the fourth Stone?"

"It's on the Jasmine planet."

"Jasmine planet!"

"The fourth Stone is around one of KOGN's largest bases," said Gostler.

"Great. I dislike that planet and having to go in underneath KOGN's nose is going to be interesting. I see why he got up and started to plan out what he was going to do."

Gostler became quiet, not wanting to say more. The chefs returned with their breakfast. Sunna thanked them and she watched Gostler start to eat.

Picking up her utensils, Sunna asked, "Gostler, why didn't you stay with Justin and Ghonllier when he was a child, like Dapper did? You could've done it with your abilities."

Gostler gave Sunna a thoughtful look before turning away. "I was with him until I was told to go into exile."

"Why were you told to leave?"

"I became a liability for Ghonllier. Too many people knew who I was. We thought it would be better and safer for him if I was never seen with him. I went into exile against my hopes and desires."

"Exile was hard, wasn't it?"

Gostler took a bite of his breakfast and nodded. "It was the hardest thing I've ever had to do."

Adamite entered and interrupted their conversation by talking to Sunna. Gostler was relieved to have him do it. He didn't like where Sunna was taking their conversation. It made him uncomfortable as there was little he could tell her. If he offended the Master Stones, they would extend his time with them.

Gostler kept on eating as he listened to Adamite telling Sunna how he located a server stone for her to use at home. They talked during the time it took for him to eat his meal. Finished, Gostler left before Sunna had an opportunity to continue her interrogation. He left, hoping Sunna would never talk to him again about his life in the way she did this morning.

Chapter 12

The Music Box

*W*ith Gomper's depression, Ghonllier mentally never left his side. He was away searching for an answer to keep Gomper alive until he became the Master. The Stones let him know the moment anything changed in his brother's environment that would warrant his complete attention. Ghonllier napped when Gomper was awake, secluded in his private quarters with his staff.

When Gomper was asleep, he created dreams for him, trying to give him hope to hold on a little longer. On a subconscious level, Ghonllier was always aware of what was happening in Gomper's life. It frustrated him that he wasn't coming up with something to stop Bog. In his heart, he knew something was there and it motivated him to continue his search.

The personal staff of Suzair the Great was also concerned about Gomper. They noticed his quiet and distant behavior becoming more prevalent as he seldom joined them in casual conversations. The staff also missed his humor that they had come to love, since Suzair the Great never showed it.

The depression was obvious and they were concerned for all of their lives. Bog had brought Gomper close to death more than they wanted to count and it weighed heavily on all those involved. More than once, they would leave him alone and return to find him passed out. They knew it was Bog because he always had his hand on his stomach.

Brewster seemed to be able to bring Gomper back. With it happening quite often, they decided not to leave him alone. Now, they seldom left his private quarters, unless Gomper had to. They knew if the demon really wanted to kill them, all he had to do was attack Gomper in their presence. They felt the demon would betray them. It was only a matter of time.

With the attacks, Gomper had lost weight. His stomach hurt too much afterwards, often lasting for hours. Thus, Gomper refused to eat and drink. However, after Brewster threatened to insert an apparatus into him if he continued to keep it up, Gomper tried to regain his appetite.

Gomper's weight loss showed and they tried everything to keep him eating and looking fit to avoid the appearance of weakness. With the depression and Gomper's stomach hurting, Brewster could see he was losing the battle.

The staff knew Gomper was holding out for them and they loved him for that. Everyone always seemed worried and Gomper could see the fear in their eyes. It weighed on his heart and he kept trying to go forward, wondering how long he could keep doing it.

There were other reasons to stay away from the crew. The devoted personal staff noticed Gomper's ability to move things, like a Moveling, diminishing. Without his stepping stone and books, Bog was losing his abilities to use his powers through Gomper with each passing day.

Bog controlled people around by using his Moveling abilities. This could mangle or kill someone without them seeing it coming. And the fear this brought had kept everyone in his control.

Ghonllier was aware of everything, including his officers plotting Gomper's death. The weight of the situation was on Ghonllier's shoulders. It was so easy to lose the curse and have it roaming rampant throughout the galaxy, killing those it came in contract with. At least Bog kept it from killing blindly.

By not seeing Gomper, Commander Jabolt was getting braver with each day. Even if he got Bog to leave Gomper alone, his brother might not listen to him and he could walk right into a trap set up by Commander Jabolt. Ghonllier was becoming quiet like his brother.

Today, Ghonllier was in Adamite's office reading a message from Justin in the Eraphin language. Gostler and Adamite watched him read it. Finishing, he handed it to his father and walked away, going mentally back to his brother.

In a few minutes, Gomper would be waking up and Ghonllier could read his mind. He desired to stay asleep. The body was worn out from the abuse and didn't want to open his eyes.

Ghonllier had been trying to get Gomper to talk with him since the Stones had given Ghonllier the dream about the two men fighting. This was a good time to reach out once more to Gomper mentally and try to get him to talk. Again, Gomper ignored him, disappointing Ghonllier.

Gostler and Ghonllier never mentioned to anyone how bad it was for Gomper. They knew what it would do to Gomper's parents. Ghonllier didn't know how much it hurt Gostler to know about Gomper's situation because he couldn't read his mind. He didn't realize how close Gomper and Gostler had been when he was the Master.

Taking a quick break from his brother, Ghonllier noticed Adamite had given the message to Gostler. Ghonllier went back to pacing and thinking.

With Adamite knowing what was in the message, he watched Ghonllier pace. When Gostler finished, Adamite wanted to know his opinion. In asking Gostler, he hoped Ghonllier would answer. To his father's disappointment, Ghonllier ignored their conversation.

Since Adamite couldn't get Ghonllier engaged in their conversation, he decided to wait for Ghonllier to say something. Gostler sat down and got comfortable while Adamite went back to cleaning out his desk.

Adamite was there to clean out his office so Sunna could move in. Eventually, Sunna would want to come to work and she agreed to use Adamite's office, since she needed a server stone and they were getting scarce.

Secretly, Adamite had hoped Ghonllier would take over his office, but he turned him down. Ghonllier wanted Sunna to have it and she jumped on it. Sunna's newly recreated job made Adamite's services obsolete and he was ready to retire.

While Sunna was getting better, Adamite had trained Humphrey to handle it and he was going to be the next in charge. So Spencer was working with Humphrey because Sunna didn't want Spencer to know how well she was doing. Humphrey never saw her as he only received memos. He thought she was handling her job from a bed.

Adamite had installed a server stone in one of the empty bed-rooms. They took the bed out and turned it into an office for her. This way Sunna could work from home or be at his old office when she was ready to face people.

While Adamite worked, he kept glancing at his son. Gostler had told him that he was involved with Gomper and not to bother him. Lately, it had been tempting to watch Gomper on the server stone, but Adamite had lost access to him with Ghonllier here. The server stones now would only respond to the Master Stones. Ghonllier ordered this so his parents wouldn't know what was going on with their son.

At the moment, Gostler was blocked from reading Ghonllier's mind. He knew something had changed as a new expression of relief appeared on the young Master's face. Gostler intently studied him, hoping to get a glimpse of the new development.

Ghonllier had stumbled into a direction of questions that gave him possibilities. The Stones were finally able to answer his questions regarding Gomper. Letting out a sigh, his mind became flooded with questions and answers. For the first time, Ghonllier was able to cut into Bog's chances of winning.

Finally, Ghonllier paid attention to the two men before him. With Gostler being the only one watching him, they exchanged looks. Then Ghonllier walked over to the couches. Gostler could read his mind now. The former Master of the Galaxy kept this fact to himself.

Finally, Ghonllier spoke. "Father, open your vault."

Heading for it, Adamite expressed, "What do you want me to get for you?"

His question was met by silence. Ghonllier was in another trance. Adamite glanced at him as he approached the server stone. When Ghonllier didn't respond, Adamite opened the door to his vault, waiting for an answer.

Adamite's vault was a small hidden room that went behind the server stone. Waiting at the door, Adamite became impatient and met Gostler's gaze. "Do you know what he wants?" he asked.

"He wants everything that we took out of Bog's books," answered Gostler.

Adamite quickly disappeared inside, only to reappear in the same manner with a carrier filled with memory chips. He headed for his desk so they could spread them out. Ghonllier commanded a chip to come to him.

Plucking it out of the air, Ghonllier headed for the amplifier and placed it inside.

"Why are you putting it in there? It isn't necessary for you to read," said Gostler.

Ghonllier ignored him as the monitors showed writing. Commanding the words to go faster, Ghonllier stared at a blur. The words started to slow down and finally stopped at one particular place.

Adamite and Gostler joined Ghonllier, watching the monitor. Adamite knew it was the transcript that Gostler and he had made from Bog's books before Ghonllier burnt them.

Confused by the words, Gostler glanced over at Ghonllier to see a big grin on his face. "You understand it, don't you?" Ghonllier nodded. Looking back, Gostler added, "What does it mean that you must go back to the original situation and repeat it? Does that mean you have to go back to the curse itself when Bog placed it on your family?"

Ghonllier faced him. "No. It means we need to go back further than that. We go back before he placed the curse on our family."

"Go back to what? Why before he placed the curse on the family?" asked Adamite.

The new Master didn't answer and Gostler wished he could read the man's mind again. He knew Ghonllier was talking to the Stones because he was blocked on part of the conversation.

Eventually, Ghonllier spoke, "I understand what we have to do."

"Tell us!" demanded Adamite.

"I've got to go back," whispered Ghonllier, looking at his father. "We're going back to the Zuffra moon."

"Are you going to face him again?" feared Adamite.

Not answering, Ghonllier said, "Father, would you give me the chip that has all the people's names in the city?"

Frustrated, Adamite retrieved the memory chip from his desk. It was one he was going to leave for Sunna. Ghonllier mentally removed it from his hand and the moment he had it, the names started to appear on the server stone without him putting it in the amplifier.

Adamite watched and thought, *Why is he showing us names?*

Ghonllier heard his thoughts and answered, "Do you see those three names, Father?"

"Yes," answered Adamite.

"Get them in here now," responded Ghonllier.

"What are you going to ask them to do?" asked Gostler.

Ghonllier looked at his father and ordered, "Those three names are men in this city who are craftsmen by hobby. I want them to make this." The new Master pointed at the server stone and added, "I need this to be made in a week."

"What's that?" asked Adamite.

"A music box," answered Ghonllier.

Ghonllier had a picture of the music box, plus the instructions on how to make it, appear on the server stone. A list of material needed was showing up on the stone as Adamite asked, "Why would this have anything to do with the curse?"

"I know," smiled Gostler.

"What's he doing?" quizzed Adamite, looking at Gostler.

He nodded toward the server stone. "It's an old-fashion music box. He's going to use some hypnotic tune to keep Bog's mind busy so he'll leave Gomper alone," stated Gostler, looking over at Ghonllier.

The new Master ignored his comment while he continued to place information on the server stone. His father joined him and asked, "Is Gostler right?"

Ghonllier looked at him. "What is he right about?"

"Is this a music box for Bog?"

"Yes."

"How are you going to get him to accept it, Ghonllier?" asked Gostler, flanking his other side.

"This was a gift Bog once gave his daughter. It was the only present he really gave her and she took it with her, not understanding why. He thought it was because she wanted to remember him," answered Ghonllier thoughtfully.

"Why did she take it with her?" asked Adamite.

"She had hidden something in it that she didn't want her father to find. It was something that Sethus gave her. She didn't have time to take it out, so she took the music box with her," answered Ghonllier.

"How long do you think the Stones can distract him for you?" asked Gostler.

"Hopefully long enough for me to become the Master," stated Ghonllier, distracted. The three men were silently studying the picture, when Ghonllier added, "Father, have the men come here and build it in your office. Get all possible staff to collect their materials. I'll leave everything on the server stone and I want them to follow the instructions."

"What if they have questions?" asked Adamite.

"Tell me and I'll place the answers on the server stone," informed Ghonllier.

Adamite took out his C-Stone and started to make the call. "What do I tell them exactly?" asked Adamite.

"Tell them I-Force needs this built now. They'll need to drop everything they're doing to come and do this. They aren't going home until it is done. So make them comfortable with cots and food," answered Ghonllier, looking at his father. "Make sure they have everything they need here."

Finished, Ghonllier headed for the door. Adamite stopped him as Ghonllier faced his father, seeing his questioning eyes. "How will this music box save your brother's life?" questioned Adamite.

"I'm taking Bog back to when he was a little boy, happy and carefree. This music box means something to him."

"What?" asked Gostler, joining them.

Looking at the server stone, Ghonllier educated, "The music box was like the one his mother had and it made her very happy. It

Bog's daughter's music box

was destroyed before she died. He has anchored a lot of memories with the music box to his mother and happier times in his life."

"He'll destroy it before you can affect his mind, if he knows it came from you. How do you plan on getting it to him?" quizzed Gostler

Glancing at Adamite talking to one of the men, Ghonllier answered, "This time I'm going to let the Vanishers do the job."

"Why not take it in yourself?" asked Gostler.

Ghonllier smiled. "It isn't necessary for me to do it this time. So why risk it?"

"How complicated is his mind? How long do the Stones think they can hold him?" quizzed Gostler.

"Bog's mind is very complicated so the Stones can only guarantee me two months. Anything past two months is a risk and they'll lose him," answered Ghonllier.

"I hope you can become the Master of the Stones by then," commented Gostler.

"I do, too," stated Ghonllier, letting the air out of his lungs. Then he continued, "It's risky, if I can't become the Master in time. When Bog comes out of the trance, he'll know it's me that caused him to be in it. He'll kill Gomper without hesitation."

"Are you sure?"

"He has a worse temper than you had, Gostler," smiled Ghonllier.

"Ghonllier, could you take over for Bog and control the curse?" asked Gostler.

"I don't think so, but it's a question Bog wonders about, too." Gostler nodded. Ghonllier added, "He really wants me to face Gomper. That's the only way he can guarantee the curse will transfer to me properly."

Adamite put his C-Stone away while listening to the last part of the conversation. He asked, "Ghonllier, when we transcribed those memory chips from Bog's books, it never mentioned Jaclyn's mother. What happened to her?"

"It was custom for a sorcerer to have arranged marriages. She never fell in love with Bog. Can you imagine what it would be like to be in a loveless marriage with Bog? He only wanted a child from the woman. He forced himself on her when he knew from the stepping stone that she would conceive. Once she had the baby, he ignored them until Jaclyn was older.

"Bog started to be cruel to her mother. He treated the servants better than her. So she left, taking her young daughter with her."

"But he found them, didn't he?"

"Yes. He used his stepping stone and found them. In his anger, he killed his wife, leaving the little girl. He just needed the girl to pass on his legacy."

"Is that why he forced himself on Suzette? He knew she would conceive from the stepping stone?" asked Gostler.

"Yes, and he did it for the same reason. He could preserve the curse."

"Did he hurt the little girl?" asked Adamite.

"She reminded him of his mother. So he treated her better than his wife," answered Ghonllier.

"Why didn't he go after Jaclyn when she left with Sethus?"

"They were in a spaceship and he couldn't reach her. He could only go from one stepping stone to another stepping stone. The other sorcerers destroyed or hid their stepping stones, trying to contain Bog."

"So why the curse?" asked Gostler.

"The Master Stones. Sethus found the Master Stones and Bog wanted them. When he couldn't steal them from Sethus, he put the curse on our family, determined to steal them after Sethus was gone and couldn't stop him."

"Was Bog's daughter in love with Sethus when she left with him?" asked Adamite.

"She left to get away from her prearranged marriage and her father. Sethus took her because she saved their lives by helping them escape from prison. They didn't realize that they were in love with each other until later."

Adamite received a call and they watched him take it. Moving the C-Stone away from his ear, he asked, "Son, how soon do you want them to start on this?"

"Yesterday," stated Ghonllier, facing his father. Pointing to the server stone, he added, "Everything they need to know is on the server stone, including the timetable. The timetable is important. Make sure they understand it, Father, if you want to save Gomper's life."

"You've given them a week. Are you sure they can do it that fast?" asked Gostler as Adamite repeated Ghonllier's words.

"Tell Father I'm leaving in three days for the Zuffra moon. I'm taking these men with us. I need to go, Gostler. Contact me if you have more questions," responded Ghonllier, leaving.

"You're going to make them finish it on board the ship?" questioned Gostler.

Ghonllier didn't respond and was almost at the door, when Adamite stopped him. "Son, they say it can't be made that fast."

"That's exactly what they'll tell you every time you ask them. Trust me, those men can do it if they are pushed to perform. So I want it done," ordered Ghonllier, arriving at the door. Stopping, he added, "Tell them this box will end the war in the galaxy in three months, if they can get it finished on time. If they are late, Bog has

237

won. It might help them realize how important this is to the war efforts. Remember, Father, your son's life is in those men's hands."

"Where are they going to be able to work on board the ship?" asked Gostler, seeing Adamite going back to his call.

"They'll use my office and conference room. Sunna will have to work somewhere else," answered Ghonllier.

Gostler held up the message from Justin and stopped him. "Ghonllier, how do you want me to answer Justin's message? Apparently, he can't do what you requested."

Ghonllier replied, "Tell him to send in just the *Liberty Pursuit*. Justin needs to know that Houser is aware of me being alive, but not his captains. So remind him to tell Houser to make them take the same oath he took." Pausing, he added, "The captains will be able to read my energy waves. I'm programmed into the *Liberty Pursuit*."

Attempting to exit the room, Adamite stopped him. "Son, why don't you stay and explain this to these men if it's so important," suggested Adamite.

"I don't want them to see me as an authority figure right now. Let them think Justin is ordering it," explained Ghonllier. "Don't expect us for dinner. Today, we're having our first family outing. Sunna and Sooner are out in the transport waiting for me, so that's why I'm in a hurry to get out of here."

"Oh, Sunna is starting to get out and around people?" asked Gostler.

"No, not really. We're going where there aren't any people."

"Where is that?" asked Adamite.

"Sunna is totally fascinated with every aspect of my life for some reason, especially my past. She wants to see where Dapper and I entered through the waterfall. She has Sooner excited about seeing it too, so I'm taking them to look at it. We're staying out there for awhile and we'll be eating there as well," answered Ghonllier.

"If you decide to climb back through the doors, you might find it interesting to see what was really written on the door that led out of the cavern," smiled Adamite.

Ghonllier faced Adamite with a questioning look. In his mind, he read what was on the door. Smiling, he left the office thinking,

I can see why Dapper didn't tell me the full truth. I would have refused to open the doors. No way then would I have accepted the statement, WHO EVER OPENS THESE DOORS WILL BE THE NEW MASTER OF THE STONES.

Outside, Gabala stood next to the transport, waiting for him. The windows were darkened so no one would see his family inside. While walking down the steps, excitement rippled through his body because this was their first family outing.

With Sunna well, Ghonllier and her had set up rules for the family and their private lives. They decided to take one whole day or night together as a family with no interruptions. Sooner picked the time each week and the family discussed what they would do.

Then Ghonllier promised Sunna that she could pick one or two nights a week with no children, outside family, or business for either one of them. He promised to take her on a romantic date.

They needed a lot of romantic dates, since Ghonllier and Sunna never dated before they got married. Ghonllier promised himself to create a way for Sunna to fall in love with him more and more each day. He promised to take Sunna on a date at least once a week for the rest of their lives. It was important to guarantee quality time for their relationship, if they were going to be successful with it.

He knew from the Stones that he needed to get Sunna to fall in love on a constant basis to keep her walls from reappearing. She needed to know she was more important than his title.

Even though he knew at times in the future he wouldn't be able to do it, Ghonllier wanted to take every moment to build their relationship. Sunna and Sooner were very precious to him and any success in his career meant nothing if he let them down. He agreed to go on this journey of being the Master for his family. Neglecting them would only weaken him and he knew it.

Inside the transport, they were excited to be going and Ghonllier was relieved to finally understand what he needed to stop Bog a little longer.

Chapter 13

Asustie Left Behind

Sunna was pleased with getting back to working out at the pace she used to before marrying Ghonllier. With a medic in-house, the rules were that he had to be there to make sure you were spending the correct amount of time for your body that day. The monitors could read everything that was going on inside. She liked working out with Cid and knowing exactly how it was affecting her.

This was why Cid wanted to record Ghonllier's workouts. Ghonllier didn't like it and purposely would do it when Cid was busy. The new Master felt he had enough information to make his documentary. Ghonllier had decided to leave without taking Cid with them while he bonded with the fourth Stone.

It frustrated Cid to learn Ghonllier started to exercise during the night or at times when he was busy. So the medic learned to carry his portable analyzer in his pocket in hopes to get a peek at Ghonllier's body. Ghonllier knew when he wanted to check him and sometimes he would let him take a reading. Cid was fascinated to watch first-hand how the man and Stones meshed together.

Cid wasn't the only reason for mostly changing his workouts to nights. Ghonllier needed less sleep now with the third Stone. Since he needed to watch Gomper's enemies, it was a good time for Ghonllier to exercise so he could be by himself.

While they were waiting for the music box to be built, Ghonllier still tried to talk with Gomper when he was asleep. So far, his brother ignored him and Ghonllier knew Gomper didn't trust him. With Bog talking directly to his mind, he was suspicious of a new person and Ghonllier wasn't allowed to tell him he was his brother.

Even though he was awake most of the nights, Ghonllier promised Sunna he would always go to bed when she did. If he wasn't tired, Ghonllier would wait for Sunna to fall asleep before he would disappear. Then he would return and sleep his five hours. Ghonllier knew with the four Stones, he would sleep about two hours at the most. Sometimes, he longed for his body to be the way it was before the Master Stones. At night, he felt a little lonely. Gostler told him that he would get used to it and like it.

Sunna was feeling so well that she wanted to go to the office to decide what she would need. Ghonllier told her that Spencer wouldn't be at the office the morning before they left to deliver the music box. Adamite had agreed to go with her and she waited for him out on the patio.

Stacy had the baby, whom they named Jopert. She wanted to visit with the two while waiting for Adamite.

To avoid people, Ghonllier spent his night on the roof. He had just come out of the trance with Gomper to see Sunna was waiting to leave the house for the first time. Able to take a break from his brother, Ghonllier left to say good-bye to her. Once he was off the lift, Ghonllier used his Vanishers speed to find her.

Sunna had her back toward the door and had just given Jopert back to Stacy. When she felt the bonding fires, Ghonllier had his arms around her waist and was kissing her neck.

She faced him and he grinned, "So you're leaving me here alone today?"

"Yeah, you're alone," cajoled Sunna, reaching out to touch his face. "I feel like I'm missing you already." Pausing, she added, "I thought you would've been out here. Where were you?"

"On the roof. I was talking to Gomper when the Stones informed me that you were leaving," answered Ghonllier, pulling her in for a hug. He whispered, "Have a good day. I wanted you to know that I was thinking about you."

Sunna closed her eyes, listening to his words, while feeling the warmth from their marriage contract. Suddenly, Ghonllier started to kiss her on the neck again. She giggled and tried to get out of his grip. Sunna's neck was her ticklish spot and he knew it. Ghonllier wouldn't let her pull away. Then they looked at each other before they kissed.

Pulling away, she made a quick examination of him to see he was wearing his exercise clothes. Grinning, she teased, "You smell great."

He responded with a smirk, "Would it matter?"

"Of course it would," she countered, digging her fingertips into his ribs.

Jumping, he grabbed her wrists so she couldn't use her hands. Sunna tried to get out of his grip while Ghonllier said, "Hi, Gostler. What can I do for you?"

Sunna stopped wrestling with him to look over his shoulder. He was right; Gostler had joined them. Ghonllier relaxed his grip and she stepped back to allow him to face Gostler.

In the background, Jopert let out a cry. He seemed upset about something and Stacy was frustrated. Everyone looked at Stacy as she asked, "Jopert, what's bothering you?"

Jopert answered with another cry that didn't seem to stop.

Gostler glanced over to see Ghonllier studying the baby. Gostler stated, "Ghonllier, the men working on the music box are nervous about your timeline. Can you give them more time?"

Facing the former Master, he put his arm around Sunna and responded, "They can do it, Gostler. Tell them to stop worrying about the sound. Just follow the instructions and do it."

"How did you know that I was going to ask you about the sound? Can you read my mind?" questioned Gostler hopefully.

"No," replied Ghonllier. "I'm just aware of their concerns. They're more afraid of flying on the *Liberty Quest* than they are on getting it done, Gostler."

Smiling, Gostler nodded and left. Jopert let out another cry while Stacy tried again to comfort him.

Going to his mother's side, Ghonllier informed, "Mother, he's hungry."

"Are you sure? I fed him an hour ago," informed Stacy.

"Yes. He's on a growth spurt right now. Expect him to eat more often for the next couple days. Then he will level off again," educated Ghonllier, looking at his wife.

She grinned at him. "You know so much about babies. It might be smart to keep you around," teased Sunna, wanting another kiss.

He was glad to give it to her.

Asustie happened to be sitting on an outdoor couch. Stacy looked at her and requested, "Would you hold him while I page for someone to bring me a container of food?"

Asustie stood, looking pale. "I'll get it for you, Mother."

Ghonllier noticed Asustie for the first time and studied her while she began to move. Asustie gave them a weak smile while she passed Ghonllier and Sunna in each other's arms. Sunna and Ghonllier went back to being caught up in each other, when Jopert let out another cry.

Stacy looked over at the door, wondering where Asustie was.

In the doorway, Stacy saw Asustie lying still on the ground. Stacy screamed, "Ghonllier, help her!"

Using his speed, Ghonllier arrived next to his sister. He scooped her up in his arms, knowing nothing was broken in her body. Ghonllier headed for the medical center while he said, "Honey, get your brother. I'm taking her to Cid."

Then he disappeared.

Before he entered Cid's medical center, Ghonllier slowed down. Cid met them at the examination table. Ghonllier placed her body gently on the table while Cid activated the large analyzer that was above it.

"What's wrong with her?" he asked.

"She's pregnant, Cid. Make sure Jason is the first person to know that," informed Ghonllier, leaving.

Ghonllier hadn't gone too far when he met his mother and Jopert, who was crying in her arms. Stacy blocked Ghonllier from leaving and asked, "What's wrong with her?"

"You'll have to ask Cid," replied Ghonllier, stepping around her.

"No, Ghonllier. You can tell me. What's wrong with my daughter?!" shouted Stacy.

Just then, Carrie, Jopert's nanny, arrived to take him from Stacy's arms. Ghonllier took advantage of the moment and disappeared. After Stacy told Carrie what to do for him, she ran to the medical center. Cid wouldn't tell her anything.

She exited the medical center, angry and frustrated. Walking back, Stacy saw Ghonllier in the exercise room, starting a workout. It angered her to see him. *How dare he tell Cid not to tell me anything*, thought Stacy, opening the door.

Arriving next to the machine, Stacy challenged, "How come you told Cid not to tell me anything?"

"I didn't mean to hurt your feelings, Mother. I just think this is serious enough that Jason will want to know first."

She repeated, "What's wrong with my daughter?" Ghonllier looked away, letting her know that he wouldn't talk. Tears filled her eyes and her voice trembled, "No, Ghonllier, please don't do this to me this time! What's wrong with my daughter?"

Ghonllier stopped the machine to respond, "I refuse to tell you anything. You need to hear it from Jason."

Stacy stormed off as Ghonllier watched. She opened the glass door in time to greet Sunna. "What's wrong with Asustie?" she asked.

"I don't know!" spat Stacy, moving past her.

"What did Ghonllier say?" quizzed Sunna, watching him exercise through the glass walls.

"He won't tell anyone. We have to find out from Jason," stated Stacy, leaving.

"Oh, really?"

Sunna entered and slowly approached Ghonllier. "Are you going to tell me what's wrong with her?" she questioned.

"Yes," replied Ghonllier, looking past her to see Jason. They both watched him run into the medical center. Sunna looked back at him. "She's pregnant," he divulged.

"Why wouldn't you tell your mother?" asked Sunna.

"It means a lot to Jason and Asustie to tell her themselves. So act surprised."

Sunna left and Ghonllier knew something wasn't right with her. He jumped off the machine, stopping her from leaving. "Sunna, you're upset. I can feel it. I want to talk about it now."

"I'm not upset," countered Sunna, not looking at him.

"Sunna, I know you want your own baby. Ever since Jopert has come to the house, your heart aches for one and it's a new feeling for you. Asustie being pregnant is going to bother you more than you want to admit."

She stepped around him, but he blocked her escape again. "Please, Ghonllier, I don't want to talk about it. I haven't had time to evaluate my feelings yet."

"We can have a baby as soon as I get permission to tell everyone who lives here in this city that we're married," assured Ghonllier.

"When do you think that will be?" spat Sunna, not wanting to admit her anger had been smoldering and he was triggering it.

When she saw he wasn't going to let her pass, Sunna looked up. She saw love and total acceptance in his eyes, something Sunna didn't expect to find for some reason. In her thoughts, Sunna assumed he wouldn't accept this side of her. But he did and she knew it.

Ghonllier took his time to say, "I'm not sure. I do know that I have to be the Master of the Stones before we can tell them."

"Every day I'm getting older and I'm afraid I won't be able to have children if it doesn't happen soon."

"I want a baby, too, Sunna. I promised Sooner that he would have siblings."

"Do you know why we have to wait to tell the crew that we're married? Jason says they're starting to wonder why I live here. They've heard the rumors about Cid and I. I don't like the lie. I'm in love with you, not Cid."

"And that's all that matters," said Ghonllier, going into a trance.

Sunna took this as her time to leave. Ghonllier didn't stay there long and stopped her from leaving. He stated, "Sunna, the Stones told me to tell you to cherish this time. You need it to adjust to being a mother and wife before everyone knows you as Commander Sunna, assistant and wife to the Master of the Galaxy."

Sunna knew it was true and let her forehead fall into his chest. "When I agreed to this, I didn't realize how hard it would be."

Ghonllier nodded and gently rubbed the back of her head. "Sunna, do you understand what's going to bother you on this next mission the most?" he asked.

"What?"

"Me acting indifferent toward you. I'll be in my stern old image," said Ghonllier, placing his hand on her neck while running his thumb along her jawbone.

Slowly, Sunna nodded. "You're right. That's going to be hard."

Taking her in his arms, Ghonllier whispered, "Honey, I knew this was going to be the hardest on you. I'm so grateful it was the Master Stones who explained it to you."

Enjoying being in his arms, Sunna closed her eyes and cuddled into his neck. The bonding fires felt particularly strong when Ghonllier spoke those last words.

He whispered, "The extra warmth is the Stones confirming to you that I've spoken the truth on needing to keep our marriage secret a little longer." Inside, Sunna resigned herself to be patient. "I love you, Sunna, and you're my motivation to be the Master. Now, I strongly desire to control the powers well so I can protect you from the evils that want to destroy our very existence. I love knowing what your desires are and then having the opportunity to give them to you. Without you here, there would be no enjoyment for me to be the Master."

Melting, Sunna silently cried. It felt good to have her feelings validated and Ghonllier knew what he was doing. He didn't let go of her until she finished crying.

Sunna pulled away to gaze into his loving eyes.

"Do you want to go and congratulate your brother?" he asked.

Sunna nodded. Ghonllier put his arm around her shoulders and they walked together to be with Jason and Asustie. When they came up to the door of Cid's medical center, Stacy exited.

She gave Ghonllier a disgusted look and asked, "Why couldn't you tell me that she was pregnant?"

"I didn't because it would've upset Jason. This is something that means a lot to him and he wanted to tell you personally," answered Ghonllier.

Stacy's face softened. "Is the baby healthy?"

"Yes, she is going to be a beautiful girl, Mother. But you need to keep that to yourself. Jason will want to tell you that information himself. So don't tell Father."

Stacy smiled. "Thank you, Son. You're forgiven," she stated, leaving.

"Your welcome, Mother."

Jason lit up to see them enter. He thanked Ghonllier for taking his wife to Cid. Sunna came forward to give Asustie a hug. She could honestly congratulate Asustie and Jason.

When Ghonllier went to hug Asustie, she asked, "Ghonllier, have you known about this for awhile?"

"Yes, I knew you were pregnant soon after we arrived here on the Suzair planet."

"Can you just look at a woman and know she's pregnant?" asked Sunna.

"I can know if I want to." Then turning to his sister, he said, "With you, I wanted to know when it happened."

"Why?" she inquired.

"Ever since you got married, I've been concerned about you getting pregnant. You can't fly in space and be pregnant."

Jason looked at him. "Jenny did it. Why can't Asustie do it?"

"Jenny was a seasoned space traveler. You're not, Sister."

"Wait," responded Sunna, looking at him. "What constitutes a seasoned space traveler?"

"At least two years of spending ninety percent of your time in space," answered Ghonllier.

"What will happen if Asustie got pregnant or flew now on the *Liberty Quest*?" asked Jason.

"Space will cause her to lose the baby," stated Ghonllier.

"Is that why Cid was so upset about Suzette?" asked Jason.

Ghonllier nodded. "Your body changes while you're in space. That's why Mother doesn't like it. She swells and feels uncomfortable and it's only because she doesn't give her body time to adjust."

"And Jenny and you met on a ship that seldom landed," reminisced Jason.

Ghonllier nodded. "So for her, space was normal and comfortable," said Ghonllier.

"Was Sooner born in space?" asked Asustie.

Ghonllier nodded. "After his birth, we all were transferred off to a base ship. So we were only gone for a couple of months at a time," answered Ghonllier.

"I remember you both had spent a couple of tours before the ship was taken out by your brother," reminisced Jason.

"You mean Bog," reminded Ghonllier.

"So I won't be able to fly with you if I became pregnant?" Sunna asked, studying his eyes.

"No, honey, you can't come with me. You've spent too much time on land."

"I didn't know that," replied Sunna thoughtfully.

Jason started to chuckle and everyone looked at him. "I remember you trying to get Jenny's attention. You faked an injury so you could meet her."

"Did Jenny ignore him?" asked Sunna.

"Something like that. I think it was his rank that made her not pay any attention to him," smiled Jason, seeing the scowl on Ghonllier's face.

He didn't want Jason talking about his past to Sunna. She would start peppering him with questions. He rolled his eyes when Sunna asked, "So she had to be older than you?"

"Yes, she was older," answered Ghonllier, putting his arm around her.

"I didn't realize she was older than you. By how many years?" asked Sunna, looking at him.

"The same as you, my dear," said Ghonllier. Then, changing the subject, he added, "Asustie, I'm going to miss you on board my ship. You're a bright spot for me."

"And I wasn't?" cajoled Sunna, poking her fingers in his ribs.

Ghonllier grabbed her hands while Jason said, "I don't like the idea of leaving Asustie behind—"

"I'll be okay, Jason. We have a server stone to see each other," interrupted Asustie.

Ghonllier reached out for Sunna's hand and ordered, "Jason, reschedule Janet for the trip. I want Cid to stay with Asustie."

"Thank you for reading my concerns and giving me Cid," Asustie smiled.

"My pleasure, Sister," smiled Ghonllier, guiding Sunna out of the room.

Ghonllier held Sunna's hand as they walked toward the door to the exercise room. There, he stopped to face her. "My father is waiting for you. He's already seen Asustie and Jason."

Sunna gave him a quick peck on the lips and left. Ghonllier wished her a good day.

"Thanks," stated Sunna, disappearing out of sight.

Twenty-four hours later, Ghonllier was on the *Liberty Quest,* ahead of everyone else. Knowing Jason didn't want to leave Asustie any sooner than he had to, Ghonllier offered to go ahead and set the ship up for the mission.

He left a lot earlier than necessary. His real motivation was to talk with Justin in private. When he spoke to his father, using the Master Stones, people weren't aware of it and interrupted him. This time, Ghonllier wanted his legal father's full attention and he didn't want Adamite to hear his words. Ghonllier knew it bothered Adamite that Justin and he were so close. Adamite didn't quite feel the same closeness from Ghonllier yet. The years and hours together weren't there for the two of them.

Ghonllier relished the moments as he talked to Justin. With the problems he had with Gomper, Ghonllier hadn't spoken to him since his marriage. They used the Eraphin language, allowing Justin to get caught up on Ghonllier's life without anyone understanding what they were saying. This also guaranteed that they wouldn't be interrupted. Justin's opinion had always been valued in the past and Ghonllier felt the same today.

Justin hooted on hearing how Ghonllier let Houser know he was alive. He was pleased to know how well Sunna and Sooner were doing. Justin liked the idea that Jasper and his family had been brought into Ghonllier's city. They talked for a couple of hours.

During the conversation, Ghonllier read something from Justin that he didn't expect and it bothered him. Justin didn't think Ghonllier belonged to him anymore. Looking back, Ghonllier could see that Justin always knew he wasn't his son but loved him anyway. Now,

Justin was confused on where he really stood. During the conversation, Justin was more concerned about Adamite than he was about Ghonllier.

Noise in the background brought Ghonllier out of his thoughts and he looked in the direction of the corridor to see Jason and Asustie. He smiled to see the couple, wanting them to stay together as long as possible. Instantly, Ghonllier read their reluctance to say good-bye. The moment reminded him of Jenny and himself. It was hard to say good-bye to the person you shared your life with and dearly loved.

A call coming in distracted him. He knew it was from Houser, hoping to get through to him. Luckily, Jason was on his way over.

Ghonllier had the captains put Houser on hold while he said, "Jason, the call is for you, from Houser. Tell him you'll allow me to speak to him."

Jason picked up an earpiece and sat in the chair by the console to talk. Asustie had followed him, wanting to talk with her brother. Ghonllier stood to greet her.

"You had a rough morning, didn't you?" he smiled.

Asustie nodded. "Has Cid given you something for morning sickness? It will get worse if you don't talk with him."

She nodded. "We saw him on our way to the ship." She wrapped her arms around Ghonllier and expressed, "I love you, Little Brother. Have a good trip." Letting go of him, she added, "Is there something that I should watch this time on the server stone?"

"Yes. Have Jason tell you when we arrive at the Jasmine planet. I would expect a show when I pick up the fourth Stone," he smiled.

She nodded and looked behind him. Jason was handing him the earpiece so he could talk with Houser.

"I'll handle the boarding, Ghonllier," said Jason, leaving with Asustie.

Ghonllier sat back down and talked with his old friend Houser. He wanted to understand why Jason wanted him to track Ghonllier's signal. Jason told Houser to do it without question.

Finishing his conversation with Houser, Ghonllier was disappointed to see Asustie there. For some reason, Asustie's emotions and the ability to read her were very strong with him. On the inside,

Asustie was crying, not wanting to be left behind. She loved to fly like Ghonllier did.

Ignoring them, he left for the bridge to enter the corridor. He found Sunna looking back at them. Jason and Asustie had entered the OSA to open the reading panel. They heard Spencer's voice. With a lament face, she turned away and left. Sunna wasn't ready to face him just yet.

The new Master wanted to follow her, but hesitated. For some reason, he didn't want Spencer to see them together, even in the corridor. Before Spencer exited the OSA, Ghonllier returned back to the bridge. Watching him walk past the command center, Ghonllier wondered why he was told to bring the Tron. It would be easier on Sunna and himself if Spencer weren't on board.

Ghonllier decided to stay on the bridge until Jason returned. When he finally did, he joined Ghonllier at the NV table. "I can chart the course if you want."

"I know," answered Ghonllier, glancing at him. "This trip is going to be different without Asustie."

Jason nodded. "A lot of changes for both of us," he countered.

"Yeah."

"Do I need to know what Houser and you talked about?"

"Yes," answered Ghonllier, requesting vanishing paper.

He wrote while he said, "Jason, I've worked out the details with Houser at the Jasmine planet."

"Are you going to make him take another oath?"

"He's already put the captains under oath after telling them I'm alive. My signal is in their ship's system and I need them to know where I am."

Jason nodded. "Why not use the *Liberty Quest* and disguise her signal?"

"A Galaxy Creeper can do what I need far better than a Star Screamer," said Ghonllier.

"Will Houser be safe?"

"As long as he stays out of the atmosphere and leaves when I tell him to."

"Do you want me to give him the orders?"

"No, I'll do it. We have complete trust in each other and Houser will do what I need faster than he will for you," answered Ghonllier.

"I understand. So my job is to run your ship and give Houser a bad time if necessary?"

"Correct," smiled Ghonllier, stepping away from the table. "Take over. I'm leaving the bridge."

"Oh, a little tired?" smirked Jason.

"Yeah, something like that," countered Ghonllier.

Jason grinned once more before Ghonllier left. Then, as they headed to their next destination, Jason's thoughts returned back to Asustie.

When Ghonllier entered the corridor, he found Spencer pacing close by. Upon seeing Ghonllier, Spencer greeted, "Commander, may I talk with you?"

Ghonllier nodded and asked, "Do you want to talk here or in my old office?"

Spencer looked around and said, "I would prefer the command center. I don't want someone walking in on us."

Ghonllier knew he was referring to Sunna. Entering the command center, Ghonllier took him over by the indigo beam pad. Facing him, Ghonllier asked, "What can I do for you, Spencer?"

"Did I understand Commander Jason correctly that you personally requested me this time?"

"Yes."

"He wouldn't tell me about this mission. Is it dangerous?"

"Yes. Bert and you both will receive extra points."

"Good."

Spencer paused. "Who is going with you? Commander Jason did say you were leaving the ship at the Jasmine planet."

"Spencer, why don't you ask me the question you really want answered?"

"At the office before we left, I heard Commander Sunna tell General Humphrey that she planned on going with you on the Jasmine planet."

Giving Spencer a disappointing look, Ghonllier questioned, "I haven't asked her to come. What did she exactly say?"

"I don't know more than that, Commander. You'll have to ask her," said Spencer.

"I will," snapped Ghonllier, leaving.

It angered him that he hadn't paid attention to Sunna's thoughts. He had been so busy with Gomper that it hadn't occurred to him.

Spencer stopped him. "Are you upset?"

Ghonllier nodded. "Yes. I don't want her to come with me."

"Good. I don't want her to go."

"Spencer, you need to understand right here and now. I can't stop Sunna from going with me if she insists."

"Why?"

"We're both commanders. She is in charge of my security. The only thing that I can do is try to convince her to stay back," answered Ghonllier.

"Are you sure, Commander? Sunna says you have ways of getting things done," implied Spencer.

"What do you mean by that?" asked Ghonllier, wanting to understand his thoughts better.

"Justin, he's your father, right?"

"Yes."

"So you have more power than her?" questioned Spencer.

"I used to, but I gave her my power. It was the only way we could get along. I promised not to interfere with her job. The only thing I can do faster than Sunna is transfer someone out of here."

"Then transfer Sunna out," challenged Spencer.

"I promised my son that I wouldn't. He's very fond of her."

"So there is nothing you can do to stop her from going with you?"

"I'm bound by military law and I have to let her come," reminded Ghonllier. Then he added, "I'm going very hard to persuade her to say. Thank you for the warning."

"Thank you, Commander, for listening to me," responded Spencer, leaving with Ghonllier joining him.

Behind them, they heard, "Commander Ghonllier, I need to talk with you."

Spencer kept going while Ghonllier faced Jason. The commander watched Spencer disappear around the corner before he whispered, "Did Spencer talk to you about Sunna and Cid?"

"NO. HE WAS ASKING ABOUT THIS NEXT MISSION."

Jason watched Ghonllier leave.

In his mind, Ghonllier searched for Sunna. He found her in his old office, working. Ghonllier decided to see if she wanted to talk and entered. She shot him a glance before going back to work at his old desk. Humphrey was just leaving and Sunna didn't seem to want to talk with him. She was putting her things away so the men could use the server stone to finish the music box.

He opened a drawer next to her to retrieve a yellow stone that was left by Gostler. Taking his time, Ghonllier commanded the vault to open. Then he took his time placing the stone inside.

He knew Sunna was mentally trying not to look or talk with him. She was successfully keeping her attention away from him so her feelings wouldn't show. Before he left, Sunna heard, "I LOVE YOU."

Sunna smiled and glanced up to see he was gone.

As he exited, the Master Stones let him know that Gomper needed him. So he left to go back to the bridge and focus on his brother.

Ghonllier entered the command center, requesting the ship's hullercasts. The ship's stones instantly responded to the Master Stones. Butler was surprised to see them come on because the captains were the only who could do it. Relieved to see Ghonllier, he smiled and went back to work.

It was a peaceful sight to see the ship jumping through fields. Ghonllier wasn't in the mood to reach out to his brother, but he was going to do it. He wanted to be with Sunna more than he had previously thought.

Slowly, he took his time to sit in his flight chair, getting in rhythm with Gomper.

Eventually, Gostler wandered into the room, looking for something to do. He immediately knew Ghonllier was there because he could read his mind. Arriving at his side, Gostler saw Ghonllier had his eyes closed as he thought about Gomper.

Reading something was bothering him, he debated if he should talk with him. After a moment, Gostler decided to leave and heard, "What do you want, old man?"

"Oh, so you are upset?" replied Gostler.

"Yeah, sit."

Sitting, Gostler inquired, "What has you upset?"

Spencer, thought Ghonllier.

"What did he say or do?" asked Gostler in the Eraphin language.

"He's upset with my wife and talked to me about it," answered Ghonllier in the same language.

"Is he still in love with her?"

"Yes."

"What did he say?"

"It's not what he said, Gostler. You know what it's like."

"Oh so well," replied Gostler. "Is he suspecting anything between the two of you?"

"No, I wish he would. Maybe it would help him let go of her. For some reason, he's having a hard time believing Sunna would fall in love with Cid."

"So he doesn't really believe it?"

"He wants to hear from her before he accepts the fact. If it's true, he's hoping it is a phase."

"Why doesn't he give up?"

"If Sunna really fell in love with someone else, then Spencer thinks it's possible that she might fall for him, too," said Ghonllier, looking at Gostler.

"Why is he here, Ghonllier?"

Ghonllier shook his head. "I don't know. I was told to bring him and it has me a little upset."

"Sunna told me about her concerns about being around the crew. I keep telling her that the fourth Stone will give her a break," replied Gostler.

"Do you think the fourth Stone will be as dangerous for me as it was for you to receive?" asked Ghonllier.

Thoughtfully, Gostler stated, "I think it will be worse."

"Why?"

"Because it has been a long time since the Stones have been together. Plus, you will be behind enemy lines and they destroy anything they perceive as an enemy."

"Could the fourth Stone mistake Sunna as an enemy?"

Gostler was very slow to answer and Ghonllier waited. Eventually, he guessed, "I do think it could be a possibility."

Ghonllier sighed. "Thanks, Gostler," he expressed, closing his eyes.

Gostler knew he was through talking and he decided to leave him alone.

It was hours later when Gomper finally woke up for the day. Ghonllier had been talking to him most of the time, trying to keep his brother willing to live another day. He glanced at his timepiece to see it was late and Sunna was asleep in bed.

Getting up, he decided to get his sleep in now before Gomper needed him. The minute he walked through the hullercasts of his sleeping quarters, Sunna stirred and opened her eyes. The two looked at each other and she smiled.

The next day, Gostler entered the dining room to see Ghonllier sitting alone. Gostler sat down and informed, "The men are on schedule, like you said. They'll have it done in a few minutes and want your approval, especially the sound of the music box. Would you come and give it to them?"

"Why would they want my approval, unless someone told them that it was I who wants the music box?"

"They want some kind of approval. They requested the commanders of the ship," countered Gostler.

Ghonllier shook his head. "I can see from here and it's exactly what I need. Please tell Sunna or Jason to thank them and say that we're deeply appreciative of their dedication and skills."

"Why won't you tell them personally?"

"They don't even know I'm a commander. I want it to stay that way."

"Okay," responded Gostler, leaving.

Ghonllier watched him leave through the fish aquarium as Sunna entered. He quickly looked away, deciding to watch her through the Stones. Sunna was with Spencer and Humphrey. He could tell they were talking business.

They ordered something light and sat, continuing with their conversation. Sunna found her gaze innocently going over to Ghonllier. She wished that she could go sit at his table. She hadn't seen him all day and wanted to just touch his hand. The bonding fires would be appreciated right now.

Looking back at Spencer and Humphrey talking, she would've enjoyed their conversation in the past. It wasn't the same, now that she was married. She wanted to be with her husband now, not her past. Sitting with them, she kept an eye on them and noticed Ghonllier never looked in her direction. The conversation Spencer and Humphrey were having bored her.

Finally, she mentally asked while watching him out of the corner of her eye, *Ghonllier, can you hear me?*

Instantly, she heard, "YES."

Smiling, she glanced between Humphrey and Spencer, feeling like they heard or saw her light up. They seemed to ignore her and kept talking. Mentally, she asked, *Do you have time for me?*

"YES."

Her eyes flickered toward Ghonllier, in hopes he was looking at her. He wasn't. The two men stopped talking when Sunna moved her chair back.

Sunna stood while Spencer asked, "You're leaving?"

"Yes, if you don't mind. I have a headache and need to take care of it."

"Are you going to see Cid?" responded Spencer coldly.

"No, Cid didn't come on this trip," informed Sunna.

"Oh," replied Spencer, softening. "I wondered why I didn't see him. I heard he had to fly with Commander Ghonllier."

"Ghonllier requested Cid to stay back with his sister. She's pregnant," smiled Sunna.

"Asustie's pregnant! I didn't know. I'll have to congratulate Jason," stated Humphrey.

"Does that mean he won't be flying anymore?" asked Spencer, leaning forward.

"I don't know. You'll have to ask Commander Ghonllier. He's his medical tech, not mine," countered Sunna, leaving.

Spencer watched her walk around them while Humphrey said, "I hope you feel better, Sunna."

"Thanks, Humphrey," responded Sunna over her shoulder.

After she left, Humphrey said, "You look angry, Spencer. What's bothering you?"

"Nothing. I just wonder why a commander has to have his own medic."

Humphrey noticed Spencer watch Sunna pick up something at the galley and leave. When she left, Spencer looked at him and they continued their conversation.

Ghonllier waited for Sunna to leave the room before he stood. Stopping at Sunna's table, he requested, "Humphrey, would you come with me? I need to talk with you." Immediately, the Vanisher stood. Ghonllier nodded and smiled, "Spencer."

"Commander," greeted Spencer, watching the two men leave.

When they were away from Spencer, Ghonllier informed, "Humphrey, I want to show you where I want this music box placed in Bog's castle."

"Will it be difficult to place?"

"It shouldn't be," responded Ghonllier, entering the office.

The room was empty of personnel. On the server stone, Humphrey could see the floor plan of the castle. The general looked at Ghonllier and asked, "Will he be able to see us?"

"He's like an ungifted person, so he won't be able to see you like I do when you blend in with nonliving material or move quickly."

"Good."

Gesturing toward the server stone, he informed, "I suggest you go through the main entrance, where we went the first time. Follow the line I'm drawing up the staircase and down the hallway to this room." He tapped the noted room on the plans. He paused. "Be careful when you enter. It was his daughter's, and no one has been in this room since she left. I don't want him to know that someone left the music box in the castle. I want him to think he discovered it."

"I understand, Commander."

Humphrey stared at the floor plans while Ghonllier glanced at the music box. Then he said, "If you have questions, ask Jason."

"I will," sounded Humphrey, studying the server stone.

Ghonllier was pleased to leave and head for his quarters.

After closing the door to his quarters, Ghonllier found Sunna waiting for him. The two looked at each other.

"What took you?" she smiled.

"Business. We're close to the Zuffra moon. I needed to pass on last minute information to Humphrey," answered Ghonllier, reaching up to unfasten his uniform top.

She had their pillows propped up and snuggled into them. Ghonllier slipped his uniform top off and sent it mentally over to the chair. The two still were locked in a gaze as Ghonllier sat next to her on the bed.

"If we're close to the Zuffra moon, don't you need to still be working?" asked Sunna.

He nodded. "Do you want to watch the Vanishers with me?"

"Yes."

"Do you want to watch it from here or the command center?" smiled Ghonllier.

"I want your attention, so let's watch it from here."

Ghonllier leaned into her and stated, "As you wish, my dear."

The two kissed. Afterwards, Sunna reached up and ran a fingertip along his ear and down his neck, feeling the burning fires. He leaned into her for another kiss. The warmth from their contract increased. Tears came to Sunna's eyes to know their marriage was intact. In her heart, she still needed reassurance that everything was real. The Master Stones allowed her to feel his intense love for her and she appreciated it.

He read Sunna wanted to feel the warmth of the bonding fires more than anything else. It pleased him to give her the desires of her heart. After their kiss, Ghonllier pulled her closer to his chest. Cuddling, she let out a sigh, being satisfied.

Immediately, Sunna felt his body cool down to the right temperature for her to be comfortable in his arms. It felt so peaceful that she found herself wanting to take a nap.

Not wanting to wake her up, Ghonllier lied there, holding her, while he watched Bog and Gomper. Sunna woke up when she heard the landing chimes announcing their arrival to the Zuffra moon. "Are we there already?" she inquired, looking up at him.

"Yes," answered Ghonllier, opening the doors to the monitors.

Sunna saw the Vanishers with the music box as they appeared outside the ship. Humphrey, along with five of his men, stood momentarily at the fallen gates, with fog bellowing around them. Then they disappeared within them.

The monitor showed the floor plans of Bog's castle. Ghonllier used blue dots to represent the Vanishers. Sunna could follow them, amazed at their speed.

Looking at him, she inquired, "I never realized how fast a Vanisher could really move. What's it like to be one?"

"I like it. I think it's my favorite gift to have from the Stones," whispered Ghonllier.

"Where is Bog? Is he aware of us?"

"No, he isn't aware," answered Ghonllier, showing her where Bog was in the castle with a red dot.

Sunna intently watched Bog's dot. Suddenly, Bog moved quickly to where the music box was in the castle.

"Ghonllier! Does he know we're there?"

"No, I opened the music box."

Ghonllier was pleased to see the hypnotic sound draw him to the room. He entered, displaying a mean and angry expression. However, the minute he gazed at the music box, his whole demeanor changed. It was taking him back to his youth, before his mother died and his life changed.

Slowly, he ran his fingers along the edge. Reading his mind, the new Master was pleased with what the Master Stones were doing to his mind. Gomper had totally been forgotten and didn't exist in Bog's mind.

Ghonllier let out a sigh of relief to see he had bought some time for his brother and himself. Now, he only had to warn Gomper of Commander Jabolt and try to get Gomper unafraid of his voice.

The landing chimes were heard again, meaning the Vanishers had been picked up and they were leaving. Sunna cuddled more into Ghonllier and closed her eyes again. He lightly ran his hand up and down her arm while watching and listening to Bog and Gomper's thoughts.

Chapter 14

The Fight

*T*he ship was in night-mode as it grew late. Ghonllier leaned against the navigational table, watching the Master Stones mentally take him through the different caverns he had to get through to reach the fourth Stone. Being engrossed in the scene, he didn't see Gostler approach him.

Gostler waited for him to come out of the trance. When he did, Ghonllier asked, "Why aren't you in bed?"

The former Master shrugged his shoulders. "Sometimes you don't feel like sleeping." Seeing Ghonllier go back to staring at the floor, he added, "Have you spoken with Houser lately?" Ghonllier shook his head. "Why is Jason talking to him right now? I just left the office."

"Houser wants to know why Jason's sending me into a dangerous situation."

"Oh, so that's why Jason's threatening him to stay out of it and obey orders."

"Yeah. He's trying to protect me. Houser knows the coordinated belong to a KOGN base."

"Are you going to need Dapper with Houser?" questioned Gostler. Ghonllier shook his head. "How far away are we from landing?"

"About nine hours."

"Is Houser going to make it in time?"

"We will get there before Houser. I don't want Houser hanging around. He needs to back me up if I need him and then get out of there before KOGN converges on him."

"Do you have a backup plan if KOGN picks up his presents?"

Ghonllier looked at him thoughtfully. "He'll be fine. He's going in under code red. They won't know he is there unless he enters the atmosphere and fires on them."

"I assume you told Justin, what you're doing? Are you going to broadcast to him the event?"

"Yes, he knows," replied Ghonllier, facing Gostler. "I plan on broadcast but I think he would like to share it with you all here. Would you call him?"

Gostler nodded. "How is Gomper doing?"

Smiling, he responded, "He's improving a lot with Bog leaving him alone. I'm hoping he'll talk with me soon."

"Can he tell a difference between your thoughts and his?"

"No and he's not ready to accept me."

"Sunna was talking about going with you at dinner. Have you changed your mind?"

Giving him a cold stare, Ghonllier replied, "No. I just haven't discussed it with her yet."

Gostler chuckled. "Why not?"

"Guess, Gostler," answered Ghonllier sarcastically.

"When are you going to do it?"

"Soon," said Ghonllier, getting impatient with the questions. He was about to say something, when he looked past Gostler. The former Master followed his gaze to see what he was looking at.

"Commander, am I interrupting?" inquired Spencer.

Ghonllier shook his head. "Go ahead and ask me your question."

"What time is the meeting?"

"In the morning, around eight."

Spencer left while Ghonllier and Gostler exchanged looks. "Do you know why you were told to bring him yet?" asked Gostler in the Eraphin language.

Shaking his head, Ghonllier responded in the Eraphin language, "I think I'll go and have a talk with Sunna."

Gostler nodded and watched Ghonllier leave. He wondered how events were going to unfold. He was the only one who understood

262

how dangerous the next twelve hours would be for Ghonllier and those with him.

Ghonllier entered the room to find his wife already asleep. Being able to see perfectly in the dark, he got ready for bed and slipped underneath the covers without turning on a light. Moments later, a hand touched his chest.

Instantly, he opened his eyes and saw Sunna looking at him. "I didn't want to wake you. I'm sorry," he apologized.

Sunna requested soft light. "I've been dozing off and on, waiting for you. Is everything a go for tomorrow? Is Houser going to be there?"

"Yes, Houser will be there."

"Are you nervous about going for the fourth Stone?"

"No and yes."

"What time are we leaving? You haven't mentioned it to me."

"There's a meeting at eight in the morning. I'm leaving after it."

Sunna studied his face, listening to his words. She picked up the *I'm* and was angry. Not sure what to say, he looked away. In his mind, he could hear Sunna being very angry with him.

Looking at her, he said, "Sunna, it wasn't necessary to tell you."

Sitting up on her knees, she search his eyes. "Ghonllier, are you interfering with my job again?"

He reached to take his hand in hers and she pulled it away, giving him a cold stare. "Sunna, I want to go in at night so I can slip in and leave with the Stone without anyone seeing me. If you come with me . . . I don't want any distractions."

"Distractions? When did I become a distraction for you?" Ghonllier stayed quiet, studying her face. "You've used those words before. When we first met, you called me a distraction. Maybe that's how you really feel."

"I didn't mean it to sound the way it came out . . . Sunna, I really need to go in alone. You'll slow me down if you come."

"So you're now making the decisions on how I run my job?" stated Sunna.

Ghonllier shook his head. "No. I'm not. This time, I don't need anyone to go with me."

"Then why did you bring Bert and Spencer?"

"Sunna. I do not know why they are here. I was just told to bring them . . ."

She stared at him. Slowly, she said, "Finish your sentence."

Ghonllier looked away trying to figure out a way to explain to her what was about to happen. Sunna didn't want to wait for his answer. She headed for the foot of the bed to stay in Sooner's room. Ghonllier instantly moved and blocked her escape. "Sunna, don't leave being angry. Let's talk."

"Why do we need to talk? You've already made the decision for us. I'm not a part of the partnership!"

"Sunna," pleaded Ghonllier, "don't leave like this. There are things you don't understand."

"Understand?! I wonder why. You won't talk with me."

"Sunna, I knew you were planning on coming with me and I didn't know how to approach it. If I handled it poorly, I'm sorry," apologized Ghonllier.

His apology for some reason didn't satisfy her and she wanted to leave. Again, Sunna attempted to get off the bed, but Ghonllier blocked her with a pleading expression. "Honey, please don't do this. Let's talk about it."

"Why? Apparently, I'm not important enough to you to be a part of the decision process. You know everything. Why do you want to talk now?"

"Sunna, that isn't true. I'm not making the decision. Please hear me out. Once you know what I'm being faced with, you'll see that I haven't broken my promise to you. If you will hear me out, I will not interfere with your decision to stay or come with me."

She looked back at the pillows and Ghonllier sighed. Without another word, Sunna went back and he joined her. Resting his back into the pillows, he put his arms out to her. Reluctantly, she snuggled into his arm and waited for him to begin.

This was hard to explain something to Sunna that he or she had never seen. A Stone with the power to rip a ship in two if it so desired. He had to learn to control it but before he could. All the Stones had to come together with the same understanding. They had to setup rules on how they would work together. The fourth Stone could match the other three Stones in power in some areas.

He started off by explaining this to Sunna. Patiently, she listened and asked questions to how the Stones worked together. He explained, telling her the fourth Stone would not respect his wishes and it would take the other three Stones with him to convince the fourth to work together.

Sunna was surprised to hear him tell her that the fourth Stone needed to accept her too and it might see her as a threat to it. This confused Sunna after the Stones told her that they would always protect her. Ghonllier reminded her the three Stones promised it. The fourth Stone agreed to nothing.

After listening, she studied him. "I don't believe the Stones would hurt me."

"Sunna, is the risk worth it? The fourth Stone could kill you and I couldn't stop it. This is why I won't allow Houser to enter the atmosphere. The fourth Stone will kill him if I need his help to get out." She gave him a doubtful look. He added, "Would you please do it out of respect for me? This time, let me go alone." Gazing into his eyes, she saw his love. "Sunna, we have waited so long for each other. Let's not lose what we're trying to build. I saw our children and I love them already."

"Ghonllier, if you think I'll die on you, I won't—"

"Are you guaranteeing it to me, Sunna?"

She studied his face and said, "I believe with all my heart I won't die on you."

"That's what Jenny said before she felt. Yet, she died. So your feeling might not be telling you what you need to hear. Your desires are drowning out common sense." Sunna studied his face and became quiet. In reading her thoughts, Ghonllier added, "Honey, I really don't want you there. I don't want you hurt again and I know my limitations right now. I can't guarantee anything." Sunna stared at him.

"I'm not afraid, Ghonllier."

"I am. . . . If you knew you would get hurt, would you still go?"

She turned her head away from him. Ghonllier placed his finger underneath her chin, guiding her face to look into his eyes. Sunna followed his finger. There was so much love there that her anger melted and he knew it.

Sunna sat motionless, feeling the warmth of their marriage from his finger underneath her chin. With her heart melting, she fell forward into his arms. The bonding fires extinguished her anger.

Ghonllier pleaded, "Stay back and let me do this alone. I need to have you here waiting for me. If something happened to you, I'd have no desire to be this man the galaxy needs."

Lying in his arms, she whispered, "You cheated. You don't fight fair."

"I love you," soothed Ghonllier, holding her tightly.

Sunna reached down to pull the cover up. She kept eye contact with him. The orbiter started to dim and Sunna asked, "When you ask the Stones about the future on the Jasmine planet, what do you see?"

"It's like it was with the third Stone. I see myself with the fourth Stone in my hand and then everything goes blank," replied Ghonllier.

"I see, but I know you can see more of the future. What do you see?" questioned Sunna, looking deeper into his eyes.

"The future depends on people's choices. That's why I have Houser there, in case I get trapped and need a diversion."

Sunna was thinking about their conversation. Ghonllier ran his hand through the ends of her hair and she watched his fingers play with the ends. Slowly, he assured, "I meant it Sunna. I will not interfere with your decision. If you insist on coming, I'll support you. I'm just pleading you not to be with me in a situation where I can't completely protect you. I don't like feeling vulnerable and I feel it with you coming."

The room darkened while Sunna stayed silent, thinking about his words. She listened to his breathing change and knew Ghonllier had fallen asleep. Eventually, Sunna joined him, but it wasn't a restful night for her. She heard Ghonllier's words, but it bothered her to let him go alone. She made a promise to herself to always be there for him. Finally, by morning, she fell into a deep sleep.

When she awoke, Ghonllier was gone like always. Getting out of bed, she thought about their conversation and his request for her to stay on board.

Leaving, she could hear water running in the bathroom. She thought about confronting him once more, but instead went into Sooner's quarters to use his bathroom and get dressed. In case someone ever happened to enter Ghonllier's quarters, Sunna didn't want any trace of herself there. Thus, she exited for her bathroom, expecting to hear Ghonllier in the other room. All she heard was silence.

Peering around the corner, Sunna saw the door to his bathroom open and he was gone. Usually, Ghonllier took his time to leave their quarters, but not today. She wondered what it meant. Going to her closet, Sunna opened it and looked between her KOGN and Special Services uniforms.

This morning, Ghonllier didn't wait for Sunna, because he didn't want to talk about her not coming with him. He knew she hadn't made up her mind and he had a lot to deal with besides her. He wanted to be alone so he could mentally prepare for picking up the fourth Master Stone. They were rushing it because of Gomper. The Master Stones had awakened him a couple of times during the night because his brother needed him. So he secluded himself in the conference room, waiting for the meeting.

Problems with Gomper's officers had increased. Gomper was asleep and Ghonllier needed to let him know what they were doing behind his back. So Gomper was prepared for the morning in dealing with them. So far Gomper had followed his suggestions and he hoped it would continue.

Gomper's officers were confused by his new behavior. He wasn't using his Moveling abilities to hurt or kill people like in the past. The only thing that seemed the same was Suzair the Great's ability to know about their traps, but he wasn't retaliating against them. This gave his officers courage to try again until they succeeded. Some were questioning Suzair the Great because Gomper wasn't quite matching Bog's voice at all times.

Gostler was first to enter the conference room where the meeting was going to take place. It didn't surprise him to find Ghonllier facing the window with his eyes closed. He knew Ghonllier was using the Stones and assumed it was for Gomper's benefit. Trying not to bother him, Gostler sat and quietly waited.

Humphrey and Spencer were next to join him. Gostler nodded in acknowledgment and they returned it. They all sat silently together, waiting. Then Adamite and Bert entered, with Jason following close behind.

When Jason entered, Ghonllier faced everyone and commanded the door to shut. Then he opened the door to the monitors and spoke, "If you look at the monitor, you'll see the valley that I'm going alone into—" Right in the middle of the sentence, Ghonllier stopped and stared at the door. Everyone joined him to see the door open for Sunna, who wore a KOGN uniform.

Ghonllier felt sick on the inside. "No, SUNNA, PLEASE," pleaded Ghonllier softly for her ears only.

I believe in the Stones. They'll protect me. We're partners. I can't let you go alone. You mean too much to me. Ghonllier lowered his eyes to the table after reading her thoughts. He was silent as she came over to the table and sat down.

Taking a deep breath, he ordered, "Spencer and Bert, you are now going with me. I want you both in KOGN uniforms incase you need to be men." Ghonllier paused to look thoughtfully at Spencer, before he asked, "Spencer, would you be willing to carry us both?"

Spencer stammered, "Yes."

Glaring at Sunna, Spencer never felt so much anger toward her. All he could see in his mind was Sunna and Cid kissing behind the privacy screen. *She's willing to do this just to be with him again,* thought Spencer as Ghonllier brought him back to the meeting.

He looked away from Sunna to see everyone looking at him. "Spencer, what is your answer?" asked Ghonllier.

"Sorry, Commander. Please repeat your question."

"Spencer, I want you to take an oath that you'll follow Bert's instructions to the letter," repeated Ghonllier.

The Tron flickered a glance at Bert before he stated, "No offense, Commander, but I can take care of myself."

"Spencer, I'm well aware of your strength and skills, but you have never been on the Jasmine planet. It's different than the other planets in the galaxy. Bert has spent years there and survived. That in itself is a huge achievement." Ghonllier was concerned about Spencer now. He was aware of his anger toward Sunna and he didn't need it. Now that he had his attention, Ghonllier added, "Spencer, you'll stay here, unless you take the oath. Sunna and I can walk there if necessary."

"I'll take that oath," retorted Spencer, leaning back in his chair and staring at the table.

"Good, because I also want you to agree to another one," informed Ghonllier.

"What is it?" questioned Spencer, shooting him a quick glance.

"That you won't come to Sunna's and my rescue for any reason. If Bert tells you to leave for the ship, you do it. You bring Bert back as a human. Bert, I don't want you flying after I leave you."

Bert nodded while Spencer spoke, "So you only want me to carry you there and do nothing else?"

"Yes. You won't live if you don't follow Bert's orders to the letter. I'm putting him over you, even though you two have the same rank. Can you handle it?"

Spencer looked at the table. "Yes," he grumbled.

"How close to the valley are we landing the ship?" quizzed Jason.

"We'll be landing about ten miles away," said Ghonllier.

"Why so far?" asked Jason.

"There are numerous caverns in and around that valley. KOGN has connected them together with pipes carrying the flammable fuel. I want you far away from those caverns so you don't get hurt."

Gostler let out a groan and shook his head. Everyone looked at him. He stopped and gazed at Sunna. "You're making a mistake, Sunna, by going with him. This is too dangerous for you," he affirmed.

"Gostler, I have to do this, no matter what the risks are," she defended.

"Where do you want us to wait for your possible return?" questioned Bert.

"I'll communicate with you, Bert, so just follow my instructions."

Ghonllier could tell Spencer was about to say something that would start a fight of words with Sunna. So he said, "Spencer and Bert, you need to leave now to get ready. Meet us in the OSA as fast as you can."

The two Trons left and Sunna expected to talk with Ghonllier with them gone. But, to her surprise, Ghonllier disappeared the minute they exited.

Jason put his hand on Sunna's and stated, "I hope you're doing the right thing, too, Sister. You just found happiness."

"I believe I'll be protected," defended Sunna, hoping Ghonllier wasn't angry with her.

Gostler stood while she talked and hoped she was right.

Ghonllier was steaming and wanted his anger gone by the time they left. They were close to coming out of jump speed. He knew their relationship would be in trouble by him going back on his promise to stay out of her job. Sunna wouldn't understand the dangers, unless she went with him. Ghonllier felt vulnerable about protecting Sunna and he couldn't believe she had done this to him and the Stones.

Right now, he needed to get his anger out and then he needed to talk with the three Master Stones. He went to the exercise room and was pleased to find the running tunnel empty. Entering, he ran and didn't take the time to program it for weather or terrain. He just wanted to run. The whole time, he pleaded with the Stones to help him find a way to keep her alive.

They were concerned too and told him that they would try, but couldn't promise anything. All of them knew it would depend on the fourth Stone and what happened out there. The three Stones might be pushed to use all their powers to counter the fourth Stone and save her life. It disappointed Ghonllier to hear the Stones couldn't tell him how it might end. They were going into uncharted territory, too. This was the first time they would have to challenge the fourth Stone before they had bonded together.

He lingered inside the RT, or running tunnel, until the Master Stones told him it was time to meet the others in the OSA. Ghonllier entered the corridor and could hear voices shouting in the OSA.

"Why Sunna? I want to hear why you want to do this!" shouted an angry voice.

"Stay out of it, Spencer. This isn't your business," matched Sunna.

"You're selfish, Sunna. All you care about is your desires. You want to get hurt so you can be with Cid? Tell me the truth."

Using his Vanishers speed, Ghonllier appeared between Sunna and Spencer. Facing Spencer, he snapped, "I want this stopped right now!"

"Why should you care about this conversation, Commander? Everyone knows you two just tolerate each other!" matched Spencer.

"It's my place to care about the safety of all my crew! I'm the one in charge and I'm supposed to bring you all back alive. No one is leaving this ship if they're angry. It's a blinding emotion and someone will die and I can't have it," replied Ghonllier. Then, after pausing, he added, "Do you have problems with who is in charge?" Spencer glared at him. "Spencer! Are you allowing your personal feelings for her to interfere with this mission?" questioned Ghonllier.

Backing down, Spencer mumbled, "I'm sorry, Commander."

"You know the rules, Spencer. There must be harmony with everyone when you are facing a dangerous mission." Listening to his thoughts, Ghonllier added, "Get control now or stay back."

"Leave all of us out of it and go alone," retorted Spencer.

"No!" Sunna answered, moving out from behind Ghonllier.

Ghonllier blocked her with his arm. "Spencer, I warned you about not accepting her decision. If your emotions for the commander are interfering with your job, I'll transfer you out of here before we land again. You'll get us all killed or hurt if you're not with us."

The two men kept eye contact and Spencer softened. "I apologize, Commanders. I'm sorry for my behavior to you both."

Bert entered the room and instantly knew he had walked in on something unpleasant. He felt uncomfortable and went over to wait by the door. Spencer turned away from Ghonllier's gaze and joined Bert. Ghonllier went to his compartment, not looking at Sunna. He took his time, trying to get composure and take his own advice. They couldn't have anger and Ghonllier had been as angry as Spencer was with her.

Finally, he reached for his belt last before he shut the door. The landing chimes were heard. Facing the main loading door, he found Sunna staring at him with questioning eyes.

Mentally, she asked, *Are you angry with me, too?*

Not smiling, he winked at her. Sunna sighed and asked, "Can I wear my field glasses, Commander?"

"Yes," he answered. "I would rather you see in the dark, since we're with Snacker Vines."

Sunna reached for her field glasses from her compartment. She already had her blaster. The KOGN didn't have field glasses and she was relieved to be able to take some of her I-Force equipment.

She was the last to join everyone on the ramp. The night felt hot and muggy as she exited the ship. Bert watched for her and upon seeing her, he faced Ghonllier and requested, "Requesting to change, Commander."

"Fly, Bert."

Bert changed into a large gray eagle and flew to the nearest branch while the rest of the group walked down the ramp. The humid heat of the night was all too familiar to Bert. A slight breeze brought a whiff of peppermint and chocolate fragrance. He ruffled his feathers, knowing Snacker Vines were close by.

When Spencer arrived at the end of the ramp, he requested, "Permission to change."

"Granted," answered Ghonllier.

Instantly, Spencer changed into a muscular black horse with a wavy mane and tail, just like his hair. Ghonllier mentally lifted Sunna on his back with himself right behind her. The new Master used the Stones to speak to Bert and told him the direction to fly so Spencer could follow.

Bert communicated with Spencer through their spy earpieces. Ghonllier wished Spencer knew who he was so he could talk directly to him through the Stones, but he couldn't. Snacker Vines were scattered throughout the trees and Bert took them purposely away from them. One mistake and the Snacker Vines would've sent out their vines, wanting to devour them, forcing Ghonllier to expose his powers to Spencer.

Being this close to Sunna, Ghonllier couldn't help reading her mind and knew she was thinking about Spencer and their fight. She was upset with everyone for disapproving of her decision. Ghonllier wanted her to focus away from what happened on board. When he knew Spencer and Bert couldn't see them, Ghonllier kissed Sunna on the neck, knowing it would distract her thoughts.

It worked. Sunna struggled not to laugh. Ghonllier leaned forward so she could feel him sitting behind her. The warmth of the bonding fires increased and she smiled. He achieved his goal and Sunna started to relax.

Knowing how much Ghonllier didn't want her there, Sunna didn't expect to feel his acceptance so strong. It touched her heart and she felt herself tumbling more in love with him. She leaned back into him, finding it comfortable with him lowering his body temperature, giving her some relief from the heat.

Eventually, they left foliage and started to crest up a hill. When Bert stopped Spencer from arriving at the top, Sunna signed to Ghonllier, asking why. He answered, "THERE'S A SMALL GROUP OF KOGN ROBOTS JUST OVER THE RIDGE, WORKING ON A DYSFUNCTIONAL VALVE. THEY'LL SEE US."

Sunna signed, asking if they were close to the base.

Spencer arched his neck in time to see her question as Ghonllier answered, "Yes."

The Tron stared at Bert intently, waiting for the signal to continue to the top. Ghonllier decided he didn't want to wait to long

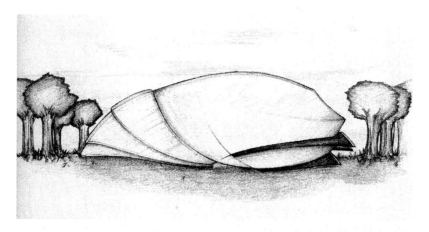

The Liberty Quest landed on the Jasmine planet

and told Bert to fly along the ridge until he found a safe place for them to walk along the hilltop. Spencer followed along the base of the hill. Finally, Bert stopped on a branch and gave Spencer the signal to join him.

When they did, the sound of a door shutting on a transport caused Sunna to jump. Everyone waited to hear what would happen next. All they heard was silence. Bert told Spencer to move faster as the bird stopped, landing on another branch, while waiting for them to catch up.

Ghonllier had his arm around Sunna's waist, staying in rhythm with Spencer's stride. Sunna searched for lights from the KOGN base as Bert kept moving them faster and faster.

A few raindrops landed on Sunna's face. She looked up to see the sky cloudy, as the air was heavy with moisture because of it. Glancing down, she saw a few lights flicker through the trees and wondered if Ghonllier saw it.

Mentally, she asked, *Do those lights belong to the base?*

"YES."

The lights let them know how large the KOGN base really was and Sunna was taken back by its size. With every step, they were hearing the sounds of a full and functioning base. Four Galaxy Creepers and nine Star Screamers were being worked on or waiting to be repaired.

Do they work around the clock? mentally asked Sunna.

"YES."

Robots did most of the repair so it was easy to run a crew constantly. There were humans there, but they didn't handle the repair, only the supervision.

Sunna mentally asked, *What time is it?*

"ELEVEN O'CLOCK, THEIR TIME," Ghonllier replied, arriving to the end.

They had reached the edge of the base. Since they had come along the top of the ridge, the group looked down upon the base and had an excellent view. It was almost too good and Ghonllier was concerned about leaving Spencer here.

After a short discussion with the Stones, they agreed it was the safest place for them. So Ghonllier floated himself and Sunna off Spencer's back.

"Change back, Spencer," ordered Ghonllier. He did and looked up at Bert in the tree. Ghonllier was aware Spencer was wondering why Bert hadn't received orders to change. So he signed to Spencer, "I want Bert and you in the tree. Bert will only change if he has to take you out of here alone." Spencer nodded. "Do not get out of the tree for any reason, unless Bert tells you to. There are carnivore plants and robots on this hill. You need to become invisible."

Spencer signed back, acknowledging the orders, and reluctantly began climbing up to where Bert was waiting for him. Then, after Spencer finally reached him, Ghonllier turned around to find Sunna waiting behind him.

He said, "WALK IN FRONT OF ME. I'LL GUIDE YOU AWAY."

Sunna left, with Ghonllier following. The minute they were out of sight from Spencer and Bert, Ghonllier held her hand.

"SUNNA, ALWAYS KEEP IN CONTACT WITH MY BODY SO THE STONES CAN PROTECT YOU. IF YOU LET GO OF ME, THEY'LL HAVE NO LEVERAGE WITH THE FOURTH STONE."

Sunna mentally asked, *Are we going in now?*

"NO."

Are you waiting for Houser?

"YES. HE'S ALMOST HERE."

Suddenly, Ghonllier stopped her. She faced him and asked mentally, *Is something wrong?*

"NO. WE'RE GOING TO WAIT A LITTLE LONGER IN PRIVATE FOR HOUSER TO JOIN US," informed Ghonllier, pointing to a tree that had fallen.

They sat down to wait while Ghonllier held her hand. She leaned into him, watching the activities below. With Snacker Vines around, Ghonllier was glad Sunna wanted to be close to him. He didn't want to fight with them tonight for her. It would expose their presence before he had the Stone.

Eventually, Ghonllier nudged her and divulged, "HOUSER'S COMING OUT OF JUMP SPEED."

He led while holding her hand. They moved down the rest of the hill and toward a fence that surrounded the base. Behind the fence, Sunna saw a parking lot of transports and a tall tree standing by itself. When they reached the fence, Ghonllier stopped and removed his knife from his belt. *He can't cut that thick fence with that knife,* Sunna thought. However, before she knew it, the knife sliced right through the metal fence.

Did the Stones just help you? she asked mentally.

Ghonllier nodded while keeping an eye on the activity inside the fence. They entered, hoping not to be detected. The robots working on top of the ships would be able to see them if they looked in their direction.

They maneuvered around two transports and stopped next to the lone tree. Two large boulders sat at the base of the tree, appearing like potent bodyguards. Sunna quickly turned away to see if anyone had noticed them, when she heard a scraping sound. Looking back, she saw Ghonllier had mentally removed the boulders and was lifting a metal lid that guarded the entrance to the caverns.

She attempted to go first, but Ghonllier stopped her. "YOU'LL CAUSE AN EXPLOSION. I NEED TO GO FIRST."

She nodded and watched him disappear into the blackness. Entering herself, Sunna was pleased to see that there were steps cut into the narrow tunnel that descended straight down.

Changing her field glasses from night-mode to black lights, Sunna knew her training had taught her to look for the invisible things that could stop you from completing a mission. Within minutes, the black lights exposed wires going down the sides of the steps. She continued down, following the wires. Then they crossed over on the steps and Sunna froze.

She recognized the wires belonging to a device that would cause an explosion. Where she had her foot, she should've triggered it. Ghonllier looked up at her while holding onto her ankle.

"SUNNA, YOU'RE OKAY AS LONG AS WE'RE TOUCHING. KEEP GOING, YOU'RE OKAY."

She continued on to find the tunnel getting smaller. Now, she discovered something new about herself. Being in the narrow underground tunnel triggered a phobia that she wasn't aware of until now. The smell of mold and wet soil was almost choking her. She had done this before, but never with the strong odors.

The lower they went, the stronger the smell became. She struggled to breathe and Ghonllier could feel it himself, since he was tied to her. He needed Sunna to relax. Thus, he started talking to her in his altered hypnotic voice, transforming her. Knowing Ghonllier was helping her cope; she wished that she'd stayed back.

Finally, Ghonllier's hand started to move up her leg, which gave her hope. They were close to the bottom. With both feet on the ground, Sunna wrapped her arms around his neck and said, "I'm so sorry. I didn't know that I would react this way. It's never happened before."

"Sunna, stop shaking. You're okay," said Ghonllier. She let go of him as he added, "Don't let go of my hand as we cross this cavern."

Sunna saw the same wires crossing back and forth on the floor of the cavern and knew why Ghonllier reminded her to hold on to him. They had only taken a few steps, when Sunna jumped. A heavy thud echoed throughout the cavern. "What's that?" she asked.

"I put the metal lid back to hide the opening," explained Ghonllier.

"Let's do this and get out of here," requested Sunna, moving away from him.

He pulled her back, going first. "Isn't the Stone in this cavern?" she asked.

"No," responded Ghonllier, not stopping.

They entered a tunnel that didn't make Sunna very happy. The phobia came back again, causing her to hold her breath.

On the base, the fence deterred Snaker Vines, but it didn't stop them from getting through. Dogs were always on the prowl, trained to detect Snacker Vines approaching. They had trackers surgically implanted underneath their skin, allowing the control tower to know where the dogs were at all times, in case they started barking.

The fence had sensors that would detect anything touching them. Ghonllier had the Stones disable it before entering. After Ghonllier put the lid back on the entrance, the control tower noticed the dogs leaving the fenced area. They manually set off the alarms, causing security lights to scan the area outside of the base.

They assumed Snacker Vines had breached their fences and taken their dogs. Robot ran to the place to find a hole cut into the fence with a precision tool. The tower was miffed to learn the dogs were found outside the fence, romping through the grass.

Those in charge were concerned. The sensors or the dogs should have detected someone breaching their fence. Apparently, they didn't or the dogs would have had the trespassers pinned up against the fence. So who had successfully entered their base and why?

The dogs obeyed and returned to their handlers. Quickly, they put leashes on them before asking them to find the intruders' scent. It didn't take long for the dogs to take them to the entrance of the cavern. The boulders were back in the same place and the handlers were perplexed as to why the dogs kept digging at the base of the boulders.

With the dogs digging, they found a part of the metal rim. The humans with them called in what they found to the tower. Instantly, the tower manually turned on the sirens, letting everyone know that security had been breached. All men and robots were called out to find the intruders.

The Master Stones vibrated to let Ghonllier know about what happened on the surface. He was pleased Sunna wasn't close enough to feel them. She had enough struggles of her own with trying to control her phobias without knowing the dangers that awaited them aboveground. It disappointed him that they weren't going to be able to walk out like he had hoped.

He picked up his speed, moving through the tunnel faster. Moments later, the commanders entered a spacious cavern. Sunna was relieved to be there. Ghonllier let go of her hand while he searched the ground, letting Sunna catch her breath.

Sunna searched the cavern while she took in deep breaths. The cavern was made out of tall lime stone structures. In one direction, she stared at a place that seemed to be swallowed up in blackness. She headed for it so she could see it better.

"Don't go over there, Sunna," warned Ghonllier, aware of her decision.

She stopped to look at him. He was mentally causing a large boulder to float up in the air. Sunna had thought the rock was attached to another and was surprised to see it wasn't.

Arriving at his side, she asked, "What's over there? I'm getting a whiff of something."

"You're smelling methane gas," explained Ghonllier, falling to his knees to rummage in the dirt.

"Is that why the cavern was sealed?"

"Yes." He glanced at her. "Stay with me, Sunna."

"Is there a lot of methane gas here?"

"About a thousand feet down, you'd find a good-size underground lake."

Sunna looked away to see Ghonllier lifting out a miniature coffin. He opened the container and they saw the fourth Stone already pulsating. He stood while Sunna started to lift up the front of his uniform.

While Sunna exposed the belt, Ghonllier ran his fingers over the Stone. Knowing the belt was exposed, Ghonllier placed the Stone in the proper place. Instantly, all the Stones started to pulsate with different patterns.

"What are they doing?" asked Sunna, watching him put his uniform back into place.

"They're trying to find a common ground of communication with each other. The other Stones are trying to connect with the fourth Stone so they can save your life," replied Ghonllier. He placed his hands on her shoulders. "Stay right next to my body. We're about to have visitors."

Voices filled the caverns and Sunna fell into Ghonllier's arms as he wrapped them tightly around her. *The wires,* thought Sunna as an explosion went off. Dirt and rocks went flying all around them, along with deafening sounds. Sunna struggled to breathe from the lack of air as they were instantly buried.

She also had another problem. During the explosion, Sunna moaned after a rock struck her on the hip. Ghonllier felt it within his body, along with her inability to breathe. He commanded the Stones to make it possible for her to breathe fresh air.

Suddenly, the air was clear and she started to take in deep breaths. Looking over Ghonllier's shoulder, she saw a clear dome had encased them. The dirt and rocks were still falling, but she wasn't feeling them. Glancing at Ghonllier, she saw he was looking up. The debris still fell against the dome, making it impossible to see out. Then she realized that they were buried alive, causing panic to set in on her.

"RELAX, SUNNA. YOU'RE OKAY," said Ghonllier's hypnotic voice. She responded to his words instantly and Ghonllier pulled her in tighter. "REMEMBER, YOU NEED TO STAY AS CLOSE TO ME AS POSSIBLE SO THE FOURTH STONE CAN FEEL YOU."

"What happened?" she questioned.

"They found my hole in the fence and followed us here. They opened the tunnel and attempted to follow us. You saw the wires."

"How are we going to get out of here?" asked Sunna.

Ghonllier finally looked down at her. "I don't know. We're staying here until the Stones agree on something. The fourth Stone isn't sure about either one of us."

Dirt started to filter down, letting them know that they weren't completely buried. Ghonllier and Sunna looked up through the top of the dome to see the ceiling had caved in on them. *The explosion must've been massive,* thought Sunna.

The face of a man appeared. Sunna gasped while Ghonllier said, "Great!"

The man was a robot and could easily see them. He recognized Sunna's I-Force field glasses. Quickly, he responded by exposing his blaster. Others joined him as he fired a blast. It only went halfway, returning to the robot, hitting him. It didn't cause him to explode, because Ghonllier wasn't involved in the blast. The fourth Stone interpreted the blast as a threat and was defending itself.

The others pulled out their blasters and Ghonllier knew this wasn't going to get them out. Therefore, he reached out to Houser. Luckily, the *Liberty Pursuit* was in position and Ghonllier needed him. Houser had his field glasses on and his comset working, just like Ghonllier had requested.

He used the Stones to talk with Houser's comset on his field glasses. Ghonllier said, "YOU HAVE MY SIGNAL, HOUSER."

"Yes."

"TELL YOUR CAPTAINS TO SHOOT JUST TO THE RIGHT OF ME."

"Squirt, are you sure? That's too close. I don't want to kill you."

"BEANPOLE, HIT RIGHT NEXT TO MY SIGNAL WITH EVERYTHING YOU GOT AND THEN GET OUT OF THERE. A KOGN GALAXY CREEPER IS GOING TO BE COMING OUT OF JUMP SPEED AND YOU'RE IN ITS PATH."

"Squirt, I don't want to do this."

"TRUST ME, HOUSER. I'M TRAPPED AND I NEED A DIVERSION. TRUST ME, MY FRIEND. I WILL BE OKAY." Houser hesitated. "DO IT NOW!" repeated Ghonllier.

Ghonllier could hear Houser giving the order and knew how painful it was for him to do it. However, the *Liberty Pursuit* hit the mark, which had been the transports. Immediately, they burst into flames, causing the KOGN robots to leave.

The new Master didn't expect what happened next. The fourth Master Stone stopped its arguing with the other three Stones and looked at the *Liberty Pursuit*'s attack as an all out war. The fourth Stone looked at everyone as its enemy. In its anger, the clouds overhead started to swirl together as the ground of the base started to shake.

The mammoth power was out of control. Ghonllier knew the three other Stones were concerned along with him. They wouldn't be able to convince the fourth Stone to save them. All the Stones along with Sunna and Ghonllier were in question to survive. The fourth Stone did not understand consequences of its actions, which was they needed a man to bond with.

Chapter 15

Buried Alive

G ostler, Jason, and Adamite stared at the server stone, dismayed. When the explosion took place, Adamite quickly stood and paced. The former Master ignored everyone's questions as he read the chaos from Ghonllier's mind. He knew the power of the fourth Stone and he was impressed by the demonstration of its power.

Nervously, Jason spoke, "Gostler, please tell us anything about what's happening. Is my sister alive?"

Finally, he whispered, "I have no idea. The Stones have been passed on in peaceful time. This . . ." Gostler shook his head. "I'm not sure about anything."

When the fires broke out from Houser firing on them, the KOGN sent up emergency shuttles, trying to stop the fires by dousing them with chemicals. The fourth Master Stone took the procedure as a threat. It caused lightning to fulgurate within the clouds before it shot bolts that struck the emergency shuttles.

They crashed on top of the transports, causing them to explode on impact. The fires were getting out of hand and couldn't be stopped. The men in the towers fired off an emergency stress call for working ships on the planet to come in and evacuate the base.

The fourth Stone wasn't happy with the robots being programmed to fire on them. It caused the ground to shake, rendering the KOGN unable to stand. This compounded Ghonllier's problem by the ground surface caving into the caverns below. In some places, the fuel tanks were exposed while fire was raging everywhere. If the fires made it too hot for the fuel, then an explosion would erupt underground.

KOGN faced another problem. The pipes carrying the fuel to the base were weakening from the ground shaking. One pipe cracked from the ground shifting, causing fuel to shoot up like a geyser. Fire soon reached the fuel, sending a blaze through the pipes. One Galaxy Creeper had been fueling up when the fourth Stone started to unleash its power. Fire reached the linking fuel and shot through the flexible hoses before the robots could remove them from the Galaxy Creeper.

Fire entered the ship, causing it to explode, as the fourth Stone perceived it as a threat. It shot lightning bolts from the clouds, hitting anything that moved. The tower that brought ships in was hit by consecutive blasts. Once the tower was hit, all communication with the outside ceased.

Sunna had no idea what was happening outside. She only saw Ghonllier in a trance, assuming he was working on a way to get them out alive. She was very frightened, feeling the movements and hearing the ground groaning. Sunna was envisioning scenarios that she wondered if they were right. She wished Ghonllier could validate her thoughts. With him in the trance, she couldn't bother him.

In fear, she closed her eyes hearing thunder vibrate overhead. Looking above through her small opening, Sunna saw everything go a bright yellow. When she opened her eyes, she saw flames leaping high into the air on one side. She strained to look around Ghonllier's shoulder, hoping it wasn't all around them.

She couldn't tell but she soon guessed it was very close with their space heating up. Glancing up again, Sunna saw the flames all around them. She pressed her body against Ghonllier's as his temperature dropped to compensate for the heat. Inside the dome, the heat increased. She struggled to breathe.

Ghonllier felt her physical discomfort and finally whispered, "Sunna, stay with me."

"You could walk out of here and the fire not affecting you if I wasn't here, couldn't you?"

"Yes."

"Ghonllier, I wished I would've listened to you. You're right . . . I should've stayed back. I'm sorry, honey. You better leave—"

"Never! We die together or live. Do you understand, fourth Stone?! This includes you. We all know that if I die, you'll be destroyed with the methane gas that's here. And I carry you—"

Sunna didn't hear him finish his words as she went unconscious. Ghonllier picked her up, looking into her face. He knew the heat was too much for her. He could stay in the engulfed dome, but not her. The clear dome's temperature was rising quickly.

The tearful Master tenderly held her closer to his body, looking at the fire they were being consumed in. He listened to the other Stones telling the fourth Stone who Sunna was and what they had all agreed to in the beginning.

A cold breeze swept over Sunna's body, causing her to shiver. She didn't know how long she was unconscious, but found herself coming back to life. The cold moisture on her face had awakened her.

Opening her eyes, Sunna saw Ghonllier's face. She gasped for a deep breath to feel cool moisture fill her lungs.

"RELAX, SUNNA, YOU CAN'T MOVE," he stated while Sunna realized she was in his arms.

She looked around to see they were in a fog. Perplexed, she asked, "Where are we?"

"Inside a cloud," answered Ghonllier.

"What are you standing on?"

"Nothing, so don't move."

"How did we get here?" she asked.

"The three Stones lifted us up here to bring down your temperature," answered Ghonllier.

"The fourth Stone?"

"It's wild, so don't let go of me. It has only agreed not to interfere with you and I."

Lightning lit up the cloud, frightening Sunna. Cuddling into Ghonllier, she asked, "What is the fourth Stone doing?"

"Hitting the ground at will. So please hold on to me. We aren't sure the fourth Stone understands who you are and it's still not sure about me."

"When will it stop?"

"I don't know. It won't talk to me and little to the other Stones," answered Ghonllier, seeing they were descending below the clouds.

Sunna saw the raging fires for the first time as they floated over them. Their wild intensity briefly struck her, along with the burning destruction it caused.

Eventually, the Stones gently brought them down to the ground by the log they sat on when waiting for Houser to arrive. The log was a welcomed sight for Sunna.

Thunder rumbled above them as Ghonllier set her down, keeping his arms around her. Sunna gazed up at the dark green clouds. She gasped to see several funnels drop from them. They touched the ground, wiggling around, before retracting up.

They started up the hill and Ghonllier could feel the pain in her hip from being hit by the first part of the cave-in. Suddenly, Ghonllier picked her up in his arms and moved in his Vanisher-like speed. Before Sunna realized it, Ghonllier had her on the ground and was on top of her.

The next thing she heard was a huge explosion, the ground groaning as it shook. When it stopped, she found Ghonllier looking at her. He tenderly brushed the dirt from her face while she studied his face.

"What just happened?"

"See for yourself," he expressed, getting off of her and then helping her up.

Sunna was stunned to see a huge crater where the base once was. They were standing at the edge. At the bottom of the crater, a light glowed from under the ground that looked deep.

As he guided her away, Sunna asked, "What's causing that glow?"

"The lake of methane gas is burning underground," answered Ghonllier.

"We were just there," gasped Sunna.

Ghonllier suddenly stopped, pulling Sunna behind him.

Out of the foliage, Sunna saw four KOGN men appear and one spoke, "Why do you have a woman with I-Force field glasses on?"

Ghonllier answered, "She's my prisoner."

They pulled out their weapons on them as the one man said, "We want her."

"I suggest you put those blasters away if you want to live. They seem to attract lightning," warned Ghonllier, giving the Stones orders.

The men ignored Ghonllier's suggestion. Instead, they demanded, "Give us the woman!"

Ghonllier was already moving away while he kept his body between them and Sunna. Holding tightly to her waist, he kept going. Suddenly, Sunna was blinded by intense white light. It took a few moments to clear before she had her vision back. Ghonllier kept her walking while they were engulfed in the white light.

When it cleared, she noticed everyone was gone. She whispered, "What just happened?"

"We were all hit by lightning."

"And we lived?" asked Sunna as Ghonllier moved her away from the scene.

"None of the elements will affect me anymore, Sunna," answered Ghonllier, moving his arm from her waist to her shoulders to give her more protection.

Sunna looked at the raging fires and explosions. The ground underneath them groaned at the explosions that were taking place in the caverns from the fires and shaking of the ground.

Looking at Ghonllier, she asked, "Did you see this before you came?"

"It was one of the scenarios I saw."

"Did the worst case scenario happen?"

He looked at her. "Yes."

"How did those four KOGN men survive the explosion from the base?"

"They weren't at the base. They're four robots that were in the area, checking on equipment below," answered Ghonllier.

She asked, "Did Spencer see what you just did?"

"Yes."

"Great!"

Looking away from Ghonllier, Sunna jumped. They had just entered a patch of Snacker Vines and they had brushed up against them. Instead of sending out vines to carry them away, the large, flowering heads touched the ground as they approached. Sunna studied them as they passed. Looking over her shoulder, she watched them raise their huge heads, following their movement. They seemed to be watching them, waiting for something. Sunna wasn't sure.

Then it started to make sense to her. The plants detected who he was and they were giving him respect. It was the most reverent sight she had ever seen. *How would they know he was the Master of the Stones? Is this how everything will treat him from now on?* Sunna looked back at her husband with questioning eyes. *Who did I really marry? I never imagined every living cell in the galaxy would respond with respect to the Master of the Stones.*

Ghonllier didn't look at her or respond to her thoughts as he guided her up the hill.

Finally, they arrived at the tree where they had left the Trons. Bert joined them by landing on Ghonllier's shoulder. He stated, "It's good to see you again, Your Grace. That was impressive."

Ghonllier didn't answer, listening to Spencer's thoughts. Sunna watched him climbing down, concerned about what he saw. When Spencer arrived on the ground, he faced Ghonllier and slightly bowed. "Your Grace, I am honored to server you. Now I understand why you have bodyguards and medics."

Spencer kept his eyes fixed on Ghonllier as Sunna studied his expression. "I can see you have figured it out, Spencer. Will you give me your allegiance?"

"Yes. I'm honored to serve you."

"Will you take an oath to not reveal to anyone who I am until it is announced throughout the galaxy?"

"I will."

"Do you understand that you are making an oath to the Master Stones? As part of my elite force, you're obligated to not talk about them or me and they'll protect you. But if you break this oath, it will be instant death."

Spencer nodded. "I'll take it."

"Good. Now change back into a horse and get us out of here. There's going to be a major explosion in a few minutes."

The humble Tron changed into the black horse as Ghonllier floated Sunna and Bert upon his back. Spencer quickly took off with them. Suddenly, the sky lit up. Spencer paused to watch it.

Within the clouds, they saw a silhouette of a Star Screamer being attacked by lightning from all directions. Suddenly, the ship descended below the clouds and exploded, sending burning pieces in all directions. Ghonllier urged Spencer forward. He charged forward only to find a large piece of burning ship hit the ground in front of him, catching the trees on fire. With the winds blowing, the fire quickly spread, blocking them from leaving.

"Spencer! Charge the fire!" The Tron slightly went up on his hind legs and pawed the fire, letting Ghonllier know he wasn't sure about it. "Do it now!" he ordered.

The Tron put his faith in Ghonllier's words and charged the fire. He disappeared into it, expecting to come out shortly on the other side. But it was a huge fire and he found himself surrounded by burning debris. He couldn't see an end to the flames. Panic momentarily consumed him as he heard, "RELAX AND KEEP GOING FORWARD. YOU'RE OKAY AS LONG AS I'M TOUCHING YOU."

A sudden comfort spread through him as he went to a full gallop, moving around large pieces of twisted metal and burning trees. Eventually, they exited. It took everyone some long moments to realize that they weren't even touched by the flames. But they weren't out of it yet.

The wind had increased, causing fire to readily leap from one tree to another. Fire again spilled into their path and without hesitation, Spencer entered it only to exit shortly. Fire had now filled the valley and the winds were sending it their way.

Spencer galloped down the hill toward a large patch of Snacker Vines. Before they arrived, they started to bow their heads. Sunna gasped as Spencer leaped over one. The jump made her feel the pain in her hip from the cave-in, as well as a sudden pain in her back. Ghonllier wrapped his arm around her tightly and lowered his body temperature again.

"RELAX, SUNNA, AND LEAN AGAINST ME. YOU NEED A COLD PACK ON YOUR INJURY," said Ghonllier so everyone could hear him.

She obeyed, fighting back the tears from the pain that shot through her hip and back. Soon she started to breathe easier, baing against Ghonllier's cold body. Ghonllier used the Stones to talk with her mind, stopping her injured muscles from going into shock. Before Ghonllier was through, Sunna was fighting to stay awake.

In the meantime, Bert spent his time looking at the destruction that was behind them. Finally, they were moving faster than the fires were spreading. Bert was relieved to have the experience behind them. He didn't mind saying it was quite an emotional event. He mentally requested from Ghonllier permission to fly, but the Master denied him.

Bert was concerned about digging his talons into the Master's shoulder. Ghonllier read his thoughts and consoled him. He explained that his talons could not hurt him. After another mile, he heard thunder rumble overhead and asked Ghonllier if the storm was natural or caused by the Stones. The new Master assured him it was natural.

The rain started to fall. Bert was use to the rain since it happened a lot on the planet. He ruffled his feathers thinking back on the days, when he lived here. Bert was grateful to have left here and ended up working for the Master. He became aware of Ghonllier title when Dapper asked him to join his elite force.

It didn't take long for the warm rain to wake up Sunna. She moved away from Ghonllier and moaned lightly. Glancing over her shoulders, she asked, "Did I break anything?"

"No," answered Ghonllier, not looking at her.

The rain started to fall harder and, in a way, she was glad to have a shower. *If only I was off Spencer's back,* thought Sunna. Watching Spencer gallop through the trees, she realized they were in dense trees. The low branches were moving out their way. So it wouldn't slow him down. Sunna sighed, leaning against her husband. The bonding fires were comforting to her.

Eventually, she saw the *Liberty Quest* and was relieved to see her. Finally, Bert received permission to left Ghonllier's shoulder. He flew for the ramp. Instantly, he changed into a man, entering the ship. Spencer stopped at the edge to have Ghonllier float Sunna and himself off his back.

The minute they lifted off, he changed into a man. Sunna's feet touched the ramp and she moaned lightly to take her first step.

"How bad are you hurt, Sunna?" asked Spencer.

She looked at Ghonllier and he answered for her. Sunna looked away from Spencer and entered the ship. Spencer watched her disappear as Ghonllier waited for him. He knew the Tron was processing a lot of information. He was also surprised at what Spencer was thinking.

With Sunna gone, Spencer looked at Ghonllier and gestured to him to go up the ramp ahead of him. "You first. I want to protect your backside."

Spencer looked away from him and followed orders. Inside the OSA, he waited for Ghonllier to enter the ship. When he did, Spencer was miffed see he was totally dry. Everyone was soaked to the bones.

"Why are you dry?"

"It goes with the territory of being the Master of the Stones. . . . Spencer, I can see you want to talk . . ."

"Do you have time to do it right now?"

Ghonllier nodded as the door to the ship started to seal. Spencer followed Ghonllier to his compartment and asked, "Can we go somewhere and talk where we won't be bothered?"

Ghonllier placed his weapons belt in the compartment and shut the door. Then he faced Spencer. "Let's go talk in my old office," suggested Ghonllier.

"Will Sunna be in the office?"

"No. She getting help for her back."

Spencer remembered now. He was thoughtful as they entered the commander center on their way to the commander's office.

The two men walked up to the open office door. Ghonllier stopped and gestured for Spencer to enter first. Everyone stopped talking when they saw Spencer and not Ghonllier.

Stepping around Spencer, Ghonllier requested, "Do you men mind leaving while Spencer and I talk?"

Jason, Gostler, and Adamite had been watching the events on the server stone and wanted to talk with him regarding it. Everyone exchanged looks before they stood.

Looking at Jason, Spencer requested, "Commander Jason, I need to have you stay for this conversation."

Jason sat back down while Gostler and Adamite left. Ghonllier shut the door and gestured for the Tron to sit. Spencer did and Ghonllier joined him. They looked at him as water for the rain trickled down his face.

Spencer wrapped it off and pulled his long hair back before he said, "Does everyone on board know who you are?"

Commander Jason stared at Ghonllier, wondering how he was going to answer this. Ghonllier leaned back and let out a sigh. "Spencer, everyone aboard knows about me being the new Master of the Stones but you."

"Why not me?"

"You came late. Everyone on board knew about me before I did. The Master Stones hand-picked each person on this ship, including you."

"Why didn't you tell me?"

"In the past, the other Masters weren't allowed to tell anyone, including their wives or children. In my case, it's different. People only knew if they were directly involved with my security. You weren't directly involved until today. This is why you know now."

Spencer let the air out of his lungs and expressed, "So Sunna has always known."

"Yes. She knew five years ago when she took the assignment to be Asustie's bodyguard," replied Jason. Then he looked at Ghonllier and added, "I knew Ghonllier was the Master ten years ago because I was in charge of guarding him by using a server stone."

The Tron looked over at the server stone in the wall and stayed quiet. Ghonllier listened to his thoughts and Jason wished he knew what was going on. Was Ghonllier going to tell him that he was also married?

After a moment, Ghonllier commented, "Spencer. Why don't you ask me what is in your heart? I can tell you feel torn and I want you know that I understand and I'm not upset with you."

He looked at him. "Even what happened in the OSA before we left?"

"Yes."

"I want to be a part of your elite force more than anything else, but—"

"It's obvious you have feelings for Sunna, Spencer. But I really want you to be a part of the elite force. The Stones highly approve of you being with me." Spencer looked away. So Ghonllier added, "I can also see you're deeply hurt about something with Sunna. Am I right?" Spencer nodded before he faced him. "Do you want to talk about it?" Ghonllier asked.

Spencer shook his head before he said, "I can't work around her any longer, Commander. You saw what happened before we left. . . . Yet, I really want to work with you. I . . ."

"Spencer. I can see you're very confused right now. There is something gnawing at you and you feel like you might miss something if you don't act now."

The Tron was surprised by Ghonllier's words. He said, "You are right! Until you said it that way, I didn't realize that I need to go do something or . . ."

"I want you with me and I want you to do something for me." He leaned forward and expressed, "I am going to give you a leave of absence."

"I'll lose points . . ."

Ghonllier shook his head. "According to the records, you will be doing something for Commander Jason here. If you return back to me the minute, you get things resolved in you personally life. I'll give you points for your time away."

"Will it make me a general?"

The new Master nodded. "Thank you . . . I don't know where to . . ."

"Let me send you to the place that I feel help you get your life back into focus," suggested Ghonllier.

Spencer nodded. Then he smiled and asked, "Where are going to send me, Your Grace?"

"I need to tell your superior first. I made a promise to not interfere with her job."

"Are you referring to Commander Sunna?" Ghonllier nodded. "I don't want to say good-bye to her."

"Spencer, I'll go talk to so I can keep my promise. I want you to go pack because I'm dropping you off in a couple of hours," stated Ghonllier, looking over at Jason. He added, "I will have Commander Jason prepare your transfer chip."

Spencer smiled, "Thank you, Your Grace."

Ghonllier gave him a serious expression and Spencer noticed it. "Are you okay . . ."

"Please do not use *Your Grace* again." Spencer sat back as Ghonllier continued, "I do not want my friends, family or elite force calling me by that name when we are not in front of the public." Spencer nodded and Ghonllier stood, he reached out his hand and added, "I see you as a friend."

Spencer smiled and accepted his handshake. "Thank you, Commander, for thinking me as your friend."

With the Master reading his mind, Ghonllier said, "Spencer. I will tell Sunna good-bye for you. Is that acceptable to you?" He nodded. "The captains will beam you down."

He saluted and left. Jason looked at Ghonllier for some answers. He had a lot of questions. Ghonllier stood and glanced at Jason. "He doesn't suspect anything," informed Ghonllier.

With Spencer leaving, Adamite and Gostler rejoined them. Ghonllier started to follow Spencer. He nodded as he passed them. Jason stopped him. "Where are you sending him?"

Ghonllier smirked, "Do you think I'll tell you before she knows?"

Jason cajoled, "I see. So you're afraid of her."

Facing him, Ghonllier countered, "You would like that, now wouldn't you?"

Jason chuckled and grinned. "I would." Ghonllier continued out. Jason asked, "We want to talk with you. Will you be back?"

"Yes. Get Spencer's transfer while I help your sister," Ghonllier said, before he disappeared.

He knew they wanted to talk about the Jasmine planet and it would keep. Entering his quarters, he went to Sooner's old room. Leaning in the doorway, he arrived in time to see Sunna exiting the bathroom in a robe. She ran her hand through her wet hair while looking at him.

Then she grinned, "I knew the moment you entered my room. I didn't realize, until the shower, how bad you and I smell of smoke."

"And you don't like that smell?" cajoled Ghonllier.

"No," smiled Sunna.

She headed for her drawers to retrieve a nightgown. Since the ship was on night-mode, she wanted to go to bed. Holding the gown in her hand, she asked, "Are you going to tell me, 'I told you so'?"

"No, I came in to look at your back. Turn around so I can see it."

"Do you need me to take off my robe?" asked Sunna.

"No, I can see through your robe," replied Ghonllier.

Soon after Sunna did as he requested, she heard, "Wow!"

"What's wrong?" asked Sunna, looking over her shoulder.

"Before, I understood what was wrong with you. Now, I can actually see everything underneath your skin."

"What do you see?" she asked, whirling around.

"I actually see the broken vessels and torn muscles. Blood in some areas are still seeping into your muscle tissue. The muscles are bruised right down to the bone. I can see a slightly torn ligament that's attached to your hip joint, which was why you needed me to lower my body temperature."

"It hurt to have the warm water touch it. How do we fix it?"

"I'll tell Janet how to make up a patch that will be exactly what you need."

"Would you administer the patches for me?"

"No. I will have Janet do it. I don't want rumors to start flying about us. It's her job."

"Oh, so the rumors are true about Cid and you."

Sunna just smiled as he left. Being alone, she sighed.

Ghonllier entered the medical center without being announced, knowing the medic wasn't busy. Janet was startled when she turned around. Stuttering, she inquired, "Can . . . Can I help you?"

"Yes. Would you make up two patches of Sweet Lil and William Dust," ordered Ghonllier.

"So you have a deep bruise?"

Ghonllier followed her to the doorway of the medicine room and answered, "No, they're for Commander Sunna. I want the patches made up differently than you were trained to make them." Janet entered the medicine room and looked at him.

"Shouldn't I still see her first?"

Ghonllier shook his head. "I do not like you questioning my orders, Janet." She went back to work. "Janet. I can see you were offended with my last comment. I'm not use to a medic questioning me."

"I know. I just forgot it was you I was talking to. Please forgive me, Commander."

"You're forgiven," said Ghonllier. Then he added, "To be exact on your doses, I want two and a half grams of Sweet Lil on each patch, along with three grams of Sweet William Dust."

She nodded as Ghonllier watched her. He could tell it was making Janet feel uncomfortable but he didn't care. This patch was for Sunna and he wanted it just right. When she had made them to satisfy the Stones, Ghonllier left so Janet could administer the patch in Sooner's room.

He made sure Janet saw him headed back into the office to talk with Justin and the other three men as he promised. After their talk, he left and entered his quarters. Sunna was in their bed and he could see she felt a lot better. The patches were doing their job successfully.

Sunna was lying on her stomach, partially covered with a blanket. He knew it was still too tender for her to sleep on her side or back. Leaving, he went to the bathroom to shower, knowing Sunna didn't like how he smelled.

Returning with his robe on, he paused to see she was still asleep. He got dressed in pajamas to cover the Stones and lifted the covers up so he could slip underneath them. Instantly, Sunna stirred and opened her eyes.

"It's still quite tender, isn't it?"

"Yes."

"Despite what you think, Sunna, I'm sorry that you're in pain and you got hurt."

"It's only because you can feel the pain."

"No, it's not and you know it," he stated, slipping underneath the covers.

"Why did it take you so long to come back?"

"I was talking to Justin."

"About what?"

"Spencer."

"What about him?"

"He's requested a leave of absence."

"He can't have one. There isn't a big emergency in his family."

"In a way, yes, he has an emergency and I gave it to him."

"Without running it past me first?!" Raising her eyebrows, she quizzed, "Are you interfering with my job?"

"Sunna, relax and hear me out," replied Ghonllier. He paused for a moment and continued, "Spencer is deeply hurt by your relationship with him not going anywhere. He keep having dreams about something that isn't clear to him. He just knows that he needs to move and do something or he'll miss an opportunity. This is why he was going to ask you to marry him again. He thought that was what was bothering him. In truth it isn't. Spencer needs to relax and stop trying to hard to find happiness with a woman."

Sunna was quiet, knowing Ghonllier was right. Slowly, she asked, "How hurt is he?"

"Hurt enough that he doesn't want to say good-bye to you."

Sunna sighed. Then she said, "I wish we could've told him that we were married."

"I know why we couldn't."

She gave him a startled look and asked, "Why?"

"The Stones knew he might choose to leave us. They couldn't have him out in the galaxy, knowing we were married. The Stones never want the rest of the galaxy to know that I'm married or anything about my personal life."

Sunna smiled. "Where are you sending him?"

"You've sent him to the Thinball moon and to a specific place there. According to his records, you have sent him there to do a top secret mission for Justin," answered Ghonllier, leaning in to kiss her on her shoulders.

"Why am I sending him there? What is his mission?"

Ghonllier chuckled. "You know the answer to your question. You like to tease, Sunna."

"What happens if he doesn't come back? He knows you're the Master. . . . I thought no one out of your elite force would know?"

"Spencer will come back. I told him that I would make him a general if he returned the minute his life was back in focus."

"Why the Thinball moon?"

"A woman who is desperately looking for him as much as he is looking for her is there."

"Will they get married?"

"I'm going to give him the opportunity. They should get married, if he doesn't mess it up."

"Like me?"

"Yes, my dear. Like you."

Sunna smiled, "I like that. It makes me feel good to know that we're making it up to him."

Ghonllier nodded. "That was the goal." Reading Sunna's mind, he cajoled, "He should be as happy with her as you are with Cid."

Sunna instantly poked her fingers in his ribs and he gently pulled her into him. "Come here," he whispered as they kissed.

Chapter 16

The Nightmares

*A*couple of nights later, Sunna abruptly came out of a deep sleep. The bed shook and she sat up and ordered the orbiter on.

The light showed Ghonllier sitting on the edge of the bed, holding his head, while resting both elbows on his knees. She went to his side, placing her hand on his back. He looked in her direction with bloodshot, moist eyes.

Sitting next to him, she asked, "What's wrong?"

"I'm sorry. I didn't want to wake you up," he choked out.

Gently, with her fingertip, she wiped away a tear from his cheek. "What's going on this time?"

"It's Sooner."

"What's wrong?"

"Nothing now. I just had a dream about the future, regarding him."

"What did you see?"

"He was unconscious, close to death, and we weren't there."

"Tell me about it," she whispered.

Holding his wife, Ghonllier cleared his throat and said, "The dream started out with Sooner playing outside Jasper's house. They entered Jasper's house and went to his room. Sooner sat on the bed and fell into unconsciousness. They called home for Cid to come and get him. He didn't make it in time before Sooner died."

"Where were we?"

"In space somewhere."

"Why did the Stones let him die and not tell you?"

Ghonllier shook his head. "It happened too fast. He was attacked by something that moves fast to kill its victims."

"Are the Stones trying to warn you about something?"

"I think so."

"What is it?"

Ghonllier shook his head. "I don't know. I need time to think it out in my mind to understand what they're doing. All I know is my dreams are stronger and more realistic than with the earlier Stones."

Letting go of Sunna, he went back to resting his elbows on his knees. Sunna ran her hands through his hair until he would look at her. Seeing his glistening cheeks, she said, "Honey, it's the future. You're aware of it now. You'll be there. Come to bed. There is nothing you can do right now."

Taking her suggestion, he returned to his pillow. This time she covered him up while they kept eye contact. Staying on his side, she leaned into him and they kissed. He smiled at her. Sunna smiled back, cuddling into him.

The bonding fires were soothing to his troubled heart. Sunna quickly went back to sleep, leaving Ghonllier awake. He stared at the ceiling and eventually joined her.

They both thought his dreams were over with for the night. However, as soon as he fell asleep, he went into another dream. This one took place in a meadow on a mountainside. It reminded him of the place where Jenny and he had their vacation right before she died.

He expected to see her any minute, but instead saw a deer wander out of the trees that lined the clearing. It ate the grass, not paying any attention to him. Ghonllier watched it work its way over to him, eating as it went. They were about to touch when it sharply brought up its head, looking behind him.

Suddenly, in the distance, he heard laughter. The deer bolted for the trees as he whirled around to witness four children running out of the forest. They seemed to fall into the grass, laughing. He chuckled to listen to them teasing each other. Then they stood up and started to chase one another. All the children seemed to be the same age as Sooner.

One child yelled out a word and they abruptly fell to the ground again. After a few moments, one of the children yelled something and they stood up, chasing each other again. He smiled to understand they were playing some kind of game that he wasn't familiar with.

As they repeated the game, Ghonllier wanted to go to them and ask why they were there. Stepping forward, he found himself restrained. Before he could ask the Stones why, they ran toward him. There were three girls and one boy. Staring into their faces, he felt something familiar about them. Yet, he knew he had never seen these children before.

They started to play around him and he became perplexed as to why the children were in his dream. *Who are they? What are the Stones trying to tell me now?* he thought as the boy caught his attention.

Ghonllier started to understand why they looked familiar. The boy reminded him of himself as a child. Smiling, he noticed the boy handled the situation with the girls like he would. *Is this me as a child? If it is, who are the girls?* One girl giggled and Ghonllier was immediately drawn to the sound. *Sunna!* It was then he started to connect the dots and understand that these children were Sunna's and his.

Stones, why are you showing them to me? What are you trying to tell me?

THEY ARE A PROMISE OF WHAT CAN HAPPEN. IT'S OUR CHOICE TO GIVE THEM TO YOU OR WE CAN ALLOW YOU TO NEVER SEE THEM.

Then why show them to me? snapped Ghonllier.

The Stones didn't answer as he watched the children playing at his feet. He desired to look away, but found himself mesmerized by their movement and laughter. *Stones, why are you telling me that they are only a promise? Why are you showing me Sooner dying? Why isn't Sooner here if they are my children with Sunna?*

WE WANT YOU TO KNOW WHAT MAKES YOU STRONGER OR WEAKER.

Why show me this? What do you want from me?

GHONLLIER, WE'RE GIVING YOU A LOT OF RESPONSIBILITY AND YOU CAN'T TAKE IT LIGHTLY. WE'RE GOING TO ASK AND TEST YOU WITH THINGS BEFORE WE SUBMIT OURSELVES COMPLETELY TO YOU.

Tell me everything that you want from me.

THERE ARE TWO THINGS THAT WE WILL ASK OF YOU. THE FIRST ONE IS WE NEED YOU TO GIVE US EVERYTHING, INCLUDING YOUR WILL. AND, IN RETURN, WE'LL MATCH YOU WITH EVERYTHING, INCLUDING OUR WILL.

Are you kidding?

NO. THIS IS WHAT WE REQUIRE FOR ANY MAN TO BE THE MASTER OF US.

Won't I lose control of my life . . . of who I am, if I give you my will?

WE ARE PERFECT IN KNOWLEDGE AND HAVE ALL POWER. THINK ABOUT THE POWER YOU HAVE ALREADY SEEN. GHONLLIER, YOU'LL HAVE MORE FREEDOM AND CONTROL OVER YOUR LIFE THAN YOU HAVE NOW. THIS IS WHAT HAPPENS WHEN YOU'RE A PART OF PURE SOURCE OF LIGHT AND KNOWLEDGE. FOR YOU TO BE GREAT, YOU NEED TO MATCH WHAT WE'RE WILLING TO DO FOR YOU.

I'm confused to why you are asking for my will. I thought I gave it to you when I accepted the fact of being the Master.

YOU HAVEN'T GIVEN US EVERYTHING. THERE IS A PART OF YOU THAT YOU HOPED WE WOULDN'T TOUCH.

Where do I have more to give?

THERE IS A PART OF YOU THAT YOU'VE NEVER SHARED WITH ANY-ONE IN YOUR LIFE. IT'S HIDDEN DEEP IN YOUR SOUL AND WE'RE ASK-ING YOU FOR IT. TOGETHER, WE'LL MATCH YOU BEING IN PERFECT BALANCE SO WE CAN WORK TOGETHER WITHOUT ANY HIDDEN AGENDAS.

I don't have a part of me that I never shared with anyone, defended Ghonllier.

YOU ARE LYING TO YOURSELF. THERE IS A PART OF YOU THAT'S VERY MUCH HIDDEN WITHIN YOU. SEARCH FOR IT. YOU WILL FIND IT.

Are you asking this so I will totally understand myself?

THAT IS WHY WE'RE ASKING.

It angered Ghonllier that he had to go deeper inside to under-stand himself. He wasn't sure what he would find. Hidden away, he had a lot of feelings. They were things life had taught him, but there were also things that he didn't want to deal with. They meant some-thing to him and he didn't want people criticizing him. He didn't realize how sacred they were to him.

GHONLLIER, IF YOU DON'T DO IT, YOU'LL BE A WEAK MASTER. WITHOUT DOING THIS, IT WILL BE EASY FOR YOU TO BECOME SELFISH AND WE CAN'T WORK WITH A MAN WHO'S WITHHOLDING A PART OF HIMSELF. YOU NEED TO SHARE IT ALL—YOUR FEARS, DREAMS, AND DESIRES—IN ALL AREAS SO NOTHING COMES UP AND BECOMES AN ISSUE FOR YOU IN THE FUTURE. AND YOU NEED TO ACT WITHIN A MOMENT'S

NOTICE. WITH THIS KIND OF POWER, YOU'LL BE DANGEROUS AND WE'LL BE FORCED TO LEAVE YOU.

So I have no choice?

YOU ALWAYS HAVE A CHOICE. THIS IS WHY WE ARE TALKING TO YOU NOW. WE NEED TO KNOW EXACTLY WHERE YOU STAND ON ALL ISSUES BEFORE WE GIVE YOU THIS KIND OF POWER. WE CAN'T WORK OUTSIDE OF LOVE AND WE WON'T FORCE YOU. WHEN YOU FORCE SOME- ONE, IT'S THE FIRST STEP TOWARD HATE AND EVIL. WE NEED TO KNOW IF YOU'RE CROSSING OVER TO THE DARK SIDE.

Why did you pick me out of all the men in the galaxy?

YOU WERE NEVER INTERESTED IN BEING POWERFUL. YOU HAVE A STRONG LOVE FOR OTHERS, ESPECIALLY YOUR FAMILY. YOUR GREAT LOVE WOULD DETER EVIL, WHICH MAKES IT EASY TO WORK WITH YOU. WITH YOUR PASSION FOR OTHERS, YOU WILL BE THE MOST POWERFUL MASTER OF THE STONES, BUT ONLY IF YOU UNDERSTAND EVERYTHING ABOUT YOURSELF.

What will make me so powerful?

A PERSON WHO DOESN'T SEEK POWER RESPECTS IT AND WON'T MIS- USE IT. WITH YOUR CAPACITY FOR LOVE, EVERY CELL IN LIVING MAT- TER WILL RESPOND TO THIS LOVE INSTANTLY. YOU'RE A VERY PATIENT PERSON AND YOU HAVE A GREAT KNOWLEDGE OF TRUTHS AND LOVE FOR THE ONES THAT GOVERN THE WHOLE UNIVERSE.

YOU UNDERSTAND THE POWER OF CHOICE, SO YOU WON'T GIVE YOUR PERSONAL POWER AWAY VERY EASILY. YOU AREN'T A MAN WHO BELIEVES IN THE WORD CAN'T. YOU BELIEVE ALL YOU NEED IS SOME TIME TO FIGURE IT OUT.

YOU HAVE ACCOMPLISHED THESE SKILLS BY NOT SUBMITTING TO EVERY WHIM YOUR BODY REQUESTED OF YOU. YOU TRIED HARD TO KEEP EVERYTHING IN MODERATION. YOU UNDERSTAND BALANCE BETWEEN YOUR SPIRIT AND BODY. BY US ADDING OUR POWER TOGETHER, YOU'LL BE INCREDIBLE.

YOUR BIGGEST PROBLEM IS YOU DON'T BELIEVE IN YOURSELF. WE CAN WORK ON THAT TOGETHER. BECAUSE YOU'RE GRATEFUL FOR EVERY- THING IN YOUR LIFE, WE'LL BE ABLE TO WORK WITH YOU.

The words of the Master Stones burned in his mind. Watching his children pulled at his heartstrings. He loved being a father and his heart was tumbling in love with them. Tears came to his eyes at the thought of never seeing them and being a part of their lives.

In frustration, he finally was able to look away. Somehow, he sensed the act of giving his complete will to the Stones was tied to his children. It surprised him to learn how a simple request was so intimidating. The Stones were giving him a glimpse of his future and were putting pressure on him to not make the decision lightly. *How do I let these children go and not allow them to exist?* Ghonllier thought, glancing back at them.

His eyes couldn't leave them again. He found that he ached to have them not know of his existence. They played at his feet, totally unaware of his presence. His mind was learning everything about their different personalities and needs. Each second he was exposed to them made him not want to lose them.

The similarities between the children were noticeable. One of the girls stopped playing and stared at him. She seemed to look right through him as if she was searching for someone. *I wish she could see me.* For a moment, she appeared to see him and his heart soared.

Suddenly, she looked away. A wave of sadness swept over him to realize she couldn't see him but was aware of his presence. He felt her love for him and Ghonllier wanted to take her into his arms.

He watched the girl a little longer and decided she looked so much like Sunna. The boy came up and taunted her in a loving way. He accomplished getting her attention the way he wanted and Ghonllier smiled. It was so like him. The girl who looked like Sunna was aggressive like her mother. The boy was clever enough to miss her attempts to grab him and tease her back.

He compared Sooner and this boy. Sooner had Jenny's eyes and lips, which he really didn't mind. This boy looked like Ghonllier. He was pleased to see that his next son would look more like him. The children bolted in another direction, leaving him behind. He desired to follow, but found it impossible. They entered the trees and he wanted to call them back. His voice choked in his throat. They disappeared, their laughter fading away. His heart ached for them as he listened to the deafening silence.

The experience of his children leaving him left Ghonllier with a haunting sadness and a chilling loneliness as the scene faded from his mind. Opening his eyes, Ghonllier saw the ship was still in night-mode. He rolled onto his side, hoping to go back to sleep. Every time he closed his eyes, the faces of his future children were there, along with the Stones' words.

He tossed and turned, eventually drifting off to sleep, but not until he realized the Stones were right. He had held back a part of himself. It was a part that he had never shared with anyone, including Jenny. It bothered him to be asked to share everything with others and keep nothing for himself.

When Ghonllier awoke again, he found himself troubled. Glancing at Sunna, he saw her asleep. Not wanting to go back to sleep, he slipped out of the covers and left.

Already, he felt the effects of the fourth Stone on his ability to sleep. It was obvious to him that he could get by on less sleep than he could the day before. He wondered what it really was going to be like for him in the future. *Will I really ever sleep again? And, more important, will I want to, if I always have dreams like I had last night?* thought Ghonllier, entering the bathroom.

When Sunna woke up, she was disappointed to find Ghonllier gone. She was aware of him waking up the second time, after his first dream, but didn't want to bother him. So she stayed quiet and watched before falling back to sleep herself. *Now,* she wondered *what was in his second dream. Was it about Sooner?* She exited their bed, wondering if he was going to tell her.

Once she was dressed, Sunna stepped into the doorway that separated their quarters to hear water running. *Good, Ghonllier is in the bathroom.* Approaching the door, it opened without her asking. She found Ghonllier standing in front of a mirror, shaving his face.

Leaning in the doorway, she said, "I wanted to say hello and good-bye before I left."

He vocalized, "Come here."

Whirling around, he took her into his arms, holding onto her tightly. Then he started to kiss her all over her face and neck, smearing his shaving cream. Sunna burst out laughing, pleading for him to stop. Eventually, he let go and the two looked at each other, smiling.

She responded, "You got me good this time. I'll learn to come to visit you when you're shaving." A towel floated into her hand from behind him. She plucked it out of the air to wipe her face as she added, "Thank you." Seeing he was still staring at her, she commented, "Your second dream must have been better."

"You noticed?"

"Yeah, I did. What was it about?" asked Sunna, handing back the towel.

"I saw our future children."

"Really?! Were they gorgeous?"

"There was a little girl who looked just like you and our only boy looks like me."

"So everyone will know who their parents are. Good. I don't want them to question they're Cid's," cajoled Sunna. Ghonllier didn't respond while he came forward for a kiss. "Did you see anything more about Sooner?" she inquired before he kissed her.

Sadness clouded his eyes as he moved back, without speaking, and faced the mirror to start shaving again. Sunna felt so sorry that she had asked that question. She wanted to take it back, but the remark was out there.

"No, the Stones won't show me the outcome of Sooner and he wasn't there with his brother and sisters," lamented Ghonllier, placing more shaving cream in his hand.

"I'm sorry, Ghonllier. I shouldn't have asked you about that," apologized Sunna, watching him lather up his face again.

Not leaving, Sunna studied his face in the mirror. She noticed the faraway look in his eyes and things were different. Without saying more, Sunna left to go find Gostler. She could've easily paged for him from their quarters, but Sunna didn't want Ghonllier to know. So she headed for the bridge to talk with the captains in person.

The corridor was empty this morning. Usually, Spencer was there to greet her for the day. It felt a little strange to have him gone. She never saw Spencer after she entered the ship from the Jasmine planet. Spencer was on her mind as she entered the bridge. They were good friends and she hoped he would find happiness like she had.

Arriving on the bridge, the captains paged Gostler for Sunna. They didn't immediately use the ship's con-speakers, because of the time of the morning. With Gostler not being in the military, they didn't know where he was then. Luckily, they found him in his quarters.

Sunna waited while looking at the reading panel. It showed her husband still in their quarters and she was on the bridge. Suddenly, panic consumed her. *The captains have known that I've been staying in Ghonllier's quarters. Great, are the Stones upset with us?* She looked at them. *They have to know something.*

Sam glanced at her, causing her to quickly look away. Right now, she didn't know what to think, or how much the captains knew, and it bothered her. Feeling uncomfortable, Sunna decided to meet Gostler in the corridor.

She was almost to the dining room door, when she saw Gostler coming toward her. When he saw Sunna heading in his direction, he stopped to wait. Sunna arrived and inquired, "I hope I didn't get you up."

"No, I always get up early. What do you want?"

"Gostler, are you hungry? If you haven't eaten, I would like you to join me."

"A beautiful woman asking me to eat breakfast with her? Sure."

Sunna headed toward the dining room, when Jason exited her office.

"Sunna! Good, I've been looking for you."

"What do you want?"

"Breakfast, do you mind?"

"Sure, join us, Brother," answered Sunna.

Gostler nodded as Jason joined them.

Sunna entered the dining room first and ordered her breakfast from the galley. Gostler stood back, watching Sunna closely. He suspected why Sunna requested to have breakfast with him and wondered if he was right.

When Sunna coded him into the galley so he could eat, he leaned into her. "Do you want to talk or just have someone to eat with?"

"Talk," whispered Sunna.

He nodded before he went to pick up his food. His breakfast was ready before Sunna's, so he was there before she arrived. As she sat, she asked, "Do you mind me asking you to breakfast so we can talk?"

Gostler smiled. "I expected it," he replied. As Jason joined them, Gostler added, "I suspect Ghonllier had a rough night."

"Is that normal?"

Gostler nodded. The former Master expected her to continue with his opening question, but she surprised him. Sunna directed her next question to Jason. "Brother, have the captains mentioned to you that they know I'm not sleeping in my quarters?"

Jason shook his head. "No, they haven't and won't. The reader panel shows you in your own quarters, not Ghonllier's. I've checked," he whispered.

"How could that happen? I thought you couldn't override the navigational stone."

"The Master Stones can override the navigational stone. It's easy for them to do that," assured Gostler.

Jason started to chuckle. "What's so funny?" asked Sunna.

"You should've seen your face. I've never seen you that embarrassed before," smiled Jason.

"I'm glad you enjoyed my moment," cajoled Sunna and then looked at Gostler. Then she asked, "Is it normal to have random dreams with the fourth Stone?"

"Yes. He'll have numerous dreams," answered Gostler.

"About what?" asked Sunna.

"They'll be about anything they want."

"Can you tell me what his dreams mean?" questioned Sunna.

"Maybe," commented Gostler, setting his utensil down while playing with the suction piece on his container. "What did he dream about?"

"Sooner dying was one dream. Another was about our children together," reminisced Sunna, staring at her plate of food. Then she looked at Gostler. "Does Sooner really die? Is that what it means?"

Gostler leaned back in his chair. "Maybe."

"No!" whispered Sunna, getting emotional.

Reaching out, he laid his hand on hers. "What's the dream about with Sooner? Give me any information you can," soothed Gostler.

"That's just it. Sooner died. There isn't anything more," snapped Sunna, pulling her hand away. Placing her hand on the edge of the table, she spat, "Why show him something like that? Something . . ."

"That tears at his heart," stated Gostler.

"Yeah," whispered Sunna.

"Sunna, the Stones are playing with the strings of his heart."

"Why?" Sunna asked through clenched teeth.

"What was his dream about your children?" questioned Gostler.

She shook her head. "He didn't say anything more than that he saw our children," informed Sunna.

"I bet he was told they were a promise," whispered Gostler.

Sunna leaned forward and requested, "Why would they show them as a promise? Is something going to happen to me?" The former Master looked away. Sunna repeated, "Gostler, tell me everything that the Stones are asking of him."

Gostler shifted a glance in Jason's direction before he answered, "The Stones are trying to examine every aspect of Ghonllier's soul. The fourth Stone bonds to his soul. They're giving him dreams to see how he functions under those situations. They want to know everything about him, even under certain circumstances."

"Why?" Sunna snapped back.

"They need to know him and he needs to know himself."

She leaned back, folding her arms. "I think it's cruel."

"They need to understand his weaknesses and show him where he needs to grow. They're going to push him and possibly you to your limits before the bonding is through."

"Why me?"

"You're a part of them. They have tied you two together. That's why they went to you when he refused to be in harmony with them."

"I still don't understand why they're doing this to us."

"Ghonllier and the Stones need to know how he will react under any situation. So when the situation comes up, the Stones and he both have an understanding of each other's needs. That way, they can work together smoothly," answered Gostler. Sunna shot him a long glance. "They won't push him or you past your abilities to handle it."

Sunna stared at her plate and contemplated Gostler's words. With tears in her eyes, she looked up and quizzed, "So you don't know if the dreams are real or a test?"

"Correct."

"I'm sorry, Sunna," whispered Jason.

Sunna looked at him while wiping away a tear. "When will we know if Sooner isn't going to die?"

Gostler stated, "Before he completes the bonding. When and how, I have no idea. Just know they cause things to happen to test your depths within your soul."

"I still can't believe they'd do this," she whispered.

"Don't be too hard on them. They know fear is a problem with humans. Most of us make our most important decisions in a moment of fear. They need to know what causes it or if he ever makes a decision in a moment of fear. A Master can't utilize power and be fearful."

"That is a question I couldn't answer," sighed Sunna. "Fear, it's a strong emotion."

"I've never known you to be a fearful person, Sunna. When did this happen?" asked Jason.

She gazed at him thoughtfully. Then she stated, "I never felt it until Sooner and he came into my life."

"And Ghonllier? How would you feel if you knew he could be gone from your life without notice?" asked Gostler.

Sunna nodded. "I see your point," she expressed.

"Is there another reason the Stones are doing this besides understanding his level of fear?" asked Jason.

"Maybe, if they detect something there. The fourth Stone will expose everything about your personality. By the time he's the Master, Ghonllier will know everything about himself in a way that you can only learn from being the Master."

"While he's the Master, will they keep our children's lives hanging over our heads?"

Gostler studied her face before he said, "No, Sunna. They are looking for something else. They'll ask a sacrifice from him. He'll have to give up something that's very dear to his heart to be in the position to protect this galaxy. They are looking for it and it might be his children. But he will know before he's the Master."

"What was your sacrifice, Gostler?" asked Jason.

"I can't tell you until the Stones release me from their service. When they do, then Ghonllier can tell you his or after the sacrifice has been taken by them."

"It seems so unfair," stated Jason.

"I felt that way when I was your age and bonding to them. Now, I have hindsight. I can see the Stones were very merciful to me and fair by what they asked me to sacrifice," reminisced Gostler, getting a faraway look.

"Why would you say that after being in exile and the punishment people gave you for the Stones being gone from the galaxy?" questioned Jason.

"The Stones designed my trials for me. I'm a better man today because of them and I wouldn't trade my trials. I might have changed some choices I made, was all."

Sunna shook her head. "This is so hard."

"No, it's not," whispered Gostler. "You're saying that because of fear. Am I right?"

Sunna studied his face. Slowly, she nodded. "I didn't realize how much I allowed fear into my life."

"Is it a new feeling?" asked Gostler. Sunna nodded. "It's because you have something in your life that you don't want to lose."

"Ghonllier and Sooner," whispered Sunna.

"Now that they're in your life, are you afraid of the unknown?" asked Gostler.

"Yes," answered Sunna.

"The Stones are showing you things that you haven't dealt with in your life yet. They have thrown them at you without being prepared to show you your response to them. Is your fear that you might not be able to handle the loss of the happiness you've found?"

Not wanting to admit he was right, she looked away. "Is Ghonllier afraid?"

"He's been like you, Sunna," informed Jason.

"The fourth Stone will find any fears that he has," replied Gostler.

Sunna played lightly with the suction piece of her container and said, "If your words are correct, I now understand more deeply what the Master Stones were trying to teach me those days I was with them." Glancing at Gostler, she added, "Would the Stones ever take me away from him?"

"I doubt it," answered Gostler.

"Why?" asked Jason.

"They've already passed on Sunna. She proved worthy to be a partner with them by coming back when they gave her the chance to die."

Sunna nodded. "You're right," she whispered. "I almost died three times on him."

"Two," reminded Jason.

"No, three," corrected Sunna.

"What was the third time?" asked Jason.

"When we went to get the fourth Stone. I was wrong and should have listened to Ghonllier and stayed back," divulged Sunna.

Gostler nodded. "It's too bad you couldn't hear his conversation with the Stones when you were trapped inside the fire," whispered Gostler.

Jason looked at him. "How did you hear Ghonllier talking to the Master Stones? I thought you couldn't hear him talk to the Stones."

Gostler nodded. "I know. But this time the Stones allowed it. I think they wanted me to learn something and I did," divulged Gostler, looking at Sunna. "The fourth Stone was being belligerent and refused to save your life. Since he had control of the other three, he ordered them to kill him if you died. The three Stones played back to the fourth what they had already gone through to get together. When you went limp in his arms, the fourth Stone lifted you up with him."

Sunna lifted her eyelids and smiled, "It was interesting to be in the fire. It was so hot for me and he was so cold."

"How did he handle the heat they were in?" asked Jason.

"By changing his body temperature, it kept his organs on the inside from being affected," educated Gostler.

Jason sat back and expressed, "The power that we saw was incredible. I would think it would be hard to control forces like what I saw."

Gostler nodded. "You guys haven't seen anything. There is much more he can do when he has control."

"Gostler, what is it going to be like when we land again? Will he have control of the Stones by then?" asked Jason.

"No, he won't. It takes time for them to work together consistently, especially after being separated for so long."

"So we should expect the same weather again when we reach land?" asked Sunna.

"Yeah," informed Gostler.

"Okay," said Sunna, "I don't want to bother Ghonllier with details. Let's plan out how we're going to handle it. We should have the

Star Skipper packed and ready to leave when we land. Then we can go and not leave the ship."

Gostler and Jason nodded in agreement. They went back to eating, but Sunna played with her food, using her utensil. She thought about everything, what both Ghonllier and she could be faced with in the near future.

Setting her utensil down, she asked, "What will happen to his personality this time? Will he be indifferent with me and irritable like with the first and second Stone?"

"He might be slightly irritable only because of his lack of sleep and the Stones playing with his heart. The dreams he is having can be very hard on both of you."

"Will they get worse?" inquired Sunna.

Gostler shrugged his shoulders. "I have no idea what those Stones will do."

"What will his personality be like after he becomes the Master of the Stones?" asked Sunna.

"He'll be a better man than he was before. You'll find him focused on the galaxy but very aware of your feelings and needs. When the Stones find a common ground of communication, every cell of his body will ripple with power and knowledge. He will be better at handling more situations at once," reminisced Gostler, thinking of his reign.

"How can I help him the most?" asked Sunna.

"Give him room and space to work with the Stones, during this time of bonding. He isn't going to have the luxury that I had. I could take my time and work into them. Ghonllier has a lot of pressure on him with this war and his brother carrying this curse," said Gostler, reaching out to touch Sunna's hand. She looked at him. "He might seem distant for awhile. Don't bother him and demand his attention. It will only be a few weeks. When he's the Master, it won't matter if you bother him."

Sunna gave him a half smile and nodded. "Thanks for your advice."

She went back to staring at the food left on her plate. Gostler let go of her hand and took a sip from his container. Jason thoughtfully looked at his sister, thinking about what the future would bring to them all.

Finally, Jason stated, "Well, it will be different to have Ghonllier gone for awhile. In a way, I'm looking forward to being with Asustie and knowing I won't have to leave her for some time."

Sunna ignored Jason and asked, "Gostler, will the Stones require him to leave without me while he completes this last stage?"

"I don't know. But if you go with him, it will be hard on you," said Gostler, looking at something behind her.

This made Sunna turn around to see Ghonllier at the galley.

Facing Gostler, she asked, "How will we know when the process of bonding is complete?"

"He'll know. The Stones will tell him that he is the Master and the process is complete," informed Gostler, looking away from Ghonllier.

Jason motioned Ghonllier over to sit with them. Sunna leaned over to Gostler and whispered, "Gostler, I appreciate you talking with me and admire what you go through to become the Master of the Stones. The rest of the galaxy has no idea."

"Thank you, Sunna. I really appreciate you saying that," smiled Gostler, squeezing her hand. "If you want to talk, Sunna, I'll answer as many questions as I can," he assured her.

Ghonllier joined them and everyone greeted him, but Sunna. She stood and announced that she was going to work. In her mind, she said, *Sorry, honey. I'm leaving because I don't think it's a good idea we're here together. I want to beam at being in your presence.*

"I KNOW. I LOVE YOU AND SORRY THAT WE CAN'T BE HERE TOGETHER," said Ghonllier, sitting.

She nodded toward him and said, "Commander, have a good day."

"You, too, Commander," responded Ghonllier.

Jason and Gostler watched her leave. "It's too bad you two can't be friendly with each other in public," said Jason, looking around. "Why don't you? There is hardly anyone here."

"We're concerned that we might slip up at the wrong time again. I don't want another Spencer on our hands," informed Ghonllier, taking his first bite.

Gostler smiled and didn't tell Jason about the mental conversation the two had before Sunna left.

Chapter 17

The Storm

*A*fter the day, Sunna spoke to Gostler about Ghonllier. She had noticed her husband had become very quiet and reflective in his mood. He didn't participate in causal conversations and she knew he had more dreams. When she asked about them, Ghonllier refused to tell her. She wondered if it was because they were about Sooner. The Stones were making her sensitive toward Ghonllier's moods and feelings. She was being given the chance to feel his emotions without understanding what he knew.

It became their last night on the *Liberty Quest*. Going to bed first, Sunna fell into a deep sleep. Then, all of a sudden, she felt something hit her hard in the back. Quickly, she sat up, commanding an orbiter to light up the room.

She did it just in time to see Ghonllier's hand coming toward her. Pressing her back up against the wall, she avoided his fist. Then, staying quiet and watching him, Sunna realized Ghonllier was really asleep. She could see that he was experiencing a lot of anger.

Without notice, his arm came toward her again and she just missed it. Watching him intently, she thought, *He's dreaming again. I wonder what it's about this time.* She watched him for a few moments longer to see his body relax. *Maybe he's through with this fight and maybe he's not*, thought Sunna, looking at the foot of the bed. *I'm glad this bed is so big.* Picking up her pillow, she decided to sleep at the foot of the bed so he wouldn't bother her.

With the pillow in her hand, Ghonllier's arms came at her again. Her first instinct was to wake him up, but Gostler had warned her against it. Gostler had talked with her for a couple of hours in the office, without Jason, after breakfast.

Ghonllier relaxed and she headed again for the foot of the bed. Clutching her pillow against her chest, Sunna watched him as she moved. The bed was big enough to make it possible for her to lie below Ghonllier's feet undisturbed.

Before she got too far, Sunna heard Ghonllier yell, "No!" Then his arm came swinging in her direction with a lot of force. Not being able to move out of his way in time, she dropped her pillow and deflected his fist. By blocking his first swing, he came at her with his other arm. Sunna blocked it too. Wanting to get away from him, but being unable to, she lunged forward and applied a grip on his shoulder, blocking the nerves to his arms. His arms went limp.

The grip to Ghonllier's shoulder hurt and Sunna knew it. The defense tactic was something she taught when she trained spies. It could make a person momentarily unable to move in order to put restraints on them.

She only used it out of desperation. Ghonllier suddenly opened his eyes as Sunna let go of the pressure point. He stared at her with glassy eyes. They seemed to look right through her and she wasn't sure if he was asleep or awake.

Moments later, he closed his eyes and asked, "Why did you do that?"

"I'm so sorry. You had me pinned here against the wall and came at me with your fists. Were you dreaming about a fight?"

"I was. I'm so sorry. Did I hurt you?" questioned Ghonllier, rolling over on his back.

"No, you didn't hurt me; I protected myself. Who were you fighting with?" asked Sunna, lying next to him on her stomach.

"Bog," answered Ghonllier, staring at the ceiling.

"Gostler warned me about not waking you during a dream. Did I do something wrong just then?"

"I don't know," replied Ghonllier, looking at her. He rolled on his side and put his hand on hers. "I'm so sorry, Sunna. Maybe I better sleep in Sooner's room for awhile," he added.

Sunna reached up, lightly running her fingers over his stomach, and replied, "I think we better stay together. If we start separating because one of us is going through a tough time, I'm afraid we won't stay close to each other. It's too easy to ignore the other person's needs if we remove ourselves from the situation."

Ghonllier watched her eyes as she spoke. Smiling, he responded, "The Stones agree with you. You're a very smart woman." Ghonllier ran a finger along her cheek as she smiled. Then he added, "Now, I know why I love you so dearly."

Reaching up, he pulled her in for a kiss. After their kiss, Sunna gazed into his eyes and asked, "We both know you have to face Bog again. Are you upset about your meeting with him?"

"No. I'm not concerned about meeting him as I am about the outcome."

"What do you mean by 'outcome'?"

"I need to give Bog two choices—"

"Why? He didn't give one to Gomper or all the people he's killed and hurt."

"That's how the Stones work. I have to give him at least two choices. How he chooses could have some deep repercussions with different people in our galaxy," informed Ghonllier.

"Like who?"

"Like his descendants. We all might lose what we call our special talents, if he forces me to end his existence," informed Ghonllier.

"Will it affect Gomper's life?" asked Sunna.

"You mean with him being a Moveling?"

"Yes."

"Yeah, he won't be one, just like Asustie won't be a Mingler."

"You need Asustie to be a Mingler to stop the curse, don't you?"

"Yes, and that's the part that bothers me. I need him to choose the right way and I can't force or control that."

"Are you going to trick him?"

Ghonllier shot her a quick glance. "I can't do that. I need to present the facts and let him choose what is best for him. I need to present the facts so Bog can see past the evil that's inside him."

"What happens to the curse with these choices?"

"If I'm forced to destroy Bog, then the curse will spin out of control. Gomper will become the Bog, killing everyone he sees. If someone manages to kill him, then the curse goes to one person to another until there is no one left."

"Could you avoid it and hide a group of people?"

"No, it will seek me out and when it finds me, I'll become a part of the curse. Then it'll continue until there's no one but me. No one will be able to kill me."

The two looked at each other and Sunna was stunned. Trying to encourage Ghonllier, she smiled, "I can see why you're upset." Ghonllier looked away. "What can I do to help you?" she inquired.

Ghonllier knew he had frightened Sunna by talking out loud and vowed not to do it again. He reached for her hand and said, "Don't worry about it. It's my problem and I'll find a way around the obstacles. It's my job and there's always a way through every situation, darling."

She smiled, "I wish I knew what goes through your mind."

"Why would you want to know that?"

"I feel like I could help you more. Right now, I don't know what to do for you."

"You're feeling insecure," whispered Ghonllier, knowing the truth. Sunna didn't like that statement, because she wasn't ready to admit it. She attempted to defend it, when Ghonllier stopped her. "Sunna, I know I'm changing on you. Every time I change, it will make you feel insecure. It isn't your job to protect us anymore. It's my job to protect us."

Sunna thought for a moment and said, "You're right. I do not like feeling insecure."

"Do you want to know why?" She nodded, being curious. So he added, "You are learning new things about me and yourself. When you aren't sure how to handle a situation with me, you are concerned you might not be able to handle it. Then you wonder if Jenny could do a better job if your places were reversed. Or maybe, I love her more than I do you and wish she was here." Sunna rolled onto her back, realizing how true those words were. He got up on his elbow to look at her. She looked the other way. "She isn't here and I don't know how to measure my love for you both. I just love you with everything I have, Sunna. So please don't question the depth of my love for you."

She faced him. "Are you always going to know that much about my feelings before I do?"

"Yes. We're tied together by a thin thread that lets me know about your physical pain too."

"It unnerves me to have you understand me so well and I really don't know anything about you."

He smiled, "You have a lifetime to discover my love." He leaned in closer. "Do you want to know how I feel about you?"

"Yes."

"Look deep into my eyes, what do you see?"

After a few minutes, she started to giggle. She saw his love and he knew it. So he added, "If all I wanted was companionship, there were many women I could have asked to walk with me through this life."

"How many girlfriends did you have?"

"It doesn't matter how many I had. After Jenny, I waited six years for you. That's why I never dated and you know it. Please stop questioning me."

He lightly ran his hand down her arm. The bonding fires were extremely strong. Every part of her knew he had spoken the truth. It bothered her to discover how much she needed to be reassured. A grin spread across her face as she stated, "Thank you for waiting."

Ghonllier leaned into her for a kiss. Sunna kissed him back tenderly.

When Ghonllier's morning arrived, he woke up to find they had stayed asleep in each other's arms. Rolling over on his back, Ghonllier stared up at the ceiling. He had another dream earlier. He was getting used to them, so he wasn't necessarily waking up Sunna.

In fact, this last dream was pleasant. It was about Asustie and her new baby. He watched the two of them together and it reminded him again of his future children and the warning to not take his responsibility to the galaxy lightly.

After thinking about it, he gently kissed Sunna on her head. Then he mentally lifted her head to remove his arm, not waking her. Quietly slipping out of the covers, he left to get ready for the day.

When he came out of the bathroom, he found Sunna gone. Glancing over at the time sync stone, the stone sent the information to his mind. He knew they had four hours until they would be home. He started to tell Sunna last night that he wasn't going to allow her to come with him while he bonded to this last Stone. For some reason, he couldn't bring himself to tell her after she expressed her need to help him the night before.

Leaving, he decided to find a moment when she would fully understand that he didn't want to burden her with the last stage. Ever since realizing how close they were to being home, Ghonllier felt uneasy. He suspected it was his worries of leaving Sunna home and how she would take it.

He left to find her and found himself stopping at his old office. Ghonllier entered, not knowing why. Once inside the room, it hit him that the uneasiness wasn't Sunna. It was something else.

The room reminded him of everyone in his past. The memories of Sooner and Dapper were in this room. They had spent a lot of time together here. He seldom entered his old office. The night he received the fourth Stone was his last time. Now, Sunna and Jason worked out of his old office. Sadness seemed to shroud his heart as he looked around, reminiscing old memories.

Taking in a deep breath, he left. It bothered him that the room agitated his troubled heart. Frustrated, he entered the dining room. With each day, Ghonllier was loosing his appetite. When he became the Master, he wouldn't need to eat again. He could but it wouldn't be necessary. Entering the dining room, he was in search of companionship.

Adamite smiled at him as he walked up with something from the galley. Sunna and he were eating together. Sitting down, he used his Master Stones and said, "Good morning, my love."

She quickly shot a look at him and went on eating, smiling.

Adamite asked, "Ghonllier, how did you sleep last night?"

"Same as always."

"In and out of sleep?" asked Adamite.

"Yes."

"Adamite, did Ghonllier talk in his sleep when he was a child?" asked Sunna, playing with the suction piece on her container.

Ghonllier looked at her sharply to see why she would ask that question.

"When Asustie and Ghonllier were younger, one of you two would talk very clearly at night and the other one would moan or mumble in their sleep," answered Adamite.

"If those are my choices, I think Asustie moans and your son talks," suggested Sunna, making sure no one could hear them.

Sunna's opening question got Adamite talking about the twins' youth. He reminisced about all the cute things they did. Sunna didn't expect it, but was pleased she had started him talking. She found it interesting that Asustie and Ghonllier behaved a lot in the same way. Yet, they never lived together.

Ghonllier ate slowly and listened to his father's stories. It entertained him to hear about Asustie and realized they were truly twins. Listening to his father allowed him to let go of his concerns and enjoy the moment.

When he finished picking at his food, Ghonllier pushed away his plate and leaned back. Adamite's stories were fun to listen to. Somewhere in the stories, Ghonllier's thoughts went to Sooner and the Stones showed him where Sooner was at the moment.

Suddenly, Ghonllier shut out his father's voice. Concerned, he stood and left in a hurry. Sunna called out his name, but he didn't respond to her.

Seeing him disappear through the hullercast, she requested, "Adamite, take care of the dishes while I go see what's wrong."

Entering the corridor, she found Ghonllier wasn't there. Nowadays, Ghonllier spent most of his time on the bridge. So she headed there first. Stopping just inside the room, she searched for him. She was about to leave, when she saw his arm reach out to the ship's C-Stone from his flight chair. Sunna ran to face him.

Ghonllier had his earpiece in so she could only hear his side of the conversation. Jason and Humphrey happened to be on the bridge. They joined Sunna in listening intently to his conversation.

Confused, Jason questioned, "What's wrong?"

"Did he say anything to you?" quizzed Sunna.

"No," answered Jason.

"I don't know then," assured Sunna, stepping around Jason so she could get closer.

She heard Ghonllier say, "Cid, you have ten minutes to get that patch on him."

Suddenly, they heard Cid's voice over the speakers on the bridge as he explained, "I've sent the emergency shuttle. I'll have this ready for him and be outside, Ghonllier, just like I did for Sunna."

Sunna went white and limp. Jason grabbed her and Humphrey joined him. They helped Sunna to a flight chair. After she sat, Sunna put her hand up to her face.

Jason inquired, "Sunna, what is this about?"

When there was a break in Ghonllier's conversation with Cid, Sunna whispered, "Sooner dying."

"Did Ghonllier tell you about this?" asked Humphrey, leaning in.

Sunna nodded. "He had a dream about it and told me to watch out for it," choked Sunna.

"My men are with him. Why didn't you tell me?" retorted Humphrey.

She shook her head. "There is nothing your men can do about it. This is something between Ghonllier and the Stones," answered Sunna, facing Humphrey. "He didn't know when it would happen. I just learned about it and didn't think it would happen this fast or I would've warned you about it, General. Sorry." Looking at Ghonllier, Sunna requested, "Please, let us see what's going on."

Ghonllier just sat there, motionless, as the huge monitor behind the control panel showed home. Tears came to Sunna's eyes to watch Sooner playing, knowing he would die soon. She closed her eyes after seeing them enter Jasper's home. Everything was like Ghonllier had described.

The two boys grabbed a cookie from the cupboard and then ran upstairs to Jasper's room. Humphrey was the only one who saw his Vanishers following them upstairs. They moved quickly, blending in with the walls so no one would see them.

When the two boys entered Jasper's room, Sunna opened her eyes to watch and realized everything occurred like Ghonllier said. She bit her lower lip to see Sooner headed for the bed while Jasper looked for what they came into the house to get.

Just like Ghonllier described, Sooner sat on the edge of the bed and started to fall back. The Vanishers appeared out of the walls and caught him. They saw the flashing lights through the windows, letting Sunna know the emergency shuttle was there for him. Silently, tears glistened her cheeks as Adamite arrived next to Jason and her.

Before Jasper could turn around, the Vanishers had left with Sooner in their arms. They met the medics as they exited the shuttle with Jasper's mother following them. One Vanisher paused to tell her what was happening. Then he disappeared into the shuttle before the door closed.

The pilot took off the moment the door was shut. The two Vanishers stood back to let the medics work. They closed up the control temperature blanket and activated it. One of the medics had a C-Stone and was talking to someone. As they activated the blanket, the medic moved the C-Stone away from his ear and ordered, "Cid wants the blanket on manual. Set the temperature so he goes into hypothermia."

"Are you kidding? Why?" asked the other medic, reaching for the controls.

"Cid says he has a section bug," answered the medic, going back to the C-Stone.

"What's his proof? He hasn't seen the boy. I can't do it; I'll lose my license."

The Vanishers pulled their blasters from their belts as one ordered, "If Cid told you to do it, then you follow his orders now!" The medic stared at them, stunned. "Hurry!" repeated the Vanisher.

The medic did it while the other one said, "Who are you and why are you with this boy?"

"This boy is part of our crew from the *Liberty Quest* and if Cid tells you to do anything in the future, you never question him again or you'll be answering to us. Do you understand?"

The head medic glanced at the control blanket's controls and asked, "Is he going into hypothermia, Doug?"

He glanced away from the monitor and sighed, "Yes, he's there." He looked at the Vanishers and added, "You know this boy could die from this?"

"He could die if he has a section bug."

"We don't know if he has one."

"He has one, trust us," replied the Vanisher, listening to Ghonllier as he talked with him.

After Sunna heard the conversation, she looked over at Ghonllier to see how he was holding up. He remained still as he stared at the floor, a lament expression spreading over his face.

At the moment, Sunna felt completely hopeless. Tears turned into light sobs. Jason was upset too and it showed on his face. Sunna's tears caused him to want to join her.

Humphrey put his hand on Sunna's shoulder and said, "Sunna, I know Sooner meant a lot to you . . ."

Jason interrupted, "Sunna, let's go back to your office so you can watch in private."

Sunna took Jason's hand and left. Adamite joined her by putting his arm around her. With Adamite with Sunna, Jason stopped and went back to Humphrey, wiping away his tears. He wanted to be there in case Ghonllier needed him.

Humphrey and Jason watched the emergency shuttle land by the steps where Cid was waiting. The door opened and Cid entered. The head medic glanced at the Vanishers to see them putting away their blasters.

While Cid applied a patch to Sooner's jugular vein on his neck, the head medic leaned in and whispered, "Cid, do you know that I can pull your license?"

"Try doing it, Doug. You won't be able to touch me," stated Cid, reading the monitor to see what the patch was doing in Sooner's body.

"Why?"

He flickered him a glance and stated, "I'm now military and this boy is my responsibility, since he's a part of the *Liberty Quest* crew."

Doug shot the Vanishers a glance and stated, "Yeah, I've heard that already, but—"

Cid was moving Sooner out of the shuttle. "Cid, if he dies, I have to report this," warned Doug.

"Do what you have to!" shouted Cid, running up the steps.

The Vanishers were the last to leave. One looked at the medics and said, "I suggest you leave Cid alone. He has equipment that is a military secret and it is far superior than your analyzers. So I suggest you let things go."

The medics watched Cid disappear inside while Doug said, "I don't care who you are. That child dies and we're bringing him up on charges of murder."

Nodding, the Vanisher said, "We understand."

They disappeared and the medics shut the doors and left.

Sooner and Cid entered his medical center with the room ready for surgery. Ghonllier had his stats on the monitors for Cid and his staff to see. Cid placed Sooner on the table and ordered, "Don't touch that blanket until I get back. Is everything ready for surgery?"

"Yes," responded one of his assistants, helping Cid into his gown.

Cid left to sanitize his hands while looking at the monitor. Ghonllier had the bug that had burrowed underneath Sooner's skin on the monitor. He had no equipment that could show this and he appreciated Ghonllier's abilities.

The section bug got its name because it burrows underneath the skin for the heat of a mammal. Underneath the skin, the bug starts to divide out in all directions. Each split of the bug carries a deadly poison. The different sections repeat this process numerous times, spreading the poison. If the bug reached a vein or artery, the section of the bug would enter the blood, killing the person or animal.

As it enters the body, it renders the victim unconscious. The only way the bug can be detected is by an analyzer being put on an unconscious person's hand. By then, it was usually too late. With Cid placing Sooner in hypothermia, he stopped the bug from splitting. The patch was an antidote for the poison that the Stones had given Ghonllier.

Now Cid needed to surgically remove the bug from the boy's body. A little piece left behind could kill him when Cid moved Sooner out of hypothermia. Sooner faced death again if Cid warmed him up too fast.

Cid wasn't aware of the kind of patch that Ghonllier had requested him to make for his son. He didn't hesitate since the budding Master had requested other unknown patches for Sunna and they had worked. The medic felt a lot depended on Sooner's father, and Cid had no idea just how much was on Ghonllier's shoulders.

They moved back the control temperature blanket enough for them to reach the entrance of the bug. Picking up his surgical knife, he started to cut. Cid found the bug had partially spilt right where Ghonllier said it had. With Sooner's body so cold, it was a bloodless surgery. And as Cid and Ghonllier conversed throughout the operation, the medic was relying on Ghonllier more than he was on his own equipment.

When Ghonllier was satisfied that his son was free from the insect, Cid stopped, allowing his assistants to finish up. They sealed the blanket up around Sooner's neck and started to bring his body back slowly.

Sunna sobbed throughout the surgery while Adamite held her hand, crying too. Gostler joined them about halfway through, as they didn't talk until after it was over. Sunna asked, "Gostler, can you read Ghonllier's mind?"

He shot her a glance and asked, "What do you want to know, Sunna?"

"Does he have any idea if he's going to live?"

"He doesn't know," answered Gostler.

"Why won't the Stones tell him?" snapped Sunna.

"Sunna, I warned you about this part. Don't let anger blind you. Let it go and believe in the process. This is between Ghonllier and the Stones. They're testing to see how deep his feelings are for his son. They want to know if he will be a sacrifice that will strengthen or weaken him. "

"That's cruel," retorted Sunna.

Gostler shook his head. "No, it's not. None of us know how deep our wells are on the inside until we're asked to go there," stated Gostler, looking at her. Then he added, "Have you lost a friend, Sunna, that you didn't realize how much they meant to you until they were gone?"

She studied his face before nodding. Then she paused before asking, "Will they do the same to him, regarding me?"

Gostler smiled, "Sunna, what do you think the last two poison-ings were all about that you received? You both needed to learn how deep your feelings went for each other."

"So they won't test him again?"

"No, they passed on you or the three Stones would've fought for your life with the fourth Stone," answered Gostler.

"He never told me," whispered Sunna.

"I wouldn't expect him to," said Gostler.

"Ghonllier usually shuts you out of his thoughts. Why do you think he's not doing it now?" asked Adamite.

"As long as he's bonding with the fourth Stone, he won't be able to shut me out," answered Gostler.

"Is he pleading with them?" she whispered.

Gostler nodded. Sunna looked at the server stone, switching it to Ghonllier. The same lament expression showed on his face. Sunna ached to go put her arms around him to offer support. However, it wouldn't look right if they weren't supposed to be friends.

Ghonllier was alone with Humphrey and Jason on the bridge. Sam happened to return from a food break to see Cid watching Sooner's monitors. Instead of going to his station, he joined Jason and Humphrey and asked, "What's going on? What's wrong with Sooner?"

Jason didn't look at him as he responded, "Sooner might be dying."

"No!" replied Sam, looking at the monitor with concern.

The legal commander of the ship grabbed a hold of Sam's arm and asked, "Can you get this ship to fly faster so he can get home to his son?"

"I'll see. I love that boy. I taught him to read," responded Sam, heading for the purple stones embedded into the control panel of the ship. Over his shoulder, he requested, "I need someone to tell me what our time is now."

Humphrey ran to the time sync stone and requested the time of arrival. He shouted, "Two hours and ten minutes!"

Sam touched the black jump stone. Then he touched the purple navigational stone, intently looking at them. Eventually, he looked at Humphrey and ordered, "Try the time sync stone."

The general requested the time again. Humphrey shouted, "We'll be home in one hour and a half!"

Sam nodded. "Good. She's getting us there faster," he whispered, lovingly patting the stones.

Jason and Humphrey looked at Ghonllier, expecting to see a change or response from him. His demeanor remained the same. They lost interest in Ghonllier when they saw Sunna walk up toward Sam and kiss him on the cheek.

"Thank you, Captain," she smiled.

"Thank you for the kiss. I don't get those very often," he grinned.

"I don't give them very often," answered Sunna, looking up at the monitor.

Chapter 18

Sooner's Fight

*T*he last hour and a half to get home seemed to drag on forever. Adamite stayed with Ghonllier on the bridge while Sunna made plans with Jason to pack the Star Skipper for the family. Jason was aware that Ghonllier had planned to leave by himself.

Sunna wouldn't hear of it and Jason agreed. Things had changed and they weren't going to check with Ghonllier. They prepared for Sunna, Cid, and Sooner to go with him. It helped Sunna to deal with the situation, planning on taking Sooner. In her mind, he was going to live and she didn't want to accept anything else.

Therefore, she and Jason packed in their two rooms. When they were finished, Sunna shut the door between the two rooms while Jason paged for Humphrey and the few Vanishers with him to help get the Star Skipper packed for the family.

Sunna left her quarters by dropping her bag by the door and joined Adamite on the bridge. Ghonllier never changed his expression or position. Adamite assumed Ghonllier was mentally with Sooner, like he was with Sunna, in order to keep him from slipping away.

The moment the captains sounded the landing chimes, Adamite and Sunna ran for the OSA. An emergency shuttle waited for them outside. The minute Sunna and Adamite stepped inside, they saw Ghonllier appear. One medic shut the door while Doug came up to Adamite.

"Sir, this isn't what an emergency shuttle is supposed to be used for . . ." stated Doug, seeing he had better drop the subject. So he asked, "Is your grandson alive?"

"Yes, I watched you talk to Cid. Don't you dare ever question him again. He brought Commander Sunna back when you thought it was impossible," snapped Adamite.

Doug looked at Sunna and nodded. "You're right. Congratulations, Commander. We didn't think you would live."

The shuttle began landing, but Ghonllier didn't wait for it to come to a complete stop as he opened the doors and disappeared. Doug looked at Adamite and asked, "Where . . . ?"

"Don't ask and do not leave. You'll be shipping my grandson to the *Liberty Quest*."

"We know, sir," answered Doug.

Adamite left as the medic watched.

Adamite entered the house to see Sunna waiting at the lift. He joined her and asked, "Did you see him?"

"No," stated Sunna, seeing Sarah, Cid's assistant, coming from the medical center. Then she fully turned to her and asked, "Sarah, is Sooner still alive?"

Sarah offered a faint smile. "His vital signs are still showing in the medical center."

"Thank you," answered Sunna, seeing the door open as she and Adamite entered.

After exiting the lift, they ran to the room where Cid had brought Sooner after the surgery. His lifeless body shocked Sunna back to the realism that he might not make it. She looked between Ghonllier and Cid. The medic watched the monitors while Ghonllier held his son's hand.

Sunna joined Ghonllier to see tears trickling down his cheeks. She wanted him to look at her, but his eyes were closed. Sunna looked at Stacy watching and joined Adamite with her.

"Has Ghonllier said anything?" asked Sunna.

Stacy shook her head.

Cid hoped Ghonllier's presence would improve Sooner's stats, just like it had with Sunna. Finally, he saw a small increase. Cid glanced at Ghonllier to see him touching the patch on Sooner's neck. Sooner responded to his touch, just like Sunna had. *So does this mean the boy will live?* Cid thought.

Ghonllier interrupted his thoughts. "Cid, keep the patch at that level until I tell you otherwise."

"He's going to make it, isn't he?" questioned Cid, seeing relief on Ghonllier's face.

Ghonllier nodded and, for the first time, looked at Sunna, who stood silently beside him. Sunna buried her head into his shoulder, crying for joy. Looking at Cid, Ghonllier responded, "Thank you, Cid, for not wasting any time in following my instructions. You saved his life."

"You're welcome."

"How close was the insect to his arteries?" asked Sunna.

"I removed a section of the bug that was close to a big artery," answered Cid, glancing at Ghonllier. "If your husband hadn't told me about it, and if we didn't lower his body temperature, we would've lost him. Those bugs can kill within five minutes of entry if they enter close to a large vein or artery."

Sunna looked over Ghonllier's shoulder at Stacy and asked, "Did you pack everything?"

"Yes. Gabala arrived at the ship as you left," answered Stacy as Sunna let go of Ghonllier.

"Does that include Cid's things?" asked Sunna, looking at him.

"I always have a bag packed since I became your medical tech. Did Gabala get it?"

"Yes," answered Stacy.

Sunna looked for Ghonllier so she could ask him how long he thought it would be until the storms hit, but he was gone.

The relieved new Master left the room to be by himself. Taking in a deep breath, Ghonllier slowly walked down the steps of the patio. Speaking just above a whisper, he addressed the Stones. "Thank you for accepting my soul and sparing my son."

GIVING YOUR WILL IS A PROCESS, NOT A DESTINATION. THIS IS WHAT YOU NEED TO LEARN. WHEN WE SEE YOU'VE DEVELOPED A STRONG PATTERN OF GIVING UP YOUR WILL, THEN WE'LL GIVE YOU OURS AND YOU CAN RULE OVER US.

"Are you going to allow me to have my future children?" whispered Ghonllier.

YOU HAVE SHOWN US THAT SUNNA AND ALL YOUR CHILDREN ARE YOUR ONLY MOTIVATION TO EXIST. YOU HAVE MORE STRENGTH WITH THEM SO WE HAVE PASSED ON THEM. GUARD THEM WELL. THEY ARE YOUR BIGGEST STRENGTH. WE'LL KEEP LOOKING FOR YOUR SACRIFICE THAT IS MORE APPROPRIATE.

The news that his children had been spared thrilled him more than he could ever imagine. Tears of joy trickled down his cheeks, allowing his mind to completely relax. Relieved, Ghonllier walked on the paths through the garden, enjoying the peace and beauty of his mother's work.

Suddenly, he felt a new sensation taking place within his body. It took him a moment to realize that he was feeling new power surging to every cell. The power became all-consuming to his body and mind.

The four Stones had found a common ground to work with Ghonllier and they were bringing him into them. The bonding of the fourth Stone had begun. Power surged through him, causing Ghonllier to feel dizziness. As it consumed him, he closed his eyes, hoping his body would adjust soon.

The dizziness only increased. He opened his eyes to find a safe place to sit before he would fall down. A short distance away, he saw a bench tucked away among some foliage. He fell onto the bench and was relieved to be there.

Wanting relief, Ghonllier leaned over, holding his head in his hands while resting his elbows on his knees. He planned on staying there until the dizziness stopped. Ghonllier didn't know, or care, how long he stayed there as he waited to regain stability. Eventually, he opened his eyes and wiped the tears from his cheeks.

He took in a deep breath while sitting up. Immediately, he noticed his vision grew sharper, along with his senses. Every cell of his body was taking in information of his surroundings. The energy waves of a passing butterfly came to his attention, as did a raindrop falling from a leaf next to him. He had never heard the sound of a single raindrop before.

Standing, Ghonllier heard another raindrop land on a leaf close by. He raised his eyes to look at the shield to witness rain slowly filtering into their dimension from the outside. Asking to see above the shield, Ghonllier saw a dangerous storm forming, caused by the fourth Stone. Winds were swirling together from different directions and he knew this place was in trouble and he had to get out now.

Tornadoes or twisters would shred the shield and they were quickly forming. Using his Vanisher-like speed, he entered the house. The front door was open and he could see emergency lights from a shuttle, still waiting outside.

He was surprised to know the emergency shuttle was still here. Ghonllier saw they were about to shut the doors and his family was inside.

"Cid, Sunna, I can't have you go with me," Ghonllier stated, entering the shuttle.

Sunna looked at Doug and ordered, "Tell the pilot to fly and get us out of here." Then she looked at Ghonllier and added, "I know that you weren't planning on taking Sooner or me. But do you really want to leave him after almost losing him?" Ghonllier looked at Sooner and shook his head. "If you're taking him, then Cid and I need to come to take care of him," explained Sunna.

"Then leave the gurney. I don't want it on the Star Skipper," responded Ghonllier.

Cid looked at Doug and asked, "Do you mind returning it to my medical center?"

"No," replied Doug, pausing. Then he said, "Congratulations, Cid. You saved someone from another impossible situation. What's your secret?"

Ghonllier left to go sit while he half listened to Cid skirt around the truth. They were up in the sky and rain was pounding the shuttle. The medics were complaining about it and how strange this weather was. The shield was supposed to protect them from bad weather.

The new Master wanted to test his new powers out on Gomper. He thought about him and was surprised to see that his connection to his brother was stronger. Gomper was safe at the moment, so Ghonllier asked, *Stones, show me what happened when they reported to Gomper what happened on the Jasmine planet.*

Ghonllier suddenly found himself in the room with Gomper. He was at his desk on the Galaxy Creeper, working. Pappar wasn't far from the desk when Pursy, his personal military assistant, reluctantly entered the room. He handed Gomper a memory chip.

Gomper gave him a sharp look and snorted, "Why did you give this to me, Pursy? I didn't ask for anything new to see."

"I know, Your Grace. This is a report regarding a major attack by I-Force on the Jasmine planet," he stated, slightly shaking. Then he added, "Commander Jabolt wanted you to see it."

"An attack by I-Force on the Jasmine planet? Are you sure?"

"Yes, Your Grace," he assured.

Giving him a cold stare, Gomper took the chip from him. The timid assistant left as Gomper watched him. When he shut the door, Gomper placed the memory chip into an amplifier.

"Why are you questioning an attack on the Jasmine planet?" asked Pappar.

"I've been reading old reports so I could understand what has happened in this galaxy since I lost my memory. From the reports, I-Force abandoned the planet, so why would they attack it?" replied Gomper, leaning against the window. Comfortable, he added, "Amplifier, show me what is on the report."

Pictures of the base appeared after Ghonllier had entered the caverns. They witnessed the explosion caused by the robots. Then they saw Houser's hit on the base in a place that made Gomper curious. *A parking lot of transports? That doesn't make any sense.* The chip went on to show the destruction by the fourth Master Stone, tearing the place apart by using the elements. They saw Ghonllier and Sunna being lifted out of the fire and it stopped when the methane gas took everything out.

"Who recorded this?" asked Gomper.

"You have everything recorded automatically everywhere. It's a way you keep a tight rein on your troops," explained Pappar. Gomper had a thoughtful expression. "It's impossible for anyone to live in a fire and then float up into the clouds. What do you make of it?"

Gomper faced him and sighed, "I don't know." He went to his desk and wrote: THE TRUE MASTER OF THE STONES CAN DO THAT.

Pappar wrote back: Are you saying this weird weather was done by your brother?

Gomper nodded and answered on paper: YOU BETTER KNOW WITH ALL YOUR HEART WHICH SIDE YOU'RE ON. IT'S ONLY A MATTER OF TIME UNTIL HE'LL BE HERE.

Pappar read it while Gomper asked, "Memory chip, were their any survivors?"

The answer came back as a no.

Pappar reminded, "Your Grace, you have to attack I-Force. Your officers will expect it and you'll be out of character to not get revenge."

Gomper went to the window and became quiet. "Can we say it was a freak of nature and leave it at that?"

"No, they saw your brother."

Gomper studied him before he stated, "Have Pursy tell them I will attack and I have something special for I-Force. I'll do it in my own sweet time and when I'm ready, I'll give instructions."

"Yes, Your Grace. I think that will work," replied Pappar, leaving to deliver the message.

Being alone, Gomper grinned while looking down at his desk. *Well done, my little brother. You're getting stronger. I hope it isn't too long until you come and get me.*

Ghonllier wished he had the ability to appear to Gomper so they could talk now that Bog wasn't a part of his life. Thunder caused the shuttle to shake and it brought Ghonllier back.

"Ask the control tower to explain why we're having weather like this," demanded Doug.

Cid and Sunna exchanged looks while Ghonllier stood. He went to the pilot and stated, "If you're not comfortable flying in this kind of weather, I'll be glad to do it for you."

Thunder shook them again and this time lightning hit the shuttle, causing the pilot to lose most of his instruments.

"Great!" shouted the pilot.

"You're okay. You're okay. Lower your altitude to two hundred feet and you'll see my ship," informed Ghonllier.

The pilot did what he said and saw the *Liberty Quest*. Ghonllier pointed, "Take her into the bay. They're expecting you."

"Yes, sir. Thanks for your help," stated the pilot.

Ghonllier left for Sooner and ordered, "Cid, get him into the Star Skipper now. Sunna has everything ready."

As they entered the bay, Ghonllier opened the door and disappeared again. Cid removed Sooner from the gurney and Sunna stayed with them. Humphrey joined them at the shuttle and Sunna asked, "Where is Commander Ghonllier?"

"I saw him leaving the bay, Commander," answered Humphrey, walking with them to the Star Skipper.

Sunna glanced back at the shuttle and ordered, "Humphrey, tell the shuttle that it's okay they wait here until the weather clears."

"Yes, Commander," replied Humphrey, disappearing.

They entered the Star Skipper to find the other Vanishers and Jason. He arrived at his sister's side and asked, "Is he going to live?"

"Yes. Where is his bed?" asked Sunna.

"Let me show you," offered Jason, heading for one of the storage rooms.

They entered to see three cots floating above the floor. She looked at Jason and said, "We need four cots. Where is the other one?"

"We put it in the other storage room for you, Sister."

"And the food and supplies?" asked Sunna.

"We split them up in both rooms," answered Jason.

Humphrey joined them and asked, "Sunna, Gostler told us what it would be like for you. Would you like me to go in your place?"

She looked at him sharply before she answered, "Thank you, Humphrey. But I can't leave that little boy. It's my responsibility as his bodyguard."

Humphrey smiled, "I understand."

Sunna nodded and said, "Please thank your men for getting him to Cid so fast and defending him."

"I'll do it," replied Humphrey.

"Did Cid's medicine make it on board?" asked Sunna.

"Yes," answered Jason, pointing to a container at the head of Cid's cot. Then he added, "Cid's medicine is in that container."

Sunna came in to give her brother a hug. "Thanks for your work here. I'm sorry to take Cid from Asustie."

"She'll be okay. Janet is going to be taking over for Cid at his center."

"Tell Mother what happened and that I didn't have time to call her, but I will when we land," requested Sunna.

"This is a change, you reporting in to Mother," smiled Jason.

Giving him a smirk, she countered, "Do you have enough food for the three of us?"

"Yes," said a voice to the side of her. Sunna looked to see Gostler. "I told them to place ten weeks of food and water for you. I think we have everything for you, Sunna," smiled Gostler.

"Ten weeks. I hope it doesn't take that long," she expressed.

Gostler motioned them to leave. "He's ready to leave and you need to get out of here or this place will be destroyed by the weather," he warned.

"Is Ghonllier here?" replied Sunna.

Gostler nodded.

Sunna waited for everyone to leave before she shut the door. The suction sound of the door sealing swept over her with a feeling of sadness. Stepping away, Sunna returned to Cid and Sooner.

Touching Sooner's cheek, she asked, "How is he, Cid?"

"He isn't back to his correct body temperature. His numbers are climbing fast, so I expect the Master Stones are helping him. I'd expect him to be waking up soon."

Suddenly, lightning turned the windows of the ship to a bright color of yellow. Standing, Sunna left to go see what Ghonllier was doing. Sitting down in the seat next to her husband, she watched him finish putting in coordinates for their destination. She expected him to say something, but he didn't.

Wanting to hear his voice, Sunna asked, "Have we taken too much time? Is the storm tearing the shield apart?"

Ghonllier didn't answer but lifted the ship from off the bay floor. They were facing the open doors and suddenly everything went a bright yellow outside. "Activate your safety straps. You're going to need them," said Ghonllier, leaving the bay.

He took the Star Skipper straight up and then started to climb at an angle that threw Sunna hard against her seat. The pressure on her chest hurt and she wanted to talk, but found it difficult. All she could see were the constant white or bright yellow windows around her.

Sunna dug her fingers into the arm of her seat. When she thought she couldn't take it anymore, Ghonllier started to level out, making it easier to breathe. She took in a deep breath as the blue sky appeared.

Ghonllier encouraged, "Sunna, take in more deep breaths or you'll pass out. You're going to have a bad headache, too, if you don't breathe deeply."

She did and realized how much better it felt. Looking over at him, she asked, "Why did you fly at that angle?"

"We were flying up a lightning bolt," informed Ghonllier, looking at the numbers spinning next to the stationary set of numbers.

"That's impossible," said Sunna.

Ghonllier gave her a smirk and said, "You just did it, so how is it impossible?"

"Have you done it before?"

"No, only the Master of the Stones can do it."

"Why did you do it?"

"So we could get away from the city faster by using the energy of the lightning bolt," answered Ghonllier.

"How did Cid and Sooner survive that takeoff?"

"They're fine. I suspended them in mid-air so it was more comfortable for them than it was for you."

Sunna looked out the window to see how far above the ground they were flying. Ghonllier's voice brought her back into the ship. "Honey, would you look at this and tell me if you approve?"

She gave him a smirk. "You want my approval?" Ghonllier handed her an image from the navigational screen. While taking it, he said, "Yes, we're a partnership. I most definitely want your approval. This is going to be hard on the three of you and I'm so sorry for putting you through this."

After a few minutes of looking at it, she asked, "When did you get this?"

"When I disappeared."

"Why?"

"I wanted your approval of this place. If you don't like it, I have a couple of more in my head that we can go to," said Ghonllier, looking at her.

"What are the other ones?"

"I can show you on the small monitor in front of you, if you'd like," answered Ghonllier.

Sunna looked at the picture, stunned to realize that Ghonllier was insisting on her approval. It meant a lot to her and she didn't realize it until now. Looking back at him, she stated, "Are you telling me that you took the time just to get my approval?"

"Yes," answered Ghonllier. "Why? Don't you trust me?"

She studied the image, not answering him. Eventually, she expressed, "It looks like from the image that this place is the highest point in this mountain range. Is that true?"

"Yes," answered Ghonllier.

"It looks wonderful. There isn't a lot you can damage here, correct?"

"Yeah."

Sunna handed the picture back and he stated, "You keep it so you can remember this place."

She giggled, "Oh, after ten weeks, you think I'll forget?"

"Ten weeks?"

"Yes, Gostler said it might take that long."

Ghonllier shook his head. "I can see it took Gostler ten weeks, but I can't take that long."

"Why?"

"Bog. I can't keep him hypnotized that long."

The two exchanged looks and Sunna looked away, understanding what they were up against and hoped Ghonllier could pull this off. She gazed at the image, thinking Ghonllier had made up his mind to go here before Sooner became sick.

Suddenly, she felt him tipping the ship sideways. Looking up, she saw they were there and Ghonllier was letting everyone know. The place looked more spectacular than it did from the print that came off of the navigational screen.

The highest point on this mountain range looked like an old dormant volcano. Seeing the crater, it looked deeper than what she thought from the picture. Flying over it, she saw light blue water at the bottom. She had never seen that color before with water.

Looking at Ghonllier, she asked, "Why does the water have such a strange-looking blue color?"

"The water is shallow and trapped. It has algae growing in it."

The water disappeared from her sight as Ghonllier started to set the ship on the highest point. Looking out the window, Sunna saw the crater covered with dark pine trees. The blue sky made the contrast in color feel peaceful. She regretted seeing this place be ruined and hoped Ghonllier wouldn't do it.

Behind her, she heard, "Sunna!"

Whirling her head around, she saw Cid standing next to Sooner's door. She stood to join him as Cid smiled, "He wants his mother."

Grinning, Sunna ran to his side and greeted, "Sooner."

"Mother, why are we here?" asked Sooner, pointing at the window.

"Your father had to leave home before the power of this new Stone almost completely destroyed the city. So we're staying here with him until he gets complete control of this Stone."

"How long will that be?"

Sunna shook her head. "I don't know. We are planning on it taking as long as ten weeks."

"What about school?"

"Your grandfather, Adamite, contacted your school. He's made arrangements for you to attend a school at home."

"Home? But we aren't home."

"Yes, but they don't know that. They think you're using the server stone," answered Sunna.

Sooner was getting upset. "Mother, we don't have a server stone."

"No, you have something better. You have your father and he's going to broadcast school here and you'll be able to be a part of it," she assured.

"Did you bring my C-Stone?"

"Yes, so you can keep in touch with Jasper." Afterwards, Sunna reached out to touch his face as Sooner looked back with tired eyes. "How do you feel?" she added.

"I don't feel anything right now," replied Sooner.

"And you won't feel anything for a couple of days," interjected Cid.

"Cid said I picked up a dangerous insect, Mother. Was it like yours?"

Sunna smiled and shook her head. "No, it was a different one, but just as deadly."

"We're lucky, aren't we, Mother."

"Yes, we both are alive because of your father."

"Where's Father? Can I go outside?" asked Sooner, looking at Cid.

Cid shook his head and Sunna noticed it. Looking at Sooner, she said, "He's securing the ship to the ground. I'll go find him for you. I know he wants to see you."

As Sunna left, she half expected to see Ghonllier still in the pilot's seat, but he was gone and the door to the ship was open. She exited the ship to be greeted by a warm breeze. *Oh, this feels good. I wish we would be able to keep this weather,* she thought, walking slowly down the short ramp of the ship. She paused. *This place is so beautiful.*

Thinking about the Jasmine planet and their experience, Sunna wondered if the solid rock they had landed on was smart. She headed around the ship, looking for Ghonllier. The vista caught her attention and she slowly made her way on, taking in the beauty.

At the front of the ship, Sunna stopped. *This place is so peaceful,* thought Sunna. Somewhere in the daydream, Sunna felt arms wrap around her shoulders. Instantly, they felt the bonding fires. She leaned into him and he started to kiss her on the neck lightly.

Sunna giggled and expressed, "This place is so beautiful."

"So, you like the mountains?" asked Ghonllier.

"I haven't spent much time in them before. This is restful," replied Sunna. Pulling away, she faced him. "I like this place. I don't want you to destroy it. Maybe we should leave."

"It won't be any different than any other place we'll go."

Sunna looked at the rock they were standing on and asked, "Are we going to be able to withstand the winds and stay here?"

Ghonllier nodded. "I manually secured the ship to the rock." Taking her into his arms, he stated, "Besides, the Stones won't hurt it, just like they didn't when I was inside the lightning bolt."

Sunna smiled, "I keep forgetting who I live with." Then she paused a moment and added, "Will anything hurt you now?"

Ghonllier placed his hand on her neck and ran his thumb along her jaw. "Losing you. It was important that we both were tested to see how loyal we would be to each other. I've given you everything, Sunna."

Sunna smiled. "Do you think I've given you everything?"

"To a point, I can see you're coming forward each day with more. You need to build trust from your own experiences. It's normal for you to have a trust issue," stated Ghonllier.

"I'm sorry. I didn't realize it until you mentioned it."

"As long as you keep coming forward each day, we'll be fine," said Ghonllier, pulling her into him.

Sunna rested her head on his shoulder. "I love you and I'm so grateful that I feel your love."

"I HOPE YOU ALWAYS DO BECAUSE I'LL ALWAYS LOVE YOU."

Thunder could be heard rumbling in the distance. Sunna cringed to hear it. She looked up to see Ghonllier staring off in the distance.

"How long do you think it will take for that storm to reach us?" asked Sunna, looking in the same direction.

"It looks like about ten minutes. Take a good look at the sun. It might be awhile before you see it again," sighed Ghonllier, looking at their surroundings.

"What is it going to be like for us here?"

"We'll find out how much we really like each other. We'll be cooped up with each other for weeks," answered Ghonllier.

"Where will you be through all this bad weather?"

Ghonllier looked back at her. "I'll be inside with you."

"What about being with yourself and working things out with the Stones?" inquired Sunna.

"How did you know about that?" questioned Ghonllier.

"Gostler told me everything that you'll be going through during this time. I'll understand if you shut us out."

"Thank you for understanding me. That's why I was going to leave without you to do this . . ." Then he paused a moment and added, "If I really need to be by myself, I'll go outside so this won't be on you."

"Outside alone? Will it be safe?"

"Totally. The weather won't bother me, Sunna."

"Yeah, I've noticed."

"Know that when I'm inside, I want to be a part of your lives. When I leave for the outside, please don't bother me."

Sunna nodded. "I understand."

"I want Sooner and you to know that you're important to me. I don't want to shut you two out," whispered Ghonllier.

"Thank you," smiled Sunna, touching the side of his neck.

Understanding her thoughts, Ghonllier leaned forward to kiss her. The wind started to pick up, making a high whistle as it moved through the pine trees below. A shiver ran through her body because of the rapidly changing temperature.

Feeling it from her, Ghonllier stopped kissing her and pulled Sunna into him. He inquired, "Does this feel better?"

"Yes," smiled Sunna, feeling the heat from his body. "You're hotter than normal, aren't you?"

"Yes. I felt you shiver before you did. So I increased my body heat to keep you warm," countered Ghonllier.

Being in his arms, Sunna felt that there was a shield between her and the wind. She looked up into his face. "Inside your arms, I can see the wind whipping the trees, but I don't feel it. Is this how the wind feels to you?"

He nodded and said, "I don't feel anything except your discomfort."

"Even if we aren't together?"

He nodded. Sunna snuggled back into his neck and watched the clouds gathering. Lightning lit up the clouds in different places, announcing the storm. He put his arms around Sunna's shoulders as they headed for the ship. The moment Sunna left his arms to enter the ship, the thunder vibrated through her body.

Chapter 19

The Bonding

*G*ostler told Sunna this was going to be hard. It was more than she had imagined. Even the experience she had with Ghonllier on the Jasmine planet did not prepare her for this moment. Somehow, she had pictured it differently.

It had been weeks since they had seen the sun. The ship was always in a cloud, the nights and days quickly melted into one. She felt like they were in space, except for the pounding sound of thunder or hail playing outside the small ship. Like the *Liberty Quest*, mood lights were the only indicators of day or night. Sunna wondered if they coincided with the area or were set to match the *Liberty Quest* mood lights. She thought about asking Ghonllier but didn't.

Everyone but Ghonllier had their ears covered, causing them to communicate in sign language. At first, Cid was left out, but he was a quick learner. Ghonllier helped by telling the others what he was trying to sign. Sunna taught Cid to speak directly to Ghonllier's mind so he could feel more a part of the group.

The military sound covers for the ears weren't always the most comfortable things to wear, but they did help to filter out the agonizing noise. Music from the ear covers helped to control the frustration. They couldn't believe Ghonllier wasn't bothered by the noise. He had the ability to tune it out.

They could look outside and see either rain, snow, or hail. Thunder, wind, and lightning were always present with what was happening outside. The cloud was always prevalent. Cid and Sunna especially ached to see the sun. They weren't used to space like Sooner and Ghonllier, who could go for months without seeing it or feeling its warm rays.

So they wouldn't be too bored, Sunna and Cid focused on Sooner's studies and classroom work. During Sooner's classroom time, Ghonllier would disappear outside. Sunna would watch him quietly leave without saying a word to them. For some reason, every time he left, she cringed inside. She would watch him disappear into the cloud. A chill would shiver through her body as she felt that she would never see him again. The Stones were testing her as she thought about how she would handle it. Sunna knew she could live alone and be fine. Now, she didn't want to do it. She realized how much she wanted to be with him.

The time outside was good for Ghonllier. He watched the elements working together or against each other. Through the Stones, he was gaining more information than he thought possible. He had no idea how deep the laws were that governed the elements. The elements wouldn't obey him without this basic knowledge of how they worked. This time was important. He needed to understand their limits in order to have them respond to his commands.

When Ghonllier finally understood the laws, he needed to move on to the next level of becoming the Master. He was frustrated because he didn't seem to ask the right questions to understand what he was supposed to be doing.

He never talked about it, but Sunna could see it in his eyes. Ghonllier could feel the elements and energy waves of the storm. When he tried to connect with them, the elements shut him out. The Stones wouldn't tell him if it was them or the elements that denied him access. This was his biggest frustration.

Bog was always in the back of his mind and in his dreams. Time was ticking away and he needed to figure this out. In searching for the positive, Ghonllier was grateful that the Stones kept the elements there for him to learn. Yet, why was he able to feel the energy waves, but he wasn't able to get in harmony with them?

Every time Ghonllier entered the ship, he saw the suffering of his family and friend. Ghonllier took it personally. He had the power to stop it if he could get in harmony with the storm. Ghonllier was aware of their thoughts and feelings, even though no one ever said a thing to him.

When Sooner was through with school, Ghonllier would always enter the ship. He stayed with them until they went to bed. He would sleep for a couple of hours and then disappear outside.

Ghonllier's family and Cid went to sleep with deep sleeping patches, so they could sleep through the noise without their comsets. When morning would come, they kept their comsets next to their beds so they could put them on quickly. Every morning, Sunna hoped that they wouldn't need them. So far, it wasn't getting any better and she was disappointed.

Every morning, Sunna was the first one up and Ghonllier always entered the ship to greet her. Each morning, she saw the disappointment in his face become more apparent.

After the fourth week, Ghonllier changed his habits and Sunna noticed it immediately. He stopped showing up the moment Sooner was through with school and it concerned Sooner. Sunna was surprised to see Sooner waiting by the window for his father to come home.

She would watch from behind Sooner. When Ghonllier appeared out of the clouds, she could tell by his walk and expression that he was angry. Sunna assumed he was upset with himself and she never asked how it was going for him. His face told the whole story.

He stopped returning in the mornings and she cringed. With him not there, she wondered if the ship would be torn apart by the constant storms. They never saw twisters, but Ghonllier said they were all around the ship. After the Jasmine planet, Sunna was nervous to have him outside. She knew it was impossible for the storm to touch them with Ghonllier inside.

The clouds would move around and she could see him standing there amongst them. Sighing, Sunna was starting to wish that she had kept Sooner home and stayed with him. Maybe, she wouldn't be worrying that Ghonllier wasn't going to pull this off in time to save Gomper and the galaxy.

To keep her mind off their isolation and Ghonllier, they played games. Gostler made sure they had enough and Sunna appreciated it now. Sooner would insist on playing near a window so he could watch his father. It helped them all to watch Ghonllier while playing their games. In a way, they could still be connected to him.

It frightened Sooner to see his father disappear into white light from a lightning strike. Even though he would reappear unharmed, Cid expressed privately to Sunna how uncomfortable he felt watching Ghonllier do it. He explained how a lightning bolt could chemically affect a body. When Sunna told him that she experienced it first-hand, Cid pumped her for information on how it felt. She answered his questions, as long as he didn't talk about it in front of Sooner. Cid kept his promise.

When his father finally joined them, Sooner would ask him what it felt like to be hit with lightning and live. Ghonllier would smile and ruffle his hair, but never answered his question. After Sooner would push it, Ghonllier would say, "I don't know how to explain it. There is nothing I know for you to compare the experience to."

He never said more than that. With each day, Ghonllier became distant and seldom acknowledged them. He stopped interacting with them and would sit by himself with a faraway look on his face.

Sooner missed his father and would push the point that he wanted him to play. The most he ever got out of Ghonllier was, "It isn't the same anymore."

He would move farther away. Ghonllier would go sit by the window, watching the storm. Sometimes, he would leave and go outside again. The weeks in the clouds had now reached five and frustration had become pronounced on his face.

Ghonllier felt he hadn't gained much headway. He needed to understand why the elements wouldn't obey him. And Gomper and Bog never left his thoughts.

Moving into the sixth week, Ghonllier's frustration turned into anger. He still wasn't any closer to controlling the elements and the Stones couldn't stop Bog much longer. In his anger, he wanted to quit, but knew it wasn't an option. During this time, discouragement wanted to bury him and he kept fighting back.

The problem was that he hadn't done something to activate the process of getting in harmony with the elements. He couldn't think what it was and he began getting more impatient with himself.

In his dreams, he would see Bog killing Gomper stupidly out of anger. Now, the curse was released into the galaxy without him being able to stop it. In the dreams, he held his family, dying, and he couldn't stop it. When he awoke, Ghonllier would find himself pleading with the Stones to help him understand.

In the middle of the sixth week, Ghonllier awakened after his usual two hours of sleep. He rolled over to watch Sunna sleep. For some reason, this relaxed him. Eventually, Ghonllier rose from the cot and went to the window. He stared at the storm raging outside.

Usually, he went outside after he awoke. But tonight, he didn't want to leave Sunna's side. He felt like he couldn't throw off his discouragement this time and keep going. Tears streamed down his cheeks as he repeated everything in his mind, trying to see what he had missed. Nothing made any sense to him. In silent anger, he closed his eyes and tried to stop the sobs, aching to save those he loved.

His anger burst forward as he shook his fist at the storm and shouted, "What am I not understanding?! What do you want from me?!"

The storm drowned out his words. In complete despair, Ghonllier fell to the floor of the ship. Moments later, he felt the bonding fires and brought his head up sharply. Before him, Sunna was on his level, smiling at him.

Miffed at why she was there, he touched the patch on her neck and signed, "You shouldn't be awake with this patch. Why are you here?"

"I heard you call my name. You said you needed my help," signed back Sunna. Then she removed his hand away from her patch and added, "What do you need?"

"I never called you."

"Someone did. So talk to me. Tell me what you're thinking."

Looking away, he paused and then signed, "Time is running out. I need to start controlling the elements. If I don't do this soon, Gomper and you will die."

"Do you know why you're not controlling them?"

"I'm missing something," signed Ghonllier, shaking his head. "I don't know what it is."

"Are you arguing with the price to be the Master of the Stones?"

"What do you mean?" questioned Ghonllier, shocked by her question.

"What is your sacrifice that the Stones will require from you?"

"How did you know about that?"

"Gostler told me."

Ghonllier let out a sigh and let his head hit the wall. Using his hands, he said, "I don't know what it is. I haven't asked."

She countered, "So you're afraid." Ghonllier glared at her. Then she smiled and signed. "Ask."

"What if it's something that I don't feel like I can give up?"

"Do you know what Gostler's ultimate sacrifice was?"

"No."

"He was asked to give up the opportunity of having a spouse while in the service of the Master Stones. Would you want that one?"

Ghonllier leaned in to kiss her. He told her no by shaking his head.

She signed, "Well, you know it isn't that one."

Putting her arms around his neck, they kissed. Afterwards, she touched his face fondly and added, "You can do this. Let go and give your heart completely to the Stones. Your sacrifice will make you invincible. I know it." Sunna slowly moved in for another kiss.

After the kiss, Ghonllier glanced out the window at the raging storm. When he looked at Sunna to thank her, she was gone. It miffed him to see her in the same sleeping position she was in before coming to him. Staring at her, he knew she was right. He had been arguing with the price for success and refusing to ask what his sacrifice would be from the Stones. They weren't going to give him access to the elements without him asking. Looking back at the storm, he knew what to do.

In the morning, Sunna awoke to silence. She placed her hand on the comset next to her bed and waited for the next thunder. Looking at the window, she watched for lightning. The cloud looked like it was farther away from the ship. Sitting up in bed, she realized that the cloud looked different. It was a lighter gray.

She left her ear protection by her bed and grabbed a robe, running to the windows. Quickly, she scanned the area in search of Ghonllier. He wasn't there, so she left. Everything looked different from the windows. Sunna wrapped the robe around her and decided to leave the ship in search of her husband.

The ground was covered with ice and Sunna wasn't sure about it, but decided to go anyway. Stepping onto the ramp, she slipped and caught herself. Then, deciding to sit down, she eventually slid down the ramp. At the bottom, she hung onto the ramp as she carefully worked her way to the front of the ship. As she reached the front, Sunna looked up at the icicles hanging from the ship and wished she had put something warmer on.

She worked herself forward by hanging onto the ship until she saw Ghonllier standing on the edge of the cliff. He was looking up into the sky and didn't acknowledge her. A warm breeze swept over her and she wondered if it was her husband who sent it. She decided not to bother him.

Before she left, Sunna shot a quick glance up at the sky. The clouds were parting, allowing a small ray of sun to appear. She smiled and thought, *It has been so long since I've seen the sun.* Leaning against the ship, she looked back at her husband.

A shiver ran through her body, reminding her it wasn't warm enough for pajamas and a robe. Glancing at the door, Sunna decided to retrace her steps and now wondered how she was going to get up the ramp.

Suddenly, Ghonllier appeared to give her a kiss. It surprised her and she pulled back from him. In his face, she saw something different in his eyes. *Hope!*

"Thank you for last night. You were wonderful," he whispered.

"What did I do?" Sunna questioned, raising an eyebrow. Then she added, "I don't remember being with you last night."

"You don't remember getting out of bed to talk with me?"

"No."

"Do you remember telling me what Gostler's sacrifice was to the Master Stones?"

Sunna shook her head. "What was it?"

Ghonllier could see now what had happened last night. He had to figure out on his own how to break through the door to the elements. They talked to him through Sunna. She had to be willing to do it or it wouldn't have been possible.

"I'll tell you after I release Gostler from the Master Stones," he whispered, holding her again.

After a long hug, the humbled man looked fondly into her eyes and smiled. Sunna praised, "So you did it."

"Maybe."

She looked behind him and asked, "How long are you going to keep the sun out?"

"For a while. There is a lot of snow and ice that needs to melt," responded Ghonllier as Sunna felt a drop on her head.

She felt the warm breeze again and looked over at the vista. "Are you controlling the wind and the temperature?" she questioned, looking at him. Ghonllier nodded. Smiling, she snuggled into his shoulder and he felt warm to her. She added, "I'm happy for you, Ghonllier. I always knew you would do it." Then she pulled away and asked, "I want to get dressed and get out of the Star Skipper. Would you help me get up the ramp?"

He nodded and leaned in to kiss her again. Then he said, "I want Sooner to join us."

"What about school?"

"I'll rebroadcast it later. I want him outside today with me. Have everyone come out," he requested.

Sunna jumped as an icicle fell right behind her. Ghonllier picked her up in his arms as they looked at each other. "Do you want me to carry you inside or just let you float up to the door, Commander?"

"I like being in your arms. It's been a while since you even touched me."

"I'm sorry. The bonding fires feel really good right now, don't they?"

"Yes," smiled Sunna.

Ghonllier carried her to the ramp and stopped at the door. Tenderly, he kissed her again. "I would like your attention."

In the background, Sunna heard Sooner calling out to her from his room. She smiled, "Later."

The relieved Master let her float out of his arms. When she was on her feet, she left, glancing over her shoulder at him. He didn't leave until Sunna disappeared. Then he went back outside to practice some more.

Everyone was excited to hear that Ghonllier had control of the elements. Cid was first to arrive outside. He saw the sun and brought out some portable chairs. Cid planned on sitting in the sunlight, watching the ice melt.

Sooner beat Sunna outside and ran to his father. Ghonllier met him halfway and Sooner was asking questions faster than Ghonllier could answer. Watching the two of them together, Sunna observed Ghonllier was behaving like his normal self. *I wonder if the worst is over with.* Ghonllier sidestepped most of his son's questions, only because they were too complicated to answer.

This was a day for celebration and they spent it outside. It was great to even eat their meals under the sun. The next day, Sooner went back to school while Ghonllier spent his whole time practicing. Cid joined him by reading or going on short walks. It was too muddy to leave the rock the ship was anchored to.

The medic found it interesting to watch Ghonllier move the elements. He kept all storms over the lake at the bottom of the old volcano crater. Now the water wasn't shallow like it had been in the beginning. It had swollen halfway up the walls. Waterfalls from the melting snow and ice spilled into the lake.

On the third day, everyone woke up to see the dark clouds back. Sooner was up first and ran to the window, searching for his father. Seeing him by the edge of the cliff, Sooner exited the ship.

Running, he shouted, "Father!"

"Yes, Sooner," Ghonllier responded.

"Where's the sun?"

"I sent the sun away so I could make fresh snow for you to play in," smiled Ghonllier, looking at him.

Sooner grabbed his arm with enthusiasm and asked, "You can really make snow?"

"Yes, and it will be the kind that you can play in," assured Ghonllier. Gesturing toward the ship, he added, "Go get your warm clothes on."

Sooner gave him a hug and replied, "Thank you, Father, for keeping your promise."

Ghonllier smiled, watching him leave. He thought about the last time they talked about Sooner playing in the snow. It was the day Dapper died and he wished his old friend and bodyguard was there. In a way, Ghonllier felt like he was. He never felt alone when he was in the clouds, trying to learn.

Sooner passed Sunna on her way out. He hurriedly explained what was happening while Sunna studied Ghonllier. Joining him, she inquired, "What about school? I thought you didn't want him to get behind."

Glancing at her, he added, "It will be okay. I need him today. His school has a break coming up in a couple of days. Sooner can make it up then."

She searched his eyes. "Have the Stones told you what your sacrifice is?"

"No, but because I asked, they're allowing me to handle the elements."

Sunna shivered a little with Ghonllier lowering the temperature so he could make snow. Noticing her plight, he pulled her into him. Instantly, she felt the warmth of his body. Cuddling underneath his chin, Sunna asked, "How far away are you from producing snow?"

"About ten minutes," answered Ghonllier, looking down at her. "We can stay this way if you want. But you'll get pelted with snowballs, I'm thinking."

She smiled and left, understanding what was going to happen. Ghonllier joined with his arms around her, trying to keep her warm. When they reached the door, Ghonllier squeezed her hand as the two gazed into each other's eyes, smiling.

The excitement in Ghonllier's eyes made everything they had endured worth it. Hope had filled their hearts and she knew now how insecure she felt when he couldn't control the weather. A heavy weight had lifted off of Ghonllier and Sunna. They were the only ones who understood the timetable he was under.

Sooner was the first one to return to find his father. When Sunna returned, she sensed an eerie stillness outside. Joining Ghonllier and Sooner, she heard, "Sooner, I want you to watch those trees on the other side of the lake."

Thunder rumbled above them and Sunna looked at him. "Did you cause it to thunder?"

"Yes, I did it to get your attention," answered Ghonllier, keeping his gaze on the other side.

Sunna chuckled and looked in the same direction to see a lightning bolt shoot from the clouds, hitting a single tree. Instantly, it burst into flames, standing like a huge candle among the other trees.

"You did that?" questioned Sooner.

"Yes."

"Can you put the fire out?" challenged Sooner.

"Yes."

Instantly, the fire disappeared.

Amazed, Sooner asked, "Father, how did you do that?"

"I just removed the oxygen from the space around the tree."

"How did you stop the fire from spreading to the other trees?" asked Cid, joining them.

"I controlled the air and the winds to keep the flames exactly where I wanted them."

Sooner smiled, pleased with his father's answer, while Ghonllier watched his expression. Suddenly, a single snowflake landed on his eyelash. Sooner looked up to witness thousands of little tiny snowflakes starting to fall.

"Father!" cried Sooner, putting out his hands to catch some. "Are you doing this?"

"Yes, Son. I'm doing it just for you," smiled Ghonllier.

"This is awesome!" stated Sooner, looking up and letting the snowflakes fall on his face.

Quickly, the snow went from light to heavy. The rock underneath their feet turned white. Sooner moved his feet and noticed they left a print of his foot. Excitedly, he walked in a circle. Stopping, he looked back at his design and then grinned at his parents as they watched him.

Instantly, Ghonllier read new feelings from him and was perplexed by them. The new Master stepped toward him and Sooner stepped backwards. Stopping, Ghonllier quizzed, "Sooner . . . are you afraid of me?" The boy stayed silent. So he added, "Sooner, I don't want you to be afraid of me. I won't hurt you."

Seeing he needed reassurance, Ghonllier got down on his son's level. Keeping eye contact, he repeated, "Sooner, ask me your question."

His son hesitated for a moment and then asked, "Can you ever lose control of this power . . . ?"

"And hurt you or someone else?" finished Ghonllier. Sooner nodded. "Son, this is how the Master of the Stones protects the galaxy from those who want to destroy it. He uses the elements that are already in the galaxy. I don't need ships and armies of men, so people don't have to die because of war. If the people of the galaxy respect the Stones and give them their allegiance, the Stones will protect them."

All of a sudden, Sooner was hit with a snowball in the back. Whirling around, he saw his mother making another one. Quickly, Sooner copied her, but she beat him and this time threw it at Ghonllier. It went about halfway and returned to Sunna, hitting her in the face. Everyone started to laugh.

Sooner could see Cid making one and he threw his at the medic. After a long, good snowball fight, everyone was tired but Ghonllier. He watched, regretting that the Master Stones wouldn't allow anything to touch him. It was a rule that Ghonllier couldn't override. This was why Gostler and Ghonllier weren't allowed to face Gomper with Bog in control.

Seeing they wanted a break, Ghonllier asked, "Sooner, what else would you like me to make?"

"Hail, make it hail!" shouted Sooner.

Immediately, hail started to fall, hitting the rock so hard that it made sparks. Everyone jumped except for Ghonllier. The hail was the size of Sooner's fist and looked like fire while hitting the rock. Sunna grabbed Sooner, pulling him into her for protection. They both looked at each other when they realized the hail wasn't touching them. It was only hitting around them.

Looking at Ghonllier, Sunna quizzed, "Do you have that much control that each piece of hail lands where you want it to?"

Ghonllier nodded. "I also have control on how hard it hits the ground," replied Ghonllier, looking at Sooner. "Son, you don't need to be afraid of me. I have that kind of control so I can protect you and the galaxy," assured Ghonllier.

Sooner broke away from Sunna's arms to reach for his father. With the hail on the rock, his feet went out from underneath him, causing him to fall back. Before Sooner could reach the ground, his father mentally caught him in mid-air. Slowly, Sooner floated through the air, back to Sunna.

"SOONER, IT'S TOO DANGEROUS FOR YOU TO WALK AROUND WITH SUCH LARGE HAIL STONES," he heard his father say.

Sooner stared in shock at his father. He heard his voice by the side of his ear, but didn't see him move his mouth. Finally, he asked, "How did you speak to me?"

"I have many powers now, Son. It doesn't matter where I am in the galaxy. I'll always know where you are and what you're doing. So be careful about what you do. There will be little you'll get past me," smiled Ghonllier.

"Will you always be there to catch me when I fall?" asked Sooner, reaching up to take hold of his mother's hands.

Ghonllier shook his head. "No, I won't. Sometimes, it is important for you to fall. How you get up will determine what kind of a man you are." Sooner gave his father a thoughtful look. Ghonllier read Sooner was searching for some kind of resolution toward his changes. Smiling, Ghonllier inquired, "Are you hungry, Son?" Sooner nodded. "Let's go eat."

Ghonllier brought in a warm breeze that quickly melted the hail so they could walk inside the ship without falling. Ghonllier also brought the sun out before they ate. The men entered the ship first, leaving Sunna at the door. She wanted to stay there and compare how it looked today in contrast to the day they arrived. The waterfalls were getting smaller but they were very beautiful.

Ghonllier glanced at Sunna looking outside and knew what her deepest thoughts were. She wondered if she had lost him to the galaxy. He had spent most of the time being distant toward her. It was the same question he had, but he wasn't ready to talk about it with her. He wouldn't know the answer until he had completed the process of becoming the Master.

Sunna was his motivation to be the Master of the Stones and if he became indifferent toward her, he wasn't sure about being the Master. There were a lot of issues that Ghonllier and the Stones needed to come together about before they turned their power over to him.

She entered the ship and joined Cid and Sooner for lunch. Now that he had the fourth Stone, Ghonllier didn't need to eat or drink water, but he could do it. He planned on doing it only to be social in the future.

During lunch, he watched Sunna's reaction toward him. The thought that surprised him the most was Sunna's concern about losing her identity. While she lived in his shadow, he could see they both had issues that needed to be resolved before he became the protector of the galaxy.

After lunch, they went back outside to watch Ghonllier practice with the elements.

The next day, Sooner went back to school. It was hard for him to concentrate. He wanted to watch his father. So Ghonllier came into the ship and worked from there, not letting Sooner know what he was doing. They stayed together until everyone went to bed. This was Ghonllier's time to practice and talk with the Stones.

At the beginning of the second week of controlling the elements, Sunna noticed a change in Ghonllier. He totally withdrew from everyone, more than he did before. Cid and Sunna tried to shield Sooner from it, since he always wanted to be with his father. They came up with things for Sooner to do, distracting him from Ghonllier.

Finally, they had to tell him not to bother his father and he couldn't understand. This time, Sunna was frightened of the changes that were taking place in Ghonllier. She always talked positive to Cid and Sooner about it, keeping her feelings away from them. She hoped to talk with Ghonllier when he was ready.

One day, he disappeared without telling her when he would return. He was gone for hours. When he finally did return, she stayed silent and knew if he wanted to tell her, he would. Ghonllier kept to himself.

Cid saw more changes than Sunna did. She didn't realize that something was happening to her, too. During the times of his absences, Sunna would curl up at the window with a blanket, staring out. She, too, stopped talking.

Sometimes, Cid would see Ghonllier appear outside the window and the two would stare at each other for a long time. He didn't realize they were talking to each other.

Ghonllier said, "I CAN SEE YOU NEED TO TALK."
Maybe.
"SUNNA, PLEASE ASK ME ANY QUESTION."
Do you know about our future?
"WHAT DO YOU WANT TO KNOW ABOUT OUR FUTURE?"
When we go home, can we tell the crew that we're married?
Ghonllier shook his head. *Why?*
"I NEED TO BRING GOMPER HOME ALIVE OR DEAD FIRST BEFORE THE STONES WILL ALLOW IT."
Sunna looked away, causing Ghonllier to come inside. He took Sunna in his arms as she continued to talk to him mentally. *I'm scared of the unknown in our future. I'm in a territory that I've never been in before.*
"I FEEL THE SAME WAY. THIS WHOLE EXPERIENCE IS NEW TO ME, TOO. WE'LL GET THROUGH IT TOGETHER. SUNNA, I'M SORRY TO IGNORE YOU LATELY. I DON'T THINK THIS IS A SIGN OF OUR FUTURE."
He released her and she looked at him. *Ghonllier, I know you have to leave us. Will you be leaving us soon?*
"I'M NOT SURE," answered Ghonllier.
Please tell me when you need to go. I need to know . . .

"I KNOW AND I WILL."

They gazed at each other for a moment and then he left for outside again. Sunna went back to watching him through the window. This time, he disappeared from her sight. She leaned back into the seat and closed her eyes. She was tired and wanted to go to bed, but wanted to wait up for him to come home.

After hours of waiting, she gave up and went to bed. She started to drift off when she heard his voice in Cid and Sooner's room. She waited to see if he would come to her and he did.

He entered, not looking at or acknowledging her. She was relieved to see him, even if he wasn't talking. After he got ready for bed, Ghonllier and Sunna exchanged looks. The Stones were causing her to reflect on her life in the same way they made Ghonllier reflect. Neither one of them really didn't want to talk about what was happening to them. Ghonllier lied down on his cot and closed his eyes while Sunna shut hers as well.

When she awoke in the morning, Ghonllier was gone. Sitting up, she realized a note was on her pillow.

It read:

> *Sunna,*
> *I have been told what my sacrifice is and it's something I'm struggling with. I have left and I won't return until I can openly embrace my sacrifice and until the Stones and I understand each other completely. I won't appear again until the Stones and I are together on every level. I don't know how long it will take.*
> *I love you and don't worry about me. I don't need food or water anymore to survive. There is nothing that can harm me. Please know the sacrifice will only affect me and not you.*
> *My love is yours forever,*
> *Ghonllier*

Sunna showed the note to Cid and Sooner so they wouldn't worry about Ghonllier. But the hours of waiting for him were long and hard on Sunna. This was harder than the raging storms outside.

She appreciated Gostler telling her about this part of the bonding, so it wasn't a complete surprise. In her way, Sunna withdrew inside herself, mirroring what Ghonllier was going through.

Cid kept Sooner busy and away from her. He spent the time with Sooner, either playing or working on schoolwork. Being a part of the partnership with the Stones, Cid sensed what the Stones were doing to her. She was also being prepared.

When she would join them, Sunna never lasted long. The window always seemed to call her back. If she weren't there, Sunna would go outside and walk around the ship for hours.

On her walks, she searched the vista. All she wanted to do was know he was there. Now, she wished they had brought the *Liberty Quest*. The ship had a server stone and she would be able to watch him.

With Ghonllier gone, the weather went back to normal. It made her feel like he had totally disappeared from the area. To ease her heart, she pictured him in her mind, not too far away.

A week went by with no sign of him. For some reason, she awoke one night while feeling troubled. It was dark, but the light from a clear night shed softly in their room. Looking at Ghonllier's cot, she realized it had been slept in. Right now, it was empty.

She ran to the window to see a slightly pink horizon appearing and a silhouette of a man standing outside. "Ghonllier!" *It has to be him*, she thought, running from the room in her pajamas.

The door was left open and she knew it had to be her husband outside. Running around the Star Skipper, she stopped when she saw the silhouette. The man didn't move and something felt different. Concerned, she stepped forward and the man ignored her. Her Ghonllier would've acknowledged her by now. *So who is this man?*

Suddenly, the man spoke in an unfamiliar voice. "What do you want, woman?"

"Who are you?" countered Sunna boldly.

"I'm the man you seek."

"And who is that man?"

"I'm the Master of the Stones and your husband," he replied, facing her.

Sunna was silent and studied his face in the darkness. In a quiet tone, she asked, "I'm not sure who you are. If you're my husband, then show me," challenged Sunna.

With his face still in the shadows, he reached out for her hand. Instantly, she felt the bonding fires. "You're my love," he whispered.

He took her into his arms and she silently rejoiced. "Oh, Ghonllier, I've missed you so."

"I've missed you, too. I won't be leaving again."

Looking at him, she asked, "Has it really happened? Are you the Master of the Stones?"

"Yes, and at a price," assured Ghonllier, holding her tightly in his arms. "I'm so glad you're not my sacrifice. I couldn't do it."

"What happens to us next?" asked Sunna, cuddling into his neck.

"I need to go back home as soon as possible."

"Why?"

"It's Bog. The magic of the music box won't be able to hold him much longer. He'll kill Gomper when he realizes what I've done to him."

"Is Asustie ready for this?"

"I hope so."

"Then let's go home now. I'm getting tired of field food," expressed Sunna.

"I was about to ask you if you wanted to eat breakfast first. But I can see you've had enough and you want to go home. Thank you for putting up with so much."

Sunna didn't want to answer him and was grateful he knew her answer. Instead of leaving, they both held each other and watched the sunrise.

This was the first day of their new life, a life that they had long prepared for. Now, they hoped they were ready.

Chapter 20

Old Friends

*S*unna awoke the next morning to see the drapes open and Ghonllier standing in front of the windows, looking out on his city. At first, he reminded her of the silhouette she saw the morning before. The sun was bright and she wondered what time it was. Sunna's body was off because Ghonllier had the mood lights set to coincide with the crater, not home. Looking at the timepiece by her bed, Sunna decided he was right. She should be getting up.

When they arrived yesterday, the welcome home was fun. Stacy had her server stone set to let her know when the Star Skipper flew again. The family had a private celebration set up at home, since the crew couldn't know about their marriage. It was important to Sooner and he wasn't going to let them forget. Sunna's family was the only ones invited.

Sunna was pleased to see her parents. Bonnie was especially warm toward her daughter and it took Sunna back a little. Gratitude was expressed in every word she used. It was a big improvement and Sunna was pleased. While they were away, she took a page out of Sooner's book and contacted her mother weekly.

They talked and shared their experiences and this was something new for both of them. Sunna could see how unfair she had been to her mother by shutting her out of her life. In Sunna's career, it was easy to do. There was so little she could tell her mother and with her being so negative, she was always relieved to avoid the subject. Now, she wished she had tried harder to talk with her.

It really surprised Sunna to see Bonnie give Ghonllier a hug the minute they walked through the door. This was the first time she had ever acknowledged he was in the room, let alone hug him. She wondered if it was because of what she did or because of his title.

After the party, Ghonllier assured her that it was because Sunna had shared her experiences with her mother. Bonnie wasn't sure about his title and was concerned Sunna was going to be neglected. If he did neglect her, she planned on having a talk with him.

Sunna was relieved to know how much Bonnie loved her. Watching her mother, Sunna was looking forward to the future. Until now, she didn't realize how much she wanted her mother's acceptance and she liked it. Sunna realize her mother changed when she gave her unconditional love.

Closing her eyes, she stretched and rolled over on her back, deciding to get up. Sunna expected Ghonllier to look at her, but he didn't. She threw the covers back and watched him. He didn't move. Assuming he was deep in thought, she left for the bathroom.

Sunna entered the bathroom and paused to close the door. *What's wrong with him? Is this going to be my husband from now on?* Before, Ghonllier almost smothered her with attention. Since Ghonllier told her that he was the Master of the Stones, something was different and it wasn't anything like what Gostler described to her.

He was very quiet around the family yesterday and it still hadn't changed. The only person he went out of the way to talk with was Jason. It was only to tell him to prepare his complete elite force for departure to help Gomper. He didn't give anyone a time for when they were leaving. The night before, all she got from him was a quick kiss goodnight before he disappeared.

Sunna shut the door, deciding that this was the way he was going to be, and found herself already missing the attentive man. Shortly, she returned to find Ghonllier gone. Seeing she was alone, Sunna rolled her eyes and entered their closet, wondering what was happening.

With him being attentive, she always knew how Ghonllier felt about her. Now, she wasn't sure.

Ghonllier didn't mean to avoid Sunna or be rude. He had major problems that he wasn't quite ready to talk about. They were leaving shortly for the Zuffra moon to face Bog and he couldn't see the sorcerer. The Stones weren't showing him, because he had missed something in his understanding. They wanted him to figure it out or things wouldn't go well when he faced Bog. He was running out of time. Bog was already starting to resist the hypnotic music.

When he left their sleeping quarters, he headed over to the other side of the house, looking for Gostler. His room faced the garden on the third floor and Ghonllier wanted to talk with him. He wanted to talk with someone who had been in his shoes before. Maybe Gostler could tell him how to figure out what he missed.

The former Master of the Galaxy was asleep as Ghonllier barged into his room. Gostler was startled to see Ghonllier by his bedside and asked, "Why are you here?"

"I have a problem. I need your help."

"I knew you were upset when you came home. Why didn't you talk to me then?"

"I thought I could figure it out . . . and wasn't ready to talk then. What do you know about what's bothering me?"

Gostler rolled over on his back, studying Ghonllier's face. "I know you couldn't see Bog or your brother yesterday. You mean to tell me that you still can't see them?"

"The Stones seem to be stonewalling me this time. They said I've missed something very crucial. They told me to talk with the person who helps me the most. I've spent most of the night going through everything. I can't figure it out. I know you saw my life . . ."

"Not this part. I didn't know about Bog when I was the Master," interrupted Gostler. Ghonllier gave him a disgusted look. Gostler defended, "Ghonllier, I have nothing for you. I don't know what they meant by that statement, unless I'm not the person who helps you the most."

Grunting, Ghonllier left. Gostler was concerned as to why he came to him. Getting up, he decided to go after him and get him to talk more. Maybe together, they could figure it out.

Frustrated, Ghonllier stopped at the door of the garden and listened to those in the kitchen talking about setting up breakfast. Tuning out the noise, Ghonllier stared at the garden. He was planning on going outside to think. Suddenly, he decided not to go outside. This morning, he wanted to be with people.

Knowing his family would gather in the dining room, Ghonllier entered. One of the chefs saw him and instead of sending someone out, he exited the room and greeted, "Your Grace, may I please get you something?"

Ghonllier smiled, "Please don't call me 'Your Grace.' I don't want people I live and work with all the time to use that title."

"Please forgive me. Can I get you something?"

Ghonllier could see he really wanted to please him, but he wasn't hungry. So he stated, "Please just get me something light."

"Yes, sir." The chef nodded and left.

Ghonllier waited in front of the huge windows. It was relaxing to have huge windows that made you feel like you were eating outside. The windows gave Ghonllier a great view of the garden and he loved how his mother had designed the garden right there. She was working outside, even now, and while staring at her, he allowed his mind to drift off in a daydream.

When he heard someone enter the room, Ghonllier's mind paid attention to that person. Without looking, he knew it was his father watching him. Ghonllier faced him and the two men searched each other's eyes.

Then Adamite spoke, "Son, I was on my way down here when I ran into Gostler. He told me about your conversation, wondering if I knew what you were talking about. I told him that I would talk with you, since I knew where you were."

Ghonllier faced the window. "You've always been an early riser, haven't you, Father?"

"Yes," replied Adamite, joining him. "How did you know that?"

"I asked the Stones to show me your whole life. They showed me everything, except for the time Mother and you met," answered Ghonllier, glancing at him. Then he added, "Do you know why?"

Just then, someone from the kitchen asked Adamite what he wanted for breakfast. Adamite ordered his meal while Ghonllier's attention went back outside to his mother. When Adamite finished, he faced Ghonllier to answer his question. He found Sunna in his arms, kissing him. The scene reminded him of Jenny and Ghonllier and he smiled.

Finishing, Sunna smiled, "So you aren't upset with me?"

"No, why would you think that?" Sunna stared at him. "Oh, I see. You thought my being quiet meant that I was upset with you."

Sunna nodded. "Where did you go this morning when you left our room?"

"I have a problem, Sunna. I missed something that made me unable to see Bog or Gomper," confessed Ghonllier, placing his hand on the back of a chair. Then adding, "The Stones said I'm missing something important and it would be dangerous to face Bog without understanding what it is."

Again, the chef interrupted Ghonllier's conversation. Sunna gave him her order for breakfast and went to Ghonllier's side. She asked, "Ghonllier, did you ever go back to the fight that you had with Bog in your dreams?" He looked at her, perplexed. So she added, "The one I woke you up from. Remember, you hit me in your sleep."

Ghonllier looked away and thought. Then a grin emerged on his face. The Master Stones were assuring him that Sunna was right. *So you're the person who the Stones were referring to.* He pulled Sunna into him and whispered, "I love you." He knew Sunna had replaced Gostler. *I'm so glad it's you.*

Cuddling into Ghonllier's chest, Sunna gazed out the window with him. When she felt Ghonllier slowly nodding his head, she looked up. Someone entered from the kitchen and said, "Commander, your breakfast."

"Thank you," replied Ghonllier, letting go of Sunna.

He took his plate from the kitchen help and sat. Adamite and Sunna joined him. Staring at his plate, Ghonllier went into a trance.

They didn't have to wait long for their food. Sunna and Adamite had their breakfast gone by the time he finally came out of the trance.

The first thing Ghonllier did was take Sunna's hand as he praised, "You're priceless. Thank you."

"What did you miss?" asked Adamite, leaning forward.

"The dream was important for me to understand. I needed to see how to present the different possibilities to Bog so we can end this with him. Now, I can move ahead with him in confidence," answered Ghonllier, standing.

"Is Bog bothering my son?" asked Adamite, joining him.

"Not yet. I need to leave now, if Gomper is to live."

"Are you going to eat first?" asked Sunna, following.

At the door, Ghonllier stopped and looked at his plate. "I'm not hungry. I don't know why I ordered it. I only eat to be sociable."

He left with Sunna looking at Adamite. She inquired, "Are you going?"

"There is no way I'll miss this. I've waited a long time to see my son be freed from Bog," stated Adamite, following.

Sunna and Adamite exited to discover Ghonllier standing in the middle of the room in another trance. Afterwards, Adamite quickly headed off to tell Stacy good-bye as Sunna stood beside Ghonllier, waiting for him to explain what they were doing. She was ready to go, since she had left her things on the *Liberty Quest*.

Suddenly, Ghonllier came out of his trance and asked her, "Are you ready?" Sunna nodded. "Let's go."

"Are we taking the crew?" asked Sunna, following him to the door. "No."

She grabbed his arm. "Don't you want to see Sooner before you leave?" she asked.

Ghonllier looked at the ceiling and commented, "Yes, he'll be upset if I use the Master Stones to tell him we're leaving."

Sunna ran for the lift, but Ghonllier beat her and had the lift waiting for her. Before getting in, Ghonllier saw Gabala. "Gabala, would you take us all to the *Liberty Quest*, including Jason?" requested Ghonllier.

"When do you want to leave?" asked Gabala.

"Now. Just give us enough time to say good-bye to our son," informed Ghonllier, entering the lift.

Sooner was still asleep as they entered. When Ghonllier sat on the edge of the bed, he opened his eyes. Surprised to see his father, he asked, "What's going on?"

"Son, your mother and I need to leave. Do you want to come with us?" asked Ghonllier.

"No, I want to see my friends. Do I have to come?" questioned Sooner, rolling onto his back.

"You can stay home," replied Ghonllier, standing.

"Why are you leaving?" asked Sooner.

"There's a man who's terrorizing the galaxy. I need to go stop him," said Ghonllier.

"This is your job, right?" asked Sooner.

"Yes, this is my job."

"If you need us for any reason, please call," said Sunna with a warm smile.

Sooner smiled back. "I will."

"Thank you, Son," smiled Ghonllier, patting him on the leg.

"Are you taking Grandfather with you?" asked Sooner, sitting up.

"Yes."

"Grandmother, is she going?"

"No, so your grandmother is in charge and I'll know if you disobey her," answered Ghonllier, standing at the door with Sunna.

"I'll take care of her and do what she says."

"You'll need to take care of Aunt Asustie, too," smiled Sunna, going to the side of the bed to give him a kiss on the forehead.

"I love you, Mother."

"I know you do," stated Sunna, leaving.

Sooner rolled over on his side, wanting to doze for a few minutes longer.

Ghonllier and Sunna returned to the main floor and left to find Gabala waiting with the transport. Sunna entered while Ghonllier waited for Jason. By the time he arrived, Adamite and Gostler were heading down the steps of the house. They all entered the transport, allowing Gabala to leave for the ship. Everyone was quiet on the ride to the *Liberty Quest.*

Sam had the door to the ship open. Jason entered first to open the reader panel so Sunna and he could check into the ship. He couldn't do his job without the ship reading he was there. Adamite and Gostler passed by it, since they weren't military. Ghonllier waited with them. Sunna thought he was waiting for her. However, he surprised both commanders by checking into the ship after Sunna.

"Isn't this the first since Dapper's death?" asked Jason, putting the panel away.

Ghonllier nodded. It really didn't matter to have Ghonllier check into the ship. He just wanted to do it to symbolize that he wasn't dead to I-Force anymore and that he was ready to take over the galaxy. The ship's stones were always aware of his presence, since they acknowledged the Master Stones.

Sam noticed his name come across the reader board and smiled. He hadn't seen him since Ghonllier became the Master of the Stones. Sam was excited to see if he seemed different. The captain watched with anticipation for him to pass by the command center. Instead, Ghonllier entered, coming directly toward him.

Sam greeted, "His Grace is on the bridge."

Ghonllier smiled. "Sam, don't you dare do that again. Only strangers call me 'Your Grace.' You can call me anything you want. I'll respond."

"Acknowledged."

Sam looked past Ghonllier to watch Jason join them. "Sam, let's leave. This is all who's going," ordered Jason.

"Which one of you is going to chart the course?" he asked, facing the control panel.

"Jason, you chart it," ordered Ghonllier. Jason left for the NV table while Ghonllier waited for Sam to look at him. When he did, Ghonllier ordered, "I want you to take us to the same place you picked us up from on the Zuffra moon. I want you to indigo beam me down and *absolutely* no one else."

Sam nodded. "I noticed Commander Sunna entered the ship . . ."

"Especially not her," informed Ghonllier, leaving.

Ghonllier left, hearing the chimes ringing throughout the ship, indicating they were leaving. It felt good for him to be on his ship again and flying in space. Entering his sleeping quarters, he found Sunna not there. Going over to the doorway to her room, he stopped and watched her looking through her bag from the Star Skipper.

Glancing over at Ghonllier, she asked, "Do you want something?"

"Always, I want something," he smiled.

Sunna heard a playful tone in his voice. It hadn't been there for such a long time that she had almost forgotten about it. She looked away from her bag and stared at him. With him being the Master of the Stones, she wondered if he would change on her in every aspect of their lives.

"What are your plans for the next three days?" Ghonllier inquired.

"I planned on working. In fact, I was about to go into the office when I put these clothes away. Why?"

"Do you remember we were going to discuss what our roles will be now that I'm the Master of the Stones?"

Looking at him thoughtfully, she responded, "I don't remember, but I would like to talk about it."

"I want to have our talk before we reach the Zuffra moon."

"Why?"

"I think you know why." Sunna gave him a puzzled look. "Sunna, I'm picking up from you that you're thinking about going with me to see Bog."

Looking away, she commented, "Is that a problem?"

"Yes, it's a problem. I can't be seen with you anymore outside of our city."

Giving him a sharp look, she stated, "And Bog is going to tell the galaxy."

"We'll never be seen together in this galaxy outside of our city," he repeated.

Sunna faced him. "So, I'll never be able to be with you now?"

"You can be Commander Sunna, my assistant of Special Servers, if it is required. But you'll never be seen alone with me. We'll always need to have someone else with us. You'll never be known to the galaxy as my close friend, lover, and mother of my children. The Stones have been very specific about that."

"I remember them telling me that. Do you know why?"

Ghonllier shook his head. "They haven't told me why. I think someday we'll understand the wisdom, but not today."

"I agreed to it with the Master Stones. But I don't understand why with Bog. He isn't a part of the galaxy anyway. He lives in a state all of his own."

"Sunna, trust me. You'll cause problems with Bog if you come with me," explained Ghonllier. Reading her thoughts, he added, "Sunna, this is between Bog and the Stones. They have been working toward this fight for over four hundred years. Bog doesn't handle crowds well."

"I'm not a crowd!" countered Sunna, shooting him a sharp glance.

"This time you're a crowd. I need to do this alone."

Sunna faced him. "I thought we were a partnership."

"We are," smiled Ghonllier.

"Then I'm unclear on our partnership," responded Sunna, stepping forward.

Ghonllier chuckled, "Sunna, you're playing games with me. We both know you're aware of your role in this partnership."

Knowing their conversation would turn into a fight if they continued in this direction, Ghonllier started to kiss her on the neck. It surprised her and she forgot about what she was going to say. Sunna's neck was her ticklish spot. She didn't like him getting the best of her, so Sunna pushed him away.

Seeing she was fighting to find her thoughts again, he came forward to kiss her on the neck again. He timed it just as Sunna was pulling her thoughts together. The giggling caused Sunna to forget them.

Facing him, she stated, "Do you want my attention?"

Grinning, he said, "Always."

"It's been a long time since you've wanted my attention," she smiled.

He kissed her and she passionately returned it. When they finished, Sunna looked at him. "What's my biggest role in this partnership?"

"I need you to keep me humble."

Sunna threw back her head and laughed. "How do I keep *you* humble? The most powerful man in the galaxy."

"Your presence humbles me and you give me the desires to be a better man. You bring me to my knees just at the thought of you."

Giving him a smirk, Sunna stated, "Whew, you are good. Jason is right. You were a ladies' man."

"I love you," Ghonllier said, leaning in for a kiss.

When he finished, she gazed into his eyes and inquired, "Are you going to stop me from going to the office?"

"Do you want me to?"

Sunna answered by putting her arms around his neck and kissing him. During the kiss, Ghonllier reached down and picked her up. When she stopped kissing him, she was pleased to see they were by their bed.

"So, you're going to interfere with my job," she whispered.

He looked fondly into her eyes and let go of her while she floated onto the bed. "Sunna, I'm glad you're on my council. I need you to advise me."

"I advise you to let me go with you to see Bog."

Ghonllier quickly joined and put his arms tightly around her and started to tickle her ribs. She begged him to stop and he did. Then the two just looked at each other. Sunna put her arms around his neck and pulled him into another kiss.

Chapter 21

Collette

*B*efore Ghonllier went into exile, he requested Gostler and his father not to inform Justin of him becoming the Master of the Stones. This was something that he wanted to tell his legal father personally. And, after figuring out how to handle Bog, he was ready to have his talk with Justin.

Ghonllier waited to talk with him when Justin was alone and had time to spend with him. It happened during the ship's night, soon after Ghonllier awoke from two hours of sleep. While he got ready, Ghonllier thought about his two fathers. He was pleased Adamite was asleep. Justin and Ghonllier were close. On a deep level, Adamite was bothered by their relationship and by the fact that his children were taken away and raised by others.

He still hadn't completely embraced his life without his family around him. Ghonllier could see Adamite hadn't forgiven himself for what happened to his family. Even though he knew he had nothing to do with it, he held himself responsible for what happened to his children.

Entering the command center, Ghonllier was pleased to be alone there as Butler left. Afterwards, Ghonllier sat down in his flight chair to contact his legal father. He reached for his earpiece before activating the C-Stone.

Justin was waiting for his call because Ghonllier notified him with the Stones first. They decided to use the C-Stone because Justin would be constantly interrupted. It was early in the morning for Justin and he was awake, waiting for Ghonllier. Even though Justin and Ghonllier were alone, they used the Eraphin language to talk with one another.

"Hello," spoke Justin cheerfully.

Ghonllier answered, "Father, I wanted to hear your voice. Thanks for coming to your office to talk with me."

Justin was so touched by his words that he choked up on his response to him. The two talked for hours. Close to the end of the conversation, Ghonllier noticed Gostler had joined him. It happened as Justin signed off to take care of business. Ghonllier watched Gostler, wondering why he was there. It was the middle of the night on the *Liberty Quest*.

He still couldn't read Gostler's mind. Then, as he put away his earpiece, Ghonllier asked, "Can I do something for you?"

Gostler gave him a perplexed glance and stated, "I thought you wanted me."

Ghonllier shook his head. "I've been talking to Justin."

"The Stones awoke me and said you needed me. I was going to ask you what I could do for you," replied Gostler, sitting down in the chair next to the C-Stone.

The Master stared at him while he spoke with the Stones. Finally, Ghonllier leaned forward and stated, "I think I know why they woke you up."

"What do you need?" Gostler asked, rubbing his eyes.

"I just finished talking to Justin about me becoming the Master of the Stones. I asked the Stones to tell me where Becker was in the galaxy. I wanted to find him so I can talk with him. The Stones are telling me that he is alive and you know where I can contact him."

"Why would you want to talk with your old teacher?"

"He meant something to me and I want to know where he is. The Stones told me to talk with you."

Gostler looked away. "I don't think it's necessary for you to talk with him. He understands more than you think."

"Tell me where he is," repeated Ghonllier. "I'll make that judgment call."

"I'll think about it," answered Gostler, standing up.

Gostler was stunned by Ghonllier's next thoughts. Abruptly, Ghonllier stood and stared at Butler's empty chair. With his ability, Gostler could read the anger and pain that Becker had caused by leaving Ghonllier without saying good-bye. Ghonllier needed closure with Becker and needed to talk with the teacher of his youth.

It took him a few minutes to gather his thoughts before Gostler stated, "Son, I already know about you being the Master."

Facing Gostler, Ghonllier saw Becker standing next to the chair. Anger consumed Ghonllier and he shouted at him. "WHY DID YOU LEAVE ME?!" he cried in anger.

At that moment, Ghonllier stepped into his past, being fourteen-years-old in his emotions. Becker stayed silent while Ghonllier continued, "In the middle of the night, you just disappeared and didn't leave me a note explaining where you went. How could you just walk out on me, Dapper, and Justin?"

"You know why," answered Becker.

Silently staring at him, Ghonllier started to realize he wasn't the fourteen-year-old boy hurt by his disappearance. Slowly, Ghonllier whispered, "So, you're Becker."

Becker changed back to Gostler. "I'm sorry you didn't know that Becker was really me, the former Master of the Galaxy. Without permission from the Stones, we felt like we couldn't tell you the truth," explained Gostler.

"I should've figured it out when I learned you were a Mimette," grunted Ghonllier.

"You probably would've figured it out, if you weren't reeling from Dapper's death." Ghonllier shook his head in amazement. Gostler continued, "I'm sorry I left without saying good-bye. I didn't realize how much it upset you. Why did it?"

"You were there every day of my life until I was fourteen. I loved you like I did Justin and Dapper. Do you really think she would have betrayed you and me?"

Startled, Gostler quizzed, "Who would have betrayed you and me?"

"The reason why you left me and went into exile: your love. You know, the woman you had loved ever since you were the Master of the Galaxy."

Stunned, Gostler eventually stated, "I would've betrayed you even if she wouldn't have . . ."

"It was Dapper and you who took me from my parents and brought me to live with Justin. You should've lived at our house like Justin wanted you to."

"Why would you say that?" asked Gostler, realizing the Stones had to be feeding him this information. *Maybe, it means they're finally releasing me from their services*, thought Gostler, knowing that the Stones would tell Ghonllier about his life if they were releasing him. So Gostler pressed forward by adding, "She couldn't have gone into exile with me. It was because of something that I—"

"If you're talking about your sacrifice, I know about it," interrupted Ghonllier, pausing. Then he added, "The Master Stones planned on you taking her with you into exile."

"Why didn't they let me do it?" snapped Gostler.

"You made choices that tied their hands," countered Ghonllier. Tears started to well up in Gostler's eyes and he wanted to scream. Listening to the Stones talk to him, Ghonllier continued, "They planned on you taking her into exile and they warned you about it when you insisted on going after Gomper."

Gostler moaned, remembering. He choked, "I forgot about that. You're right. They warned me that my decision would alter my future. At the moment, I was so angry that I told them I didn't care."

"Do you think the Stones were too severe on you?" asked the Master.

"No, I knew better." Gostler smiled, "I had the knowledge to know better, but I let my emotions get the best of me."

Ghonllier nodded. "They warned you about getting more in control of your temper. This experience has taught you that, hasn't it?"

Gostler nodded. "I wish I had learned it better when I was younger."

"You went into exile because of her, didn't you?" Gostler nodded. "The Stones are showing me that you entered Justin's building, looking like Becker. Collette had transferred to the moon and was at the building, getting something relating to her job. She got off the lift and you didn't see her until you accidentally bumped into her. Recognizing her, you momentarily lost Becker and switched back to Gostler. She recognized you as Gostler.

"She started to ask questions about you and learned you always went to Justin's private residence. It was a place she could never go, so she started to ask questions and started to follow you, after you left Justin's building. Did you know that?"

"No," Gostler whispered.

"She followed you to the place where you lived. She moved into your building, didn't she?" Gostler nodded. "You should've moved in with Justin then for a while and disappeared, but you didn't."

"I know. That decision has haunted me for years," whispered Gostler.

"Gostler, the Stones aren't going to release you tonight from them. They are going to do it in segments. What I need to say to release you is going to be hard for you to hear." Gostler stared at him with tears trickling down his cheeks. He nodded to let Ghonllier know he understood. So the Master continued, "After Collette studied your habits, she appeared at the place you frequented to see if you would talk with her. You didn't. So she went to other extremes, wanting to get your attention."

Gostler sighed, "It was hard to ignore her. I thought she was still beautiful, even after so many years of not seeing her. I so wanted to take her into my arms and just hold her. I was still in love with her."

Ghonllier smiled, "She felt the same way about you." Gostler reached up and wiped away his tears. "You started looking for her on the street and frequenting the place more often where you saw her." Gostler nodded. "Soon, the two of you started to talk. One day, she asked you to help her bring home some packages." Ghonllier watched Gostler wipe his cheeks on his sleeve. "Do you know why she was using a different name than the one you remembered?"

"No," choked Gostler.

"Since she wasn't using her real name, you should've had Justin run a check on her, but you didn't. You didn't want Justin to know about her. Justin would've made sure you never saw her again." Gostler nodded. "You loved having Collette this close to you. It was a dream come true."

"Do you know why it meant so much to me to have her around?"

"You wanted her close so when you were out of the service of the Stones, the two of you could be married without you courting her. But . . . you didn't take into account what happened next. Collette knew who you were and you thought she was being friends with Becker." Gostler leaned his head back and closed his eyes. "She talked you into staying for dinner one night. After the two of you cooked the meal, she divulged her heart to you and told you that she knew who you were and that she loved you.

"This terrified you, since the Stones told you not to let anyone know. Now, everything was different and you had to change plans. Stunned that she came forward for a kiss, you lightly pushed her away and defended the point that you weren't Gostler, the former Master of the Galaxy.

"She called you a liar and you left, devastated. This time, you went to Justin. She expected you to go home. When your housekeeper acted surprised to see her and he didn't know where you were, she left. When you arrived at the house, I wasn't home, was I?"

"No, you were expected home soon."

"You told Justin about her and said that you were weak and you had to get away for a while. Justin happened to have a Star Screamer leaving in thirty minutes for the Zircon moon. Lucas was an old friend of yours and Justin's. After he made a call to Lucas, Justin put you on the Star Screamer. Justin was going to get her to leave and then you would return after she left. But you didn't return, did you?"

Gostler shook his head while making sure he didn't look at Ghonllier. The Master continued, "You went with just the clothes on your back and they didn't tell anyone. When you never returned, your housekeeper reported you as missing. The authorities started to talk to neighbors. They traced you to Collette's place and she wasn't surprised that you disappeared. The former Master of the Galaxy wasn't a popular man in those days."

"He still isn't," mumbled Gostler.

Ghonllier smiled, "Collette was in trouble with KOGN at the time. Justin did his research on her and before he got back the information, Collette turned herself into the authorities."

"Why?" questioned Gostler, glaring at him.

"She was a KOGN spy, Gostler. For some reason, we fall in love with spies."

"Why would she turn herself in?"

"She wanted out and wanted your help. She never got a chance to ask you. With you gone and KOGN pressing in on her to do something that she didn't want to do, she decided to end it all.

"She gave them information that would force her to hold court and end it. Justin had to be the one who held it. He recognized her name immediately and panicked. Justin couldn't have her talking about you under the Truth Test."

"I can't believe she was a KOGN spy," expressed Gostler.

"Yeah, she was not really out of choice. It was a way of being able to live that she became one," whispered Ghonllier.

"Now, her last words make sense. She told me that she had something to tell me. When I tried to leave, she said there was more. But I ran before she could tell me."

"I'm sorry for what you had to go through, Gostler. I can see Sunna and I coming together has been hard on you, along with everyone blaming you for the Stones leaving the galaxy . . ." Then Ghonllier paused for a moment and added, "I even misjudged you in the beginning and I'm sorry. Do you forgive me?"

Gostler nodded. "I was used to it by the time I met you again. Was that how she died?"

"She was brought before Justin because he was over spies, Special Services. She refused the Truth Test and told them everything that would force Justin to sentence her to death. He was sick."

"Why couldn't I come back after that?"

"Justin couldn't bring himself to tell you and knew you would find out if you returned."

"So he waited for you to tell me," sighed Gostler.

"Yeah."

"What were you told about Becker after I left?"

"Nothing. Dapper came to tutor me the day after you left. When I asked about you, he told me Becker was gone for a while. Justin told me the same story. Then a couple of days later, Justin told me that you weren't ever coming back. He refused to discuss it with me after that. I was hurt . . ."

"Yeah, I read how hurt you were. I'm sorry." Then Gostler paused, "Do you have more to tell me?"

Ghonllier looked at him and shook his head. Gostler stood and said, "Good, I think I could take not hearing the rest of my life right now." The new Master watched him leave, but Gostler stopped. Ghonllier stood as Gostler asked, "Did Justin order her execution?"

"Justin didn't execute her. He couldn't do it. He removed himself from the situation when she told those in the room that she had killed you. He knew it was a lie and couldn't tell others why. If he had, then he would've been forced to tell everyone where you were hiding. A representative from the Senatorial Board happened to be visiting that day and was a part of the court. Justin turned it over to him."

"Is that really why I couldn't come back? She told them that she had killed me?"

"Partly. We both know you could've come back as someone else, but not Becker."

"Why would she do that? Why tell them that she killed me?" he asked.

"She felt trapped by KOGN and there wasn't anything to fight for in her life. She believed you didn't love her."

"I really altered my future, didn't I?"

"Yes, and you know that you must forgive yourself for those mistakes if you want peace in this life."

"You know, once you've been the Master, you can choose when you die."

"Yes, but it's granted by the Stones. You have to go with peace. You don't have it, Gostler, if you can't forgive yourself," informed Ghonllier.

This time, Gostler left.

Finally, he was alone and Ghonllier was pleased to know that the Stones weren't going to make him tell Gostler everything. It was hard to talk about what he just did. He knew he had to be hard on Gostler. *I want to know what else they have to tell me so I can release him*, thought Ghonllier, looking at the time sync stone.

It revealed they were close to the Zuffra moon and would be coming out of jump speed shortly. Butler walked past him so he could take the ship into the atmosphere.

Ghonllier got his attention by saying, "Butler, wake up my family for this and I'll tell Gostler."

"Acknowledged, Commander," responded Butler, arriving at the control panel.

While he walked down the corridor, Ghonllier mentally saw Butler notifying Jason and Adamite but not Sunna. It pleased him to see Butler didn't even put Sunna in the equation.

Ghonllier had promised Sunna that he would wake her when they neared the Zuffra moon. Sitting on the edge of the bed, he took a moment to watch her sleep. He thought about Gostler and Collette and was so grateful that Sunna chose to face her walls instead of keeping him out. Finally, Ghonllier reached out to her with the Stones, softly calling her name. She opened her eyes and stared at him, trying to wake up. Ghonllier waited for her to engage.

Finally, she responded, "What do you want?"

"It's time for me to leave."

Quickly, she sat up and expressed, "How soon will it be until we arrive?"

"Hullercasts, on," commanded Ghonllier.

The room showed they were in the atmosphere of the moon and Sunna knew Ghonllier hadn't left her a lot of time. Throwing back the blankets, she ordered, "Move. I don't want to watch from here."

Standing, Ghonllier reminded, "Sunna, I can project everything for you to watch here and the *Liberty Quest* will be hovering a short distance away."

"No, I want to see everything up close," answered Sunna, disappearing into her room.

He followed her. Seeing he was there, she stated, "I want to watch on the server stone."

He smiled, seeing she had her uniform almost on. She could've easily watched in her robe and pajamas since family members were the only ones here. Since they were close, Ghonllier took a moment to focus on Bog. He was still at the music box and Ghonllier made up his mind when he was going to release him. Timing was everything since Bog still had the power to kill Gomper.

He stared at the hullercasts in his room and thought. Shortly, the terrain of the moon appeared. He looked into one direction to see the mountains that guarded the valley of where Bog's castle stood. Suddenly, Sunna blocked his view. She had her arms around his neck. Smiling, he leaned in to kiss her good-bye.

When they finished kissing, Sunna cuddled into his arms and asked, "How close are we now?"

"We are about five minutes away from his castle."

"Are you nervous?"

"No."

"Are both the captains on the bridge?"

"Yes."

Looking up at him, she inquired, "For the first time, can we walk out of your quarters together?"

"Yes, and they aren't my quarters. They're ours."

"Not until we can tell others about our marriage, they're your quarters. I don't want to slip up and make a mistake."

Ghonllier put his arms around her and expressed, "It won't be long now and we'll be able to tell the crew that we're married."

She smiled while he let go of their embrace. Taking her hand in his, he commanded, "Hullercast, open."

At the office door, Ghonllier let go of her hand. Then he used the Stones and whispered, "MEET ME IN OUR QUARTERS WHEN I RETURN. I DON'T WANT TO TALK TO ANYONE, BUT YOU, AFTERWARDS."

She grinned and stepped back, expecting him to leave. Ghonllier didn't move and she knew he was waiting for her to enter the office. Sunna slowly backed through the hullercast, smiling at him. When Ghonllier disappeared, she faced the room to see Adamite and Jason already there. They had the server stone on and were watching Bog in front of the music box.

Jason glanced over and greeted, "Good morning, Sister. Finally going to join us?"

"Yeah," responded Sunna, looking at the hullercast door.

Adamite switched the server stone to Ghonllier. They could see him waiting in the beaming pad area. The hullercasts were on in the room and Ghonllier was watching the floor, so he could tell the captains where he wanted them to wait for him.

Jason glanced over to see Sunna's gaze bouncing between the server stone and the hullercast door. Finally, Sunna took a step toward the door and Jason questioned, "You're not going to watch from here?"

"I want to see him before he leaves," answered Sunna, leaving.

Adamite and Jason exchanged looks.

Sunna slowly worked her way to the command center, waiting to see the indigo beam lights. When she saw them, she waited at a safe distance before entering the room. The minute they disappeared, Sunna entered the room and ordered, "Captains, quickly beam me down, too."

"No, Commander," replied Sam, calmly keeping his eyes forward.

"Captains, I gave you an order. Beam me down to the surface!" demanded Sunna.

"No," responded Butler, looking up at the monitor in front of him.

"Why are you disobeying my orders?" snapped Sunna.

"Because His Grace outranks you and he gave us strict orders to not beam you down to the Zuffra moon," countered Sam, keeping his gaze on the monitors.

Seeing Ghonllier had appeared below her, she shouted, "Aw!"

Sunna entered the office to hear Jason gloating to Adamite about Ghonllier winning this time. Seeing Sunna, he smiled.

The commander countered, "Are you having fun, Jason?"

"Maybe," he grinned.

"Did you watch me on the server stone just now?"

"Yes, but I also heard Ghonllier tell the captains to keep you from following him before he left the Suzair planet," he informed.

"He knew then?!"

"Yeah, Sister. You won't get anything over on him now. And I love it," chuckled Jason as Gostler entered the room.

Sunna watched him enter, expecting Gostler to give his usual warm greeting. The former Master was still reeling from Ghonllier's news. Like Ghonllier expressed, he had a very hard time listening to his words.

The commander studied him long enough to notice his red and swollen eyes. She was about to sit next to him and quiz Gostler about what had happened to cause the red eyes, when Jason pointed out that Ghonllier was moving.

Instead, Sunna sat down and watched her husband.

Ghonllier stopped before the fallen gates of Bog's castle. He was remembering how this place looked today in comparison to the dream he had with Bog being a little boy. This place was well taken care of back then. Today, it was in poor shape. It had been hundreds of years since a human had been here for more than a few minutes. In the distance, he could hear the music coming from the box that he had left there for him. Ghonllier listened to the words that were programmed only for Bog.

While he listened, Ghonllier surveyed the area. The new Master could see clearly past the gate. The Stones gave him the ability to cut right through the fog that always lingered in this valley. Bog had created it to keep people away from him and his castle.

Today, the Stones made the castle crystal clear to him. Feeling he was ready to face Bog, Ghonllier commanded, "Stones, release him." Then he disappeared, using his Vanisher-like speed.

Chapter 22

The Choice

*B*og suddenly came out of the trance to discover where he was. Bewildered, he wondered why he was in his daughter's room. It had been years since he had ever entered it, after vowing never to do so when she left. *So why now?* Looking around, he tried to search for the answer.

Eventually, he looked down at the music box and found himself lifting up the lid. Music began to play and it was different from what he remembered. This was his mother's, for he had been very familiar with the music. Quickly, he shut the lid and searched the room while shouting, "Ghonllier!"

Bog wanted to get back to his room, where he had the best connection with Gomper. He was concerned Ghonllier had visited Gomper when he wasn't aware of it. Maybe he had lost his chance to transfer the curse, or maybe Gomper was with Ghonllier already and it wasn't too late.

The angry sorcerer was a short distance from his room when he heard the music box again. Whirling around, he said, "How did that lid get opened? Unless . . ."

He decided to go back into his daughter's room, but he didn't make it. A power consumed him, pulling him in another direction. Fear overwhelmed his emotions. This had never happened to him at any time.

Against his will, Bog moved through the walls of the castle. With every room he passed, Bog's fear increased. The power took him from the top floor and brought him outside. Slowly, he floated down to one of the inner courts; the one where he fought with Ghonllier before. *This has to be him. He's here!*

Arriving, Bog found the inner court empty. Reaching the ground, he tried an incantation to break the hold, but it did nothing to release him. In fear, he searched the inner court and saw no one. The only thing there was had been a music box from his daughter's room. When he noticed the box, Bog found it hard to look away from it.

Then, after finally forcing his gaze away from the box, Bog shouted so he would be heard above the music. "Ghonllier! I know you're here. Show yourself!"

He expected to see Ghonllier appear from his hiding place. Instead, he heard thunder rumbling overhead. The noise was so loud that Bog felt it bounce off the walls and vibrate through him.

Bog looked up at the sky and saw dark, angry clouds had replaced his fog. Lightning fulgurated within the clouds and he had seen this before on his stepping stone. Bog realized he hadn't stopped Ghonllier from becoming the Master of the Stones.

The thunder repeated itself with more force. Somehow, Ghonllier had channeled all the sound to stay within the inner court and Bog could feel it, even though he was just a ghost now.

"SO YOU'RE IMPRESSED, BOG," a soft voice spoke from behind him.

Whirling his head around, he found no one there. Something did catch his eye, however. Bog noticed the music box floating up to a broken window above him. When the music box disappeared, Bog searched the inner court again.

Feeling braver, he shouted, "Where are you, Ghonllier?!"

Almost as soon as he shouted this, the new Master of the Stones appeared at the edge of the court. The two men locked gazes as Ghonllier casually walked into the middle of the court.

When he arrived, the sorcerer inquired, "What do you want?"

"You know what I want," responded Ghonllier, stopping to face him. "You were on your way to kill my brother and release the curse within the galaxy. I told you to leave him alone."

"You're wrong. I wasn't on my way to kill him," lied Bog.

Thunder rippled through Bog, causing him to shudder. "HOW DARE YOU LIE TO ME, BOG!" The sorcerer wanted to move away from Ghonllier but couldn't. "YOU WON'T BE ABLE TO MOVE, BOG. YOU'RE IN MY POWER AND I CAN DO ANYTHING I WANT WITH YOU. YOU ALWAYS WONDERED ABOUT HOW MUCH POWER THE MASTER OF THE GALAXY REALLY HAD. TODAY, YOU WILL SEE IT."

"Ghonllier, why are you here? You coming to me isn't going to cause the curse to leave your brother."

"TRUE. I NEED TO SEE YOU BOTH AND I'M STARTING WITH YOU."

Bog was impressed that Ghonllier had the ability to talk to him without moving his lips. He witnessed other Masters do it on his stepping stone and he tried to find a way to copy them, but never found out. The experience unnerved him to hear his voice all around at different places. One time, it was soft and then it would sound like thunder. He found it very intimidating.

Ghonllier brought him back when he explained that he wasn't going to release him and that he wanted Bog to make a choice. Bog still desired to win this battle with the Stones, the one he started when he was alive. He reached out for one last try.

Bog stated, "Look, Ghonllier, you took my books and stepping stone. Without my things, I'm weak like you said the first time you were here. I can't do anything to this galaxy. I'm not a threat. It's your brother you need to go see, not me."

Ghonllier didn't respond with words. Instead, the thunder rumbled, releasing a bolt of lightning that squarely hit Bog. Stunned, he stared at Ghonllier. Being a ghost, he was surprised to feel the lightning. Any minute, he expected to be hit with another one.

When it didn't come, Bog asked, "Why aren't you going to end it for me?"

"SO, YOU BELIEVE I CAN DESTROY YOUR EXISTENCE?" smiled Ghonllier.

"Yes, I know it," surrendered Bog, finally being truthful.

This was what Ghonllier had been waiting for. Bog needed to know his fate was in Ghonllier's hands. The dreams of Bog having the Stones quickly dissipated.

So Ghonllier spoke, "IT UPSET YOU THAT GOSTLER NEVER CAME AFTER YOU WHEN HE WAS THE MASTER OF THE STONES. HE RUINED YOUR PLANS BY STAYING AWAY. YOU KILLED MY OTHER TWO BROTHERS, EXPECTING GOSTLER TO COME AFTER GOMPER. GOSTLER KNEW IT WAS A TRAP AND HAD NO INTENTION OF COMING AFTER HIM."

"He ran from the galaxy because he was afraid of me and my powers," boasted Bog.

"WRONG. THE MASTER STONES HAD BEEN WAITING FOR THIS. THEY KNEW YOU WOULD EXECUTE THE CURSE DURING THIS TIME AND ON ONE OF MY BROTHERS. THEY UNDERSTOOD IT HAD TO BE SOMEONE IN GOMPER'S FAMILY WHO COULD ONLY STOP THE CURSE. THAT'S WHY YOU KILLED MY BROTHERS AND THEN TRIED TO KILL MY MOTHER WHILE SHE STILL CARRIED ME IN HER WOMB."

"Apparently, I didn't. How did you live?"

"THE MASTER STONES SAVED MY LIFE AND THEN HID ME FROM YOU AND YOUR STEPPING STONE."

Bog looked away. *They did a good job. I thought you were truly dead,* Bog thought. He expected Ghonllier to say more, but he didn't. Then, the sorcerer looked at him and asked, "What are you going to do? We both know that we can't stay together in this galaxy."

Thunder crackled like a whip through the sky and lightning bolts shot all around Bog. The sorcerer gasped, expecting them to hit him directly like before. Fear consumed him as he stared at Ghonllier.

The new Master's silence made him angry and he shouted, "Why are you playing with me?! Finish it and end my existence."

"I JUST WANTED YOU TO UNDERSTAND THAT I HAVE ENOUGH ENERGY ABOVE YOU TO INCINERATE YOUR SPIRIT."

"Okay, I understand. . . . Are you going to torture me with it?"

"YOU'RE AFRAID OF TORTURE, AREN'T YOU?" Bog didn't answer, so Ghonllier continued, "YOU WERE TORTURED AS A CHILD AND THAT'S WHY YOU'RE AFRAID OF IT."

"You're right. So why don't you just get it over with."

"I WANT SOME ANSWERS TO MY QUESTIONS FIRST. IF YOU DO NOT TELL ME THE TRUTH I WILL TORTURE YOU UNTIL YOU DO."

"What do you want to know?"

"WHY DID YOU PUT SUCH AN UGLY CURSE ON YOUR OWN FAMILY?"

"Sethus! He stole from me!" answered Bog, shaking his fist at Ghonllier.

"HE STOLE WHAT, BOG? WE BOTH KNOW IT WASN'T YOUR DAUGHTER. YOU AREN'T CAPABLE OF LOVING. WHAT DID HE STEAL THAT MADE YOU SO ANGRY?"

"My life!"

"YOUR LIFE!" echoed Ghonllier's voice, bouncing off the walls. "He had the life that was meant for me."

"YOU STOLE YOUR OWN LIFE FROM YOURSELF BY THE CHOICES YOU MADE."

"What choices? Sethus ended the era of sorcerers. I had no choice. I had to defend the honor of all sorcerers."

"YOU DIDN'T CARE THAT THE ERA HAD ENDED. BY IT ENDING, YOU WOULD GO DOWN AS THE MOST POWERFUL SORCERER AND THAT WAS WHAT YOU WANTED. YOU WANTED YOUR DAUGHTER SO YOU COULD KEEP LIVING THROUGH YOUR POSTERITY."

It surprised Bog that Ghonllier used those words. He had never told a soul about how he felt with the ending of the sorcerer's era.

"If it didn't bother me, then why did I put the curse on our family?" challenged Bog.

"YOU WERE JEALOUS OF SETHUS. SO YOU PUT A CURSE ON YOUR DAUGHTER BEFORE YOU CHALLENGED SETHUS TO A BATTLE. YOU STARTED THE WAR TRYING TO DRAW HIM IN. HE WAS DEMONSTRATING MORE POWER THAN YOU HAD EVER IMAGINED." Ghonllier spoke while casually walking in a circle around Bog. He taunted, "YOU WANT TO ARGUE WITH ME?"

Bog laughed nervously as his gaze followed Ghonllier. "I didn't say that."

"IT DOESN'T MATTER. I CAN READ YOUR THOUGHTS. YOU PUT THE CURSE ON YOUR FAMILY BECAUSE IT ANGERED YOU THAT SETHUS DISCOVERED THE GALAXY'S TRUE SECRETS; HIDDEN SECRETS THAT YOU SHOULD HAVE KNOWN ABOUT. YOU WANTED THE MASTER STONES FOR YOURSELF. YOU DREAMED CONSTANTLY ABOUT THEM. YOU BECAME OBSESSED WITH THEM.

"YOU ALLOWED OTHERS TO KILL YOU BEFORE SETHUS KNEW ABOUT THE CURSE." Bog followed Ghonllier with his gaze. The new Master continued, "DO YOU REALIZED IT WASN'T YOU, BOG, WHO PUT THE CURSE ON YOUR FAMILY?"

There was a moment of silence before Ghonllier said, "Do I TELL HIM OR WILL YOU DO IT, MAGNIFISON?"

Bog gave him a severe expression. "Why did you use the name, Magnifison?"

"YOU RECOGNIZE IT?"

"Yes."

"WAS IT THE NAME OF A MAN YOU THOUGHT TO BE YOUR STEP-FATHER, BOG? A MAN YOU THOUGHT YOU HAD KILLED."

"What do you mean the man who I thought was my stepfather? He was!" shouted Bog.

Ghonllier shook his head. "No, BOG. DID YOU EVER HEAR YOUR MOTHER TELL YOU THAT HE WAS YOUR STEPFATHER?"

"No, she called him my guardian, I mean. My gra—"

"FINISH IT."

"My grandfather," whispered Bog. "For some reason, I forgot that."

"IT WAS BECAUSE MAGNIFISON WANTED YOU TO FORGET. HE CAUSED YOU TO FORGET, JUST LIKE YOU DID WITH MY BROTHER."

"STOP IT!" boomed a different voice coming from Bog.

The voice wasn't Bog's. It had been a very long time since Bog had heard that voice and he recognized it. Ghonllier could see Bog was starting to understand what he needed him to. So Ghonllier added, "DO YOU REMEMBER YOUR REAL FATHER?"

"Barely. I don't remember much about my father," whispered Bog.

His voice sounded different and this was what Ghonllier was trying to get to. Ghonllier had sent the music box to help Bog unlock his memory of his past and undo the incantation that his grandfather had put on him. The music had taken him back to his parents before his life there at the castle. Ghonllier was pleased the music box had succeeded in reminding him of his good memories.

Ghonllier interrupted his thoughts by asking, "DO YOU KNOW WHAT HAPPENED TO YOUR FATHER?"

"No."

"HOW OLD WERE YOU WHEN HE DIED?"

"Two, maybe three."

"WERE YOU LIVING AT THE CASTLE?"

"No."

"YOU WERE HAPPY THEN, WEREN'T YOU?" Bog nodded. "DO YOU KNOW WHO KILLED YOUR FATHER?"

"He was killed?"

"YOU SHOULD'VE TAKEN THE TIME TO LEARN ABOUT YOUR ANCESTORS AND WHERE YOU CAME FROM, BOG. IT MIGHT HAVE CHANGED SOME OF THE CHOICES YOU MADE IN LIFE."

"What do you mean?"

"THE PERSON YOU KNEW AS MAGNIFISON KILLED HIM."

Bog looked away. The news seemed to overwhelm him. He tried to avoid it, but he knew it was true. "Then he deserved to die," whispered Bog, glaring back at Ghonllier.

"DID HE DIE WHEN YOU STRUCK HIM WITH A ROCK?"

"What do you mean by that statement?"

"DID YOU EVER HEAR MAGNIFISON USE THE TERM *HALF-BREED*?" Bog nodded. "HE CALLED YOU A HALF-BREED ALL THE TIME. HE ALSO TOLD YOU NOT TO USE YOUR POWERS. WHY DID HE?" Bog shook his head. "DIDN'T HE TELL YOU NOT TO USE YOUR POWERS BECAUSE YOU WEREN'T WORTHY TO HAVE THEM? AFTER ALL, YOU WERE ONLY A HALF-BREED."

That word, *half-breed*, took Bog back to his mother. In his mind, he recalled the fights she would have with Magnifison, her father.

Ghonllier answered his thoughts. "HE DIDN'T WANT YOU TO BE A SORCERER. AM I RIGHT?" Again, Bog nodded. "DO YOU KNOW WHY?"

"No, why didn't he want me to use my powers?"

"IT ANGERED HIM THAT YOUR MOTHER RAN AWAY AND MARRIED A TRON. SHE LEFT, TAKING HER FATHER'S STEPPING STONE SO HE COULDN'T FIND HER. SHORTLY AFTER SHE LEFT, YOUR MOTHER MET YOUR FATHER. THEY FELL IN LOVE AND WERE MARRIED. YOU CAME VERY SHORTLY AFTERWARDS. THEY WERE HAPPY.

"EVENTUALLY, YOUR GRANDFATHER FOUND HER AND HIS STEPPING STONE. IN THE PROCESS, HE FOUND YOUR FATHER FIRST. HE INSTANTLY KILLED HIM AS YOUR MOTHER ENTERED THE ROOM, CARRYING YOU IN HER ARMS. HE ATTEMPTED TO KILL YOU, BUT SHE STOPPED HIM BECAUSE SHE WAS A GOOD SORCERESS.

"HER FATHER PROMISED HER THAT HE WOULDN'T KILL YOU IF YOU WOULD ALL RETURN BACK TO THE CASTLE. WITH YOUR FATHER DEAD, SHE RETURNED. HE HAD TO KEEP HIS PROMISE BECAUSE ON

THE INCANTATION SHE USED, IF YOU DIED, HE WOULD LOSE HIS POW-
ERS. BUT THE RELATIONSHIP WAS STRAINED BETWEEN HER AND YOUR
GRANDFATHER."

Since Bog didn't have a body, Ghonllier found it easy to show
him everything that happened in his mind as he talked. It pleased
Ghonllier to see him shed a few silent tears for his parents' demise. It
proved Bog had a heart and that was what Ghonllier wanted to know.
It caused him to change his plans. So he asked, "DO YOU REMEM-
BER WHAT HAPPENED WHEN YOU ARRIVED HERE AT THE CASTLE?"

"No."

"YOUR MOTHER AND GRANDFATHER CONSTANTLY FOUGHT ABOUT
YOU. IN A WAY, HE KILLED HER, TOO."

"How?" choked out Bog.

"HER BROKEN HEART GOT THE BEST OF HER AND IT KILLED HER.
SHE DEEPLY LOVED YOUR FATHER AND YOU. AN INCANTATION SHE
PUT ON YOU MADE IT IMPOSSIBLE FOR YOUR GRANDFATHER TO KILL
YOU. BUT IT DIDN'T STOP HIM FROM TORTURING YOU. THAT'S WHY
YOU'RE AFRAID OF IT." Ghonllier paused before he continued, "YOUR
MOTHER WANTED YOU TO REMEMBER THE GOOD TIMES AND HER
LOVE. SO SHE GAVE YOU THIS."

Ghonllier raised his hands above his head. Above his hands, a
ball appeared. It was Bog's ball as a boy. The ball was his most favorite
item before his grandfather broke it so he couldn't use it.

Bog gasped and longingly gazed upon it. Ghonllier continued,
"SHE TOLD YOU THAT YOU WOULD NEVER FEEL ALONE AS LONG AS
YOU KEPT THIS BALL CLOSE TO YOU. SHE TOLD YOU THAT SHE PUT A
LOVE SPELL ON IT, SO YOU WOULD ALWAYS KNOW HER LOVE."

Tears flowed from Bog's eyes. Then a voice boomed from him.
"You can't have that! Where did you get that? I destroyed it!" shouted
Magnifison.

Ignoring the voice, Ghonllier continued, "YOU'RE FEELING A LOT
OF EMOTIONS: HATE, LOVE, FEAR. MAGNIFISON, I BREAK YOUR SPELL
AND RELEASE YOUR ABILITY TO CONTROL OR SPEAK THROUGH HIM."

A mournful, painful cry came out of Bog, along with a black mass.
Ghonllier reached his hand out, holding the black mass captive. Then

he slowly moved his hand up, taking Magnifison with him. The black mass went up to the edge of the clouds.

Bog watched as lightning, resembling bony fingers, tried to grasp a hold of him. "I'll find a way to get back, Ghonllier. You won't get rid of me!"

"WRONG, AND WE BOTH KNOW IT. YOU'RE BANISHED," thundered Ghonllier's voice.

The lightning fingers attacked, disintegrating the spirit of Magnifison. He let out a mournful cry before he suddenly vanished. Bog looked at Ghonllier with questioning eyes. Ghonllier was stunned to look at Bog, for he had changed. Ghonllier saw the angelic face of the young boy he had seen in his dreams with the second Stone.

The silence got to Bog and he asked, "What are you going to do with me?"

"I SEPARATED YOUR GRANDFATHER'S SPIRIT FROM YOURS. NOW, IT'S YOUR CHOICE WHAT I DO WITH YOU."

"What do you mean 'your choice'?"

"I CAN SEND YOU OUT OF THIS GALAXY LIKE I DID YOUR GRANDFATHER OR YOU CAN GO BACK TO THE PATH YOUR LIFE WAS DESTINED TO HAVE."

"I can't. I killed my half-brother that day."

"NO, YOU DIDN'T. YOUR GRANDFATHER HIRED THAT BOY TO WATCH YOU AND MAKE SURE YOU DIDN'T USE YOUR POWERS. MENTALLY, HE WAS TRYING TO DESTROY YOUR SELF-ESTEEM SO YOU WOULD BE UNPRODUCTIVE. IN THE PROCESS, HE FOUND YOUR POWERS TO BE EXCEPTIONAL AND HE CAME UP WITH A PLAN TO USE THEM."

"What did he do?"

"HE FOUND YOUR POWERS EQUAL OR BETTER TO HIS AND HE WANTED TO BE THE MOST POWERFUL SORCERER TO EVER LIVE. HE COULDN'T HAVE YOU BECOME BETTER THAN HE WAS. A HALF-BREED. SO HE PUT A CURSE ON YOU AND PROVOKED YOU TO EXECUTE THE CURSE. IF YOU KILLED HIM, THEN HE WOULD BECOME YOU."

"Is it the same curse that's on your brother?"

"IT'S SIMILAR. YOUR GRANDFATHER WAS PURE EVIL, SO FULL OF HATE AND ESPECIALLY FOR HIMSELF."

"Himself?"

"THAT'S WHERE HATE GETS STARTED WITH EVERYONE. IT STARTS WITH SELF."

"So that's why my grandfather hated me so."

"YES. HE USED YOU TO NEVER LOSE CONTROL OF THE POWER ON THE GALAXY. AND WHEN YOUR DAUGHTER MARRIED A MAN MORE POWERFUL THAN HE, THE FIRST MASTER OF THE GALAXY, THEN HE PUT THIS CURSE ON YOUR FAMILY. THEN HE HAD SOMEONE KILL YOU, WHICH ACTIVATED THE CURSE."

"Thank you for answering my questions and releasing me from the spell," replied Bog. Then he paused before adding, "What are you going to do with me?"

"I'M HERE TO GIVE YOU A CHOICE, BOG."

"What choice?"

"YOU CAN JOIN YOUR GRANDFATHER OR . . ." paused Ghonllier, looking at the ball still floating in mid-air. Then he smiled, "Or YOU CAN GO BACK TO BEFORE YOU HAD THE CURSE."

"Why are you doing this for me?"

"YOU WERE FORCED AT A YOUNG AGE TO DO SOMETHING EVIL WITHOUT UNDERSTANDING WHAT YOU WERE DOING. I CAN GIVE YOU ANOTHER CHANCE IF YOU WANT IT. YOU CAN HAVE THE LIFE THAT WAS INTENDED FOR YOU."

"I can't go back," said Bog.

"YES, YOU CAN. I CAN MAKE IT POSSIBLE," said Ghonllier, causing the ball to spin in mid-air.

The ball was designed to shoot out bright beautiful colors of light when it spun around. Only a spell could cause the ball to display the colors and Bog's heart rejoiced to see it operational. Immediately, the same emotions and feelings of joy were felt right before he killed his grandfather. It felt wonderful to feel the love spell that his mother had given him.

"My ball is so beautiful," whispered Bog.

"COME FORWARD AND CLAIM IT. YOUR MOTHER WANTED YOU TO HAVE IT. SHE GAVE IT TO YOU," reminded Ghonllier, speaking softly for his ears only.

Without thinking, Bog stepped toward the ball. It surprised him that he had freedom to move. He faced Ghonllier and requested, "Repeat my choices."

"YOU CAN TOUCH THE BALL AND IT WILL TAKE YOU BACK BEFORE YOUR GRANDFATHER ENTERED YOUR BODY. YOU CAN BECOME THE

KIND OF MAN YOU WANT. OR STAY HERE AND I DO TO YOU WHAT I DID TO YOUR GRANDFATHER."

It had been centuries since Bog had the freedom to make a choice of his own. The freedom gave him a moment of fear. He had his gaze on the ball and it gave him the courage to step forward. He ached to feel this love and be with his mother.

He was afraid to make his choice and Ghonllier wanted him to hurry. Gomper was on his mind and Ghonllier feared if Bog had too much time, he would make the wrong choice. Thunder rumbled overhead as Ghonllier spoke, "MAKE YOUR CHOICE. I NEED TO LEAVE."

Bog looked away from Ghonllier, fighting with his fear. Finally, Bog floated over to the ball and took it in his hands. He fondly gazed on it as Ghonllier let out a sigh of relief.

Bog looked at him again and asked, "Can I really go back to a life I was intended to have?"

Ghonllier smiled. "THE BALL WILL TAKE YOU TO YOUR HEART'S DESIRE. YOUR MOTHER IS WAITING FOR YOU AND THE BALL WILL TAKE YOU TO HER."

Bog nodded, still looking at him. "Thank you for helping me. Take good care of the galaxy."

"NOW YOU'RE AT THE MOMENT BEFORE HATE. TAKE THIS LOVE YOU'RE FEELING AND BRING IT TO THE PRESENT AND TAKE IT WITH YOU ON INTO THE ETERNITIES. I BANISH YOU TO YOUR NEW LIFE."

Bog heard voices calling his name and looked off into their direction. It was his mother and father calling out to him. Happy, Bog floated in their direction as he quickly faded away.

Ghonllier felt relieved to have Bog gone. A heavy weight was lifted off his shoulders and he was pleased with the outcome. With his choice, Asustie would be able to use her powers to remove the curse from Gomper.

With Bog gone, the fog dissipated, allowing the sun to touch the ground for the first time in centuries. Ghonllier had sent the clouds away and was surveying the grounds. Plants immediately responded to the sun's rays and started to come alive. Leaves and flowers soon appeared everywhere.

The sun felt good on his face as he looked up at the blackened tower. The tower would always stand as a reminder of his first visit.

"SAM, COME AND GET ME."

Suddenly, he was covered with the purple light. Then, a moment later, he was inside his beloved ship. "Home, Sam," ordered Ghonllier, heading for his quarters.

Jason, Adamite, and Gostler stepped out from the office and into the corridor to greet him. Adamite greeted, "Congratulations, Son."

"Thank you, Father," replied Ghonllier, not stopping.

They watched him enter his quarters. Sunna was there like he asked her to be. Upon seeing her husband, she ran into his arms as they both held each other. After a few moments, she inquired, "What's next?"

"I'm going to go pick up Gomper and remove the curse from his body."

Sunna pulled back and asked, "Are you just going to walk into where he is and just take him?"

"I could, but people need to believe Suzair the Great is dead. They won't if I walk in and take him."

"Will he live through the process of removing the curse?"

Ghonllier sighed and said, "I hope so."

"If he lives, will Gomper have a normal life?"

"I don't know that either. It will be Gomper's choice and I don't know what that will be, nor will he, until it happens."

"Is Gomper ready for this?"

"I hope so," answered Ghonllier, going into a trance.

Sunna watched patiently, waiting to learn what they were going to do next. Slowly, Ghonllier started to shake his head.

"What's wrong?" asked Sunna.

"I can see Gomper now," responded Ghonllier, still shaking his head. Then he stated, "He's in trouble. I can see why the Stones hid him away from my eyes. It would have distracted me with Bog."

"What kind of trouble is he in?"

"His officers are plotting to take over and kill him within the hour."

"If they succeed, does that mean you lose control of the curse?"

"I'm already on a course of losing control of the curse. Now I can see why they didn't tell me."

"What do you mean you're on a course to losing control?"

Ghonllier looked at her. "By removing Magnifison, the curse is slowly now going out of control. When it reaches a certain pitch of pain for Gomper, he'll start killing, being blinded by the curse."

"Where is he now?"

"Still on his Galaxy Creeper, coming to the Suzair planet."

"Why is he coming to the Suzair planet?"

"To attack it," replied Ghonllier, frustrated.

"How long have you known about that?" questioned Sunna.

"I was the one who put the idea into his head. I had to get him to Asustie, since she can't fly," whispered Ghonllier. Looking at Sunna, he added, "Sunna, I know I told you we would be together, but I need to talk to Gostler. Do you mind?"

"It's fine with me if I can go with you."

"Yes," answered Ghonllier, opening the door to their quarters.

"Where's Gostler?" asked Sunna, staying by his side.

"He's in the dining room."

"Do you want to talk there?"

"No."

Sunna grabbed his arm. "I'll go get Gostler and bring him to you. Where do you want to talk?"

"In your office," answered Ghonllier.

Sunna nodded and ran off. Ghonllier decided to request Jason's presence at the meeting. Using the Stones, he ordered Jason to join them.

Gostler noticed Sunna entering the dining room. He was surprised to see her, since she had gone to Ghonllier's quarters to meet him. Arriving at his side, she whispered into his ear. Gostler didn't hesitate to move as he looked at Adamite. "You'll probably want to be a part of this one, David."

They followed Sunna into the office to find Ghonllier and Jason together.

"What's wrong with Gomper?" Gostler asked.

Ghonllier stepped away from the desk. "Has things changed for your brother, since Bog has left?" asked Adamite.

Not wanting to answer his father's question directly, Ghonllier said, "Gomper is close to the Suzair planet, getting ready for an invasion from his ship only."

"Are you going to allow him to land his ship?" questioned Adamite.

"No. Gomper doesn't expect me to allow him into the atmosphere . . ."

"He expects you to kill him," interrupted Adamite.

"Yes, Father. He doesn't expect to live much longer. But—"

Adamite interrupted, "Are you going to kill him?"

"Not with that curse in him. It will still transfer to the person who kills him, so I can't allow his officers to complete their plans," stated Ghonllier, looking at Jason. He ordered, "We need to make a change of plans. I need to separate Gomper and those on his ship who give me their allegiance."

"How are you going to do that?" asked Sunna.

"I need to go put a plan together now. Jason, I want you to take Asustie to a place where there is no one around. The coordinates are on the navigational screen. Contact my officers and tell them to join you there. I want all of the elite force in the Master of the Galaxy's uniforms. This is going to be official."

Jason nodded and stopped at the door. "Ghonllier?" He looked at him. "Are Asustie and our baby in any danger?"

"Absolutely none," assured Ghonllier.

Jason left, relieved to get this over with.

Ghonllier commanded the door leading into the conference room to open and headed for it. Adamite stopped him.

"Does Gomper want to come home?"

Ghonllier looked away before he answered, "Yes. Deep in his heart, he desperately wants to return. But, as strong as he wants to come home, he believes he can't." Then he paused for a moment and added, "Do you want him, really? With all he's done to this galaxy and he killed your other two sons. Do you really want him, Father?"

Adamite's eyes watered up as he stared at Ghonllier, thinking. Slowly, he said, "With all my heart. I miss him so."

"Then I'll do my best to make it happen, Father. It will depend on him. He feels no one will accept him as Gomper, but only as Suzair the Great."

"Does he know we live on the Suzair planet?" asked Adamite.

"He has no idea of where we live. And, yes, he knows I'm the Master of the Stones by now."

"Can you face him safely now and not have the curse transfer to you?" asked Sunna.

"If Gomper dies before I can completely remove the curse, then it could easily transfer to me," replied Ghonllier. Then he paused before stating, "If things go wrong, I won't get a second chance."

Ghonllier felt for everyone, understanding what they were up against. "I hope he's ready for this," whispered Adamite.

"Which one, Ghonllier or Gomper?" asked Gostler.

"Both of them," whispered Adamite. He looked at Gostler and added, "Will it be painful for Gomper to have the curse removed?"

"Ghonllier and I have talked about it. Ghonllier knows it will be very painful for him to remove it. The curse was being used by Bog to torture him before Ghonllier stopped him."

"Torture?" Gostler nodded. "Should I tell Stacy about what's happening?" Adamite added.

Gostler paused to ask Ghonllier. Eventually, he answered, "He wants to do it himself. She has questions like you and will worry more if she knows too early."

"Did Ghonllier ever tell you what Gomper was going to be like if he does live?" asked Adamite.

Gostler sighed, "We talked about it at length. I don't think you're going to be happy with what he said."

"What will he be like?"

"Because he had so many incantations put on his mind, the curse has attached itself to his memories. Ghonllier doesn't know for sure if he can separate them successfully," stated Gostler.

"How would Gomper handle living and knowing he was Suzair the Great?" asked Adamite.

"It would be worse for him to live if he could remember," said Gostler.

Adamite and Gostler exchanged looks as they thought about the possibilities.

Chapter 23

Two Brothers Meet

*T*he mood quickly changed on the ship. Everyone went from being excited, regarding the galaxy's safety, to feeling deeply concerned. Ghonllier disappeared on the way home and Sunna hung out with Jason. Adamite wasn't fun to be around and she didn't want to think about what was facing them.

Since he had the third Stone, Ghonllier had been preparing for this moment. In Gomper's dreams, Ghonllier spent a lot of time talking to him. The reason had more than one purpose. Not only was Ghonllier trying to give him hope, but he also wanted him to get used to his voice. He knew he had to talk with Gomper sometime, and he didn't want to frighten him. They didn't have the luxury of taking their time with the curse starting to spin out of control.

Today, Ghonllier was going to speak to Gomper openly and not through his dreams. He hoped it would work and that Gomper would accept him. While Gomper worked in his office, planning the invasion of the Suzair planet with his officers, Ghonllier watched and waited for the right moment.

Finally, the officers left as Gomper thought about Ghonllier. He planned the invasion in retaliation of Houser firing on the Jasmine planet. Gomper had hoped that he had given Ghonllier enough time to become the Master and end this war.

Now, they were down to the point of arriving at the Suzair planet. Gomper hoped in his heart that somehow he would receive the answers to his questions before he died. He leaned back in his chair as Pappar watched him.

"Do you want something?" his loyal servant asked.

Gomper looked at him. "Yeah. Do you mind getting me something to drink? I'm parched."

Pappar left the room to pass the request on to Pursy as Gomper rested his eyes and relaxed. Ghonllier took advantage of the moment. Staying in the rhythm of Gomper's breathing, Ghonllier used the Stones to say, "GOMPER, I NEED TO TALK WITH YOU."

He quickly opened his eyes to find he was alone. The voice reminded him of the demon's ability to speak with him. But the demon never used his name. Just then, Pappar entered the room with his drink. He studied the man, setting the drink on his desk, while he thought about the voice in his head.

"Do you want anything else?" asked Pappar.

"Yes, please leave me alone. I'm tired and would like to rest," stated Gomper.

"Are you feeling okay? Do you want me to get Brewster?"

"No, I just want to rest."

Gomper nodded.

Pappar left, unsure about leaving Gomper alone. It had been a while since the demon had tortured him, but they weren't sure that he was gone, despite what Gomper told them.

When the door was shut, Gomper whispered, "Who are you?"

"YOU DON'T NEED TO SPEAK ALOUD, GOMPER. I CAN READ YOUR THOUGHTS."

"Gostler?" whispered Gomper.

"GHONLLIER," answered the new Master. Reading his mind, he added, "DID GOSTLER ALWAYS TALK TO YOU THIS WAY?"

Yes, answered Gomper. *Are you coming for me?*

"YES, BUT IT ISN'T GOING TO HAPPEN THE WAY YOU THINK, MY BROTHER."

What do you mean?

"WHEN YOU ARRIVE AT THE SUZAIR PLANET, YOU EXPECT ME TO STOP YOU. IN THE PROCESS, YOU EXPECT TO DIE IN A BATTLE."

Yes.

"I WANT TO ASSURE YOU THAT YOU ARE RIGHT ABOUT THE CURSE TRANSFERRING TO ME, IF WE MEET IN BATTLE . . ."

We both can't live. What are you going to do?

"YOU'RE TIRED AND ACHY RIGHT NOW BECAUSE OF THE CURSE. I DESTROYED THE DEMON WHO PUT THIS CURSE ON OUR FAMILY AND HE WILL NOT BOTHER YOU AGAIN. IN DOING IT, I'VE SENT THE CURSE INSIDE OF YOU OUT OF CONTROL."

So it's going to kill me?

"WHEN IT REACHES A HIGH PITCH OF PAIN, YOU'LL START TO KILL THOSE AROUND YOU. IF SOMEONE SUCCEEDS IN KILLING YOU, IT WILL TRANSFER TO THEM. THEY WILL CONTINUE ON THIS KILLING SPREE UNTIL NO ONE IS ALIVE."

Can't the Stones do something . . . to stop this?

"WE ARE WORKING ON IT. THE STONE HAVE NEVER HAD TO DEAL WITH SOMETHING LIKE THIS BEFORE. THEY AREN'T SURE. SO I NEED YOU TO STAY CALM AND FIGHT TO KEEP BREATHING, WHILE THE STONES MOVE THE CURSE FROM THROUGHOUT YOUR BODY. THIS IS THE ONLY WAY I CAN STOP THE CURSE. I'M REMOVING IT FROM YOUR BODY BEFORE IT CAN TAKE YOU OVER."

Will it be painful?

"YES."

Gomper closed his eyes, hoping he could do this. He had hoped Ghonllier could just come in and release him of his pain and suffering. Choking back his frustration and fears, Gomper mentally asked, *What is going to be like?*

"I NEED TO HAVE YOU LAND TO COMPLETELY REMOVE THE CURSE. WHEN YOU ENTER THE ATMOSPHERE, YOU'LL REALLY FEEL THE PAIN IN YOUR STOMACH IF THE STONES AND I ARE SUCCESSFUL. . . . WILL YOU LET ME DO IT?"

Is that the only way it won't transfer to you?

"YES."

"Do it. . . . I want—" stopped Gomper.

"FINISH IT."

"No."

"THEN I WILL. I WANT YOUR ALLEGIANCE, GOMPER."

In my heart, you know what I want. But if I give it to you, then you will be bound to save me and I don't know if that would be good for you or me.

"WHY?"

"You saving Suzair the Great, the sworn enemy of the galaxy. If someone found out, you would lose you credulity as the Master of the Galaxy. You have to kill me," reminded Gomper out loud.

"I UNDERSTAND THE CONSEQUENCES OF HAVING YOU LIVE. REMEMBER, I NEED YOU TO DO EVERYTHING IN YOUR POWER TO KEEP BREATHING. YOU DIE AT THE WRONG TIME, AND YOU'VE SENTENCED THIS GALAXY TO DOOM."

What happened to me, Ghonllier? How did I get this and what happened to our parents?

"GIVE ME YOUR ALLEGIANCE AND I'LL TELL YOU."

I can't give you my allegiance officially, but I'll do everything I can do to live long enough to keep the curse from transferring to you.

"THEN I CAN'T TELL YOU MORE ABOUT YOUR PAST. I CAN TELL YOU THAT YOUR OFFICERS ARE PLANNING ON KILLING YOU DURING THIS INVASION." Gomper thought about his officers.

How do we stop them? I want to help you save this galaxy.

"I NEED YOU TO ACT LIKE SUZAIR THE GREAT IN ALL HIS OLD GLORY. SO EVERYONE ON THAT SHIP KNOWS YOU ARE THE REAL MAN. I'LL USE MY POWERS TO MAKE YOU LOOK LIKE HIM."

My voice—

"DON'T WORRY ABOUT MIMICKING HIS VOICE. I WILL SPEAK FOR SO EVEN PAPPAR WON'T KNOW THE DIFFERENCE."

The two brothers talked on about how to accomplish the things Ghonllier needed done. Together, they came up with a plan.

After they finished, Ghonllier leaned back while thinking about their plan. He smiled to understand what Gostler said about his brother. Gomper was good and contributed a lot to the plan.

Ghonllier stood and opened the door to the office. Leaving the conference room, he found everyone was still waiting for him to return. Gostler saw him first and expressed, "I assume Gomper talked with you?"

Ghonllier nodded.

"Did he give you his allegiance?" Adamite asked.

"No, Father. He refused."

"Why?!" shouted Adamite, hitting the edge of the desk with his fist.

"He doesn't want or expect to live, knowing he was Suzair the Great. He has given his heart to saving this galaxy he loves. What happens now is in Gomper's hands."

"Then he has given you his allegiance."

Ghonllier shook his head. "Does he know I'm alive?" asked Adamite.

"He knows all of you are alive."

"Are you sure the curse will stay in check while he's in space?" asked Gostler.

Ghonllier answered, "I've changed my mind after talking with him. I'm moving the curse now very slowly to his stomach area. Then I'm removing him off his ship before I destroy it."

Jason stood. "You can't do that? Unless you are only taking Gomper."

"I'm taking everyone I know that will give me their allegiance. The others I'll kill, letting the galaxy think that I destroyed Suzair the Great." Glancing at those in the room, he answered their thoughts. "I will not be lying. Bog was Suzair the Great, not Gomper."

"Will I see him alive?" asked Adamite.

Ghonllier looked at him thoughtfully. "I would not plan on it. It will be Gomper's choice. I can remove the curse from his body but it will be Gomper's choice . . ."

"I need more than that, Ghonllier!" spat Adamite.

He was thoughtful listening to his father's concerns. "Father. I gave him a reason to live . . ."

"What?"

"I refused to explain to him what happened to him. I would only tell him if I had his allegiance and he lived."

Adamite fell to his chair, thinking about his sons.

"How far away are we from home?" asked Sunna.

"We'll be home in about thirty minutes. In about two hours, Gomper will be meeting Asustie."

Sunna looked at Jason and asked, "Is that why you told the elite force to leave with her, Jason?"

He nodded. "Why didn't you have the officers go with Asustie?" asked Jason.

"I want a meeting with all my generals and you the moment we arrive on the bridge. After the meeting, we'll fly them out to Asustie."

"Do you need Special Services at the meeting?" asked Sunna.

"No," answered Ghonllier, leaving to return to the conference room.

Sunna watched him leave, wanting to talk in private with Ghonllier. By him not needing Special Services, it meant that she wasn't invited to the meeting. Sunna took it that way because Ghonllier left abruptly for the conference room. He didn't tell them that Gomper needed him and Ghonllier wanted to be alone with him.

In anger, Sunna left and went to their quarters. She wanted to talk with him and mentally called out to him. In vain, she waited, not understanding he couldn't leave his brother. Gomper was getting more uncomfortable with the curse moving and Ghonllier needed to keep him calm.

When she heard the landing chimes, Sunna realized Ghonllier wasn't coming. She became furious. In anger, she left their quarters, arriving in the command center with her bag. All generals had arrived and were talking with her husband and Jason.

Sunna took her time walking through the corridor, watching them. She expected Ghonllier to invite her to join them. When Ghonllier didn't, she stormed off. It hurt that he wouldn't even look at her. By the time she reached the OSA, her anger had increased. *If everyone knew we were married, I could've joined them without being invited. I'm tired of this secrecy. When will it end? He's the Master of the Stones!*

Outside, Gabala was waiting to take home anyone from Adamite's place. He sensed Sunna was upset as she arrived. He asked, "Madam, would you like me to take you home now, since you're the only one here?"

"Please," snapped Sunna, getting inside the transport.

He shut the door and took one quick look back to make sure no one else had followed.

Ghonllier was well aware of Sunna's anger. Right now, Sunna needed to be reassured that Ghonllier could stop the curse from entering him. Down deep, she feared for the lives of those she loved, not realizing it. He had his reasons for not inviting her to join them and hoped she could accept them when he explained.

The minute he was finished with his role in the meeting, Ghonllier excused himself and disappeared. Arriving home on his own accord, he entered the house. Inside, Ghonllier looked at the ceiling, wondering if he should go to Sunna first or his mother. Stacy was in the dining room with Sooner. She watched Ghonllier's encounter with Bog, but turned it off after. She was well aware that Ghonllier was going after Gomper. Stacy was upset far more than she had every imagined.

Making up his mind, Ghonllier appeared in the dining room. Sooner greeted him first by giving him a hug. Stacy stayed quiet, staring at the plate before her. Ghonllier requested, "Sooner, would you go get your mother and ask her to join me here? Please give her a kiss for me. She's upset."

"Did you do something wrong?" scowled Sooner.

"No, Son. She's just confused and misunderstood my actions. Let her know that you love her and I do, too. I'm still changing on her, so she feels insecure about me. Would you please tell her what I just said?"

"Sure," responded Sooner, leaving.

Ghonllier spoke the whole time with Sooner while he stared at his mother. Stacy wouldn't look at him, instead she moved her food around with her utensil. Then there was silence after Sooner left. Finally, she glanced up to see if he was still there.

The two didn't say a word, but just looked at each other. Then Stacy looked away and sat her utensil down. "Why are you staring at me?" she asked.

"You know why."

Biting her lower lip, she asked, "How is he?"

"He's preparing to come home."

"Does he want to come?"

"On a deep level, he desperately wants to come home, Mother."

"I heard you tell your father that he wouldn't give you his allegiance."

"Officially, yes. He is holding back his allegiance. He loves this galaxy, Mother. The Stones will not kill him unless he tries to force me to do it."

Stacy put her hands up to her face and started to cry. Ghonllier went to her side and softly whispered her name. Stacy stood and he put his arms around her. Through her sobs, she expressed, "Ghonllier. We have come this far. Please . . . tell me he will live."

"Mother, understand Bog told him that he forced him to kill Manchester and Astor. Put yourself in his shoes. How does he face his parents after he was involved with so many malicious crimes."

"I don't care. I want my boy. I'll never have back . . ."

Her sobs increased. Ghonllier soothed, "Mother, I need to know if you want to come with me to get him. I'm going in space and I know how much you dislike it."

She looked at him sharply and expounded, "I'll go anywhere to get to him."

Shortly, Adamite appeared in the doorway to see Stacy crying in Ghonllier's arms. He went to her side and whispered, "Stacy."

Sharply, she looked at Adamite and left Ghonllier for her husband's arms. Ghonllier watched them until Sunna appeared in the doorway. He apologized, "Please forgive me for not coming to you on the ship. I needed to be with Gomper. I needed to stay with him."

She didn't say anything, but watched Adamite and Stacy comforting each other. Then she approached her husband as he whispered, "Sunna, I wanted to tell you good-bye when you left the ship. I didn't like you leaving upset."

"Then why didn't you? You could've spoken to me without leaving the meeting," responded Sunna.

"I'm sorry, Sunna. I'm a little upset myself," he replied.

She looked up at him. "Are you doubting yourself?"

"In a way, what I'm doing is very dangerous. One slight mistake and you'll be dead," answered Ghonllier.

"After you remove the curse, can we tell the crew about our marriage or do we have to wait longer?"

"Let me handle one thing at a time," stated Ghonllier.

Sooner immediately entered the room to retrieve his bag for school. Sunna wiped away the last of her tears, smiling at Sooner. He was perplexed to see everyone but his father crying. He gave him an unsure look.

Ghonllier answered what he read from his mind. "SOONER, EVERYTHING IS OKAY. THIS IS REALLY A HAPPY MOMENT."

Sooner rolled his eyes and left with his things. As he passed his father, he gave him a quick sign with his hand, which meant to say good luck.

Sunna noticed it and smiled, looking back at her husband. "Thank you for just holding me," she stated afterwards.

"I love you, Sunna, and I'm aware of your needs."

Reaching out for her hand, they left. As Ghonllier passed his mother, he said, "Mother, we're leaving in an hour. You can ask Cid to give you something for flying in space. Also tell him that he needs to leave with us."

They looked away from them. Arm in arm, Adamite and Stacy left to pass on Ghonllier's orders to Cid.

Ghonllier waited a few minutes before he took Sunna upstairs to their room. They needed to be alone and talk. In a very short time, their lives were about to change forever and Sunna had questions. She was glad for the time alone with him. This was what she wanted aboard the ship.

While Ghonllier answered her questions, he watched Gomper. Sunna cuddled in his arms on the bed as they talked, waiting to leave. The hour quickly passed. Ghonllier kissed her on the neck and let her know that Jason needed to talk with him. Sunna nodded to move. She was taken back to hear Ghonllier ask her to go talk with Jason. He didn't want to leave Gomper.

Sunna left with Ghonllier getting comfortable in a chair, still focused on his brother.

Eventually, Pappar became concerned that something had happened to Gomper. He opened the door to check on him only to see Gomper leaning against the window. Suzair the Great looked over at him with a steely glare.

He was really taken back to hear, "I don't remember telling you it was okay to enter."

Pappar was stunned. Gomper's voice sounded like Suzair the Great before Gomper arrived. Perplexed, Pappar asked, "Can I get you anything, Your Grace?"

"Yes, send in Pursy and I want you to wait outside the door for orders. Do not enter again," responded Gomper coldly.

"Yes, Your Grace."

Soon, Pursy entered and announced, "Your Grace, your officers are wondering when you're going to the bridge."

"Soon," answered Suzair the Great. He looked past Pursy and ordered, "Pappar! Shut the door and tell Commander Jabolt what I just said." Pappar stepped forward to shut the door. Suzair the Great continued, "I've changed my mind. Pappar, I want you to to take Jamham and Brewster to a Star Screamer on Deck Eight, Station Four now. Don't let them take anything and don't let anyone talk with them. Do not leave them."

"Sir?"

"How do you address me?" snapped Gomper.

Pappar froze because Gomper sounded just like Suzair the Great. He stammered, "Your Grace . . ."

Gomper interrupted, "I'm back, Pappar. So you better do everything I tell you."

"I've done everything—"

"I killed your young friend who has been pretending to be me. Do you understand me?" Pappar nodded. "I want a tight guard on Brewster and Jamham now! So keep your weapons exposed. There are people planning to kill them before they board the Star Screamer. If not, you—"

"I know the rules, Your Grace," interrupted Pappar coldly.

The door shut and Gomper looked at Pursy. "Did you get everyone that I told you about put on those Star Screamers?"

"Yes, Your Grace. I have everyone including the captains of this ship. Your personal staff were the only ones . . ."

Suzair the Great interrupted, "Do not repeat things that I already know."

Pursy apologized and finished his report to Gomper. When he completed the report, Gomper ordered him to stay by his side until they reached the Star Screamer. Pursy reported a few more situations as they left the office.

The minute Gomper exited his office; everything that wasn't anchored to the floor started to fly around the room. Everyone hurried underneath a desk or lied flat on the ground to avoid being hit and killed.

Pursy was stunned to see it. This was Suzair the Great before he had an encounter with the ghost at their home base. He moved in closer to Gomper, not wanting to be hit accidentally. The brothers wanted everyone to be distracted since there were people planning to kill Gomper before he made it to his Star Screamer. The old Suzair the Great tortured those around him. Many times in the past, he killed others by sending flying objects at them.

The words started to spreading quickly through the ship that Suzair the Great was angry. Some men didn't believe it as they waited to kill him. Pursy heard a moan behind him. Staying in stride with Gomper, he looked behind to see three men falling to the floor with sharp objects sticking into their hearts.

Fear and terror were on the faces of everyone they happened upon. The word of His Grace being on the rampage was terrifying to them. The staff watched him pass in hatred and anger. Everyone on board, Ghonllier knew would never give him their allegiance and they would continue to keeping fighting even with Suzair the Great's death.

Gomper entered the bridge, knowing the officers were shocked to see him. "Commander Jabolt, where are the other officers?" bellowed Suzair the Great.

Shock showed on their faces; they didn't expect to see him.

Gomper grinned, "Surprised to see me, men?"

"No, Your Grace," stammered Jabolt. Then he quickly added, "Are you ready to send out the Star Screamers?"

"No. I have a little business to take care of here," responded Suzair the Great, gesturing toward the door.

Instantly, it shut. Then he reached out his hand to have weapons came flying off their bodies. Gomper ordered the weapons to stop. They hovered in mid-air in front of him.

Gomper plucked a knife out of the air and held it up. "Men, why do you have these hidden on yourselves? It's against regulations to have weapons on the bridge," reminded Suzair the Great.

"Your Grace, we're going into an invasion. We were planning on going with you," justified Jabolt.

Gomper rolled it over in his hand and said, "Yes, but these were hidden. None of you have your weapons belt on. . . . Why do you have these weapons?"

Suddenly, the landing chimes were sounded. "The captains aren't on the bridge. Who did that?" asked Jabolt, getting more frightened by the moment.

"I did it," answered Suzair the Great. Looking at the knife in his hands, he continued, "As you can see, I have more powers than you thought I did, Commander."

Suddenly, all the weapons spun around and faced their owners. Gomper let the knife in his hands go over to Jabolt as it pointed at his heart. It hovered just out of penetration of his body.

Frightened, Jabolt stammered, "Your Grace . . ." The other weapons engaged. He stopped speaking and everyone stared at Gomper with fear in their eyes.

"Did we do something to upset you, Your Grace?" questioned Jabolt.

"Yes. You did. I want you to know that I was aware of your plot to kill me. The other officers aren't here because they are dead." Coldly, he paused, "I killed them."

Everyone shot quick glances between themselves, knowing this was the end of their lives. Gomper started to laugh like Suzair the Great. He added, "Yes. You are going to join them. But first I want you to see something first."

He left for the door and it opened before his approach. Jabot called after him. Gomper stopped to look at him.

"What are you doing?"

"You move one inch and your weapons will kill you. If I'm in the mood, I might remove those weapons," said Suzair the Great, leaving.

The door shut after him. The weapon didn't move. One-person shift on his feet and his weapon followed him. Everyone noticed it and they looked away at the closed door in fear. How long was he going to keep them there before he killed them?

Outside the bridge, Ghonllier caused everything possible to go flying to keep everyone off their guard. He kept it up until they reached the bay where the Star Screamer waited to take Gomper to his brother. Gomper was relieved to see it. His stomach's pain had increased and he hoped that he could stay alive long enough for Ghonllier to save the galaxy.

Safe inside, Gomper rested his head against the wall, rubbing his stomach. Pursy stayed with him concerned.

"Your Grace . . ."

"Leave me, Pursy," snapped Gomper, still sounding like Suzair the Great.

Pursy nodded, exiting the OSA. Being alone, Gomper sighed. Leaning against the wall, he whispered, "This is going to get worse when I enter the atmosphere?"

"YES. GOMPER. I REALLY NEED YOU TO WILL YOURSELF TO LIVE UNTIL THE CURSE IS OUT OF YOU." Gomper hoped he could keep up his pretense that he wasn't hurting. Ghonllier told him. "THEY ARE WAITING FOR INSTRUCTIONS ON THE BRIDGE."

Slowly, Gomper entered the command center. When one of the captains saw him, he announced, "His Grace is on the bridge."

Gomper leaned against an empty captain's chair, staring at those in the room. It didn't surprise him to only see Pappar, Brewster, and Jamham. In away, he wished no one was there but the captains.

"Captains, move away from the control panels. I'm releasing the security of your ship," said Suzair the Great.

The captains were surprised by his orders as they moved back. The Galaxy Creeper captains were the only ones who could release the security and they were the only ones who could fly this ship. But the ship was lifting off and heading for the bay doors.

They started to say something to Gomper when he interrupted them and ordered, "Turn on the hullercast."

Everyone in the room watched them leave the Galaxy Creeper. They witnessed five other Star Screamers exiting different bays. Jamham happened to look back at Gomper. He wanted to know what was going on and he didn't believe Pappar that the real Suzair the Great was back. He found Gomper leaning lightly over the tall captains chair. His face was white and he could see the pain in his face.

Jamham nudged Brewster as he left to go to him. Brewster followed and spoke first. "Your Grace. Let me help you?"

"Get away from me Brewster. You can't help me. No one can," said Gomper finally in his own voice.

Jamham said, "I knew it. I knew you had to be alive."

Gomper looked up him with pain in his eyes. "Jamham. I am dead. It's only a matter of time."

"Are we meeting your brother?" asked Brewster.

"Yes."

"Are we all going to die with you?" asked Brewster.

Gomper looked at Galaxy Creeper getting smaller and said, "No. It's just the opposite. I've just saved your lives, if . . . I can stay alive long enough."

"What are you saying?" quizzed Brewster, reaching into his pocket for his analyzer.

Before he touch Gomper, they heard, "KOGN, I HAVE CONTROL OF YOUR SHIPS, INCLUDING THE GALAXY CREEPER YOU JUST LEFT. THIS IS THE NEW MASTER OF THE GALAXY AND I WANT YOUR ALLEGIANCE NOW OR I'LL DESTROY YOU."

Everyone in the room stared at Gomper. He didn't look at them, but started to rub his stomach. Finally, Gomper looked at his Galaxy Creeper as they saw the *Liberty Quest* appearing.

"What have you done?" retorted one of captains, coming up to him.

Facing him, Gomper answered, "I have brokered a deal with the new Master of the Galaxy. My life for yours. That's why I hand-picked the people on these ships. If anyone on that Galaxy Creeper gives him their allegiance, he will not be able to destroy their ship."

Then he looked over at the *Liberty Quest* as it had been between them and the Galaxy Creeper, when they heard, "I'm THE NEW MASTER OF THE GALAXY. YOU'RE NOT GOING TO ATTACK THE SUZAIR PLANET. GIVE ME YOUR ALLEGIANCE NOW OR I WILL DESTROY YOU." Ghonllier's voice vibrated throughout all the ships, including the Galaxy Creeper.

Suddenly, the Galaxy Creeper fired up on *Liberty Quest* only to have the blasts go back and spilt. Fire appeared in one area. Gomper knew Ghonllier had caused the weapons to fall to the ground, giving Jabolt a chance to fire the ships cannons.

The fire meant Ghonllier had opened the hatches to the fuel that made the hullercasts possible. Shortly, the ship started to break up and Gomper felt sad. It meant no one on board would give Ghonllier their allegiance and they vowed to fight on.

As the Galaxy Creeper fell apart, the *Liberty Quest* faced Gomper's ship and the other four Star Screamers. She stayed behind, herding them to the Suzair planet. Shortly, they went through transition and saw the *Liberty Quest* disappear.

Everyone on the bridge looked back at Gomper to see him struggling to stand. Brewster reached out to let him lean on him. He said, "Your Grace . . ."

Gomper interrupted, "Don't call me by that name."

Pappar joined him and asked, "Why did you tell me that the young boy was dead?"

"Because I needed you to leave the ship without me. I knew you wouldn't leave my side if you knew that I was alive . . ." gasped Gomper, grabbing his stomach.

They started to ask Gomper questions about what was going to happen to them. He answered them until he found it too hard to stand. Brewster and Pappar were now holding him up in the chair, while Jamham felt helpless.

He let out a long moan as he clutched his stomach. "What can we do for you?" asked Jamham.

Gomper opened his eyes and stared at him. "Promise me. You'll give your allegiance to my brother so you can live." He looked into

each man's eyes before he continued, "I need to know that my sacrifice . . . has . . . saved you . . . men." They all nodded. "Good,"
whispered Gomper, closing his eyes.

Pappar and Brewster were now holding Gomper up in the chair.
Jamham looked helpless. The hullercasts got their attention as they
saw the ground appear. The ships stayed together as they slowed
down and skimmed across the surface.

Gomper moaned again. They looked at him to see tears streaming down his cheeks. *Hurry Ghonllier. I don't know if I hold on much
longer* . . . Suddenly, the ships stopped and drop from the sky.
Below, they could see a man standing in a large open field.

Without taking his gaze off of Gomper, Jamham asked, "Sir.
Did you give your allegiance to your brother?"

"No," gasped Gomper.

Jamham faced and asked, "Why?"

Gomper shook his head as he closed his eyes. He said in a raspy
voice, "I won't allow him to save my life. I just need to allow him
to remove the curse before I die. So it won't be released within the
galaxy. There is no way . . . people would never accept me as . . ."

Jamham interrupted, "Your name. What is it?"

Gomper let out another moan before he answered, "Gomper
. . . my name is Gomper."

Behind them they heard, "Move back from him."

Jamham moved back as Humphrey and others appeared on the
bridge. Gomper stood on his own accord, knowing he was there to
take him outside. It was there he heard, "Gomper!"

He looked in the direction of the OSA to see Gostler. Tears
started to scream down his face as the former Master came up to
him. They wrapped their arms around each other.

Gomper was so relieved to see Gostler. Ghonllier didn't tell him
that he would be there. He was so grateful to see him again before
he died. Gomper let go of him as Humphrey said, "The Master
wants him outside now."

Gostler nodded as Gomper looked back at his three trusted
friends one last time. The Master of the Galaxy's elite force was
standing between them and Gomper. They tried to follow but his

force wouldn't allow it. They had to watch Humphrey and Gostler support Gomper out of the room.

By the time, they reached the main loading door. Gomper was gasping for air with short breathes. His body was so racked with pain. He struggled to walk on his own accord. Gostler kept talking to him encouraging him to keep breathing.

Outside, Humphrey and Gostler stayed with him. He could see all of the KOGN Star Screamers had landed and were surrounding Ghonllier. At least, he assumed it was Ghonllier. They talked about him waiting for him right where he was standing. Gomper had always wondered what his brother looked like and wished he could get a good look of his face before he died.

He struggled to make it down the ramp. When he did, Gomper looked up to see a pregnant woman and another man standing with Ghonllier. Gomper looked over at Gostler and asked, "Who are those people?"

"The one in the middle it your brother Ghonllier. The woman is your sister Asustie. The man next to her is her husband."

Gomper wasn't aware that they were going to be there, too. He so wanted to see them both up close, but he couldn't walk. As his heart ached to see his siblings, he slumped to the ground. Humphrey and Gostler went with him. Gomper was on all fours, trying to breathe.

Ghonllier order Humphrey and Gostler back into the Star Screamer. The former Master wouldn't leave Gomper. "GET AWAY FROM HIM, GOSTLER. HE'S MINE," ordered Ghonllier, allowing everyone to hear him.

"No!" challenged Gostler, becoming emotional.

Gostler couldn't leave, after seeing him. Humphrey had already left to go back up the ramp. With Gostler disobeying orders, Ghonllier mentally picked him up and floated him inside the ship. Then Ghonllier sealed up the ship.

Jason took a hold of Asustie's hand and took in a deep breath. Asustie was awe struck to see her oldest brother. Like Gostler, she become emotional. Gomper was moaning as the last of the curse was entering his stomach. Asustie wanted to comfort her brother by going to him. Ghonllier put his hand on her arm and warned her to stay put.

Not taking his gaze from Gomper, Ghonllier said, "I need the container, Jason."

"Here," responded Jason, handing him a large container that looked like a metal bowl.

The new Master commanded the container to go to Gomper. It floated over and landed underneath him. When Gomper saw it, he was relieved to know it was time to start heaving. He started into convulsions only to see thick black substance come out of him.

Sweat poured from his face as he repeated the action several times. Then Gomper stopped and started to shake as he tried to hold his body up. Ghonllier quickly removed the round bowl before Gomper fell into it.

No one noticed that the *Liberty Quest* had appeared until she beamed someone down to Gomper. Cid quickly placed Gomper's hand on the analyzer. Shortly, he looked at Ghonllier and shook his head. Asustie let out a cry. Ghonllier put his arm around her and said, "Asustie. You need to focus on what's next. We aren't through this yet."

She nodded as she stared at the bowl that held the curse. Jason handed Ghonllier another metal bowl that matched the same size of the first one, while the captains picked up Cid and Gomper. Then the *Liberty Quest* hovered as as Ghonllier mentally set the new bowl on top of the curse.

He brought it closer to Asustie. The Master caused the metal container to hover as Asustie started to melt the two bowls together. It was fascinating to witness the edges on the containers become one. Ghonllier slowly turned it around until Asustie had completely sealed the containers. When she finished, they couldn't see a seam. Now, it looked like a ball with two flat ends.

The minute Asustie finished, Ghonllier had the *Liberty Quest* land near him so Asustie could see her brother. Then he raised the contained curse higher into the sky. Dark clouds had appeared and they were turning green and slowly swirled. The *Liberty Quest* opened her doors. Jason took Asustie up the ramp as Ghonllier watched the container up in the air.

The clouds started to fulgurate with light. Boney-like fingers started to reach out for the container. Suddenly, the clouds lit up before lightening bolts hit the ground, striking everywhere. They especially hit the container. It was impressive to have the lightening hit the ground without touching the ships or Ghonllier. At the end, one bolt of lightening hit him.

Ghonllier stood there as if nothing had hit him. Next, funnel clouds dropped down from the clouds and engulfed the sealed container. It was then Ghonllier headed for his ship. The angry green clouds left as fast as they had appeared.

The new Master unsealed all of the ships. Gostler came running out of the Star Screamer Ghonllier had sent him to. The Master entered the OSA and waited for Gostler to join him.

When he arrived, Gostler asked, "Is he alive?"

"Barely. He'll . . . I don't know if he will make it, Gostler. It will depend on much he wants too."

Gostler left Ghonllier on a run. The Master paused to look up in the sky before he followed Gostler.

Ghonllier entered to find Gostler had joined his family at Gomper's side. He was on a gurney with Cid watching his stats. The Master kept his gaze on Sunna as he walked over to the captains. She was so caught up in Stacy crying while holding on to Gomper's hand. She wasn't aware of him being there.

Ghonllier whispered, "Captains. Will you keep everything that happens in this room a total secret from the rest of my elite force?"

They looked at him with questioning eyes. Butler said, "Are you referring to your brother?"

"Yes. I do not want anyone to know about him living or about anything else that I do here in the next few minutes." They nodded. "Use the ships speaker and please request my wife."

The captains grinned before Butler reached over to do what Ghonllier had requested. Sunna was stunned to hear the captains use the word *wife*. She looked in their direction to see Ghonllier leaning against the captains control panel, grinning.

Excited, she left those mourning to join him. She ran into his arms and they kissed. Then they held each other while Sam and Butler watched.

"Congratulations, Commanders," they said in unison.

"Thank you," grinned Sunna.

She looked up at Ghonllier to see him looking up at the ceiling. Sunna joined him while he kept his arm around her. "What are looking at?" she asked.

Looking down at her, he answered, "I was just watching the container that Asustie sealed up being caught into the sun's gravity."

"Why all the lightening?"

He grinned. "It was for KOGN's sake. They were questioning me being different than Suzair the Great," answered Ghonllier.

They heard Stacy's sobs getting louder. Sunna looked back at them. "I'm sorry. Gomper didn't live."

Ghonllier looked at them and answered, "He's not dead yet."

"Are you going to tell your mother that?"

Ghonllier shook his head. "Cid and I decided to wait. He is barely picking up some kind of brainwave."

"He isn't breathing . . ."

"He's breathing. His body is in shock and it's shallow breathing. He's barely getting enough oxygen."

"Why isn't Cid giving . . ."

"I'm giving him Gomper's readings and we do it that way until Gomper can come out of the shock and decide if he wants to live or die," educated Ghonllier, looking at her. He added, "This is better for my mother. If Gomper does live, he might be a vegetable with little . . ." Ghonllier shook his head. "I'm getting very little brain activity."

"Then are we safe? What's next?" asked Sunna, expecting Ghonllier to say they could tell others about their marriage.

In his mind, Ghonllier was seeing a very clouded vision of a battle taking place on the outside edge of a another galaxy. He knew it to be another galaxy because it was hard to see. When Ghonllier asked about what this had to do with them, the Stones switched to a conversation.

"Sir, they defiantly aren't following us. What do you want to do?" asked the captains.

"Go into mock speed. We aren't going to return. I'll give you a destination when I get the reports," sighed Boras, seeing Jorvas coming toward him.

He was Boras's highest ranked officer and the only person he trusted. They had been through a lot together and were close friends before they started this quest. Boras didn't really want to talk but knew he couldn't get away from Jorvas.

"Do you know what we're going to do?" asked Jorvas, watching Boras past him.

The leader shrugged his shoulders and headed for the computers. Jorvas followed, watching Boras. He turned on a computer while Jorvas sat in the chair next to him.

The alien leader shot him a glance as he waited for his computer to boot up. "When will the reports be ready?" asked Boras.

"Soon. I have some already. I'm waiting for everyone's before we look at them."

Boras nodded as he started to search the universes known charts. There was silence as Ghonllier read their mind. Then he became upset to learn what the man was thinking. He made the decision to come to his galaxy. As he listened to their conversation, it angered him that these people were professional warriors. They knew nothing else and had no interest in peace. This was why they were being kicked out of the Chartooth galaxy.

Sunna brought him back as she repeated her question. "What is next? Are we at peace?"

"I don't want to know," informed Ghonllier.

"You don't want to know about what?" she asked.

He smiled. "This is a time to celebrate. The war is over. What happens next we take it one day at a time."

Ghonllier pushed the conversation out of mind not realizing that he just programmed the Stones to not tell him about the future invasion. At the same time he had Humphrey mentally contact him before he could finish instructing the Stones on how he wanted to handle what they had just showed him. Ghonllier was distracted and didn't finish something he would regret in the future.

Looking at Sunna, he said, "I need to leave. Humphrey has a problem that I need to handle."

"Can I come?"

He spoke with the Stones before he answered, "Yeah. You might find this interesting."

Ghonllier looked over at Jason and invited him to join them. They left together for the ship that Gomper had used to come to him.